DEATH THREAT

"We're listening," Duncan said.

The voice that echoed out in response was low-pitched, somewhere between male and female. "We have been patient, but time is running out. We want the key."

"The key to the lower level of Qian-Ling?" Duncan asked.

"Don't play games with me," Lexina said. "I have shown you just a small sample of what I can do by destroying the place you held my comrades' bodies and your last manned space vehicle. I now control the talon and I will do much worse if you do not turn the key over to us."

"You killed a lot of people," Duncan said.

"And I will kill many, many more if you do not get me the key."

"Did you destroy the *Columbia* as it approached the talon?" Duncan asked.

"No. That was the talon's automatic defense system reacting to anything that came close. But I control it *now*. I control your satellite through the talon. I warned you," Lexina said. "You ignored the warning. Do not ignore this one. Give us the key."

"Why should—" Duncan began but she was interrupted.

"Give us the key or we will destroy your country completely."

BOOKS BY ROBERT DOHERTY

The Rock

Area 51

Area 51: The Reply

Area 51: The Mission

Area 51: The Sphinx

ROBERT DOHERTY

AREA 51:
THE SPHINX

A DELL BOOK

To Deb, thank you for everything

Published by
Dell Publishing
a division of Random House, Inc.
1540 Broadway
New York, New York 10036

Dell® is a registered trademark of Random House, Inc., and the colophon is a trademark of Random House, Inc.

ISBN: 0-440-23494-8

Printed in the United States of America

Published simultaneously in Canada

February 2000

10 9 8 7 6 5 4 3 2 1

OPM

THE PAST

PROLOGUE

THE GIZA PLATEAU
May 27, 1855

The face of the Sphinx gazed enigmatically over the sand, the weathered and battered stone bathed in the rays of the rising moon. The two men approaching the statue halted, dwarfed by the large stone sculpture towering over them, their feet sinking into the desert. Beyond the shoulders of the Sphinx, the massive bulk of the three Giza pyramids filled the western horizon.

"Abul-Hol," one of the men said in Arabic, the words coming from inside the deep folds of the hood he had pulled over his head. "The Father of Terror," he repeated in English.

The head of the statue was twenty feet wide and almost the same in height. The neck and shoulders disappeared into sand that swept like an ocean around it.

"Impressive." The other man spoke Arabic also, but with an accent that indicated it was not his native tongue.

"The body is even more impressive," the Arab said. "It has been buried for many, many years."

"How do you know there is a body, then?"

The Arab shrugged. "Either you trust my knowledge or you are wasting your time, Englishman." He pointed at the scarred face above them. "The nose was destroyed by cannon fire. Foolish infidels."

"I heard it was Napoleon himself who directed that shot when he was here with his army."

The Arab spit into the sand. "Your ears have heard a lie. It was the Turks over a hundred years before Napoleon who did that damage. There are many false stories concerning the Sphinx and the pyramids."

"And you know the truth?"

"I know some truths, Mr. Burton."

Richard Francis Burton pulled his hood back as he peered up at the ancient monument. The Englishman's face was a terrible sight in the dimness, as scarred as that of the Sphinx. There was a jagged red wound on each side of his upper jaw where a spear had been thrust through less than three months before and the healing had not yet finished. Scraggly, rough beard surrounded the incomplete scar, the dark and swarthy face almost matching that of his Arab counterpart.

The Englishman's voice was low and harsh, the inside of his mouth having also suffered from the wound. As he spoke, small amounts of pus and blood oozed out of the holes on either side of his face, unnoticed by him in his excitement. "My dear Kaji, I am the only European to have been in the holy cities of Mecca and Medina. I have read documents there written in the ancient tongues and seen by no other westerner. I have stood in the shadow of the Himalayas, traveled across the deserts of Arabia, traversed to the Upper Nile and beyond the first cataracts.

"There is much more I want to see before I die—the true source of the Nile, the mines and treasures of King Solomon, the church that is rumored to hold the Ark of the Covenant, the Mountains of the Moon that are hidden in the mists."

"Some of those things and places are myths," Kaji said. He pulled his own hood back, revealing the lined face of an old man, and a bald, wrinkled scalp. He had a large, hook nose, and his eyes were black stones in deepset sockets.

"No, I don't think so," Burton replied. "I have heard of mysteries on the plateau beyond what we see here.

Hidden marvels. The whispers and ancient writings tell of a chamber under the Sphinx. A chamber of knowledge. Of truth. It is said to be the Hall of Records from the ancient and lost land of Atlantis. My quest has led me to you as one who knows the ways of the Plateau. I will not rest until I see this chamber."

Kaji's dark eyes regarded the foreigner. "Go back to England. What you seek is perilous. Sometimes it is better not to know the truth. The truth is a very, very dangerous thing."

Burton laughed. "You cannot deter me with the stories of curses that you Egyptians love to scare foreigners with. I have been many dangerous places and I have stared death in the face. I will not blink now.

"I am on the *tariqat*," Burton continued. The word he spoke in Arabic translated as the spiritual path leading to the truth, which normally meant the truth of God, but Burton wasn't certain where his *tariqat* was going. He reached into his shirt and pulled out a circular medallion that hung on a chain around his neck. On the surface of the metal, an eye was emblazoned over the apex of a pyramid.

Kaji's gnarled fingers ran across the surface of the medallion. "Where did you get this?"

"In Medina. From a man named Abdu Al-Iblis."

Kaji stiffened. "You are one of his disciples?"

Burton shook his head. "No. I spoke with him one time. A most strange person. He gave me this."

"Did you get anything else from him? A key?"

"What kind of key?"

"If you had it, you would know." Kaji remained still for several minutes, Burton waiting on him. Finally the Arab's shoulders slumped ever so slightly. "I see it is to be our fate. I will take you inside. What you seek is below us."

"The Hall of Records?"

"Yes."

Burton looked around. "Through the sand?"

"There are other ways to go where you seek," Kaji said. He pointed at the Great Pyramid. "We must go there." He began walking around the Sphinx's head.

It appeared to Burton that the middle pyramid was the highest, but he knew that was a trick of the lay of the Plateau of Giza. The one farthest to the northeast, where they were headed, was the tallest and most massive.

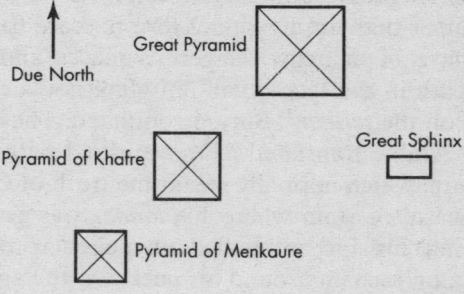

Burton hurried to keep up. Like Kaji, he wore the long robes of the people of the desert. Richard Francis Burton was a strange man, and it was no accident that he had ended up here in Egypt, searching out mysteries told of in legends and written of on decaying parchments. Born in England in 1821, he'd briefly attended Oxford, where he had been the only student at the time to study Arabic. Disgusted with the closed minds at the school, he left after two years and joined the military. In 1842 he was posted to India, where he promptly began studying Hindustani, then Persian. Because of his linguistic talents and his desire for adventure, he became a spy for the British army, scouting along the borders of the English Empire in that part of the world. During one of those missions he became seriously ill with cholera.

Given two years of sick leave, he used that time to become a Master Sufi, one who studied and searched for a universal truth in connection with God.

He was the only non-Muslim to travel to both Mecca and Medina, disguising himself as one of the faithful, his dark skin and language abilities allowing him to pose as a Persian trader. He had seen the Ka'ab, the heart of Islam, which none outside the faith were to see and be allowed to live.

From Arabia he went to Africa, hoping to start an expedition to discover the mythical source of the Nile. Because of his proficiency in languages and his willingness to go into the native areas and listen, he heard many whispers and late-night stories told in a drunken stupor, finding it difficult to separate fact from fiction. It was in Mecca that he had first read of ancient secrets hidden on the Giza Plateau. Another man, said to be a Master Sufi also—Abdu Al-Iblis—had found him—how, Burton knew not—and directed him onward to the African continent and gave him the medallion telling him to use it to gain help on his path. Al-Iblis's only request was that Burton return to Mecca and tell him what he had discovered. Burton did not trust Al-Iblis—he sensed evil from the man, and Kaji's reaction indicated his instincts were correct—but Burton had long before realized that his path would often brush up against such people and if he was to pursue his goal of the Truth he would have to use them also.

What had piqued Burton's interest were the stories of the mythical Hall of Records, hidden somewhere in the ancient complex of structures built on the Giza Plateau outside of Cairo. The Hall was said to contain the Truth, although what exactly was meant by that, Burton had no idea. To some it meant religious truth—which of the many gods man worshiped around the world was the one true God—and to others it was the truth of the Antediluvian World, the story of Atlantis and man's roots, of great civilizations before recorded history. Regardless, Burton was determined to discover it.

After his camp near Berbera was attacked by Somali bandits and he suffered his grievous wound from a spear thrust through his jaw, Burton was forced to postpone his search for the source of the Nile. On his way back to England to recuperate, he had stopped at Giza to explore this mystery before boarding the steamer. His persistent questioning had led him to Kaji, an old Egyptian he'd found huddled in a hut on the edge of the Plateau. As near as Burton could determine, Kaji was some kind of caretaker for the monuments, although the man seemed poor and had no affiliation with the local government. He had badgered the old man every day for a week, before Kaji even assented to talk to him. And then it had taken another week of pestering to get him to agree to take him to the Plateau this evening.

Burton felt the familiar stir of excitement as they closed on the Great Pyramid. He had read the report of the English mathematician John Greaves, who had visited the Pyramid in 1638. Burton had also studied the more exacting measurements of Frenchman Edme-François Jomard, who had been commissioned by Napoleon to study the structure. Jomard had deduced the Pyramid of Khufu's current height to be 481 feet, making it by far the tallest known man-made building in the world. Even more fascinating, Jomard measured each side of the base and discovered they were all 755 feet long, give or take eight inches, an incredible feat of building by the ancients—accuracy within one-tenth of one percent over such a vast scale. Just as amazing, the sides of the three major pyramids were perfectly aligned with the cardinal directions.

Burton intrinsically felt there had to be more here than what he had heard and studied. He had an instinct for mystery and intrigue and he could feel the power of both swirling about as they reached the base of the Great Pyramid. He was pleased when Kaji led him to the entrance Caliph Abdullah Al Mamum had cracked in the side of the large monument. Burton had read old scrolls in Medina about the caliph and how he had gone to the Great Pyramid in A.D. 820 and forced his way in search of secrets of a "profound science" and the "complete history of man and the truth of astronomy." The scrolls told that Al Mamum sought a secret chamber that held "maps and terrestrial spheres." Those scrolls written in the old Arabic tongue had been one of several clues that had led Burton to the Giza Plateau.

Kaji handed Burton a kerosene lantern. "We will light these once we are inside. What we do tonight it is best no one knows about, and there are always thieves and scoundrels hiding in the darkness around the Plateau. Also, the government has officially forbidden travel inside. Those in power know the danger of the truth." Kaji paused. "Mr. Burton, this is your last chance to turn around and go back. Please, sir, I beg of you, do not pursue this any further. I tell you honestly that death awaits if you persist."

"Death awaits every man," Burton said. "You cannot stop me."

Kaji turned toward the Pyramid. "It is Allah's will, then."

They passed into the dark opening and carefully made their way into the tunnel, moving a little distance by feel, before Kaji paused and lit both lanterns.

"In the ninth century, the caliph's men broke through the rock by heating it with fire, then pouring cold vinegar over the stones," Kaji informed Burton as they moved down the tunnel. "They had to break through much rock—over one hundred feet—before they reached this."

Burton ducked his head as they entered a four-foot-high tunnel that his lantern showed went up at a steep angle.

Kaji pointed. "The caliph's men then found the original entrance, hidden behind a pivoting stone door. That entrance leads to the Queen's Chamber and the Great Gallery, which ends at the King's Chamber in the middle of the Pyramid."

"Both of those had nothing in them when opened," Burton noted.

"The titles given to those chambers were made up by people who knew no better. They are rooms inside the Pyramid, but there is no evidence a king was buried in one chamber and a queen in the other. No one really knows what was in those rooms—if anything," Kaji added. "Besides, we are not going up."

The Arab placed his hands on one of the stone blocks to their right. For the first time Burton noted a large ring on the man's right hand. He was startled as, with a grinding noise, the stone Kaji had touched rotated clockwise, revealing a narrow opening.

Kaji slid through the opening, Burton following. They were in a wider tunnel, about five feet high by four wide. Burton still had to hunch over, and he waited as Kaji placed his hands on the stone and it rumbled shut behind them.

Enclosed in this tunnel, the way out now sealed, Burton felt the immensity of the Pyramid. The thousands and thousands of massive stone blocks above his head were a palpable presence. The air was stale and dry. A thin layer of undisturbed dust covered the floor of the passageway, which angled downward at what Burton estimated to be a thirty-degree slope.

Kaji headed down the tunnel, Burton following closely, their lanterns casting long shadows in both directions along the smoothly cut stone walls. Burton paused briefly and swung his lantern close to one side. The joints between the blocks were so tight that he could not get the blade of his penknife between them. Remarkable craftsmanship on an immense scale. Even the great cathedral builders of Europe had not managed such work, and this had been built while Europeans were still living in mud huts.

He had to hurry to catch up to the Arab. He heard something very faint and realized Kaji was counting to himself. Burton almost bumped into the other man, when he abruptly halted.

"We are at the base of the Pyramid." Kaji ran his hands over a particular stone block. Burton now saw that the face of the large ring was turned palm in and that Kaji seemed to be trying to place it in a specific spot.

It must have hit the correct place, because the stone block, over six feet wide, rotated, allowing space on either side. Burton estimated the block to weigh at least several tons, yet it turned smoothly, still perfectly balanced after all these years.

"To the left," Kaji said.

"What's to the right?" Burton asked.

"Death."

"A trap set for grave robbers?"

"No. A box that holds death for everyone in the Pyramid and on the Highland of Aker."

"What kind of box could do that?"

"I have seen it once. A black box inside a sarcophagus in a chamber below the center of the Pyramid. I dared not open it or even touch it. My father told me it holds a very powerful weapon. One that could destroy all three pyramids."

"What could do that?"

Kaji shrugged. "I know not."

"How could the ancients have such a weapon?"

Kaji did not answer. Burton wanted to find this b

open it, and see what kind of device could do such a fantastic thing, but he had agreed with Kaji to find something else and he knew he needed to stay on that task.

Kaji extended his arm, indicating for Burton to go ahead.

The Englishman paused. "You go first, please."

Kaji shrugged and scooted through the opening. Burton followed, pushing past the Arab, who waited to close the stone. He could smell the other man's sweat, the faint odor of spicy food on his breath, and something else, deeper and ranker. Burton had smelled that before, and he thought for a few seconds before he realized what it was—the odor men gave off just before going into battle. The smell of fear.

The air was heavier now. Burton could feel it on his skin, in his mouth and throat. The layer of dust was even deeper, almost an inch thick, undisturbed as far as Burton could tell.

This tunnel also descended, but less than fifty feet after following it, Burton noticed a change. The walls were no longer made of smoothly cut blocks, but rather had been burrowed through solid stone.

Kaji confirmed what Burton was seeing. "We are below the Pyramid, into the bedrock of the Highland."

The English explorer ran his hand along the wall. "It is perfectly smooth. I have been in many mines and caverns and never seen such a well-constructed shaft. Who made these tunnels? The builders of the Pyramid?"

"Some say these tunnels predate the Pyramid." Kaji paused and ran a hand across his forehead.

Burton could see the sheen of sweat on the Arab. It was warm, but not that warm. He wondered what was causing the other man's fear.

"It is said the three pyramids above us were built in ⁀e Fourth Dynasty of the Old Kingdom, between the ⁀rs 2685 and 2180 before the birth of our Lord," Burton said. "The Great Pyramid, built by the Pharaoh Cheops, as the Greeks called him—Khufu in your tongue."

"Before the birth of *your* lord in the West," Kaji amended. "Your Christ is just a prophet in the Koran. A man, not a god."

Burton saw no need to get into a theological discussion at this place and time. Besides, he was not a firm believer in the religion he had been raised in, and the many cultures and religions he had already witnessed in his life had shown him that if there was a god in heaven, there were many paths by which people might worship him. Becoming a Master Sufi had forced him to delve deeply into Islam, and he saw much in that faith that he admired—more than he did in his native belief. A Sufi adhered to no specific religion and dismissed no religion. The truth transcended such petty concerns of men.

"Who built these tunnels, then, if they are older than the pyramids?" Burton asked. "And were the pyramids built over them to hide the entrance to the tunnels? Or perhaps to mark the entrances?"

"These tunnels were built by those who carved the Sphinx and built the temple around it." Kaji inclined his head in the direction the tunnel was dug. "We are heading toward the Sphinx now. East."

Burton considered that information. "Then the Sphinx is older than the pyramids?"

"Much older."

"How much older?"

Kaji smiled for the first time since they had entered the Great Pyramid. "You would not believe me if I told you. Long before the Pharaoh Menes founded the First Dynasty."

"How can that be? Who built the Sphinx?"

"It was carved during the time of the Neteru who ruled in the first age."

"Who were the Neteru?" Burton asked.

"The time of the gods, of Osiris and Isis. I do not have time to give you a lesson on the history of my country."

"What of man during this time? Who lived here?"

"Those who came before from over the sea," Kaji said, which meant nothing to Burton.

The Englishman cocked his head. There was a very faint noise, a deep, rumbling sound coming from ahead. "What is that?"

"The river of the underworld." Kaji was moving once more. "Water from the Nile flows through tunnels under the Plateau and then back to the river, farther downstream. It is the second Gateway of Rostau; there is one on land and one in water."

They trod down the perfectly straight tunnel for another five minutes.

"How deep are we?" Burton finally asked, but Kaji was counting to himself once more and didn't answer.

The Arab paused and swung the light close to the wall on the right side. He pressed his hand against it. Burton stepped back in surprise as what had appeared to be unmarked stone changed and the outline of a block, five feet wide and the height of the tunnel, appeared. It didn't rotate like the others, but slid back two feet, then smoothly up into a recess above.

"How did that work?" Burton demanded, but Kaji signaled with his free hand for him to go through. The other was still pressed against the wall. There was only blackness beyond.

Burton hesitated. "You first."

Kaji went through, and Burton followed. The door slid down behind him and the outline of the door disappeared as quickly as it had appeared.

"Where are we?" Burton asked.

They were in a larger tunnel that also descended, except something was wrong. The light from their lanterns was absorbed about twenty feet away from them, fading into an utter darkness.

"I have given you my word that you will see what you seek," Kaji said. "This is the way to the Hall of Records."

"You go first," Burton said, which only brought a slight smile in response from Kaji.

The Arab walked down the tunnel, lantern held in front of him. Burton blinked. It was as if the man were fading from sight, yet he was no more than ten feet ahead. Kaji looked over his shoulder, his figure faint. "You must have faith to go this way. Do you have the faith?"

"I—" But even as Burton responded, Kaji faded from view, the lantern in his hand blinking out. There was nothing but that disquieting darkness—an unnatural black the likes of which Burton had never seen.

Burton forced himself down the tunnel, feeling the darkness press against his skin, as if the air were becoming a liquid. He pushed forward, even as the light from the lantern faded to a very small dot dangling from a hand he could no longer see. He no longer felt connected to his body, to the world. He was in another place, another time.

Light exploded into his eyes, momentarily blinding him. Burton staggered and would have fallen but for Kaji grabbing his arm. Burton blinked, his eyes trying to adjust.

"There—" Kaji's voice was a whisper.

Burton's jaw dropped. He didn't notice the pain from his wounds as he took in his surroundings. He was on a ledge along the side of a huge cavern. Light came from a five-meter-wide orb overhead that Burton could not look at for more than a second or, like the sun, it burned his eyes. The far end of the cavern was at least half a mile away. The walls were curved, consisting of red rock, cut smooth, reflecting the light of the minisun.

"There is the Hall of Records." Kaji was pointing at the floor of the cavern, a hundred feet below them.

"My God!" Burton exclaimed as he saw what was there.

It was a replica of the Great Sphinx—but this one was not covered by sand, nor was it made of stone. The skin of the creature was a flawless black that absorbed the light. The head was larger, the nose not shot off. Indeed, it was larger than the stone one above. Fuller. The eyes caught Burton's gaze. They were the only part of the Sphinx not black. Blood red, with elongated red irises, they glowed from some inner fire. For a second Burton thought it was alive, a monstrous creature, before he realized it was inanimate.

"What is it made of?" Burton asked. "I have never seen the like."

"*B'ja*—the divine metal," Kaji said.

Burton looked around. Stairs cut out of the rock itself led down to the floor on which the Sphinx rested. Its paws extended almost sixty feet in front of the head, which rose seventy feet above the floor. The body stretched one hundred and eighty feet back from the head, making the whole thing almost three hundred feet long. Between the paws was a statue about three meters tall. Burton looked closely—it was the figure of a man, but one strangely shaped, with a body too short and limbs too long. The most startling aspect, though, was the head, with polished white skin, ears with long lobes that ended just above the shoulders, and two gleaming red eyes set in a long, narrow face. The stone that covered the top of the head was also red.

"Who is that?" Burton asked. "A pharaoh?"

"Shemsu Hor," Kaji said. "A Guardian of Horus."

Burton had studied some of the ancient Egyptian

texts while in Cairo, and he knew that Horus was supposed to be the son of Isis and Osiris, the latter of whom was the supreme god of the underworld.

"And what does it say below?"

Kaji laughed, but it was not a pleasant sound. "The black box along the other Road of Rostau would destroy the Highland of Aker. That says that if one does not know what to do with what is inside the Hall within a certain amount of time, the entire world will be destroyed."

Burton had no idea what the other man was talking about. "Let us go down." Burton moved toward the stairs, but Kaji grabbed his arm, stopping him.

"I promised to show you the Hall. No one can enter."

"Where are the Records?"

"The Records should be inside," Kaji said. "But a key is needed to get into the Black Sphinx."

"Where is this key?" Burton demanded.

"That information I do not have. There are several keys from the ancients, and each is important in its own right. When the key is brought here, then the bearer will be allowed to enter the Hall. The bearer must know where to take what they will find, or else darkness will descend. Until then, no one can enter." Kaji turned toward the tunnel they had come out of. "We must go back."

"I want—" Burton paused. He saw something in the other's eyes. A look he had seen before in combat. A battle lust. It startled him; as far as he knew, he had done nothing to provoke such a reaction in the other man.

"We must go back," Kaji repeated.

Burton nodded. "All right." He would have to come back here with a fully funded expedition. He had to know what was in the Hall. He would have to find the key Kaji spoke of.

Kaji headed back up the tunnel, into the darkness. Burton looked back at the massive Black Sphinx crouched on the floor of the cavern guarding its secret and the statue of the Guardian of Horus between the paws. He walked forward, still looking over his shoulder, into the darkness. The last he saw were the red eyes of the Sphinx, glowing, before the black took him.

He was back in the tunnel.

"Quickly," Kaji urged. "We must be out of the Great Pyramid before dawn."

Burton hurried to follow, his mind swirling with what secrets might be hidden inside that massive statue he had just seen. The Black Sphinx itself was a magnificent find, one that would place his name among the ranks of other legendary explorers.

They slipped through a doorway. Up a tunnel. Through another doorway that appeared out of the solid rock as Kaji placed his hand along the wall. Along a tunnel. Another hand placed, another doorway as a block appeared and slid up.

Kaji gestured with his free hand. "Go, go."

Burton paused. This was not the way they had come. "You go first."

Kaji grimaced, then stepped into the opening, waving. "Come. Quickly! It will close soon."

Burton dashed past the other man. He heard the stone move and grabbed the Arab, who was jumping the other way. They tumbled down in a heap, Kaji struggling to get away.

The stone slammed shut with a reverberating thud.

Kaji's scream followed that noise. An undulating exclamation of pain and shock that died into a whimper.

Burton rolled onto his knees, lantern held in front. Like an animal in a trap, Kaji lay on his side, his left hand caught under the door-stone. He was alive only because the stone was so smoothly cut and heavy, it had briefly sealed the arteries that flowed to the hand at the point of impact. But even as he crawled closer, Burton could see blood bursting out of the blocked veins at the wrist where it disappeared under the stone. The flesh and bone on the appendage had to be smashed flat by the immense weight. Kaji moaned in pain, staring at his arm in shock.

"Easy, old man, easy," Burton said as he pulled off the belt that held his robe around the waist. He tied the leather band on Kaji's upper arm to act as a tourniquet. He removed a dagger from the man's waist, slid the handle through the knot, and twisted it, tightening the belt. Once he was sure he had the flow of blood stopped, Burton looped an end of the knot over the dagger's handle to keep it in place.

"How do I open the stone?" Burton demanded, placing his hands on either side of Kaji's face and trying to get his attention.

Kaji swallowed, speaking through his pain. "You cannot. We will die here together, Englishman. What you have seen this night will die here also."

The wounds on Richard Francis Burton's face grew even darker as anger gripped him. "You wanted to trap me here."

"You are one of Al-Iblis's minions. You must die."

"I do not work for this Al-Iblis. I met him only once."

"The medallion—it is one that is carried by my people, the *wedjat*. Al-Iblis kills my people. He took that off one of my comrades and gave it to you to try to find this place. He has tried many times, and always we have killed those he sends."

"If I was doing Al-Iblis's bidding, would I have mentioned his name?"

Kaji closed his eyes in pain as he considered that logic.

"Is there another way out?" Burton swung the lantern, looking around. They were in not another tunnel, but a closed stone chamber. The open space was twenty feet long by ten wide. The ceiling was slightly taller than Burton's six feet.

"No." Kaji crushed Burton's hope as effectively as his own hand had been. "This room is a dead end. The door opens only from the other side."

"Who are you? Why have you done this?"

"I am the guardian of the Highland of Aker, what you call the Giza Plateau. I thought you were from Al-Iblis. You speak our tongue and many others. I have heard of your studies of the ancient texts in Mecca and Medina and in your own country. You are a unique man, and such people can be very dangerous. If words will not stop such men, my orders are to take more extreme measures.

"No man outside of my order has traveled into this place and lived to come back out. No man who does not have the key can be allowed to live after having been on the Roads of Rostau and seeing the Hall of Records. When someone like you gets too close we bring him inside and leave him trapped, so that it appears as if he disappeared off the face of the planet."

"Where do the other tunnels lead?" Burton demanded. "You have alluded to these other places. If I will not live to see them, then at least my ears can hear your tales of them."

"I told you of those places to distract you," Kaji said. "To whet your appetite so that you would come in here with me."

"You have taken my life, then," Burton said. "The least you could do is tell me what you know before we die."

"I gave an oath, a most serious oath on my life, never to reveal the secrets I know until it is time."

"If we die, then your secrets will not have been revealed," Burton said. "You would not have broken your oath. You showed me the Black Sphinx knowing I would never be able to tell of what I saw. Let me know all of it. I was your guest. It is the law of Allah that you grant me this wish." Burton had often used the law from the Koran to get help from the followers of Islam.

Kaji considered that line of reasoning. As he did, Burton took off his wool shirt and tucked it under the Arab's head, making him more comfortable.

"I want your word, Englishman, that if by some miracle you survive me, you will never repeat the words I tell you or tell anyone what you have seen today. That you will never speak to Al-Iblis. I must have your promise before I speak. I was told you are a man of honor, and if you give me your word I will not have betrayed my oath. I kept my word of honor—I showed you what it was you sought. I did not promise that you should see it and live."

Burton waved his hand at the heavy stone walls surrounding them. "If there is no other way out, then your secrets die with me."

"I must have your word in any case."

"You have my word that I will never speak of what I have seen or what you tell me. I swear upon the life of the only person I love, the light of my heart, Isabel."

Kaji nodded. "I see in your eyes you do love her. I believe you will keep your word."

"You called these tunnels the Roads of Rostau. You say you are the guardian of the Highland of Aker. You have shown me the Black Sphinx that holds the Hall of Records. Tell me what it all means. Who built this and why?"

Kaji closed his eyes, and his voice was low as he spoke through his pain. "My order is an ancient one. Going back before the time of Mohammed. Before the Christian's prophet you call Jesus. Before even those old ones who are written of in the Koran and the Jew's Torah.

Before the twelve tribes of Israel, before the first pharaoh, Menes, before Babylon."

"You are a priest of an ancient religion?"

"No, I am a man."

Burton's confusion showed on his face. "But you said your order?"

"I am one of the *wedjat*."

Burton knew many languages, and in his time in Egypt he had studied the hieroglyphics and language of the Old Kingdoms of Egypt. "One of the 'eye'?"

Kaji used his good hand to point to his eye. "A Watcher. In the old tongue, a *wedjat*. Different names in different tongues around the world, but Watchers nonetheless."

"What are you watching?"

"There are others who walked our Earth before the dawn of time. The ones who built the Hall of Records. Who placed the Box of Death under the Great Pyramid."

"Who are they?"

"Ones Who Are Not Men."

The words echoed off the stone walls and died in the silence that followed.

Burton reached down and wrapped his hand around Kaji's right hand. "You are telling me the truth?"

Kaji nodded. "Al-Iblis. Did he seem like a normal man to you?"

"I met him only once, and it was in a dark room. I could not tell." Burton did not add the sense of evil he had picked up from the man.

"We have watched Al-Iblis and those like him since the very beginning of man," Kaji continued. "And we have guarded the special places. Places even they have forgotten as the millennia have gone by. That is my job. To watch this place. The Highland of Aker, as it was known in the old days. The Great Pyramids and the Giza

Sphinx above. And more important, these tunnels—the Roads of Rostau, which lead to the six divisions of the Duat."

Burton was trying to absorb the information. "The Duat is the sky—the night sky. How can there be parts of it down here?"

"Much has been lost over the years. I know only what I was told by my father, who in turn had it handed down to him from his father. My son will replace me and knows all I know. I have seen only three of the divisions of the Duat, one of which you have just seen, which holds the Hall of Records. The others are farther along the Roads."

"What is in the other divisions?"

"That was not part of my promise."

"Who are they? The Ones Who Are Not Men?"

"We don't know exactly where they came from, but the records say they came out of the skies. From the stars. They are called Airlia. That is one word that is not different among the Watchers, even though the name among the peoples of the world have changed. I believe it is the name they call themselves."

Burton's grip on Kaji's hand relaxed. "You are telling me a story, not truth."

Kaji's dark eyes locked into the Englishman's. "I am telling you this on death's doorstep, facing the final darkness. You can choose to believe it or not."

Burton ran a hand through his coarse beard. He thought of the Black Sphinx with the eyes of fire he had just seen buried deep under the Plateau. The statue between the paws. He did not think men had built that. In many of the places he had been around the world there were legends of powerful creatures from the stars, of "gods" with strange appearances and powers. If there was anything his travels had taught him, it was that man knew very little, particularly with regard to the past. "Go on."

"There are two groups of these creatures, the Airlia. The legends that have been handed down among the *wedjat* say they warred against each other long ago. Before the pyramids were built, before even the Sphinx above was formed. My ancestors in Egypt transformed these creatures and their wars into our gods and legends. Both sides used, and continue to use, men for their own ends in this war.

"We call one group of men who are used the Guides. These are men who have been affected." Kaji's good hand reached up and touched his head. "Here. In the mind. They no longer are in charge of themselves, but do the bidding of the aliens even if they desire not to, but there are those who desire to serve even before their mind is changed. Al-Iblis is one of these. His name has passed down through the years as an enemy of man.

"The other group is called The Ones Who Wait. They are like men, but not men. They are different not only in the mind, but their eyes are not like ours. Elongated like the large cats of the southern jungles. And the eye itself is red inside of red. I have never seen one, but the legends say it is so. And they are not born of woman."

"How can that be?"

"I only repeat what my father told me."

Burton absorbed the other man's words. It was incredible, the words of myth, but he had seen the Black Sphinx. He had read the old scrolls, talked with aged priests and monks, and they had all hinted at something like this. And he had met Al-Iblis in Mecca. Even though he had not clearly seen the other, Burton had picked up a very strange feeling from him.

"These Records . . ." Burton's excitement overwhelmed the hopelessness of the situation. "That is what

I came here for. The Hall of Records. You said it was inside the Black Sphinx?"

Kaji nodded. "The Black Sphinx is the Hall. The Records are supposed to be inside. Your search is why you have to die."

"But these Records—why must they be hidden?"

"I do not know. It is the law of my order to protect them and watch."

"Why only watch?"

Kaji looked down at his trapped hand. "I did not think it would end like this. You were very cunning, Englishman. I have left others to die in the tunnels."

"Why do you only watch?" Burton repeated.

"Two reasons. One is we cannot fight these things. They are more powerful than we are. There have been times in the past when men have tried to fight them, and every time we were crushed. Many people have died at their hands. There have been times when men have tried to look at the Records, and it has always brought a storm of evil and death. Our primary goal as Watchers is to keep the line of man alive." Kaji's last words trailed off and his head slumped against the wool shirt.

"The second reason?" Burton prompted.

Kaji stirred. Burton could see that the man's eyes were becoming unfocused. He had seen that before and knew death was not far away. "Because we don't know which side are the ones we must fight."

"But if the Hall of Records is here, why do you not just look it up?"

"It is not allowed. And as I told you, we do not have the key."

"Who has the key?"

"I know only what I need to know to do my duty," Kaji said. "I have heard there is a place to the south of here. Beyond the source of the great river Nile, where these things had a city. Under a mountain with a white top. That one of the Airlia went in that direction long ago. Legend has it that this Airlia was killed before he could complete his journey and that the key was later buried with him."

"Who killed this creature?"

"There are also some of the Guides—like Al-Iblis—who travel among men, setting up in one place, then another. Recruiting men to do their bidding. They kill those of my order when they catch them. They kill The Ones Who Wait if they find them. We know only that they work from a place called The Mission."

Burton frowned. In his travels to strange places he had heard rumors of a group called The Mission. "Where is this Mission?"

"It moves. Always going to a place where it can find humans willing to do its bidding. Where it can breed the evil that exists in men's hearts. The Mission revels in the blackness of our nature. No one in my order knows where it is right now."

"Did the Airlia build the stone Sphinx above us?"

"Men built the stone Sphinx on the surface to mark the location of the Hall of Records to those who would know the symbol," Kaji said. "But they had help from these star creatures."

"And the pyramids?"

"The same. They were built by men for these creatures from the stars. These others have influenced our development since before the dawn of time." Kaji's voice trailed off to a whisper.

"And all you do is watch?" Burton could not understand such a life's mission.

"We watch and prevent interference by men in the creatures' war."

"Then you are siding with the Airlia."

Kaji shook his head. "No. We are preventing interference. The two sides of this ancient war seem to be in balance. If that balance is upset and one side is victorious, it is written in our scrolls that doom will come upon the planet. Then all will die."

A bead of sweat dropped off Kaji's forehead onto the stone floor. Burton could see that the tourniquet had almost completely closed off the circulation to the trapped arm. The skin in the forearm was a paler color, the cells dying from lack of blood. But he also knew that releasing the band would send a surge of blood to the smashed hand and finish bursting the vessels in the wrist, quickly killing the Arab. He could tell that shock was overwhelming the old man and it might be merciful to release the constriction.

"There must be another way out," Burton said. "Or a way to raise this stone. I can get you to a doctor if you show me."

Kaji shook his head. "You can open this stone only from the other side in the tunnel we came through. And there is no other way out."

Burton considered that. Why have a room that was a dead end? And Kaji had said he had seen only three of the Duats. There were three more somewhere. Kaji did not know all the tunnels, then.

"Ah!" Kaji let out a moan and dipped his head onto Burton's wadded shirt.

Burton could see the rise and fall of the Arab's chest, but he knew the man had not much longer to live. He got up and searched the chamber, holding the lantern close to the wall, searching for any marking.

The stone was smooth.

He walked across the chamber from Kaji's body, to the far wall. Kaji had used the ring to open some of the secret doors—of that Burton had no doubt. He didn't think that this was a dead end.

"Englishman." The word was little more than a whisper.

Burton hurried to Kaji's side. "Yes?"

The Arab's eyes were closed, and Burton had to lean close to hear. "Remember, you gave your word."

"I always keep—" Burton began, but he saw that the Arab's chest was still. He slid the shirt over the man's face.

After a brief prayer for the dead that Burton had memorized from the Koran, he set the lantern on the floor and turned it to the dimmest setting possible. He pulled the ring off Kaji's listless hand. The design was intricate, with a pyramid in the background. He turned it in the flickering light of the lantern—an eye within a circle, just like the medallion. The lantern had less than a quarter inch of kerosene in it; after that Burton would be in utter darkness.

Burton began searching once more for any sort of marking on the walls, moving quickly, but thoroughly, around the chamber. By the time he made it back to Kaji's body, without success, the lantern was flickering.

He forced himself to sit still, to think. Kaji had used the ring to open the doors. But the last door had been different. There had been no sign of it until Kaji had pressed the ring against it at a certain spot. That meant—

The lantern went out and a complete blackness, such as Burton had never experienced, consumed the room. He pressed his palms against the wounds in his cheeks, the pain diverting him from the panic that threatened to overwhelm.

He remembered Kaji's last words. Why would the Arab have been so concerned that he keep his promise if he was certain there wasn't a way out? The answer was obvious to Burton—because there was a way. And Kaji had spoken of *two* gateways to the Roads of Rostau: one on land and one in the water. On hands and knees, he made his way to the far wall. Burton carefully slid the ring onto the middle finger of his right hand, turning the eye design palm in.

Then he began moving his hand along the wall, starting at the bottom right and working his way across.

There was no way for him to know how long it took, but he was certain when he finally reached the top left that he had covered every square inch of the far wall. He turned to his right and began on that wall.

An eternity later, Burton was next to Kaji's body. The dead man's flesh was cold, the body stiff from rigor mortis. That told Burton he had been trapped in this room over ten hours. He had experience with dead bodies from his time in India and knew the stages of death.

There was no place for the ring on the walls.

Burton leaned back against the stone. There was more than the weight of the Great Pyramid above him. In fact, he was sure he was no longer under the Pyramid proper, but that made little difference. He could faintly hear the roar of the underground river somewhere not too far away.

He thought of beautiful Isabel, home in England, awaiting his return. The places he wanted to see that he had not yet. Overriding those two thoughts, though, were the words that Kaji had spoken. Of the Airlia, who were not men. Of their servants walking the Earth. An ancient war still being played out.

"I will not die in this place!" Burton yelled at the top of his lungs, feeling the pus and blood flow out of the wounds on his face. He felt power from that yell and the pain. He was still alive. There was still hope.

As the sound of his voice echoed into silence, he was aware once more of the underground river. He pressed his ear against the wall, trying to tell in what direction the water was. After trying all four walls, he was still uncertain. Then it occurred to him. He lay on the floor—yes, the water was somewhere farther in the depths.

Burton began quartering the floor, right palm down, ring covering every square inch.

When he heard the rumble of stone moving, he froze. He felt a draft of cool air hit his face. Reaching with his hands, scuttling around the edge on hands and knees, he realized that a square, eight feet on each side, had opened exactly in the center of the chamber. He leaned over it, but there was still no light. Only the feel of humid, cool air striking him. The sound of the river water was louder now.

He put his arm down, but the shaft ran perfectly straight with no end within reach. It might drop ten feet or a hundred. It might end in a stone floor, or water, or stakes on which interlopers were to be impaled.

He slid over the edge and lowered himself as far as he could, stretching his long frame out, and his toes felt nothing. With a great effort he pulled himself back into the chamber and lay on his back, breathing hard, his strength still not back after the years of recovery from the cholera compounded by the wounds received at Berbera.

He knelt next to the opening and leaned over. "Hello!" he yelled, hoping to get an echo, but it was as if the darkness below swallowed up his voice. Or there was no bottom to the shaft. He had heard of such things. Of pits where a man would fall forever and . . . Burton forced his mind to stop racing. He had to accept the inevitable reality.

It was the only way out.

Burton once more clambered into the hole, lowering himself, fingers gripping the stone edge. He dangled in the darkness, feeling the cold draft from below sliding up under his robe.

"Allah Akbar!" he whispered. Praise Allah.

His fingers began to weaken.

He fell.

THE PRESENT

CHAPTER 1

WASHINGTON, D.C.

"When I was a child in Maine, my entire world consisted of my small town, and it would expand to include Bangor when my dad drove us there once a month on a shopping trip." Mike Turcotte was standing on the steps of the Lincoln Memorial, gazing at the large statue of the sixteenth president seated in the stone chair, but his mind was in a different place and time.

Next to him, the science adviser to the current President, Lisa Duncan, also stood still, peering up. She remained silent, letting her partner struggle aloud with his thoughts.

"My world didn't get much bigger when I went to the University of Maine," Turcotte continued. "It was only when I went overseas in the Army that I began to see that the world was a much larger place than I'd ever imagined. Of course, I'd read about those other places, seen them in movies and videos, but there's nothing like being there, actually experiencing something, to make it real."

It was early, before six in the morning, and the first rays of the sun were just making an appearance in the eastern horizon, touching the flat surface of the Reflecting Pool behind them, bouncing up, and highlighting the statue. Because of the hour, the two of them had the monument to themselves.

Turcotte was a solidly built man. Of average height, he had broad shoulders and his dark skin and slight accent reflected his northern Maine, half-Canuck half-Indian background. His short black hair was sprinkled with premature gray.

He turned and looked back at the Pool, the lines around his dark eyes creasing as the sun hit them. "I thought what happened in Germany when I helped stop the IRA terrorists was as bad as it was going to get—"

"Mike, it wasn't your fault innocent civilians were killed," Duncan interrupted. "You did the best you could."

"Did I?" Turcotte asked. He didn't wait for an answer. "I really considered quitting, resigning my commission. But I didn't have time to think too long, because right after that happened you sent me to Area 51. And I've been on the move ever since." He pointed to the sky. "I've even gone into space, when I stopped the alien fleet of talon spacecraft." He looked down at Duncan. "I'm not sure how much further I can keep expanding my horizons."

"Come on, Mike." Duncan took his arm and turned him back toward the monument. She led him up the stairs and through the Doric columns that lined the monument—one for each state in the country, both north and south, at the time of the president's death—halting just in front of the nineteen-foot-high statue of the seated Lincoln.

"When I lived in Washington, I always came here when I needed to think," Duncan said. She nodded up at the statue. "He was a very smart man, perhaps the most brilliant mind this country has ever had. He used his brainpower, not like Einstein in the physical sciences, but on the more complex problems of people. He saw this country through a civil war and led it to a point where the two sides could even reconcile after his assassination. Every issue he dealt with was multifaceted, with no absolutes. The only thing he had going for him was his beliefs. That's how he made decisions."

Lisa Duncan was slightly over five feet tall and slender. Her dark hair was cut short and her face pale with fatigue and stress. She pointed to the inscription carved on the south wall. "There's the Gettysburg Address. Given in November 1863, five months after that momentous battle, where there were over sixty thousand casualties—all of them Americans. Imagine the weight of that on your shoulders.

"At the dedication ceremony for the National Cemetery for many of those dead, the keynote speaker talked for over two hours. Lincoln followed him and spoke for less than two minutes. It was perhaps the greatest speech ever given. He cut to the essence of what the battle was about and what the future needed.

"We have to do the same thing," she said. "We have to make sure all those who have died so far in this struggle have not done so in vain. From Peter Nabinger and Colonel Kostanov in China, the crew of the *Pasadena* off Easter Island, to the people of Vilhena in the Amazon rain forest. And the untold millions over the centuries who have been victims of these aliens and their minions."

"A lot of Americans died *after* Lincoln made that speech," Turcotte noted.

"Always the optimist," Duncan said.

"It's my job."

"It's your nature."

"I've read a lot about the Civil War," Turcotte said. "It always fascinated me—the bloodiest war in American history was the one where we fought each other. And we're not even clear who the enemy is in this war we're engaged in."

Duncan placed her hand on the stone wall. "I'm afraid more people *are* going to die before this is over. We have to take to heart Lincoln's last line of the address, 'that the dead have not have died in vain,' but

even more important, the last eight words. *Literally.*" She
ran her hand along the words she had indicated.

Turcotte looked at the bottom of the inscription:

THE PEOPLE SHALL NOT PERISH
FROM THE EARTH.

"That's what it's about. Majestic-12 trying to fly the
mothership reignited the smoldering remnants of the
millennia-old war between the Guides and The Ones
Who Wait. Aspasia came at us with the fleet from his
base on Mars, and you stopped that. The Mission tried
to wipe us out with the Black Plague and we just barely
stopped that, but we know they—and the others—will
come at us some other way. Until we know the truth,
what really happened in the past, we have to keep fighting and trying to survive.

"I've got to go there"—she pointed to the east, along
the length of the Mall, past the Washington Monument,
to the Capitol Building—"and testify about what just
happened. Then meet with the President about what
needs to happen. From there I'll go to New York and
meet with Peter Sterling and the rest of UNAOC."

"You have to go to Area 51 and make sure we're
secure. I'll be there as soon as possible. Then we need to
decide what to do next to make sure people do not per-
ish from the Earth."

CHAPTER 2

EARTH ORBIT

In the cold vacuum of space, the only visible remains of the space shuttle *Columbia* were a few twisted pieces of metal drifting alongside the source of their destruction. Dwarfing the human wreckage, the alien talon spacecraft took its name from its long, slightly curved shape that tapered to a point on one end like an oversized claw. Over two hundred miles long, by thirty meters at its widest, the craft's black metal skin absorbed the sun's rays that struck it. Three hundred miles below, a dark crescent bisecting the East Coast of the United States indicated dawn sweeping westward across Earth.

Man's most marvelous piece of technology had been destroyed in the blink of an eye by a blast from the tip of the talon, stopping the attempt to recover what had been considered a dead ship. The alien ship *was* indeed lifeless, the crew killed in the explosion initiated by Turcotte that had wiped out its eight sister ships as they converged on the mothership, which was also floating dead in orbit. But as the shuttle wreckage indicated, that didn't mean the ship was completely nonfunctional.

Eighty miles from the drifting talon, the Warfighter IV satellite flew on a polar orbit, its imagers shifting from their task of watching the surface of the planet below to taking a look at the talon as the orbits of the two closed on perpendicular courses.

Thermal infrared imagers pointed at the talon along with low-light-level cameras, recording what they saw and passing it to stations on Earth. Over sixty feet long and fifteen wide, the Warfighter was larger than the

Hubble space telescope. It weighed twenty-three tons, a third of that weight fuel for the maneuvering thrusters designed to place it over any spot on the globe within two hours of notification from the ground.

It boasted the full complement of imaging hardware that the latest U.S. spy satellite, the KH-14, contained, but the primary mission of the Warfighter wasn't to spy but to destroy. The imagers were for pinpointing targets; due to both its size and proximity, the talon was easily acquired as Warfighter closed to within sixty miles. The last one-third of Warfighter's weight was a small nuclear reactor hooked to a powerful high-frequency overtone laser.

Launched covertly from Vandenberg Air Force Base two years previously, Warfighter IV was the culmination of decades of classified work funded under the Star Wars program. Designed to destroy enemy satellites in space and missiles in flight in the atmosphere with the laser, its presence in orbit broke every treaty the United States had ever signed regarding the militarization of space. The nuclear reactor also violated every space launch doctrine ever established.

The imagers had a solid target lock on the talon, and the reactor began powering up the laser as Warfighter closed to within forty miles. As the power level passed through fifty percent, a golden glow suffused the tip of the talon. A thin line of power leapt at the speed of light from the talon to Warfighter, enveloping it in a stasis field. All contact the satellite had with its human controllers on the planet below was severed in the blink of an eye. The power buildup held at fifty percent. Slowly the talon used the field to draw Warfighter to it until the two were in orbit less than fifty meters apart.

They moved in tandem that way for fifteen minutes. As the Earth rotated below and the two drifted, their relative position to the planet changed. Soon they were over the western United States. The golden beam slowly rotated Warfighter until it was once more oriented toward the planet below. The imagers locked on a target on the Earth's surface.

The nuclear power buildup was released, and power surged to the laser. With a bright flash, a bolt of high energy arced toward Earth.

AREA 51, NEVADA

Area 51, located approximately ninety miles northwest of Las Vegas, on the edge of a dry lake bed nestled between mountains, consisted of three major parts. The most visible was the seven-mile-long concrete runway that extended across the dry Groom Lake flats. It was the longest runway in the world, used to launch and land the most sophisticated aircraft American designers could make.

The next most noticeable feature from above was the physical plant on the surface, consisting of hangars, support buildings, and tower for the runway.

The third—and invisible from above—part was the two hangars built into the side of Groom Mountain and the underground facilities that had housed the agency that had controlled Area 51 and the alien craft headquartered there—Majestic-12—for over five decades.

The normal operations at Area 51 came to an abrupt halt as a flash of light seared down from above, hitting one of the hangars. It was through the roof in a flash.

The initial blast was followed by a string of secondary explosions, and in less than ten seconds there was no longer a hangar and it would take days to recover the pieces of bodies from those who had been inside.

CHAPTER 3

MATO GROSSO, BRAZIL

It was after three days of difficult journeying that the falls finally came into view. They had been audible for hours during the approach. There was no mistaking the sound of over two million gallons of water tumbling over the edge of the Paraná Plateau of South America, cascading down 270 feet onto the rocks below—a natural thunder that abated only once every forty years during a dry season in the middle of a drought upriver.

The vision matched the awesome sound. It was as if an ocean met an abyss, as the Iquaca River in southern Brazil tumbled over a wall of 275 individual falls, stretching two and a half miles wide, most separated only by a few craggy rocks with some trees struggling to grow in the watery mist.

Downstream, on the west bank of the river, the small party stood in silent awe for minutes, simply watching the power of nature. Finally, one of the figures, the tallest of the group, shifted his gaze from the falls to the narrow gorge beneath them, where the water was carried away.

"Garganta del Diablo!" the native guide, Bauru, yelled in the tall man's ear, struggling to be heard as he pointed at the gorge. "That is what you seek, Professor."

"The Devil's Throat," the tall black man translated. Professor Niama Mualama was over six feet six inches in height. He was slender but not skinny, with broad shoulders and muscles packed on his frame like whipcord. His face was broad and friendly when he smiled, which was just about all the time. The only indication of his age were the thin lines around his eyes and a touch of lightness in his closely cropped black hair. He was old enough to have a one-year-old granddaughter back home in Nairobi, from his only daughter. His wife had died three years before from cancer, and since the funeral and the mourning period afterward, he had spent all his time pursuing his life's obsession.

Mualama was an anthropologist affiliated with the University of Dar es Salaam on the east coast of Tanzania. The fact that the university had barely a thousand students and Mualama had been one of only two professors in the anthropology department had done nothing to dint his enthusiasm. He had gone to graduate school in the United States and England and had returned home to help run the department. Recent changes in the government had caused severe cutbacks to what the ruling powers considered unessential programs at the university, and Mualama's department had been one of the first to fall under the ax two years ago.

No longer able to teach, he had devoted all his time to his studies and research, traveling extensively around the world, searching for answers to a mystery he had stumbled over as a young man. Mualama had spent two decades following clues scattered about the world. The last clue had led him to this location, and recent events regarding the alien presence on Earth had given a particular urgency to his mission.

He turned back to the thundering water. "The first European to see the falls—a Spaniard, Alvar Nunex de Vaca in 1541—called them Salto de Santa Maria, the Falls of Saint Mary."

Bauru shrugged. He had never heard that. They had always been the Iquaca Falls, from the local tongue, in which Iquaca meant "great water." Bauru was of Indian-Spanish descent. He was a short, stocky man with dark skin. His most distinguishing feature was his bald head.

His hair had begun falling out several years before, and
he'd decided to complete the process on his own. He
shaved it every day, even when he was in the wilderness.

"Let's go." Mualama shouldered his pack and headed
toward the gorge, where the surging water passed between rock cliffs on its journey to the Orinoco River, the
third-largest river in South America, and a long journey
to the distant Atlantic Ocean.

Bauru led and the two porters he had hired followed,
scrambling across rocks, then into the thick jungle as
they swung around the most immediate cliffs.

It was an arduous three-hour journey that covered
less than a mile before they came back out on the edge
of the gorge, the water fifty feet below them. The sound
of the falls was only slightly diminished.

"That is what I wanted to see," Mualama said.

The rock he was pointing at was twenty feet long by
fifteen wide, with a perfectly flat top. It sat about eight
feet out from the edge of the gorge in the river. Mualama eyed the water. It was fast moving and full of
stirred-up silt, making the water reddish brown in color.

Mualama slipped his pack off and pulled out a
leather-bound notebook.

"What do you have?" Bauru asked. He thought the
African most strange. They had linked up three days before at Santos, on the Atlantic Coast, just south of São
Paulo. Even though Mualama had told Bauru he'd never
been in South America before, the dark man had more
than carried his load on the journey and seemed un-
daunted by the thick jungle.

Mualama pulled a piece of paper out of the notebook.
"A copy of a telegraph sent almost a century ago." He
gave it to Bauru to read.

I have but one object: to uncover the mysteries that the jungle vastness of South America
have concealed for so many centuries. We are

```
encouraged in our hope of finding the ruins
of an ancient, white civilization and the de-
generate offspring of a once cultivated
race.
```

"Who sent this?" Bauru handed it back.

"Lieutenant Colonel Percy Fawcett, a British officer and explorer." Mualama was looking about.

"Did he find what he was looking for?"

"Fawcett, his son Jack, and a cameraman named Raleigh Rimell sent that telegraph on the twentieth of April, 1925, just before setting out on an expedition. They made one radio contact on the twenty-ninth of May, reporting their position, not far from here, then were never heard from or seen again."

Bauru wasn't surprised. Many had disappeared into the jungle, particularly in this area of Brazil, the Mato Grosso, a vast, virtually impenetrable land of jungle, escarpments, and tortuous rivers.

"What is this city they were looking for?" Bauru asked. There were many tales about the Mato Grosso, ranging from lost cities to terrible monsters to strange tribes of white-skinned people.

"Fawcett said he believed that people from Atlantis had come here just before the island was destroyed. That they built a mighty city in the jungle that deteriorated over the years. He claims that he found an old Portuguese map in Rio de Janeiro that showed a stone city enclosed by a wall deep in the Mato Grosso."

"You are searching for this city?"

"No."

"You are searching for the remains of Fawcett's party?" Bauru knew that would be an impossible task—the jungle would have consumed the three men and left no trace, especially after seventy-five years.

"No."

Bauru was a patient man. "Then what are we looking for?"

"What Fawcett was really looking for." Mualama was scanning the rocky crags below them.

Bauru was intrigued. "Not a lost city?"

"Oh, I think Fawcett believed there was a lost Atlantean city out there somewhere in the jungle, and certainly the events of the past month with the alien Airlia confirm there was an Atlantis," Mualama said. "But on that particular expedition, he was searching for something else." Mualama pointed below. "We must go down there."

Bauru eyed the route down with trepidation. He pulled his pack off and extracted a 120-foot nylon climbing rope. He tied one end around the thick trunk of a tree, then tossed the free end over the edge. Mualama already had a harness around his waist and a snaplink attached to the front. The African popped the rope through the gate, wrapped a loop around the metal, then prepared to back over the edge of the gorge, his left hand on the fixed end coming from his waist to the tree.

"How will we get back up?" Bauru asked.

"I will fasten the other end to the rock below," Mualama said. "Then we can climb back up using chumars."

"Chumars?"

Mualama held up two small pieces of machinery. "They clip on the rope, then allow it through in only one direction. You rest your weight on one, slide the other up, then rest your weight on the other. It is slow, but you will get back up."

Mualama put the chumars back in his pack and edged over the side of the gorge. He rappelled down, his feet finding precarious purchase on the jagged rock wall. Twenty feet above the surface of the river, he paused. Mualama bent his knees, bringing his body in close to the wall, then sprung outward as he released tension on the rope. The nylon slid through the snaplink as he descended, and he landed directly on top of the rock. He knelt and hammered a piton into the top of the rock before he unhooked from the rope. He tied off the free end of the rope to the piton and looked up at Bauru and gave a thumbs-up.

Only then did he turn his attention to the stone below him. At the height of the rainy season the top would be submerged, and thousands of seasons had scoured the surface smooth. Centered on the downstream side, just before the edge, was a small mark. Seeing it, Mualama allowed himself to feel the excitement of making a true discovery, of another step in his long and strange path about to be completed. He had feared this entire trip would turn up nothing, as previous trips to other places in the past had, but the mark was where it was supposed to be, and that meant— Mualama stopped himself from thinking too far ahead.

Bauru slid down the rope and arrived, leather gloves keeping his hands from burning on the nylon. The two porters followed, as Mualama examined the carving.

"What is it?" Bauru asked. He had never seen such strange markings.

"It is Arabic script for the number one thousand and one," Mualama translated. The water had worn smooth the edges of the carving.

"Arabic?" Bauru touched the rock. "This has been here for a long time. What Arab would have been here that many years ago? You said Fawcett was an Englishman."

"The mark was carved there in 1867, long before Fawcett set out on his journey. But it was an Englishman who carved the numbers. An Englishman who spoke and wrote fluent Arabic. Sir Richard Francis Burton."

"I have not heard of this man," Bauru said.

"He was a famous explorer and linguist. Burton was

assigned as British consul to Brazil in 1864. He was
based on the coast in Santos. In 1867 he left Santos and
traveled alone for almost the entire year. It is known he
navigated the San Francisco River north of here for over
fifteen hundred miles in a canoe. He barely survived,
arriving at the coast suffering from both pneumonia and
hepatitis."

"Why did he do this?" Bauru thought most foreigners
quite strange. He would never travel that far in the Mato
Grosso alone. It was akin to committing suicide. He was
amazed that the man had made it to the coast, especially
given the limited equipment he must have had over a
hundred years earlier.

"To hide something." Mualama pointed down. "It
must be underneath. I think Burton traveled here during
the dry season of the drought of 1867, when the water
was much lower. In one of his papers I found in England
he described a chamber under a flat rock like an altar, in
the throat of the Devil." Mualama looked around. "We
are in the Devil's Throat. This is a flat rock in the right
place. And this mark is his."

"How do you know that?" Bauru asked.

"Burton translated the story of the Thousand and
One Nights from the Arabic. To mark his way, he used
riddles that only someone who knew about him would
recognize. I have no doubt we are in the right place. I
must go underneath and find the chamber."

"Is this what Fawcett was looking for?"

"I believe so."

"But Fawcett never returned," Bauru noted.

"He might never have made it here," Mualama said.
"The journey is easier now."

Bauru looked at the water askance. "There is much
danger in the rivers here. You cannot see more than six
inches in that muck. There are—"

"I have to," Mualama cut him off. "Like Fawcett, I

have been on Burton's trail for twenty years, and this is the next step." Mualama pulled off his shoes and socks.

"Why did Fawcett lie about what he was looking for?" Bauru asked, trying to forestall the professor's going into the water.

"Because it is a very dangerous path he was trying to follow, and because there are those who guard it most jealously." Mualama pulled his shirt over his head, revealing his lean torso, a black metal medallion hanging around his neck that featured an eye superimposed on the apex of a pyramid, and a back covered in scar tissue.

Bauru and the porters were shocked by what they saw. "What happened to your back?"

"I was caught in a fire," Mualama said. He had only his shorts on. "I am going over the side."

"Here." Bauru pulled a shorter section of rope out of his pack and handed one end to Mualama. "Tie this around your waist."

Mualama quickly looped the rope around himself and tied it off. After a sharp exchange in their native dialect, Bauru and the two porters held the other end. Mualama slid over the side of the rock into the fast-flowing, warm water. He took a deep breath, then dove down, running hands along the rock, searching.

He went down about five feet, searching carefully, but there was nothing. He burst to the surface, gasping for air. He dove once more, hands searching along the rock face. He pulled himself lower, eight feet down, and felt an indentation in the rock. Reaching his hand into the opening, he grabbed hold of the inside and pulled himself down. The air in his lungs pressed him up against the top of whatever he was in.

The way ahead was still clear, but Mualama had no more oxygen. He pushed back out and surfaced, sputtering for air.

"Have you found anything?" Bauru asked.

Mualama could only nod as his lungs worked to replenish the lost oxygen. He noted that the porters were looking about nervously, fearful of something. Bauru sat down on the edge of the rock. "It is dangerous to stay in the water too long."

Mualama was finally able to speak. "Why?"

"Snakes. Piranha. They usually are not in water that flows this quickly, but one never knows. Sometimes they congregate in tide pools along such a river and hunt meat in packs. It is not good to take chances."

Mualama had come too far to be scared off by a threat that might not be present. "I am going under. There is a chamber. If I do not surface, or pull on the rope three times, by the end of one minute, pull me back out."

Bauru nodded.

Mualama filled his lungs and dove once more. He slid along the rock and into the opening. He could tell with his hands that it was a tunnel about four feet in diameter, going into the rock itself. He pushed along, searching blindly. Suddenly his hand was free of water. He popped his head up and breathed stale air in total darkness. He tugged on the rope around his waist hard, three times. Then he searched with his hands. A rock ledge was in front of him. It went back as far as he could reach.

He needed light.

The African professor retraced his route through the tunnel and back to the surface. He surfaced and opened his eyes.

Bauru and the two porters were no longer holding the other end of the rope. The three were standing, heads tilted back, looking at the top of the gorge. Mualama followed their gaze. A tall man in dark clothes, along with a dozen Guirani Indian tribesmen armed with crossbows, lined the top. The man's face was hidden in the shadow of a large bush hat.

The man waved his hand and the Guirani raised their weapons. Bauru reacted, dashing toward Mualama and diving into the water. The porters cried out, raising their hands in supplication, in turn to be hit with several bolts each. They dropped lifeless on the stone altar.

"Come!" Bauru grabbed Mualama's shoulder as a bolt skittered off the edge of the rock less than six inches from his face. "Lead me to the chamber."

Mualama dove, Bauru's hand now on his ankle. He pulled through the tunnel, lungs bursting—he had not gotten a good breath when he had surfaced, and the going was slow—pulling Bauru through.

Mualama was starved for air. He reached ahead, hoping to touch the surface, but felt only more water. He pulled harder through tunnel. His hand broke the surface and he grabbed the ledge, pulling himself into the air. Bauru sputtered up next to him.

They hung on the edge, gasping for several moments.

"Who was that with the Guirani?" Bauru finally managed to ask.

"The Mission." Mualama spit the last word out.

"Who?"

Mualama pulled himself onto the stone ledge and rolled onto his side, still breathing hard. "They've followed me before. The burns on my back—they almost caught me in England last year. They destroyed the place where I was studying some ancient texts, and I barely managed to escape."

Bauru joined him. "Who is this Mission? I have heard stories of such a place, but no one seems to know exactly where it is. Why do they chase you?"

Mualama felt the darkness all around. Even here the sound of the waterfalls sounded like a nonending series of drums rumbling. He reached out, searching the stone ledge. "Burton left something in this place. He could get in here during the dry season that year. Every forty years or so during a drought the river dries up and the falls are silent. Burton came here during one of those occasions."

"Why is this Mission trying to kill us?" Bauru was still focused on the immediate danger.

"They work for the aliens." Mualama's fingers brushed against something. Slick cloth. Wrapped around something. He picked it up. It was about twelve inches long by eight wide by two deep and covered with a soft pliant cloth. He slipped it into the waistband of his shirt as Bauru suddenly turned on a small penlight.

Above the rock, one of the Guirani scampered down the rope to the rock. He had a length of cord over his shoulder that he tied to both of the bodies. He fastened the free end to the piton, then rolled both bodies into the river, the blood swirling into the silt-laden water, the corpses banging against the rock. Then he unfastened the nylon rope from the piton and climbed, hand over hand, back to the top of the gorge. He pulled the rope up.

The small party stood still for a few minutes, watching. Then the water around the two bodies exploded in churning red froth.

"What do we do now?" Bauru asked. He shined the light around. They were inside a chamber about four feet from the ledge, three high by six wide. The rock walls had been polished smooth when water had carved it out ages before.

"We must get out of here," Mualama said.

"They might be waiting for us."

"We cannot stay here much longer," Mualama said. "The air is growing stale."

Bauru considered the situation. "If we stay underwater and swim with the current, we might be able to get far enough down the gorge so that they will not see us."

"All right." Mualama was anxious to be moving, to get outside in the light where he could see what treasure he had uncovered.

Bauru turned the light off and slid over the edge into the water. Mualama prepared to follow, when the guide screamed and splashed about.

"What is wrong?" Mualama yelled.

Bauru screamed again, and literally jumped out of the water onto the ledge. Mualama could hear him cursing, flopping about.

"Get it off me!" Bauru yelled.

"What is it?"

"Get it off me!" There was a ripping sound, then something splashing into the water. "Oh, God." Bauru's voice was low now as he slumped back. The light came on, and Mualama saw a long, jagged tear down the other man's chest. There was another on his leg. Blood pulsed out of the wounds.

"What happened?"

"Piranha." Bauru grimaced as his fingers probed the wound on his chest. The skin was torn for almost ten inches, the edges of the wound rough. Blood oozed out over Bauru's fingers.

Mualama tried to help him, but they had nothing to stop the bleeding with.

"We have to get out of here," Mualama insisted.

"How?"

"We wait for the fish to leave?" Mualama suggested.

Bauru looked up at Mualama, his face resigned. "They have tasted me. They have the blood scent. They will not leave. I have seen such fish block a river crossing for four days after taking down the lead horse in a column. They stripped it down to a skeleton, then waited for more."

Mualama took a deep breath to steady his nerves, but all that served to do was remind him how stale the air in their small prison was. He tried to help the other man stop the bleeding, but the wounds were too wide and long. A pool of blood was forming on the rock beneath Bauru.

Mualama looked over at the dark surface of the water.

"There is no other way out than through the tunnel," Mualama said.

Bauru laughed, a manic edge to it. "I know that. The only choice to be made is to die here slowly or to go in the water and die quickly." He leaned back, hissing in pain. "What did you find?" he asked, nodding toward the packet stuck in Mualama's belt.

"I don't know."

"Is it important?"

"I believe so."

"Worth our lives?"

"Yes."

"Even though you don't know what it is?" Bauru was surprised and interested in spite of his pain and the situation.

"I have been tracking down . . ." Mualama paused. He'd never explained what he was doing to anyone, even his wife. "I have been searching for the truth."

"The truth?"

"About the aliens. About our . . . the human race's past. I think this"—Mualama tapped the packet wrapped in oilskins—"is the next clue in a long line leading me to the ultimate truth."

"Ah." Bauru nodded. "That I can understand. It is said now that Kon Tiki Viracocha, the sun god many in this part of the world worshiped, might have been one of these aliens. That they destroyed the people of the great city of Tiahuanaco in ancient times."

Mualama nodded. "The Mission has been around for

a long time. It was behind the Black Death that killed many of your countrymen in Vilhena just recently."

There was silence for several minutes. Mualama kept pressure on the wounds as best he could, but the rips were too long and wide.

"I am going to die here," Bauru finally said.

"I will go and get help," Mualama said.

"You will die before you make twenty feet. And help where? We are over a hundred miles from the nearest help. Even if I get out of here, I am still a dead man."

Mualama didn't answer, because he knew what Bauru was saying was true.

"What religion are you?" Bauru asked unexpectedly.

"I was born Muslim."

Bauru laughed softly. "I am Catholic—will it make any difference if you pray for me?"

"I think we all look to the same God with different names," Mualama said.

Bauru looked down at his wound. "I am a dead man already. I will help you escape."

"How?"

When Bauru explained his plan, Mualama did not argue. He knew that to protest would insult the other man's brave offer. And he knew it was the only chance he had to get out of the cave and away, alive, with the packet.

"Are you ready?" Bauru asked.

Mualama nodded.

Bauru closed his eyes, and his lips moved in prayer. Mualama murmured his own prayer to Allah for his companion.

Bauru scooted over to the edge and looked down at the dark water. "I am ready."

Mualama clasped the other man on the shoulder. "I thank you."

"Use my gift well," Bauru said. Then he dove into the water and disappeared from sight.

Mualama slowly began counting to ten.

Bauru made it into the tunnel before the first piranha struck. They were of the *Serrasalmus piraya* species, the largest of the deadly fish, the biggest in the pack almost twenty inches long. They had a stocky body, with a large head, sporting a domed forehead, and were also among the most aggressive of the family of piranha. Their lower jaws opened wide, revealing rows of sharp, serrated teeth. They slammed into Bauru's body, teeth clamping down, ripping flesh free.

Still Bauru pulled and kicked, getting to the end of the tunnel, pushing free into the river, his body covered with predators. He continued kicking, a trail of blood bringing those that weren't already feasting in for the kill. Even though they traveled in a loose pack, there was no love lost among the fish, some even fighting each other to get at the meat. As Bauru splashed downstream, the pack followed him.

On the ridge above, those waiting saw the bloody struggle, and their eyes followed until the body stopped flailing and the feeding frenzy drifted downstream.

Mualama reached ten and dove into the water. He made it through the tunnel unscathed. Holding his breath, he angled left, heading for the far shore. His muscles were tight; at any moment he expected to feel teeth tearing into his flesh.

He bumped into a rock, then another, tumbled about in the current, pulled himself around a boulder, sheltering him from view from the far side, and surfaced.

Sucking in a lungful of oxygen, Mualama carefully peered around the boulder. He saw those on top of the gorge looking farther downstream at Bauru's fate.

Mualama pulled himself out of the water and onto a rocky ledge, still keeping the boulder between him and the others. He waited until, after another hour, they finally turned and disappeared into the jungle, satisfied they had accomplished their task.

Mualama climbed on top of the boulder. He could jump from there to the rock face on this side of the gorge. He knew he had a hard climb, and then an even harder forced march to civilization, but there was no doubt in his mind he would make it. All he had to do was look over his shoulder and see the remains of Bauru, stripped to the bone, washed up between two rocks downstream and on the other side.

And he had the package tucked into his pants. He had to make it to the next step in the riddled path that Richard Francis Burton had left behind as his secret legacy.

CHAPTER 4

AREA 51

The gusts of wind coming off the peaks picked up sand and carried the fine particles with them, limiting visibility to less than two hundred feet in any direction. Area 51 was completely covered by the storm.

Captain Mike Turcotte kept one hand on the goggles strapped around his head, the other on the MP-5 submachine gun slung over his left shoulder. To his right, another figure braved the scouring wind, striding forward, away from the side of the mountain where the massive hangar doors that had opened slightly to allow them out, now slid closed. The doors were painted the same color as the mountain, a dull, sandy tone, and they appeared to become part of the slope as they shut.

"At our Area 51 it was snow that the wind carried," the other man yelled, his strong accent audible above the howling shrieks.

Turcotte didn't acknowledge the Russian's comment. Already the mountain from which they had emerged had faded into the brown, swirling fog. He concentrated on moving in a straight line, knowing how easy it would be to become disoriented and wander into the wasteland that surrounded Area 51.

Turcotte held up his right arm, fist closed, the military signal to stop. Yakov, the Russian, lumbered to a halt, waiting. Almost seven feet tall, Yakov seemed little bothered by either the wind or blowing sand. He wore a long black coat that flapped behind him. A short black beard covered his lower face. A fur hat, incongruous in the sandstorm, topped his large head.

"The runway." Turcotte pointed ahead at the edge of concrete that was visible in the relative lulls between the stronger gusts. He turned to the right and moved in that direction, using the edge of the runway as his guide. After several minutes he came to another stop. To the right, in between surges of the wind, they could make out the gutted ruins of the hangar that had been destroyed by the blast from space.

"With our own sword," Turcotte said, more to himself than Yakov.

"What?" The Russian leaned closer.

"We were attacked with our own weapon."

"What was in there?" Yakov asked.

"The bodies of the two STAAR personnel we killed. The scientists were still working on the bodies, trying to figure out how much was human and how much was alien. Eight people were killed in the blast."

"It is the price of war," Yakov said.

"We're not winning the war," Turcotte said.

Yakov didn't reply to that. He reached up and made sure his hat was still attached. "We could have waited in the hangar."

"Too many prying eyes and inquisitive ears in there," Turcotte said.

Yakov laughed, a deep rumble that was ripped away by the wind. "You are learning. Paranoid is good. Paranoid keeps you alive."

"Major Quinn is doing an electronics sweep of the Cube—the underground operations center for Area 51 where you met him. Once he's sure it's secure—and Dr. Duncan gets here—we'll meet there and figure out what we're doing."

"Do you trust this Major Quinn? Was not he a member of Majestic-12?"

"I don't trust you, never mind Major Quinn," Turcotte said, turning from the destroyed hangar to watch the runway, or at least the small portion he could see. "Quinn wasn't on the inner circle of MJ-12, just their military liaison in the Cube—more of a technical guy than an actual operator. And you were a member of Section Four, right? Which was the Soviet's equivalent of Majestic, so I don't think you have much right to be questioning Quinn's loyalty."

"I may be all that is left of Section Four," Yakov said. "And *we* did not try to fly the mothership. *Your* Majestic was infiltrated by the Tiahuanaco guardian computer. I do not know if Section Four was infiltrated, but I do know it was destroyed by these aliens or their minions. I no longer know what is what and whom to trust."

Turcotte nodded. "That's something we need to talk about when Duncan gets here."

"Do you trust anyone?" Yakov asked.

"Do you?"

"No one completely. You did not answer my question. Is there anyone you trust?"

Turcotte's answer was brief. "Dr. Duncan."

"Why?"

Turcotte didn't reply.

"You must think with your head, not your heart," Yakov finally said.

"I am," Turcotte said shortly.

"I have seen the way you two look at each other. Such feelings can interfere with—"

Turcotte turned, looking up at the Russian. "I'm thinking with my head, but I trust with my heart. Maybe that's something you could learn." He reached out and tapped the large man's chest. "I *almost* trust you after what happened at Devil's Island." Turcotte returned his attention to the runway.

Yakov smiled. "Almost. That is good. That is as far as we should take things. In our profession it is never good to deal in absolutes." The smile disappeared. "Let me ask you something, my almost trusted friend. Dr. Duncan got you involved with Area 51 and Majestic-12 in the first place, correct?"

Turcotte nodded, then realized the other man couldn't see the gesture as a blast of wind reduced visibility to zero. "Yes!" he yelled.

"How did *she* know of what was going on here? Of Majestic-12?"

Turcotte had never really thought about that, and he hesitated answering. He decided to get to the other thing on his mind. "What about Tunguska? Why did General Hemstadt mention that just before he died? That we didn't know what caused it?"

Yakov shook his head. "I have not been able to find out much. Maybe Hemstadt was trying to misdirect us. You have to understand—" Yakov began, but his attention was diverted; something was moving in the storm.

"There's the bouncer." Turcotte waved a flashlight, glad that the conversation had been interrupted.

A silver-skinned, disk-shaped object hovered ten feet over the runway, moving slowly toward them. There was no visible means of propulsion and no windows in the skin of the craft, although Turcotte knew those on the inside could see out, the alien technology allowing light to pass through via a technique that those who had worked on the craft at Area 51 had yet to unravel.

The bouncer, the nickname for the craft among the Air Force pilots who'd trained on them, descended until it came in contact with the runway twenty feet in front of Turcotte and Yakov. The official designation for the nine atmospheric alien craft was MDAC, or magnetic drive atmospheric craft. Two had been recovered nearby during the early days of World War II, parked in a cavern along with a massive mothership. That discovery was the reason Area 51 had been located at this remote site, since they had had no way to move the mile-long mothership from its hiding place.

Eventually, from clues discovered in the mothership cavern, the other seven had been recovered from a cache deep under the Antarctic ice. Each bouncer was about thirty feet wide at the base, sloping up to a small cupola on top. There was no doubt that the numerous test and training flights of the craft had led to many UFO sightings and contributed greatly to UFO folklore.

Turcotte had never learned if the craft had gotten that nickname because the people inside could get bounced about so badly or because the craft seemed to literally bounce off an unseen wall when changing direction. The propulsion system was something else that Majestic-12 had been unable to reverse-engineer despite decades of trying. They had determined that it worked off the planet's magnetic field, and Turcotte knew from personal experience that the bouncers lost power if they were too far from the planet's surface, but beyond that, they could not duplicate or reverse-engineer a working model.

A hatch on the top of the bouncer swung up and a slight figure climbed out, then down the side of the craft. Turcotte ran forward and handed Duncan a set of goggles, which she pulled down over her eyes.

"The Cube isn't secure yet?" She was between the two men, their bodies giving her some relief from the dust storm.

"Quinn said any minute now." Turcotte held up a cell phone. "He'll call us when it's ready."

Duncan nodded. "Good, I wanted to talk to just the two of you alone first anyway." She looked past them at the ruins of the hangar. "I had a private meeting with the President just before coming here. Cutting through the political double-talk, the bottom line is we're on our own. The destruction of the two space shuttles has shaken the entire administration. Everyone's afraid to find out how deeply we've been infiltrated by either the alien representatives—the Guides/Mission and The Ones Who Wait/STAAR—or the human group, the Watchers. Losing Warfighter and having it used against us was the final straw."

"Who directed Warfighter to attack the talon?" Turcotte asked.

"The President acceded to the demands of his National Security Council to have Warfighter target the talon. Payback for the destruction of *Columbia*. It didn't work the way they had planned. Now they're afraid of two things. One is that Warfighter can hit any target on the face of the planet. I think the President has visions of a laser blast right through the roof of the Oval Office. The other is they don't want to admit Warfighter exists. There's already infighting at UNAOC and among the members of the Security Council. The Russians and Chinese might walk out if they know we put a weapon into space two years ago."

"So, as usual, they hide the truth?" Turcotte asked.

"Did you expect something to change?" Duncan asked. "I also met with Peter Sterling, the head of the United Nations Alien Oversight Committee, in New York, and he said pretty much the same thing as the President. He's trying to build a coalition, but he's fighting the Security Council the whole way."

The bouncer had lifted and floated past them, entering Hangar One, sliding between the large doors that just as quickly shut behind it. Turcotte felt very vulnerable standing with Yakov and Duncan on the edge of the runway, the dust storm limiting their world to a small circle of concrete. He could understand the President's fear. A weapon floating above their heads in space that could strike down at any moment was unnerving.

It went beyond that, though, for him. He'd expected bad news from Duncan's Washington and New York meetings, but a small part of him had hoped that some-one in the administration or at the United Nations would step forward and take the lead. Duncan's next words effectively quashed that hope.

"The isolationists control both the House and the Senate, which limits the President's options, and China has veto power in the Security Council, which hamstrings UNAOC from taking action. Since most actions up to now have occurred away from U.S. soil—meaning primarily the Black Death in South America, Qian-Ling in China, the Airlia at Cydonia on Mars, and the shield surrounding Easter Island—the feeling in the States seems to be that if we stick our heads in the sand, nothing bad will happen if we don't see it."

"You Americans," Yakov growled. "You entered the Great Patriotic War only after millions of my country-men were dead at the hands of the Nazis, France was overrun, and England was teetering on the edge of collapse. And then it took a direct attack against your base in Pearl Harbor to get you off the fence and into the fight. What will it take this time? This is a *world* problem. One that the oceans on either side of your country will not keep at arm's reach."

A strong gust of wind hit them, staggering Duncan into Turcotte, who steadied her with an arm around her shoulder.

"I'm telling you the reality of the situation," Duncan shouted. "We can stand here and argue how screwed up it is until we're blue in the face, but it's not going to change anything. The isolationists have a very persuasive argument, using the facts *we've* given them regarding the Airlia being on the planet so long. The point they make is that if the Airlia and their human agents have existed peacefully with us for so long, why not go back to the status quo?"

"That's bull," Turcotte said. "Majestic trying to fly the

mothership upset the balance, and it's never going to be restored. This is a fight to the end."

"I know that, and that's why I'm here," Duncan said. "The bottom line is that we're on our own. I have the same presidential authorization to gain us aid from whatever government organization we need, but that's it. We also have some support from Sterling at UNAOC, but that will be limited, as even UNAOC is being pressured to toe the isolationist line. And we have to be covert about any actions we take, not only because of the isolationists but also to steer clear of The Mission, the Watchers, and The Ones Who Wait. Just be glad the President didn't shut us down."

"Would that have been so bad?" Turcotte muttered, the words unheard by the other two.

"Official policy right now," Duncan yelled, "is to gather information but take no direct action."

"That's crap," Turcotte said. "We're sticking our necks out and getting no support." He pointed at the ruins of the hangar. "We lost eight people in there."

"I know—and that's being kept under wraps also. I did get us some backup," Duncan said.

"Who?" Turcotte asked.

"A Special Forces team straight from Bragg. Your friend Colonel Mickell handpicked the team, so they should be good. They're en route now. We're to use them as we see fit."

"No limitations?" Turcotte asked. "Like national boundaries?"

"Unofficially, no limitations," Duncan said. "Officially, if we screw up, it's our ass on the line."

"Great," Turcotte said. His phone buzzed, and he flipped it open, one hand over his free ear so he could hear, then shut it. "Quinn says the Cube is secure and clear of any surveillance devices. Let's get inside, get you cleaned up, then figure out what we're going to do."

"There's something else," Duncan said.

"What?"

She reached into her coat and pulled out a piece of paper that the wind tried to rip from her grasp. "We've heard from Easter Island."

"The guardian?" Turcotte asked.

"The message is apparently from Kelly Reynolds—or whatever Kelly has become now."

KENNEDY SPACE CENTER, FLORIDA

The security guard flashed his light at the ID card, then checked the face of the holder to make sure the two matched. The security rating on the card was the highest possible in the dark world of covert operations. The organization listed was the Central Intelligence Agency.

The owner of the card did ostensibly work for the CIA, but in reality he was a member of STAAR, which stood for Strategic Tactical Advanced Alien Response. Founded by President Eisenhower, the organization had been set up to be a coordinating group for response to a potential alien assault—given the fact that aliens had indeed visited Earth in the past, as evidenced by what Majestic-12 was working with at Area 51. In reality, though, STAAR was a front organization in America for The Ones Who Wait, allowing it to infiltrate the government bureaucracy at every level. It was the way of bureaucracy and the compartmentalization of the covert world that the correct piece of paper or security clearance could override every suspicion for decades.

The operative's code name was Etor, and he quickly strode past the guard and toward the VAB—vehicle assembly building—a towering edifice five hundred and twenty-five feet tall and covering eight acres of land, one of the largest buildings in the world. The VAB was designed to withstand winds of up to 125 miles per hour. Its foundation rested on 4,200 steel pilings 16 inches in diameter driven down 160 feet to bedrock.

Etor had first visited the facility when it was named Cape Canaveral. The VAB was originally designed for the assembly of the massive Saturn launch vehicles. It had since been modified to support the assembly of the space shuttle.

Etor watched as the high bay door, 456 feet high, rumbled to a halt, opening the spacious interior to the warm night air carried by the ocean breeze. The space shuttle *Atlantis*, mated with its external fuel tank and two solid rockets, stood vertical on top of the crawler-transporter. With a very slight jar, the huge treads on the crawler began moving, edging the entire shuttle system on its mobile launcher platform out of the VAB.

Although the final destination was in sight, it would take the crawler six hours to make the short distance to the point from which the shuttle would be launched. Normally when a shuttle was moved at night, spotlights highlighted the procedure, providing a spectacle to the American public whose tax dollars funded the entire operation. This night, though, the movement was being made in blackout conditions. All roads around the space center had been blocked off since nightfall, reducing spectators to the security personnel and technicians involved—and those with the proper security clearance.

With the destruction of the shuttles *Endeavour* and *Columbia, Atlantis*, quickly brought out of a retrofit, was the only spaceworthy manned craft left in the inventory. The shuttle *Discovery* had been stripped down to the bone for an extensive rebuilding, and it was estimated that even at breakneck speed—a term astronauts didn't want to hear when someone was talking about working on a vehicle they would be riding in—it would take over a month to get it ready for flight.

The transporter was 131 feet long by 114 wide. It

moved on four double-tracked crawlers, each 10 feet high and 41 feet long. Just one of the track shoes weighed 2,000 pounds. With a maximum speed of one mile per hour, *Atlantis* cleared the VAB doors and the treads slowly crunched their way toward Launch Complex 39-A, which was 3.4 miles away. Etor turned and walked toward one of the old launch sites, half a mile away from the road, easily outpacing the shuttle on its path.

He climbed down a rusting iron staircase into an old observation bunker, his feet splashing through water that had accumulated on the concrete floor. He leaned on a ledge, peering through a narrow slit at the black silhouette of the moving shuttle. He pulled out a small black box and pressed the on button.

"It is moving," he reported.

"Do you know the mission profile?" the voice on the other end asked.

"The cover story is deployment of two surveillance satellites. The reality is that the payload consists of the latest generation of Warfighter satellite. They want to put it in orbit and take out the Warfighter you control."

"That is unacceptable." There was a short pause. "I have a lock on target. Out here."

"Out," Etor acknowledged, putting the communicator back in his pocket.

The transporter was less than a quarter mile from the VAB when a flash of light streaked down from above and hit the top of the external fuel tank. The laser beam ignited the five hundred thousand gallons of liquid oxygen and hydrogen.

The resulting explosion not only obliterated *Atlantis,* it took out the vehicle assembly building. Windows as far away as ten miles were blown, and the shock wave from the explosion was heard in Orlando, forty miles away.

Etor had ducked down, deep inside the shelter, but

even there the passing blast wave sucked the air out of his lungs. He waited a few seconds, then stood and looked out. There was nothing where the shuttle had been.

THE MOUNTAINS OF THE MOON, RUWENZORI, UGANDA

Professor Mualama took another deep drink from the canteen looped over his shoulder and looked up at the wall of heavy clouds that blocked the sky to the west as he spoke. He was a continent away from South America, but once more deep inside an uninhabited wilderness.

"The Greek historian Herodotus, visiting Egypt in 547 B.C., was told that the source of the Nile was a bottomless lake set among tall, whitecapped mountains astride the equator. He thought the story was outrageous, but—and this is a valuable lesson for you, Nephew—he wrote it down anyway."

The young man whom Mualama had just addressed was a bit worse for wear. Peter Lago's khaki shirt was streaked with salt stains. His arms were covered with scratches and his muscles ached from the eight-hour march since leaving the last sign of civilization in Kasese, Uganda. They'd been climbing up a one-track trail since getting off the plane on the unfinished dirt strip in the town, and as far as Lago could tell, they were heading into the clouds. His uncle had set an unrelenting pace, in a rush since having Lago pick him up at the airport in Dar es Salaam the previous evening, hiring a bush pilot to fly them illegally into Uganda, and setting off on the trail.

Lago—a former archaeology student at Dar es Salaam—had worked with his uncle on digs before. East Africa was where many of the oldest fossils attributable to genus *Homo* had been found. The two had spent several summers working at the established digs in the Olduvai Gorge of Tanzania, where a fossil of *Homo habilis* had been found that had been dated back two million years. *Homo habilis* was the true beginning of the lineage of current man, and so few fossils had been found that any discovery was significant.

Lago considered his uncle a very strange man with eclectic interests. Both ancient man and modern history mesmerized his uncle—he was a scientist who believed in knowing one's facts, yet he also collected every piece of legend and mythology he could find.

Lago was still waiting for an explanation why they were here, but he was used to his uncle's long silences, because he knew he would eventually get more information than he ever wanted once the older man began speaking. It appeared that time had come as Mualama began talking again, filling up the minutes of the short break that he had allowed every two hours during the march.

"In A.D. 50, Marinus of Tyre, a geographer, recorded a story he heard from a Greek merchant who claimed to have traveled inland from the east coast of Africa for twenty-five days and reached a land of mountains and snow where the source of the Nile came out of two lakes.

"The Greek mathematician and geographer Ptolemy was the first geographer to use longitude and latitude lines to identify locations on the face of the planet. He also thought the idea of snowcapped mountains lying on the hot equator most fascinating. He called these mountains Luna Montes, the Mountains of the Moon, a name many still use for where we are."

Mualama stretched his back, the bones cracking as they settled in place. In his backpack lay the package he had recovered under the stone in the Devil's Throat. It had pointed him to the next clue, back home to Africa, and he had wasted no time getting here.

"Unlike Kilimanjaro and Ngorongoro," he continued, "these mountains—also called the Ruwenzori, a corruption of the local word for rainy mountains—were not formed by volcanic action. We are basically on the edge of an enormous massif, about one hundred and twenty kilometers long and fifty kilometers wide.

"We are in Uganda, and the border with Zaire runs along the center of this massif, where the peaks are." He pointed ahead at the clouds. "There are four major summits—Mounts Speke, Stanley, Baker, and Luigi di Savoia. All named after white men, of course. The locals have their own name for them, which the Europeans ignored. Stanley was the first white man to see the peaks in the modern age. He was in this area in 1875 and told of the mountains by his native guides, but, like us today, he could see nothing but the clouds and mist they are covered in for over three hundred days out of the year. He came back thirteen years later, in 1888, and happened to have a clear day and saw the white peaks."

"Uncle . . ." Lago knew if he didn't interrupt, his uncle would fall completely into his lecture mode, and it might be hours before he got around to the information the young man most needed to know.

Mualama frowned. "Yes?"

"Where are we going?"

"Mount Speke."

That answered one of Lago's unasked questions—why he was here. He had experience mountain climbing, summiting numerous mountains in Ethiopia and South Africa. He had never been to the Mountains of the Moon, but he knew climbing Speke would be difficult, especially if the weather turned bad. So, as usual, his uncle needed his help. He decided to ask the third question.

"Why are we climbing Mount Speke?"

"Do you know who Speke was?" Mualama asked instead of answering.

Lago shook his head.

"Stanley was Anglo-American. Luigi di Savoia was an Italian duke who mapped the mountain range in the first decade of the twentieth century. Speke was an English explorer. He is best known for discovering Lake Tanganyika with Sir Richard Francis Burton in 1858. At the time, they thought it was the source of the Nile. The two had a long-running feud when Speke returned to England before Burton and announced the discovery, taking most of the credit. They were scheduled to debate the issue when, the day before, Speke was killed in a most unfortunate hunting accident. It is quite an irony that Burton would have hidden the next clue on the mountain named for his hated rival."

"The next clue?"

"You will see," Mualama said.

Lago checked the cuts on his arm from the jungle that had encroached over much of the trail, half listening to his uncle, waiting for him to answer the question as to the purpose of this expedition. His uncle was known not only in the family but at the university, for his trips all over the world, searching for something he never quite told anyone.

The journey had been more than worth it so far, though, simply to see the bizarre terrain they had passed through. Swamps and marshes had surrounded the trailhead, but as they went up, the vegetation changed to a strange world of giant plants among misshapen rocks. Lobelias grew twenty times their normal height, and many other plants that rarely topped a foot or two elsewhere towered over their heads. The almost constant moisture from the clinging clouds combined with the mineral-rich soil and high dosage of ultraviolet light, due to the altitude and latitude, to produce mutations unknown elsewhere on the planet.

Tall, writhing stems crowned with heads of spiky leaves swayed overhead, while the ground was covered with layers of pink blossoms. Tree heathers draped with beards of lichens formed with the rest to create a landscape that might have existed millions of years ago when dinosaurs roamed the Earth. It was a land out of time with the rest of the world, and one of the most remote and inaccessible places on the planet.

Lago was startled out of his thoughts as his uncle grasped his arm. Lago was surprised by the intensity in his usually easygoing uncle's face. "Men died so I could get the information that leads me here."

That got Lago's attention. "What men?"

"My guide and porters in Brazil." Mualama quickly summarized his escape from beneath the stone altar in the Devil's Throat; the walk to the nearest town; hitching a ride back to Santos; and then the flight to Dar es Salaam.

"This Bauru was a brave man," Lago noted when his uncle finished. "Who killed your porters and trapped you there?"

"I believe it was a group that has tried to stop me several times over the years," Mualama said. "They are known as the Mission."

"Why are they trying to stop you?"

"They are afraid of what I might find."

"Which is?"

"I'll know when I find it."

Lago controlled his frustration. "What are we looking for on Mount Speke? What kind of clue?"

Mualama pulled out the oilskin-wrapped package. "This is what I found in Brazil. Burton put it there over a hundred years ago." He unwrapped the covering. A thin sheaf of papers was inside a leather case. "When Burton died in 1890, his wife, Isabel, burned a manuscript. No one knows exactly what was written in that manuscript."

He tapped the papers. "I believe this is a copy of the introduction to that manuscript. The manuscript itself is the untold story of Burton's life, of his secret expeditions. I have been following clues he left, going from one to the next, for over two decades now. Even this is just another stone in the path leading me here, to these mountains." Mualama looked up from the papers toward the mist covering the mountains. "On the side of Mount Speke, something is hidden. Something important. I believe—I hope—it is the rest of the manuscript. That is where we go."

"Why did Burton go to such extremes to hide this material?" Lago asked.

"I wondered that myself," Mualama said. "These papers say that he made a promise never to tell anyone about something he had seen. Something incredible. However, he did not promise to not help others try to find what it was he saw. Of course, he knew he had to prevent those with bad motives from also following his clues, so he made it very difficult. Very difficult." The old professor stood, putting the journal back into his pack. "It is time to continue."

SMITHON HARBOR, TASMANIA

"Are we ready?"

The voice was that of one used to speaking from the pulpit, strong and deep, easily reaching those assembled on the deck. Their solid mass, standing shoulder to shoulder in the space between the ship's bridge and the forward hatch, showed their determination. There were sixty-two people on the deck. All were dressed alike, in dull-brown pants and parkas. Sewn onto the left chest of each parka was a patch that was becoming more and more familiar around the world: It was circular with a small Earth in the center; coming out of the Earth were lines to stars that surrounded the planet.

"We are ready!" they answered with one voice.

The mountains of northern Tasmania towered over the freighter on the landward side. Their rugged beauty contrasted with the rust-stained hull of the ship. Originally called the *Island Breeze,* the ship had been renamed *Southern Star* for the purpose of this journey.

Captain Halls watched the passengers from his bridge, and he couldn't give a rat's ass what they wanted to call his ship. He had his money.

The man who had asked the question turned and walked in from the small wing off the bridge. "Let us depart," he said to Halls.

"We'll be under way in a minute, Mr. Parker," Halls said.

"Guide Parker," the other man corrected him.

Halls gave the order, which was relayed to the engine room. The ship slowly parted ways with the quay and headed for the center channel of Smithon Harbor.

Besides the way they were dressed, the people on deck did not act like ordinary passengers. They didn't line the railing and watch the land fade. Instead they looked out to sea.

"It'll be a hard journey," Halls said. "And I understand the American Navy has Easter Island under strict quarantine. I'm not breaking any blockade for you people."

Parker turned. Halls stepped back from the sheen in the man's eyes. He'd seen that look before, from missionaries he'd run into in the South Pacific, where his ship had spent many a year plowing the normal island trading routes.

"We have our faith in a power greater than the American Navy," Parker said. "We will get ashore, one way or the other. Our destiny lies on Easter Island."

CHAPTER 5

Duncan handed out sheets of paper, one each to Turcotte, Yakov, Major Quinn, and Larry Kincaid. "This was the last article Kelly posted before she went underneath Rano Rau Volcano on Easter Island and became entrapped by the guardian computer. I want you to read it and compare it to the one that was just transmitted."

The five were seated inside the conference room just off the Cube—the complex deep under Hangar One from which Majestic-12 had ruled Area 51 for decades. There was the quiet hum of machinery in the room, along with the slight hiss of filtered air being pushed down by large fans in the hangar above.

Major Quinn had been the operations officer at Area 51 for many years, but he had survived the purge of MJ-12 personnel because he had not been on the inner circle taken over by the guardian, and when Duncan had finally shut Majestic down, he had assisted her. He was the one man in the room who knew all the inner workings of the Area 51 facility and the Cube, the nickname for C3, (Command and Control Central).

Just outside the conference room was the main operations center, housing the Cube center. It measured eighty by a hundred feet and could be reached only from the massive bouncer hangar cut into the side of Groom Mountain via a large freight elevator. The entire complex was self-enclosed and rested on massive springs designed to allow it to survive a direct nuclear strike on the mountain above. Like the old NORAD headquarters in Cheyenne Mountain in Colorado, the Cube had been built during the Cold War, the costs hidden in the sixty-billion-dollar-a-year black budget.

At the height of Majestic-12's operations, the bouncers were being test-flown, and part of the security force—which Duncan had had Turcotte infiltrate—code-named Nightscape, had kidnapped subjects to be sent to the sister biotech facility outside of Dulce, New Mexico.

The Dulce facility was now crushed rubble, blasted by foo fighters, and Nightscape disbanded. Major Quinn had a different job now, aiding Duncan in her attempt to find out the truth about the aliens and their influence on mankind, which even Majestic-12 had been relatively clueless about.

Quinn was of medium height and build. He had thinning blond hair and wore tortoiseshell glasses with oversized lenses to accommodate the split glass he needed for both distance and close-up viewing.

The other person waiting in the room, Larry Kincaid, had worked for JPL—Jet Propulsion Laboratory—and NASA for over three decades. He was an outsider to Area 51 and had been as shocked as the rest of the world to learn what had been hidden there for decades. He was short and overweight, and his face bore the stress of his having sat through numerous space launches. He was the one who had spotted the Airlia base at Cydonia on Mars, right next to the enigma known as the Mars Face. Kincaid looked more dour than ever, with the recent word of the loss of *Atlantis*.

They all quickly scanned the clipping of Kelly Reynolds's article:

> *The discovery of the alien computer known as the guardian, hidden here on Easter Island at least five thousand years ago, has been the most significant and most disappointing discovery in recorded human history. Significant because it conclusively tells us we*

are, or at least were, not alone in the universe. Disappointing because we can no longer access the wealth of information the computer contains. Like a hacker breaking into a top-of-the-line computer, we can read the file names but we don't have the code words needed to open those files and read the advanced secrets they contain. The guardian shut down less than forty-eight hours after transmitting a message up into the skies, toward whom or where we do not know.

The secret to the bouncer's drive system lay just a few inches away. The details of the mothership's interstellar engine lay just as distant. The technology of the guardian computer is just as jealously guarded by the machine. Control of the foo fighters also rests inside the guardian. The mystery of where the Airlia, as the alien race called itself, came from and exactly why they were here on our planet also lies within.

We know some basics, the barest sketch of what happened thousands of years ago when the alien commander Aspasia decided to get rid of all trace of his people's, the Airlia's, presence here on Earth to save the planet from their mortal enemies, who we now know are called the Kortad. Upon making that decision, Aspasia had to fight rebels among his own people who did not wish to go quietly into the night and in doing so destroyed the land that in Earth legend we have called Atlantis, where the Airlia colony was homebased. By doing this he protected the natural development of the human race, and for that we owe him a large debt of gratitude.

But beyond those few facts there are so many unanswered questions:

- *What happened to Aspasia and the other Airlia?*
- *Why was an Airlia atomic weapon left hidden in the depths of the Great Pyramid of Giza? Indeed,*

> *as we now suspect, were the pyramids built as a space beacon by the Airlia?*
> • *What really happened to Atlantis, site of the Airlia colony? What terrible weapon did Aspasia use to destroy it?*
> • *And, perhaps most important, to whom was the transmission the guardian made four days ago when it was uncovered, directed to? And what did it say?*
> • *And how do we turn the guardian back on?*

"Most of this is already out of date," Turcotte noted.

"We damn well know where the message was sent," Larry Kincaid confirmed. "And we know where Aspasia was, and we know he's dead now, thanks to Mike." He inclined his head toward Turcotte.

"Are we sure they're all dead up there?" Turcotte asked. "After what happened here and at the Kennedy Space Center?"

"We think the talon is operating on an automatic program," Kincaid said. "It's shown no indication of being able to maneuver. It's drifting in orbit."

"An automatic program that sucked in Warfighter and used it to destroy the hangar that just happened to be holding the two bodies here?" Turcotte's tone indicated his disbelief. "And took out *Atlantis* as it was prepping to go up?"

Kincaid shrugged. "I'm just telling you our best guess."

"Back to this." Duncan tapped the news release.

"We know Aspasia was the rebel, the bad guy, not the Kortad," Major Quinn said. "And that the Kortad were some sort of Airlia police, led by Artad."

"Are we certain of those so-called facts?" Yakov asked. "We have only your dead Professor Nabinger's word on that—what he learned from a Kortad guardian

Qian-Ling in China. Aspasia's guardian under Easter Island told him the opposite thing, and did you not believe that first? It is to be expected that each side's computers would make them out to be the—How would you say? Men, or in this case, aliens in white hats?"

Turcotte was tired, more mentally than physically. First stopping the flight of the mothership by Majestic-12, then intercepting Aspasia's fleet from Mars, then stopping the new Black Plague—he saw no end in sight to this war with a foe that had yet to make themselves apparent. The fact that The Mission had escaped from Devil's Island and was now somewhere in the world, preparing the next phase of battle, was something he had thought about ever since coming back to Area 51.

"Something bothers me. . . ." Quinn hesitated, as if uncertain whether to air his thoughts in front of the group.

"Go ahead," Duncan prompted.

Quinn tapped the article. "One thing that has been lost in recent events is the factor that started all this— the danger of activating the mothership's interstellar drive."

Turcotte stirred. "I destroyed the power source for the drive—the ruby sphere we found in the Great Rift Valley. So that's not a problem."

"And the mothership was damaged badly when Aspasia's fleet was destroyed," Duncan added. She pointed to the ceiling. "*And* it's also in orbit abandoned, so we got it out of everyone's reach."

"What actually concerns me," Quinn said, "is if the Kortad were actually one side of the Airlia in the civil war they fought, who is the interstellar threat that the guardians referred to? That's the one thing *both* guardians—Aspasia's and Artad's—agreed on, as far as Nabinger could determine: that if the mothership's drive was activated, there was an enemy out there"—Quinn pointed up—"who would track back along the drive and destroy our planet."

Larry Kincaid shrugged once more. "We now know for certain there's at least one other life-form out there among the stars, so it's not a stretch to accept there are others."

"Are they *still* out there is what concerns me," Quinn said.

"Aspasia and Artad went at it over ten thousand years ago," Turcotte said. "Who knows what's out there now."

Yakov suddenly stirred. "There is an ancient Chinese saying that the enemy of my enemy is my friend. Maybe this enemy of the Airlia could be an ally in our fight?"

Everyone turned as Lisa Duncan tapped the top of the conference table. "We have to concern ourselves with more immediate problems here. On Earth. We can't count on anyone bailing us out." Duncan pulled out another sheaf of papers, giving a copy to each man. "Here's the update, supposedly, from Kelly. It was burst-transmitted on the Navy FLTSCOM network off Easter Island, into the Internet, with e-mail addresses to every media outlet. It will be hitting the papers tomorrow and is already on radio and TV and posted on the Internet."

"We can't stop it?" Turcotte asked.

"Freedom of the press," Duncan said. "It's an American right."

Yakov's snort of disgust indicated what he thought of that.

"We couldn't stop it," Quinn said, "unless we shut down every Internet provider and put an absolute blackout on all media. I can assure you that Majestic-12 looked into the possibilities of doing just that and determined it would be impossible from a technological standpoint, never mind a legal or moral one."

Turcotte quickly read the short article:

The Airlia have meant no harm. They have only been protecting themselves. They have coexisted in peace with us for thousands of years. They have protected us from outside forces that would destroy our world. It has only been the interference of Majestic-12 and people from Area 51 who have caused the recent troubles.

I have talked with the Airlia still surviving on Mars, and I know all this to be true. They are trapped now, but even so, they hold no ill feelings toward us.

The recent events in South America were the results of a NATO secret experiment in biological warfare.

The Airlia can help us, but they must be left alone. In turn, they promise not to take any action that can affect us negatively.

"Jesus, talk about spin control," Major Quinn said. "According to this, *we* started the Black Death!"

"Kelly didn't write this," Duncan said. "I don't think Kelly exists anymore. That's why I had you read the earlier article. These words are from the guardian under Easter Island."

"I'm not concerned about that or the spin control," Turcotte said. "I'm worried why the Easter Island guardian sees a need to have Kelly send this."

"Why are you so sure the Easter Island guardian is the evil one?" Yakov asked in a rather mild tone.

"Because of what Nabinger uncovered under Qian-Ling," Turcotte answered.

"Which could have been as much of a lie as what he uncovered under Easter Island," Yakov noted once more.

Turcotte held up the article. "So we should believe this? We know that The Mission was behind the Black

Death. *You* talked to General Hemstadt on Devil's Island."

"I think—" Duncan was interrupted by the buzz of her SATPhone. She pulled it out and turned it on. "Duncan here." She listened for a second, her face tightening, then pulled it away from her ear. "Can we put this on the speaker in here?" she asked Quinn.

He nodded, pulling a wire out of a drawer and running it to her phone, plugging it into the bottom. While he was doing that, Turcotte mouthed the words *Who is it?*

"The Ones Who Wait." Duncan held her hand over the phone. "Lexina, their leader."

"You're set," Quinn told her as the speaker in the middle of the table came alive with a crackle of static.

"We're listening," Duncan said.

The voice that echoed out in response was low-pitched, somewhere between male and female. "We have been patient, but time is running out. We want the key."

"The key to the lower level of Qian-Ling?" Duncan asked.

"Don't play games with me," Lexina said. "I have shown you just a small sample of what I can do by destroying the place you held my comrades' bodies and your last manned space vehicle. I now control the talon, and I will do much worse if you do not turn the key over to us."

"You killed a lot of people," Duncan said.

"And I will kill many, many more if you do not get me the key."

"Did you destroy the *Columbia* as it approached the talon?" Duncan asked.

"No. That was the talon's automatic defense system reacting to anything that came close. But I control it *now*. I control your satellite through the talon. I warned you," Lexina said. "You ignored the warning. Do not ignore this one. Give us the key."

"Why should—" Duncan began, but she was interrupted.

"Give us the key or we will destroy your country completely."

Kincaid stirred. "Warfighter couldn't even come close to doing that."

"Give us the key or we will destroy your country completely," Lexina repeated. "You have forty-nine hours. If you do not give me the key by then, North America will be destroyed."

"You're bluffing." Duncan glanced at Turcotte as she said it.

"Is the Russian there?" Lexina asked. "The man from Section Four?"

"I'm here," Yakov growled.

"Tell them about *Strategicheskii Zvyezda*," Lexina said. "Deliver the key to me in forty-nine hours, or two hundred and sixty million die and your country will be an uninhabitable wasteland for centuries."

CHAPTER 6

Mualama and his nephew Lago were both startled when a long cacophony of thunderclaps rolled down the mountain, following on the heels of two dozen lightning strikes that had split the gloom in less than five seconds. If there was to be an end to the world, Lago figured it would sound very much like what he was listening to. They were in a netherworld lost among the clouds. Snow, ice, and rock were the only things visible around them.

Sweating was no longer a problem as Lago pulled his jacket tight around the neck to keep out the chill. His uncle was seated on his pack, which rested on the foot-deep snow, reading the journal once more and looking about.

They had cleared the tree line at eleven thousand feet an hour before, and it was now well past noon. Lago knew that if they did not begin their descent soon, they would be trapped on the mountain overnight. The cold did not scare him as much as the incessant lightning. He'd never seen the like. Now he knew why these mountains were avoided and why the locals believed the gods forbade travel there.

It was the worst of two worlds—Amazonian-type jungle the first two-thirds of the journey, followed by Alpine terrain with the most awful weather in an incessant mist that threatened to make them lose their bearings. Technically the climb was not difficult, but the weather made it hazardous.

Lago's eyes continued to search the misty gloom as his uncle studied his notes. It was as if the mountain were alive, telling them with the thunder to turn back, to return to the normal world.

His uncle abruptly stood and slid the book back into his pack. "Not much farther."

They tramped up the steep trail, tied together by a twenty-foot section of rope, Lago leading the way. As the altitude increased, occasionally Lago had to put in protection—a piton, a nut in a small rock crevasse—and clip the rope in. His uncle would pull the protection out as he passed.

"Uncle." Lago paused after one particularly tricky section of climbing. "We must turn back or we will be trapped by darkness."

"Not much farther" was Mualama's response. "We do not have to reach the very top."

That was the best news Lago had heard in a while. "What are we looking for?"

"We will know when we see it."

Afternoon was sliding into early evening, and Lago had no idea how far they were from the summit. The rocks were now sheathed in ice. Visibility had increased to about a hundred feet, but darkness would put an end to that.

"There!" Mualama was pointing to the right of their narrow trail. A spectacular wall of icicles over fifty feet long and twenty feet wide dangled from a rock cornice that extended out from the mountain's side. "Would you call that the Devil's Thumb?"

Lago squinted up. The spur of rock might indeed be called that when viewed in profile.

"And this is the Devil's Veil." Mualama walked to the wall of six-inch-thick icicles that covered the depression under the spur. Lago would have thought them quite beautiful if not for the fact that they were on the side of a sixteen-thousand-foot mountain, the temperature was dropping, and night was less than an hour off.

Mualama pressed his face and a flashlight against the ice. He moved along the wall, peering in.

"There it is!" The excitement in his uncle's voice was evident. Lago joined him, looking. There was a dark square on the other side, the exact nature of which was unclear. He jumped back as Mualama swung the ice ax in his hands and it splintered one of the icicles, a four-foot-long shard crashing to the ground.

"Come on!" Mualama yelled. "Help me!"

AREA 51, NEVADA
D – 48 Hours, 50 Minutes

All eyes were on Yakov, the question prompted by Lexina hanging over the table. The Russian got up and walked over to a small table on the side of the room. He reluctantly poured a glass of water. "Haven't you stocked anything stronger yet?" he asked Major Quinn.

There was no answer, nor did Turcotte think Yakov had expected one. He knew the Russian was digesting this new information. Yakov sat back down, then looked at Duncan. "Do you have the key this Lexina creature wants?"

"No."

Yakov's bushy eyebrows contracted. "Then why does this creature think you have it?"

"The first time she asked me, while we were combating the Black Death, I told her we had it, trying to get more information out of her," Duncan said.

"That was a mistake," Yakov said. "Now, if you tell Lexina you do not have the key, the creature will think you are lying and follow through on her threat."

"What is *Strategicheskii Zvyezda*?" Turcotte finally asked, tired of the verbal sparring.

"You have to understand—" Yakov began, but Turcotte cut him off.

"What is it? Can it do what Lexina threatened?"

Yakov slowly nodded. "*Strategicheskii Zvyezda*—the long form for what was called in classified circles *Stratzyda*—means 'Strategic Star.' "

Turcotte put a hand to his forehead. "This doesn't sound good."

Yakov continued. "*Stratzyda* was launched in 1988, just before the end of the Cold War. A one-hundred-ton payload over thirty-seven meters long and four meters wide.

"It was put into orbit four hundred miles up. We knew your tracking systems would pick it up, so we fed the world a cover story. We said it was a first-stage experimental platform in preparation for launching our Mir space station. But it was not that, of course. It was—is— a weapons platform designed to . . ." Yakov stopped and took a deep drink from his glass, his face tightening when he remembered it was water, not vodka.

"What kind of weapons?" Duncan's voice was cold.

"Thirty-two one-megaton, cobalt-salted, nuclear warheads with their own reentry engines, pretargeted, as *Stratzyda* passes over the center of your country, to blanket the United States with a grid pattern that will ensure every square inch is covered with a lethal dose of radioactive material."

"You idiots." Duncan's comment filled the stunned silence that followed.

"Our own sword against us," Turcotte muttered.

ARLINGTON, VIRGINIA
D – 48 Hours, 40 Minutes

The Secretary of Defense's motorcade departed the Pentagon and headed north along the George Washington

Expressway, paralleling the Potomac. A lead and trial car contained bodyguards, sandwiching the limousine holding the Honorable William Wickham.

Wickham was going to the White House to plead with the President to give him nuclear weapons release with regard to Easter Island. The Navy had a plan to attempt to probe the shield once more, but Admiral Poldan, the commander of Task Force 78, which surrounded the island, wanted to do more than just probe. Wickham agreed with the admiral. The takeover of the Warfighter satellite and the destruction of *Atlantis* had been the final shove, landing the Secretary of Defense solidly in the camp of those in the Pentagon who believed that all-out war against the aliens and their supporters had to be waged.

Wickham paused in his musings as he saw the familiar landscape of Arlington National Cemetery out the left window of the limo. He always took this route into the capital, because the numerous rows of white crosses that stretched across the green fields overlooking the capital were a constant reminder to him of the weight of the decisions he had to make and advise the President to make. It was because Wickham felt the responsibility that would be his if his recommendations caused more young men and women to be buried that he had urged caution and restraint to this point, but the attack on the hangar at Area 51, on top of the loss of the shuttles and the submarine *Pasadena* to foo fighters and the entrapment of the *Springfield,* had changed that stance.

The three vehicles turned east onto the Arlington Memorial Bridge. Wickham turned his attention from the cemetery, which was now behind them, to the Lincoln Memorial, which was directly ahead on the other side of the river. The going was slow, because one of the lanes of eastbound traffic was closed due to construction.

Wickham knew the severe pressure the President was

under from the isolationists and that it would be a hard sell to get authorization to nuke Easter Island. He was considering arguments he could use, when he was jerked forward, almost falling off the rear seat when the driver slammed on the brakes.

"What the hell?" Wickham reached for the intercom to the driver, when he saw directly ahead what had caused the halt. A backhoe had rumbled out of the construction lane between the lead car and the limo. The backhoe turned, the heavy steel shovel now pointing at the front windshield of the limousine and coming closer.

"Get me out of there, George," Wickham yelled into the intercom.

The driver threw the limo into reverse and abruptly backed into the trail car, fenders crumpling. Wickham fumbled with door as the shovel came down on the front seat, spearing through the bulletproof windshield, pinning the driver against the seat. The steel blade sliced the man in two as it buckled the frame of the car.

Wickham pulled on the latch, trying to get the door open, but the entire car was twisted, the metal bent and unyielding. He could hear shots, his guards firing at the driver of the backhoe. The blade pulled free of the front of the limousine and the backhoe advanced, large tires climbing up onto the twisted metal. Through the tinted sunroof Wickham could see the blade looming overhead.

Outside, the guards from the first car blazed away at the man driving the backhoe, partially protected by the metal roll cage that surrounded him. Bullets ricocheted off metal, the driver ignoring everything but the rear half of the car in front of him. As a round ripped through his chest, he slammed forward the lever controlling the shovel and it dropped, crashing through the top of the car.

Wickham dove to avoid the blade as it smashed down. The edge caught his ankles, severing his feet from his body and momentarily pinning him in place. The pain exploded along his nervous system, almost causing him to black out.

The driver pulled back on the lever, edging it in the direction of the Secretary of Defense. A bodyguard was climbing up the side of the backhoe. As the guard fired a fatal shot through the driver's head, the man's hand slammed the lever forward one last time.

CHAPTER 7

MOUNTAINS OF THE MOON,
RUWENZORI, UGANDA
  D – 48 Hours, 25 Minutes

Mualama slid between the sharp shards of shattered ice, the glow from his flashlight reflected a hundred times by the glistening walls of the cavern. The far wall was ten feet in front of him. A circle of blackened stones, where a fire had once burned, was in the center of the floor.

A large stone set against rear of the cavern caught his eye. He went around the fire pit and shone the light on the rock. Etched into the stone was a word in Arabic: *Sedgh*. Mualama felt a wave of excitement. The word meant truthfulness and honestly, one of the virtues of a Sufi Master.

"Help me move this," he ordered Lago.

Together they put their shoulders to the boulder and edged it away from the cavern wall. Underneath, an oil-skin-wrapped package was revealed. Mualama sat down and got his breathing under control before picking up the package. It was much heavier than what he had found underneath the stone in the Devil's Throat in South America. Carefully he unwrapped the covering. Inside he uncovered a sheaf of several hundred pages, bound by a red ribbon, preserved by the freezing air.

In bold letters that Mualama recognized as Burton's handwriting, several words in Arabic were written on the cover page. Mualama translated them as he read:

THE PATH OF A TRUTH-SEEKER
By SIR RICHARD FRANCIS BURTON

Mualama peeled off his glove and carefully turned the page. "Ahh!" he exclaimed as he saw the handwritten script on the next page that began the body of the text.

"What is wrong, Uncle?" Lago asked.

"It has never been easy to follow Burton, and even now he makes it hard," Mualama said as he quickly began thumbing through the manuscript.

"I have never seen writing like that," Lago commented.

"I have seen this at a dig in Iraq. It is an extinct tongue. It is called Akkadian and was written and spoken in ancient Assyria and Babylon."

"Why the title in Arabic and the body of the text in another?" Lago asked.

"The title is an arrow pointing in the text. It is Burton's way."

"Is there anyone who can read it now?" Lago asked.

"Perhaps," Mualama said as he stopped on a page where there was a drawing. He held up the piece of paper. "Ah! This is even better for right now. This is the piece I needed."

"What is it?"

"Burton must have copied this from another source." Mualama carefully put the page back in the manuscript. "It fits in with two other drawings I found following his trail and tells me where we go next."

Lago sat on the floor of the cavern, exhaustion etched on his face. "And that is?"

"Home to Tanzania. To Ngorongoro Crater."

"And what is there?"

"We will know when we find it." Mualama stood and slapped his nephew on the shoulder. "Come on, young man. You can't be more tired than I am, and this is exciting! We are on the trail of a great mystery!"

AREA 51, NEVADA
D – 48 Hours, 20 Minutes

"Forty-nine hours." Kincaid spun his laptop around so they could all see the screen, although no one other than he could make out what the numbers and lines displayed meant. "Lexina didn't pull that number out of the air. This is the drifting orbit of the talon and Warfighter—" Kincaid touched the left side of the screen. His finger moved to the right side. "This is the orbit of *Stratzyda*. The two will come within two kilometers of each other in forty hours here, over the Atlantic. I assume she'll use the talon to then take control of *Stratzyda* and change its orbit to coincide with the talon's. Then it will take the talon and its new satellite another nine hours to drift east on the talon's orbit, as the earth turns beneath it, to be in position over the center of the United States to deploy the nukes."

"Can't your government bring *Stratzyda* down before the talon gets control of it? Or change its orbit?" Turcotte asked Yakov.

"It is now out of maneuvering fuel. It has been just drifting up there for the past five years. We have no control over it anymore," Yakov said. "It was never designed to be able to reenter the atmosphere—the bombs, even unexploded, are simply too radioactive.

"You have to understand that things have changed in my country in the past ten years. There is no money, no working system. Only a quarter of our ground-based missile system is functional—the rest is falling into disrepair. For over two-thirds of every twenty-four-hour cycle, we have no satellite coverage of the United States and are essentially blind, as our surveillance satellites have degraded."

"Can *we* destroy *Stratzyda* before it gets close to the talon?" Turcotte asked Kincaid.

"We're a little slim on orbital vehicles right now," Kincaid said. "Lexina made sure of that. I'll check into it, but I wouldn't count on it. Also, we'd have to go through other agencies, most likely the Air Force, to get help and . . ."

Duncan supplied the answer. "And there's a good chance any plan might be compromised, as the *Atlantis* launch obviously was." She shook her head. "Forty-nine hours until we die."

"Actually," Quinn said, "forty-eight hours and twenty minutes now."

"Is there a way to find Lexina? To stop her control of the talon?"

"It is possible there is a device that might control the talon," Yakov said.

"Where?" Turcotte asked.

"Section Four recovered an alien artifact that they believed might be some sort of remote piloting device."

"Wouldn't any archives have been destroyed when the base was destroyed?" Duncan asked.

"The archive area was far underground. It might have survived intact."

Duncan nodded. "All right. You go to Russia and see if you can get control of the talon from Lexina. Any other ideas on what the key is or where it might be if Yakov doesn't succeed?"

"Obviously, the key would be an Airlia artifact," Major Quinn said. "I'll inquire throughout the intelligence community to see if anyone has found anything new regarding the Airlia or if someone has been holding artifacts in secret."

"I'll double-check the hard drives we recovered from Scorpion Base," Kincaid said.

"Anyone else?"

"Maybe the guardian on Easter Island might have some information," Quinn added.

Duncan nodded. "I've already thought of that. If the guardian is using Kelly Reynolds to send out information, maybe we can make a connection the other way. I'm going to Easter Island to see if I can contact Kelly. The Navy has a new plan to penetrate the shield around the island and find out what is going on. If they can get through, maybe I can make contact with her."

The look on Turcotte's face indicated what he thought of that plan of action. "The Navy already tried that once, and the *Springfield* is still sitting at the bottom of the ocean, trapped by foo fighters."

"I think Easter Island is important," Duncan said. "It's the center for Aspasia's faction here on the planet, just as Qian-Ling seems to the center for Artad's faction. We can't get close to Qian-Ling again due to the Chinese nuking it, but we can get close to Easter Island. As Yakov noted, maybe the enemy of our enemy can give us some information.

"Status of the Airlia base on Mars?" Duncan had already moved on to Kincaid.

"We're watching it," Kincaid said. "No visible activity. Communications between the Cydonia guardian and the one under Easter Island have continued on a pretty regular basis. The NSA still hasn't been able to decipher the code."

"Mike?" Duncan had made it around the table.

Turcotte shrugged. "I'm just the hired gun. Sitting around waiting for the next crisis. There's nothing new with me."

"Your Special Forces team just arrived." Major Quinn was looking at the screen of his laptop, which was connected to the Cube operations center.

"I'll check them out," Turcotte said.

Yakov stirred. "Until the next crisis arises, I would like Captain Turcotte to accompany me to Russia. I could use some—how do you say—backup? I do not think I will get much support from my government, given all that has happened."

"Is that all right with you?" Duncan asked.

Turcotte nodded. "Sure."

Duncan stood and leaned forward, putting her hands on the top of the conference table that the men of Majestic-12 had sat around for five decades. "Gentlemen, we're it. The five of us. I told you the President is caught in a political quagmire. UNAOC is hamstrung by isolationist governments. The message from Easter Island with Kelly Reynolds's byline will only make that worse. I'll inform the President of the new threat from Lexina and The Ones Who Wait, but I honestly don't think he can muster enough support to take decisive action before it's too late. And after what happened to the shuttles, we always have to be worried that any support might well be compromised by the Watchers, The Mission, or STAAR."

"In other words," Yakov said, "we can trust no one outside of this room."

Duncan nodded. "We keep what we know to ourselves. The President is trying to keep a lid on what happened to *Atlantis,* and I'm sure he'll definitely want to keep the information about *Stratzyda* secret to prevent a panic.

"We have to find this key." She pointed at Major Quinn. "How much time?"

"Forty-eight hours, twenty minutes until *Stratzyda* deployment."

"Let's get moving," Duncan ordered.

As everyone headed for the door, Turcotte went to the end of the table, grabbed a chair, and sat down, watching as Duncan put her papers back in her briefcase.

"What?" Duncan finally asked, noting his stare.

"So how are you doing?" Turcotte asked.

Duncan paused, hands on the top of the table. "You

weren't happy that I picked you to infiltrate Area 51, remember?"

Turcotte nodded.

"Well, I'm not thrilled that the President picked me to be his science adviser, then tossed me the hand grenade of dealing with Area 51, and now he's backpedaling. Especially considering the ultimatum we just received."

"He didn't expect you to uncover what you did," Turcotte noted. "It would have been better if we had just discovered the bodies of a couple of little green men at Area 51 instead of what we did. Do you think he will take action with this new information and the threat from *Stratzyda*?"

"He has to make a decision, Mike." Duncan was exasperated. "Straddling the fence isn't going to work. While the isolationists and the progressives argue, The Mission and The Ones Who Wait are moving forward with their plans. We're caught in the middle, and the stakes are getting higher."

"You sound like me a week ago," Turcotte said. "What's really wrong?"

"On the flight here I was wondering if we did the right thing."

"It's a little too late for that," Turcotte said.

"I know that, but . . ." Duncan's voice trailed off.

"The real problem is you're tired," Turcotte said. "When I was in Ranger school, part of the philosophy of the course was to make the students exhausted, to deny them food and sleep, then see how they made decisions, how they operated while under that stress. Sounds stupid, but given that they were preparing us for war, it actually made sense. I've seen people make tremendously stupid decisions when tired. You have to think everything through carefully."

"You think going to Easter Island is a mistake?"

"No—more a waste of time—but I wasn't talking

about that. I was referring to the speech you made at the Lincoln Memorial. Don't you think there were times that Lincoln doubted his course of action, even considered trying to make peace with the South to save the lives of his people?

"How do you think he felt when he received the casualty list from the Battle of Antietam, the bloodiest day in American history—September 17, 1862? Twenty-three thousand Americans killed or wounded in *one* day. Do you have any concept of the scope of that, especially given the weaponry of the time? That's *nine* times the number of casualties we took on the Longest Day at Normandy during the Second World War.

"You think about things like the Gettysburg Address," Turcotte continued, "while I think about the poor grunt on the ground. In the Bloody Lane at Antietam, a quarter-mile-long stretch of road, more men were killed or wounded in three hours than in all the years of the Revolutionary War. Blood ran like a stream in that lane. You think numbers like that didn't make Lincoln sit down and ponder what the hell he was doing? If he'd made the right decisions, done the right things?"

Duncan nodded. "I'm sure he did. And he used that battle, which was a victory, although by the narrowest of margins, for the North, to be the impetus for issuing the Emancipation Proclamation, not to make peace with the South."

Turcotte had hoped she would make that connection. "Which broadened the scope of the war to a moral issue and kept England and France from giving aid to the South, as they were contemplating. He used a terrible thing in a positive way."

"And the Civil War lasted two long years after Antietam," Duncan noted.

"Is the glass half full or half empty?" Turcotte asked. "Let's try to be positive."

Duncan finished putting her papers away. "So it was your turn to give the pep talk," she said with a smile.

"Hey. I'm just one of the infantrymen," Turcotte said. "I just want to make sure I'm on the same sheet of music as my boss."

"'Your boss,'" Duncan repeated, glancing at the door to make sure it was closed. She ran a hand through Turcotte's close-cropped hair. "Is that what I am?"

"Only during duty hours," Turcotte said. "Off-duty we can flip for who wants to be boss."

Duncan laughed, the lines of strain disappearing from her face for a moment. Turcotte wrapped her hand inside of his own. "Speaking of which—" He paused as her cell phone rang once more.

Duncan pulled it out of her pocket and flipped it open. "Duncan."

She listened for a few seconds, then shut it, her face tight. "Duty calls," she said to Turcotte. "The Secretary of Defense was just killed, apparently by a Guide."

"Jesus," Turcotte muttered. "Why?"

"The Mission killed the Secretary of Defense to keep the President from taking decisive action about Easter Island."

"We're getting it from both sides," Turcotte said. "The Ones Who Wait and The Mission are trying to keep us from stopping them in their war."

"I have to sit in on a conference call with the National Security Council, reference this new development and the Warfighter situation, and give them the good news about *Stratzyda*."

"Always duty first." Turcotte removed his hand from hers and stood.

She tucked her briefcase under her arm and was all business once more. "You better go check out those Special Forces guys before you head to Russia. Get Major Quinn to give them a SATPhone, disseminate the number among those who were in this room, and direct the team leader to respond to any requests for assistance he receives. Also have Quinn dedicate a bouncer to the team for their transportation."

"Roger that," Turcotte acknowledged. As she turned for the door, his voice stopped her. "Lisa—"

"Yes?"

"Be careful."

"You too."

Turcotte watched the door swing shut and took a moment to collect his thoughts, then exited the conference room. He took the elevator up to Hangar One. Of the nine bouncers, four were present. There was also a group of twelve soldiers in camouflage. Even from a hundred yards away, Turcotte knew they were Special Forces, even though they had black watch caps on instead of the traditional green beret. They gave off an air of confidence and competence that most Special Operations soldiers were cloaked in.

He walked up, and a man with the railroad tracks on his collar indicating he was a captain stepped forward. "Major Turcotte, I'm Billam. Colonel Mickell said I was to report to you and follow any orders you issued."

Turcotte took the other man's hand and shook it. Billam was a stocky man with thinning black hair. He looked old for a captain, somewhere in his late thirties. Turcotte assumed that meant he had been enlisted and gone through either ROTC or OCS to get his commission.

Billam quickly introduced his A-team.

"This is my executive officer, Chief Tabor; operations sergeant, Master Sergeant Boltz; weapons men, Sergeants Truskey and Dedie; commo, Sergeants Prevatil and Garza; medics, Sergeants Rooney and Askins; demolitions and other nefarious acts, Sergeants Metayer and Jones. Team 055 at your beck and call, sir."

Turcotte picked up no trace of sarcasm in Billam's voice, but he was sure they probably weren't thrilled to death about getting such a vague assignment. He knew Mickall had probably picked a good team, but also a team selected somewhat randomly and secretly to prevent infiltration.

Turcotte relayed Duncan's instructions and gave them directions to link up with Major Quinn and get their SATPhone and billeting information. He could see Yakov over by one of the bouncers, talking to the pilot, and he knew the Russian was anxious to go.

"Any special instructions," Billam asked, "or just be ready for anything?"

Turcotte shrugged. "I wish I could be more specific, but you guys are basically our 'if things go to crap' option." He could see the acknowledgment of that on the faces of the men. "If you get called by any of us, things are real bad, so be prepared to come in hot. Major Quinn will brief you on everything that's happened so far. I'll try to keep you updated so you can at least war-game some options for action, but we're pretty much flying by the seat of our pants here." Turcotte turned to head off toward Yakov when something occurred to him. "Captain, are any of your men trained on SADM?"

That brought Billam's eyebrows arching up. "Sir, that mission has been phased out of Special Forces."

"I know that," Turcotte said, "but do you have anyone that was on a SADM team?" SADM stood for strategic atomic demolition mission—backpack nukes, which had been a Special Forces mission prior to the advent of cruise missiles, which could do as good a job placing a nuke deep behind enemy lines and with less cost in manpower. But Turcotte didn't think they could count on getting a cruise missile strike when they needed it and where.

Billam nodded. "Sergeant Boltz served on a SADM

team in 7th Group, and I served on one when I was enlisted in 10th Group. The rest of these guys are too young to have done that."

Turcotte pointed toward the elevator. "When you meet Major Quinn, see if he can rustle you up a nuke or two."

Billam blinked. "Are you authorized those weapons, sir?"

"We won't know until you ask. Quinn got me some nukes when I needed them before," Turcotte noted. "Like the Boy Scouts, I want to be prepared. Just in case."

CHAPTER 8

Qian-Ling was the largest tomb in the world, larger than even the stone pyramids of Egypt and the dirt mound pyramids in Central and South America. According to historians, the Emperor Gao-zong, Third Emperor of the T'ang Dynasty, and his empress, the only empress ever to rule in China, were buried inside the massive man-made hill.

Qian-Ling was located west of Xian, the city that had been the first imperial capital in China and the eastern terminus of the Silk Road that had stretched in ancient times from western China across Central Asia to the Middle East and on to Rome. It was now on the border between the rebelling Muslim majority in the west of China and ruling powers to the east in Beijing.

Since the disclosure that Earth had been visited by aliens, the ethnic and religious unrest that had always simmered below the surface in China had reached a boiling point, and there were many parts of the country, particularly in the western half, that were in open rebellion. It was part of a growing pattern around the world where the upset of accepted history was leading to an upset of traditions and norms.

As an outgrowth of that unrest what had been one of China's most revered monuments of antiquity had been seared by the thousand-degree heat from a low-altitude nuclear blast several days earlier. A CSS-5 cruise missile carrying a nuclear warhead had been fired from eighty miles away, traversed the distance in less than two minutes, and exploded two kilometers from its intended target.

The outside of the tomb was now desolate, many artifacts of antiquity destroyed. The stone statues of the sixty-one foreign ambassadors and rulers who had attended the funeral of Emperor Gao-zong that had lined the way to the tomb had been vaporized. The vegetation that had grown along the slopes of the three-thousand-foot-high man-made hill that was his grave had been burned away in a flash. The hill itself, though, was relatively undamaged, hidden behind a shimmering shield-wall of alien origin.

It was a sign of the desperation of the Chinese government that they'd not only detonated a nuclear weapon inside their own borders, but they'd aimed it at the grave of an emperor and empress. The Chinese revered their ancestors and thus their dead. Grave robbing was unknown and archaeological digging was considered practically the same thing: defiling the burial place of someone's ancestors. A nuclear bomb definitely outranked both grave robbing and archaeological digs.

Qian-Ling, though, was now almost a shelter from the storm that waged around it. All around the mountain, the air shimmered from the strange alien shield that had been activated just prior to the nuclear weapon's detonation. There was nothing alive on the surface of the earth within a ten-kilometer circle of the tomb, but underneath, inside the protective mountain of earth and alien barrier, the bomb had had little effect.

Inside a large cavern filled with alien equipment, Professor Che Lu sat cross-legged on the floor, just outside the control room that led to the guardian computer. She was an old woman, her skin creased with age, but her mind was as sharp as it had ever been.

Che Lu had seen all of the history of modern China, often participating rather than just watching it go by. She had been one of the twenty-six women who had started the Long March with Mao sixty-four years before. Only six of those women had made it to the end alive. Only ten percent of the one hundred thousand men who had started the march had been alive when they arrived at Yanan in Shaanxi Province in December 1935 after walking over six thousand miles to escape Chiang Kai-shek's forces.

She knew how significant it was that her government had tried to destroy Qian-Ling. It was more than just a blind fear of the aliens—it was also a desperate attempt by the leaders to keep the country in ignorance and remain in power.

Metal beams came up from the nearest wall and disappeared overhead, curving to follow the dome ceiling around to touch down on the far side. There were numerous large objects scattered about on the floor, the exact purpose of which was still unknown, except for one large cylinder that gave off a hum—that one had propagated the shield that had saved their lives. The black metal covering it had slid back at Elek's command through the guardian. A drum had been revealed, about fifty meters long by ten in diameter. It was mounted on both ends in a cradle of black metal that attached at the center. The drum continued to rotate with streaks of color—red, orange, violet, purple—intermingled on its surface. The other, unopened containers, were in the form of black rectangles ranging from a few feet in size to one over a hundred meters long and sixty high.

Fifty feet away from where Che Lu sat there was a bright green light glowing out of the wall, brighter even than the one overhead. Inside was a control room, and beyond that, the chamber housing the golden pyramid that was the Qian-Ling guardian computer.

Che Lu reached into the old straw bag next to her and

pulled out a leather sack. She emptied the contents onto the floor with a clatter. Four pieces of bone lay there.

"Did you ever figure out what those are?" the old man next to her asked. Che Lu had known Lo Fa for most of her life. He had been branded a thief a long time before by the government, but now she supposed he might be called a freedom fighter. He wore a faded blue shirt and black pants. His AK-47 lay next to him. He had found the bones near the tomb and sent them to her in Beijing, prompting the beginning of her journey here.

She picked up one of the bones and handed it to him. The bone was from the hip of some animal, perhaps a deer, triangular in shape, with two long flat sides that had markings etched into them.

"They're oracle bones."

Lo Fa turned it in his hands, then tossed it back. "Are you a witch who throws bones to read the future now? I thought you were an educated person." He spit to the side. "I can read yours and my future without using those—we're going to die in this tomb along with that alien creature." He nodded his head toward the tall figure of Elek, wandering through the stacks of equipment and large containers that filled the floor of the cavern.

Che Lu agreed that Elek was not completely human— the red, elongated eyes confirmed that. But he also wasn't Airlia, as he was shorter than the projection of the Airlia sentinel in the upper-level passageway had shown and some of his other features were different. Some sort of hybrid between human and alien, Che Lu had decided, a bastard designed to do the bidding of hidden alien masters. Ever since Lo Fa had found the oracle bones and sent them to her, her beliefs had experienced more change than in the previous seven decades.

"You must have hope," she told Lo Fa.

He snorted. "Hope is a bad thing. Hope is what children have before they know any better. I am too old for hope."

Che Lu pointed at Elek. "They—and the aliens they work for—came to Earth a long time ago. Many, many generations before you were born. But we—humans— are still here. You have lived a long life. We must work to ensure that our children's children also have the same opportunity.

"They are not all-powerful. Look how he searches the cavern. And he cannot get into the lowest level, which is where he wants to go. He is as weak as we are."

"And as trapped," Lo Fa noted.

Che Lu indicated the oracle bones. "I could not read those at first." She reached into her bag and pulled out a leather notebook. It was battered, with burn marks on it. "This is Professor Nabinger's, the man who deciphered the high rune language. I have been using it to read the writing on the bones and on the walls of the upper levels of this tomb, since we have had nothing else to do since being sealed in.

"I always thought our civilization was the first to develop writing. In fact, the Chinese word for 'civilization,' *wenha,* means the transforming influence of writing. But the language on these bones is older than ours."

"Spare me the lecture," Lo Fa said. "You are not at the university now. What do the bones and the walls say?"

"You have something else to do?" Che Lu asked. "Perhaps a lecture will open your mind up, old man, keep it from turning into a rock."

Lo Fa laughed. "Go ahead, Mother-Professor."

The latter term was what her students at the university in Beijing had called her. Che Lu felt a pang for those she had left in the capital. She had no doubt the upcoming turmoil would make the Tiananmen Square massacre look mild in comparison. Always blood had to be spilled to grease the wheels of change. She wished it were not so, but her long life had shown her that it was the way of reality.

She rested a hand on the battered leather notebook. "Professor Nabinger was a very smart man. His mind was open, unlike yours." She picked up one of the oracle bones. "The writing on this was dismissed as gibberish by most scholars I showed them to. The same as similar writing all around the world. What we do not understand, we choose to ignore.

"Nabinger was an Egyptologist. He didn't ignore the markings that didn't fit with standard hieroglyphics. He searched around the planet and found similar writing in other places. Dating those sites, he was amazed to discover that this strange runic writing predated the oldest recorded language that was generally accepted by historians.

"The problem he had was explaining how a similar written language could be in places as far apart as Egypt and South America. Remember, old man, this was in an age when man would rarely sail out of sight of shore. Despite not being able to explain the *why,* he decided to study the *what* he did have. He gathered as many examples of what he dubbed the high rune language and tried to decipher it."

"I am more interested in the why," Lo Fa said. "Why was this same language in such diverse places? Did the Airlia leave the writing?"

Che Lu shrugged. "Some of it, maybe. But most examples Nabinger found had slight, sometimes major, differences in style and syntax from place to place, which indicated to him that they all came from a root language, and then, as people who had learned this root language spread across the planet, they made changes to it as their own societies developed.

"My fellow anthropologists at the university always argued that civilization began in such diverse places as

Egypt, China, Southeast Asia, and Central America, all at roughly the same time period. They called this the isolationist theory of civilization. Isolationists believe that the ancient civilizations all developed independent of each other. These isolated groups of people all crossed a threshold into civilization about the third or fourth century before the birth of Christ. Isolationists explained the timing with natural evolution. We particularly like that theory here in China because we believed our early civilization was much more advanced than the others. After all, we believed we were the first to have a written language, the first to invent gunpowder, the printing press—all those things we were so proud of for so long."

Che Lu rubbed her wrinkled fingers across the bone. "Now we know this isn't true. We weren't the first to invent writing, and we were not the first to invent civilization. Indeed, the earliest dynasties here and in the other places were probably just shadows of the civilization our forefathers had to abandon at Atlantis. Even if the humans were just servants to the Airlia there, they probably lived in a style greater than even our current level.

"When Artad destroyed Atlantis to stop Aspasia and his rebels, some humans escaped. They not only seeded the myth of Atlantis and the Great Flood wherever they went, they also started to rebuild civilization. This is the diffusionest theory of the birth of civilization, which we now know to be correct."

"And the aliens who survived?" Lo Fa asked. "Where did they go?"

"We believe that Aspasia and his followers went to the Airlia base on Mars. And now we think he is dead, killed by Captain Turcotte during the destruction of the Airlia talon ship fleet. Artad"—she waved her hands around the cavern—"perhaps he sleeps below us like Aspasia slept on Mars. I think that is the reason Elek desperately wants the key for the lower level."

"Waking Aspasia was a bad thing," Lo Fa said simply. "Why should waking Artad be any better?"

"I cannot answer that," Che Lu said.

"Something else," Lo Fa said. "If they used Gao-zong's tomb to hide Artad, then maybe the Airlia had much more to do with our country's growth than we could even imagine."

"True," Che Lu conceded. "Nabinger did determine that the high rune symbol for 'help' was built into the very shape of the Great Wall in western China, north of the city of Lanzhou. It is the only man-made object that can currently be seen from space with the naked eye. There is no way the people who built the Great Wall could have known the shape they were building was more than just protection against the barbarians."

Lo Fa still had one of the bones in his hands. "What do these tell you?"

Che Lu leaned close. "They give hints. Of Shi Huangdi. The First Emperor. The Son of Heaven who unified China and pulled together the Great Wall."

Lo Fa nodded. "You said earlier he might be buried here in the tomb, even though Gao-zong was of the Tang Dynasty, well after Shi Huangdi."

Che Lu simply waited. She knew Lo Fa was much smarter than he appeared, or else he would have died long ago plying his chosen profession.

Lo Fa's eyes widened. "Do you think the alien Artad could have been Shi Huangdi—the founder of the First Dynasty?"

"I told you of the legends surrounding Shi Huangdi. It is written that when he was born there was a great radiance in the sky, coming from the direction of Ursa Major. But the word 'born' can have different connotations. It could also mean when he arrived."

"From the stars," Lo Fa filled in.

"Or simply from the sky in one of the bouncers the Americans have, or even the mothership that is now floating in orbit around our planet.

"The stories say that when Shi Huangdi met the Empress of the West in the mountains of Wangwu, they invented something. But again, invented could be used to explain something no one had ever seen before. The best the storytellers could describe it was twelve large mirrors mounted on tripods that pointed to the sky. These devices were supposed to be able to manipulate gravity. When they were operated they emitted loud noises. They were also supposed to be able to look at the stars.

"And there is Chi Yu, the Lord of the South who fought with Shi Huangdi." Che Lu was excited, and some of it was rubbing off on Lo Fa. "There was indeed a chance that the old legends were stories of fact."

"Maybe Chi Yu was Aspasia—or someone from Aspasia's camp," Lo Fa interjected.

Che Lu nodded. "Yes. While Shi Huangdi ruled in the north of ancient China, Chi Yu ruled in the south. And Chi Yu was said not to be a man but a machine. A metal beast which could fly about."

Lo Fa looked about. "If Artad sleeps here, perhaps Chi Yu still exists. Perhaps the metal beast is hidden, waiting to come alive and attack us."

Che watched as Elek strode across the chamber once more. "You might be right that awakening whatever is below might be a very bad thing."

NGORONGORO CRATER, TANZANIA
D – 43 Hours

The leopard moved stealthily through the high grass, then paused. Nostrils flared wide as it drew in the scent borne on the breeze. Ears twitched and the head turned back and forth. It smelled fresh earth, which was strange, and, stronger than the dirt, the scent of the two-legged creatures, which was also rare here, deep inside Ngorongoro Crater.

The leopard had experience with the two-legged ones from its time on the Serengeti Plain to the west. It knew they were to be avoided. The leopard loped to the north, circling around the area.

Downwind from the leopard, Mualama looked up from the shovel in his hands. "Hush!" he hissed at the other man in the hole with him.

After a moment's hesitation, Lago stopped digging and slumped down, wiping the sweat from his brow. "What?"

"Shh." Mualama held a long black finger to his lips. "There is something out there in the bush."

Lago sank down to sit on the edge of the pit they had excavated. After the climb down Mount Speke, the trek to the airfield, and the return to Tanzania, the last thing he wanted to do was come here and dig, but his uncle had been insistent.

"It was a leopard," Mualama finally said as he heard a growl. He turned his attention back to the hole.

"A leopard?" Lago repeated, his eyes darting about the thick, four-foot-high grass that surrounded their location. "Will it attack?"

"It is more concerned that we leave *it* alone," Mualama said. He found his nephew amusing. The young man would climb mountains and scuba-dive for fun, but the wonders of nature on his own continent held little interest for him.

They were in the northern part of Ngorongoro Crater, a remote spot in north Tanzania. Ngorongoro was the second-largest crater on the planet. Over twelve miles wide, it encompassed more than three hundred square miles. The crater was twenty-two hundred meters above sea level, well over a mile in altitude. Geologists claimed it was the remains of a huge, ancient volcano that had been worn down through erosion. Mualama was not sure how much stock he put in the geologists' claims. All he had to do was look to the east from the rim of Ngorongoro and he could clearly see the snowcapped summit of Mount Kilimanjaro a hundred and twenty miles away. Being a logical man, he had to ask why that ancient volcano wasn't worn down as far as this one. They were equally old and experienced the same weather.

There was no doubt the crater was a spectacular and remote place. It was difficult to get to with only one, often washed out, dirt track covering the last fifty miles to it. Once the dirt road reached the rim of the crater, it switchbacked down the steep rim, in places so narrow that even Mualama, who had been here before, had feared for the ability of his old Land Rover to stay on the road.

The land inside the crater was mostly open grassland with intermittent thick bush, although near the rim there was thick forest. Soda Lake, which filled the center, was a broad expense of water, but it was not deep, less than four feet in most places. Because of its isolation, difficult access, and the resulting lack of human intrusion, the crater teemed with wildlife.

At the edge of the pit they were digging, a surveyor's scope rested on a tripod. This morning, Mualama had used it to make his final measurements, incorporating the data from the drawing in Burton's manuscript. This spot had been triangulated to within ten meters. But ten meters was still a large area when one had to dig using only two shovels, and it was uncertain how deep the object sought was.

"Are you sure something's here?" Lago asked, a

question he was asking with increasing frequency the more dirt that was removed.

Mualama paused. "We are never sure until we find what we are searching for."

Lago waved his hand about, taking in the entire crater. "This is a big place. Why *here*? This specific spot? How did you know the drawing referred to the crater?"

"I've been here before," Mualama said. "I have information from other sources. Burton's drawing was just the final piece. Even he didn't know the exact location—he just knew something was somewhere and he had some clues. Years ago I found the first sign there." Mualama pointed to the crater wall, two miles distant.

Lago looked, confused. "What?"

"The dragon," Mualama said. "Do you see its head?"

Lago squinted. "That rock outcropping?"

"Yes. With a little imagination, it could be the profile of a dragon. That was the first sign. Drawn on a piece of ancient parchment, carefully preserved by monks, who themselves did not know what they were guarding or where the dragon sign was to be seen.

"Of course I—like Burton—didn't know *where* to look for the sign, or the other signs I learned about. It was only last year that I learned that it was in Ngorongoro Crater that I could line up the signs. And now I have the last piece of alignment." He pointed. "The notch there in the crater wall matches the drawing we just found. Where Burton found that, I do not know, nor does he say. And that, Nephew, is why we are here."

"If it wasn't from Burton's manuscript, how did you discover that it—whatever it is—would be in this crater?" Lago wanted to know, not satisfied with his uncle's vague answers.

"Have you heard of the church of Bet Giyorgis?"

Lago indicated he hadn't.

Mualama pointed at the canteen hanging from Lago's

shoulder. The young man passed it across, and Mualama drank deeply before continuing.

"Legend has it that one night King Lalibela of Axum was taken up to heaven while he was asleep and ordered to build a temple, a place of worship. It was said that when he came back he ordered construction begun on Bet Giyorgis and that the workers were aided by 'angels.'

"The church is very strange. Certainly given the tools and level of technology of the time, the temple would have been impossible to make. It is constructed inside of solid rock. In a way, you could call the entire church a sculpture cut into the rock. A most intriguing mystery that has begged to be answered for centuries."

"The Airlia built it?" Lago guessed.

Mualama nodded. "Perhaps. The entire perimeter of the church is a trench cut into rock four stories deep. Then the remaining large square of stone in the center was made into the temple. The central church was shaped in the shape of a cross, but you can get to it only through passageways cut through the stone. Then the center of that cross shape was hollowed out of solid rock. There are numerous paintings and frescoes on the walls throughout. On one of those I found drawings that led me to question the monks.

"A couple in particular interested me as they would have interested an explorer like Burton. One showed two snow-covered peaks. Another showed only one such peak. The peak in both panels I recognized as Mount Kilimanjaro."

"But you said two peaks in the first drawing?" Lago was confused.

"This was the other peak. The sister of Kilimanjaro."

"But this has been a crater for ages," Lago said.

"Perhaps," Mualama said. "Perhaps not."

"There's no indication the volcano has been active for over twenty thousand years," Lago argued.

At least the student had done his geological homework while in school, Mualama granted. "Perhaps the top of the mountain was destroyed in some other manner."

To that, Lago had no answer. The thought of something powerful enough to shear off the top of a mountain as large as Kilimanjaro and leave this crater behind was beyond his ability to comprehend.

"Why did you go to the church in the first place? Why did you start following this dead man's trail?"

"That is a long and complex story that began when I was a young man—about your age—studying in England. What do you know of Sir Richard Francis Burton?"

"Only what you have told me so far."

"Your education is lacking," Mualama said. "Sir Burton translated the Book of the Thousand and One Nights and the Kama Sutra. He was quite a linguist, with a mastery of many languages. It was because of one of his trips here to Africa and an unpublished letter he left written in a tongue that no one else could read—like his manuscript, but a different language—that I was first directed to this location. At first I thought it was a work of fiction, but now I know it was not."

"But . . ." Lago paused as his uncle picked up his shovel.

"We must work," Mualama said. "It is all speculation so far."

Lago reluctantly picked up his tool and got back to work.

Two hours later, Mualama struck down into the soft earth with his spade and was startled when it reverberated in his hands, hitting something solid. He blinked away the sweat in his eyes and stood perfectly still for a few seconds, his heart racing.

He knelt and scraped with his hands, pushing the

loose dirt aside. His fingers touched stone. A flat stone, with something etched on the surface.

"Stop." Mualama said it so quietly that Lago at first didn't understand.

"Did you find something?"

"Yes." Mualama pointed at the aged Land Rover. "Bring the brush and the hand trowels."

Lago did as ordered. "What is it?"

Mualama didn't answer. He lightly scraped with a hand trowel, removing dirt, tossing it to the side. Red stone appeared, inch by inch, foot by foot. He used the trowel and hand brush to clear off the top. When he was done, he stepped back up on the lip of the hole. The stone was nine feet long by four wide. The top was smooth except where markings were etched in it. It was a dark, almost blood red. Mualama knew a thing or two about stones, and he had never seen this kind.

Mualama did recognize the markings, though—high runes. The language of the aliens.

EASTER ISLAND
D – 42 Hours, 30 Minutes

Easter Island fell under the jurisdiction of the government of Chile, but the events of the past month had superseded that rule, and frankly, the rulers in Santiago were quite happy to wash their hands of the island. They had ceded any action to be done about it to UNAOC— the United Nations Alien Oversight Committee.

Chileans weren't too concerned about losing control of the island, for two reasons. One was that it was over two thousand miles away from their shoreline, making it the most isolated piece of terrain on the planet. The second reason was that UNAOC's forces—primarily the United States Navy—couldn't pierce the opaque shield that now surrounded the entire island. It was anyone's guess what was happening inside the shield.

The last attempt to penetrate the shield, using a remote sensing torpedo from the USS *Springfield,* had resulted in the submarine's being trapped on the bottom of the ocean floor offshore of the island by several foo fighters—small golden spheres that wielded tremendous power and focused their energy on electromagnetic sources. As long as the submarine didn't move, it was safe. Of course, there was a limit to the amount of air, food, and water on the submarine, and when one of those three vitals ran out, the crisis would escalate, but that was several weeks off and UNAOC's decision had been to withhold taking any further drastic action, a decision greatly influenced by the growing planet-wide isolationist movement.

Before the discovery of the guardian computer underneath the island, the only distinction Easter Island had was the massive statues that dotted its shoreline. With no one left alive on the island—with the possible exception of Kelly Reynolds, and her latest communiqué indicated she supported the new isolationist line—there seemed little justification in taking further action.

Easter Island was shaped like a triangle, with a volcano at each corner. Its landmass totaled only sixty-two square miles, but despite its small size it had once boasted a bustling civilization, one advanced enough to have built the *moai,* the giant stone monoliths that peered out to sea. There was no doubt now that the *moai* were representative of the Airlia—the red stone caps like the red hair of the aliens, the long earlobes similar to what had been seen on the holograph of the Airlia under Qian-Ling.

The island had been called Rapa Nui by the few surviving natives, but to the rest of the world Easter Island had been its name since its discovery by Europeans on Easter Day in 1722.

It was below the Rano Kau volcano that the guardian had been secreted. Deep underneath the dormant volcano, Kelly Reynolds's body was pressed up against the side of the twenty-foot-high golden pyramid that housed the alien computer. The golden glow that surrounded her body kept it in a stasis field. The mental field had been supplemented by a metal probe that came from the guardian and ended in the back of Kelly's neck.

The line between Kelly Reynolds's mind and the guardian machine was a thin one. It was more of a spiritual separation than a physical one, as the guardian invaded her with machinery and quantum waves.

Kelly Reynolds had originally been drawn into the Area 51 mystery because of the investigation of her fellow reporter, Johnny Simmons. His death at the hand of the Majestic-12 committee that ran Area 51 and its sister bio-research facility at Dulce, New Mexico, had destroyed her professional detachment. She had believed that mankind's best hope lay in communicating with the aliens—and the best way to do that had been the guardian computer. But since coming down here just before Turcotte destroyed the Airlia fleet, she had been caught in the same field that had changed the members of Majestic-12.

The guardian computer under Rano Kau was now the centerpiece of a bizarre structure of which Kelly Reynolds's body was just one part. Metal arms reached out of the side of the pyramid, making machines out of parts cannibalized from the material UNAOC had left behind.

All around the guardian, microrobots raced about like oversized mechanical ants. A line of microrobots went up to the surface through the tunnel UNAOC had drilled. There were several types of microrobots. The carriers, three inches long, had six metal legs, and two arms for grasping and holding that could reach forward, then rotate back and hold whatever they picked up on their backs. The makers, now six inches long, had four legs and four arms. The arms were different on each, depending on what function they served in the production line making more of their own kind, each generation smaller than the one before it.

Already the microrobots had succeeded in digging a hole in the floor of the cavern to a plasma vent two miles deep from which the guardian drew more power. The fusion plant left by Aspasia to power the guardian was insufficient for the tasks now at hand.

All of the abandoned UNAOC computers were now hardwired into the guardian. Across the monitors information flashed, faster than a human eye could follow, as the alien computer sorted through what it had learned from its foray into the human world via the Interlink/Internet. The guardian also maintained its link to Mars, to its sister guardian deep under the surface of the red planet and the alien hands that controlled that computer.

Deep inside Kelly's mind there was a small place, the center of her "self" that still existed. While the guardian experimented on her, drew on her memories and knowledge to supplement its database, Kelly was able to pick up visions from the guardian, like feedback on a loop. Peter Nabinger had made "first contact" with this guardian and been fed a vision of how Aspasia had been the savior of mankind. Then Nabinger had made contact with the guardian under Qian-Ling and been given the opposite vision. But this guardian had no need to "feed" anything in particular to Kelly Reynolds. The visions she saw were inadvertent blips on the stream of data the guardian was constantly evaluating, processing, storing, moving about.

She'd already "seen" the movement of the *moai* from

the quarry on the flanks of Rano Raraku volcano where they were carved, to their position on the coastal platforms. And she understood one mystery that had plagued westerners in the centuries following the discovery of the island—*why* the statues were carved and placed there. She now knew they were warnings by the people who had inhabited Easter Island against others landing on their island, warning them of the presence of the Airlia artifacts.

The warning had failed and other people had come. Trekking down from the city of Tiahuanaco in the high mountains of South America to the Pacific Coast, these others set sail in reed boats to the west, seeking to band together to fight the guardians—one of which was hidden deep under a pyramid in the center of their city. It was an ill-fated trip. The guardians, through the power of The Mission, hit both Easter Island and the Aymara people of Tiahuanaco with a devastating plague that effectively destroyed the civilizations at both locales.

Now she was seeing something new from the guardian's memory, a vision stunning in its size and realism:

The pyramids of the Giza Plateau gleamed in the early-morning light, the rising sun reflecting off the polished limestone casings. Kelly had been to Egypt and seen the current state of the pyramids, but there was no comparing the present weathered, stripped hulks to these beautifully crafted masterpieces.

Dazzled by the perfectly smooth sides of the pyramids, it took Kelly a little while to notice other startling differences from the relics she had personally witnessed to what she was "seeing" now.

At the very top of the Great Pyramid a capstone added thirty-one feet, bringing it over five hundred feet high above the surrounding sands. The capstone itself was unique. Not made of limestone, it was of a black metal. The very top—

about four feet on each side, ending in an exact point—was a glowing, dark red and reminded Kelly of the ruby sphere that Turcotte and Duncan had recovered in a cavern in the Great Rift in Africa.

She tried to sort through her memories, feeling the intrusion of the guardian. Nabinger had postulated that the smooth, flat sides of the Great Pyramid had been designed to give a significant radar signature into space. But the small red pyramid at the top suggested something else.

She saw something else that was different. The Great Sphinx.

It was all black, with burning red eyes. Crouched on the desert floor in front of the three shining pyramids on the Giza Plateau like—

A bolt of pain seared through Kelly's mind, shattering the vision.

Kelly's body vibrated against the side of the guardian, spasming from the pain. The only part that didn't move was the metal probe into the base of her skull, the source of the agony.

After a minute the spasming subsided, her body slumped like a rag doll, the brain retreating into the deep inner core and hiding, no longer seeking out images.

AREA 51, NEVADA
D – 41 Hours

Major Quinn took the cigarette Larry Kincaid offered and slumped down in one of the leather chairs around the Area 51 conference table. He noted the photos spread out in front of the scientist. "What do you have?"

"Imagery the Department of Defense just took of *Stratzyda* using a KH-14 spy satellite." He handed Quinn one of the pictures.

Stratzyda was a long black cylinder drifting against a backdrop of stars. The hammer-and-sickle insignia painted in red on the side of the long cylinder was a throwback to a time when the world stood on the edge of destruction by divisive human hands.

"Where is it?" Quinn asked.

"A free polar orbit."

"And it's been up there for years and we never did anything about it?"

"First," Kincaid said, "the Russians said it was a test platform in preparation for launching Mir. The intelligence guys might have suspected something, but they couldn't be sure. Then the Russians said it was no longer functional after a year or so. What did you want us to do? Go up and park a shuttle next to it and check it out? You know how many things are in orbit? Or would you have preferred we shoot it down? That would have been illegal and started a war in space and probably on Earth, too."

"Will the warheads still work?" Quinn asked.

"Some have probably degraded and are no longer functional, but I suspect more than half will still detonate upon deployment. Knowing the Russians, they built the simplest—and dirtiest—possible weapon with very few parts to break down. And it's in the vacuum of space."

"What exactly is a cobalt bomb?"

"It's a nuke that has a thick cobalt metal blanket wrapped around the core. The cobalt is used to capture the fusion neutrons to maximize the fallout hazard from the weapon—the nuke guys call this 'salting' the bomb. Instead of generating additional explosive force from fast fission of the U-238, the cobalt is transmuted into Co-60—natural cobalt consists entirely of Co-59. Cobalt 60 has a half-life of five point two six years and produces energetic, very penetrating gamma rays." Kincaid paused to see if Quinn was following this technical explanation before he continued.

"The Co-60 fallout hazard is greater than the fission products from a U-238 blanket because most fission-produced isotopes have half-lives that are very short, and thus decay before the fallout settles or can be protected against by short-term sheltering. Also, other fission-produced isotopes which have very long half-lives do not produce very intense radiation. The half-life of Co-60, on the other hand, is long enough to settle out before significant decay has occurred, and to make it impractical to wait out in shelters, yet is short enough that intense radiation is produced. In terms of the people who are in the fallout area, it's the worst of both effects. And although the threat is greatest for the United States from this"—he tapped the photo of *Stratzyda*—"in reality I think it might be a doomsday device for the entire planet, since no one really knows what will happen."

"But if the bombs go off only over the States, how can it destroy the rest of the world?" Quinn asked.

"The idea for a cobalt bomb originated with Leo Szilard, who theorized such a thing in 1950 to point out that it would be possible in principle to build a weapon that could kill everybody on Earth. To design such a theoretical weapon, he needed a radioactive isotope that could be dispersed worldwide before it decayed. Such dispersal through the atmosphere takes months, perhaps even years, so the half-life of cobalt 60 was the ideal choice. At detonation, gamma radiation from an equivalent-size normal fission-fusion-fission bomb is much more intense than Co-60: fifteen thousand times more intense at one hour; thirty-five times more intense at one week; five times more intense at one month; and about equal at six months. Thereafter fission drops off rapidly, so that Co-60 fallout is eight times more intense than fission at one year and one hundred and fifty times more intense at five years.

"We thought no one had ever really developed a cobalt bomb because its effects weren't really useful—in terms of military objectives, that is. We also thought no one had ever built one or tested one, never mind deployed them. Then again, the Russians never thought we'd put a functional laser weapon in space, either. We sure managed to fool each other, didn't we?"

"These bombs hit the States, the entire continent will be uninhabitable for decades." Kincaid lit another cigarette. "Makes me glad I didn't quit smoking."

CHAPTER 9

VICINITY EASTER ISLAND
D – 41 Hours

"What's the status of the *Springfield*?" Duncan asked. She felt a depressing sense of déjà vu. She had been here before, in exactly this same place, prepared to watch almost exactly the same thing occur. She was a firm believer in the adage that doing the same thing would produce the same results. Unfortunately, she had found over the years, working within the government bureaucracy, that few others thought the same way. The President had asked her to be present for the latest attempt to penetrate the shield around Easter Island at the conclusion of the conference call. His concern had been not so much the actual attempt but rather for her to gauge the mood of the military on blockade duty, to see how close they were to violating orders and attacking the island.

Her conference call with the National Security Council had yielded little. There was even disagreement that the threat from *Stratzyda* was real, despite the example set by Lexina through Warfighter. The only agreement was that word of *Stratzyda* not be leaked. Even the cause of the explosion of *Atlantis* was being kept under wraps, with a cover story of a one-in-a-million catastrophic lightning strike during rollout being fed to the media.

The President had been in contact with the Russian president, who had vehemently denied that *Stratzyda* was what Yakov claimed. He stuck to the old cover story of its being an experimental platform for Mir.

Lies fighting lies, Duncan thought to herself. She was

beginning to understand how easy it had been for the alien groups to manipulate mankind when truth was such an ephemeral ideal.

Admiral Poldan, the commander of the task force, was seated in a black leather chair that was elevated so that he could oversee all that was happening in the combat control center, deep inside the island bridge of the USS *Washington*. He turned slightly in his chair to look at Duncan, and his gaze was not kind. Since arriving on board the aircraft carrier via bouncer flight from Area 51, Duncan had received a chilly reception from the military personnel who manned the ship.

She had also found that to be the norm. Anyone not in uniform among a large group of others who did wear one, was bound to be looked at strangely. The Navy found it convenient to blame her for the loss of the *Pasadena,* destroyed by the foo fighters, and the entrapment of the *Springfield*. Even more than that, they were angry over having their hands tied, unable to strike back with all the numerous weapons at their command.

The *Washington* was one of the most modern ships in the Navy, a *Nimitz*-class carrier that cost over three billion dollars to build, the most expensive weapons system in the world. It was the core of Task Force 78, surrounded by two guided missile cruisers, three destroyers, two frigates, and two supply ships.

The *Washington* carried the task force's most powerful punch in the form of its flight wing: one squadron (12) of Grumman F-14 Tomcats, three squadrons (36) of McDonnell Douglas F/A-18 Hornets, four Grumman EA-2C Hawkeye surveillance aircraft, ten Lockheed S-3B Vikings, six Sikorsky SH-60B Seahawk helicopters, and six EA-6B Prowlers.

And all that power had been doing for the past few days was steaming in a circle twenty miles away from Easter Island.

"She's on the bottom, not moving," Poldan said gruffly. "No change there. No change here. We're just wasting time."

"What change would you like to see?" Duncan asked.

"I say we hit the island with everything we have."

"Including nuclear weapons?"

"Including nukes," Poldan confirmed. "The Secretary of Defense agreed with me just this morning."

"And he was assassinated on his way to tell the President that," Duncan noted.

"All the more reason to blast this rock out of the ocean."

"You received the imagery from China. Firing a nuclear weapon at Qian-Ling didn't do much."

"Nuking the foo fighter base worked," Poldan countered.

"Did it?" Duncan asked. "Then where did the foo fighters that are covering the *Springfield* come from? And the foo fighter base probably didn't have a guardian computer and shield." She wondered how he would react if he knew the threat from *Stratzyda*.

Poldan ignored her, turning his attention to the operations center, and gave orders, preparing the carrier to launch the latest attempt to see beyond the shield.

Duncan stepped closer to his chair and lowered her voice so only he could hear. "Admiral, do you think this is smart?"

A muscle in the admiral's jaw quivered. "Lady, you have the clearance to be here and you have presidential authority, but I have approval from the National Security Council, which the President also heads."

"I'm not ordering you to stop," Duncan said. "I'm just asking you to think about it. What makes you think this will be any more successful than your attempt under the water with Sea Eye?"

"Global Hawk is unmanned," Poldan said. "It fails, we lose nothing but a piece of equipment."

"Admiral, I think that—"

"I allowed you to try to contact Kelly Reynolds," Poldan countered. "You've received no response. Now we try it my way." Poldan turned to an officer seated at a console in the front of the operations center. "Do we have a link with Global Hawk?"

"Yes, sir."

"Assume control."

Global Hawk had been developed by Teledyne Ryan Aeronautical and Raytheon E-Systems to fit a very specific requirement proposed by the Department of Defense. The need was for what was called in military procurement jargon a HAE UAV: high altitude endurance, unmanned aerial vehicle.

It was shaped like the famous U-2 spy plane, except slightly smaller and having no need for the cockpit since it was flown remotely by a pilot or computer on the ground. Long black wings stretched almost 120 feet, with a thin body, all painted flat black. A pod in the bottom held the imaging gear, controlled by a central computer. A jet engine gave the aircraft power.

Global Hawk was currently at sixty thousand feet and descending rapidly. Speed was relatively slow, about 120 knots. The long, wide wings gave the aircraft plenty of lift and the small jet engine had to put out little thrust to keep the vehicle moving. It had been launched from Edwards Air Force Base in California the previous day and had been controlled via satellite link from Edwards, directed to fly toward Easter Island.

As it got closer to Easter Island, the satellite link with Edwards was cut and it entered a glide path that had been determined by the computer. The jet engine cut off and it swooped down, heading for the dark gray clouds below and the island hidden underneath them.

"See those four lines that center up?" The officer who had answered Poldan inclined his head at the screen. "That's the glide path."

As far as Duncan could tell, the lines did little good, as the entire screen was filled with gray cloud. The pilot was sitting in a padded chair, surrounded by flight instrumentation and computer screens. Directly in front of him, a joystick, such as Duncan remembered her son using for computer games, rested on a small platform. The pilot's right hand was wrapped around the stick.

"I'm ready to fly it by keeping the small red figure that represents Global Hawk centered on those lines, which are projected by the computer using a satellite uplink to a global positioning satellite." He reached forward and flipped a switch with his free hand. The gray was gone. A black bubble on a blue field filled the screen. "We're looking forward now from the Global Hawk using a thermal imager. That's the shield surrounding the island. The blue is the ocean surface outside of the shield."

The image shuddered. "Turbulence," the pilot explained, his hand hovering over the controls. "Four minutes to shield."

He hit a red button on his console. "Exit program is loaded and ready to run." He hit the button again. "Computer is off and timer is set. I have complete control by radio link."

The black bubble got closer. The guardian had made the shield opaque after the last failed conventional attack by Admiral Poldan's fleet. Up to that point, it had been invisible. The best guess UNAOC scientists had been able to come up with was that the field that comprised the shield was similar to the electromagnetic one used by the bouncers. The fact that in all the years

Majestic had worked on the electromagnetic drives of those craft not a single clue as to how they actually worked had been discovered told Duncan that the key to the shield would not suddenly reveal itself.

The pilot flipped four switches one right after the other. "I'm powering down nonessential systems," he explained. "There are only two things still on—the forward heat imager, which we're watching, and my radio link.

"One minute out," the pilot said. "Going off-line completely." He hit the red button one last time. Then he let go of the controls. "Global Hawk is on a glide path that will take it through the shield. Prior to takeoff from Edwards, the central computer was shielded and a special program loaded. When I cut all links to the UAV, the central computer will go to sleep, which should allow it to pass through the shield, as the Airlia automated equipment seems to respond only to electric signals. It will wake up once inside, take the needed images, then shut down once more on the way out."

"We hope that's the way it works," Duncan said.

The pilot shrugged. "It's the best plan we have, given what we know about Airlia technology."

Duncan wasn't too sure. The foo fighters had been taken out that way, using "dumb" weapons that gave off no EM signal, but she had a feeling the guardian was learning and adapting. Admiral Poldan had used "dumb" bombs to strike at the island during the last attack, and the shield had destroyed every one of them, unlike their success against the foo fighters. The hope of the UNAOC scientists was that the guardian—if it picked up Global Hawk—would see that the unmanned plane carried no weapons and therefore would not consider it a threat.

The pilot checked the time. "Entering shield."

The microbug was no bigger than a hornet. The microrobots, directed by the guardian, had built it from parts cannibalized from one of the FM radios left by the UNAOC scientists.

The microbug flitted through the tunnel the humans had drilled from the surface into the guardian chamber. It was shaped like an elongated teardrop, with a tiny electromagnetic gravity drive, no bigger than the flat end of a thumbtack, giving it power and the ability to fly.

The microbug sped into the sky, toward the object that had just been allowed through the shield. It easily caught up to the Global Hawk and raced alongside. Global Hawk was fifteen hundred feet over Easter Island, moving at eighty knots.

The microbug slid in through an air duct in the front of the aircraft. It immediately noted the imagers now taking pictures and readings. It flew down a wiring conduit straight to the aircraft's master computer.

A miniature door on the side of the microbug slid open and a wire, no thicker than the finest of threads, punched directly into the computer's main processor.

The Global Hawk banked and headed for a landing on the main airstrip on Easter Island. Like a group of ants awaiting a picnic basket, a small army of microrobots was at the edge of the runway.

Lisa Duncan looked pointedly at the clock.

The pilot slumped back in his seat. "We're past due," he admitted. "But it went in, we know that."

Admiral Poldan pointed forward. "We need to nuke that damn place. Nothing but a bunch of old statues anyway."

"And Kelly Reynolds," Duncan noted.

"Hell, she's a traitor," Poldan snarled.

"A lot of people think differently," Duncan said.

"Who gives a damn what a lot of people think?" Poldan asked.

"That's supposedly what democracy is all about," Duncan dryly noted. "Kelly helped uncover the secret of Area 51, Admiral. We owe her."

Poldan stabbed a finger toward Easter Island. "Tell it to that thing."

Lisa Duncan checked the clock once more. Forty hours before Lexina's deadline was up. She left the communications shack.

NGORONGORO CRATER, TANZANIA
D – 39 Hours, 20 Minutes

"What is it?" Lago asked.

It had taken the two of them several hours to completely clear the sides of the stone. It was ten feet long by four wide. The edges were exact, the surfaces perfectly smooth except where there was high rune writing. Mualama doubted that any modern stonemason could do such a good job, even using lasers to cut the markings.

Mualama stepped back, wiping a hand across his sweaty brow, not caring that it left a streak of mud. "You were the student," he said. "The first thing you must consider at a dig is how old you think the site is."

Lago frowned. "It's very strange. From the depth, given the data you gave me on this area, it should be several thousand years old. But—"

"Several thousand?" Mualama interrupted him. "That is much too broad an estimation. Narrow it down."

Lago picked up a notepad from the side of the pit. He thumbed through, searching for the notes he had taken when he'd been briefed by Mualama. Then he took a ruler and measured the stone's depth.

"I'd say this had been buried here somewhere between two and three thousand years." He looked up. "But that can't be, Uncle. It must have been buried recently and—"

"Why do you say that?"

"The other geological time indicators we found on top. They indicate that this site has been disturbed sometime after it was originally established. Do they not?" Lago asked.

Mualama nodded.

"But—" Lago pointed at the stone. "How can that be? If it was so hard for you to find it, who else could have?"

Mualama knelt next to the red stone. "What do you think this is?"

Lago shook his head. "I don't know."

"You must tell me," Mualama said. "Your head professor will not be pleased if I do not test you."

"I graduated two years ago," Lago noted. "I no longer have a head professor."

"What do you think it is?" Mualama repeated.

"A marker?"

"Yes," Mualama said. "But what kind?"

"Of a special site?"

Mualama smiled. "I do not know, so I cannot say if you are right or wrong. Yes, I do believe this is a special site. But I have my own guess what kind of marker this is."

"Yes?"

"I think it is a grave marker."

Mualama smiled. "Bring me the end of the cable from the Rover's winch."

Once his nephew brought him the cable, Mualama formed a large loop, which he laid next to one end of the stone. "Come," he called to Lago. "We need to dig around so we can get this under."

After an hour of work they had the cable around the

end of the stone, four inches in. Mualama ordered his nephew back to the winch. He gave Lago a thumbs-up, indicating for him to start the winch attached to the front bumper of the Land Rover. He then grabbed the end of the metal pipe he had taken off the roof of the Rover.

The cable was taut, the winch whining, but there was no movement.

"Hold!" Mualama yelled.

Lago hit the lever, and the winch halted. Mualama dropped to his knees and used the trowel to dig a hole under the edge of the stone. He excavated as far as his arm could reach. Then Mualama slid the pipe into the hole.

"Again!"

The winch powered up. Mualama put all his weight on the pipe, his feet coming off the ground. With a loud sucking noise, the stone lifted ever so slightly.

"Hold!"

The tension went out of the cable and the stone dropped back down. Mualama repositioned the cable, making sure it was secure.

"Once more," Mualama yelled.

The winch pulled, and this time the stone lifted four inches, then froze. Mualama was afraid of breaking it. He had taken photos of the surface from every angle, but he knew the stone intact was a magnificent find regardless of what else they found.

"You must lift with the winch," he instructed Lago, "then I will move it to the left."

"How are you—"

"Just lift when I tell you," Mualama said. "Now!"

The winch pulled once more, and the stone came up. Mualama gripped the pipe in his large hands, waiting as the end near him went up six inches. Then a foot. When it was two feet up, he slid his leg under it and pushed the pipe as far as it would go to the right.

"What are you doing?" Lago yelled in alarm.

"Keep the winch going!" Mualama put more of his body under the stone. He slid the pipe around to the right side of the stone. Then he pressed against the pipe.

The stone moved very slightly to the left; only the part that was up moved. The edge was now three feet up. Mualama's feet slipped on the dirt underneath. He desperately kept his grip on the pipe. He slid it farther down the right side. The stone was now angled.

Mualama looked—the far left edge was just over the lip of the pit. He strained, putting every ounce of strength he had into pushing the pipe along the right edge. A foot of the far left was now over the lip.

The close edge suddenly came free and the stone dangled precariously, held by the cable but free of the pipe. Mualama placed his back against the bottom of the stone, his body bent double as he tried to push it sideways.

"Are you all right?" Lago's voice seemed to come from far away.

"Keep"—Mualama had to pause to take a deep breath between each word—"the—winch—going!"

Mualama shifted his feet, slowly moving to the left, most of the weight of the stone taken by the winch. He felt the scarred skin on his back against the hard rock, the inner surface rough, unlike the smooth top, and tearing into his back.

The cable around the stone shifted and the stone dropped six inches, knocking Mualama flat. He was lying on the earth underneath the marker.

"Uncle!" Lago screamed.

Mualama twisted on his side, trying to see, just a little daylight coming in the part of the opening that was now clear—not enough for him to climb out of. He was trapped. The cable was more toward the middle of the stone now. The stone was resting on the lip.

"Is the cable holding it?" Mualama yelled.

"What?"

"Is there any slack in the cable?"

"Yes."

"Pull up to the edge of the pit." Mualama spoke slowly and carefully so that Lago would understand. "Then extend the metal brace on the front of the Rover. Run the cable over the wheel on the edge of the metal brace. Do you understand?"

"Yes. Are you okay?"

"Just do it, please."

Mualama waited. He heard the wheels of the Rover move, then metal clanking. Mualama used the time to maneuver the cable to the exact center of the stone.

"I'm ready," Lago finally yelled.

"Pull!" Mualama yelled. He heard the whine of the winch, and the stone lifted, quickly now, straight up. Mualama kept his hands on it to make sure it didn't slip either way. It was clear of the edge on all sides.

"All right! Stop the winch!"

The stone stopped moving.

"Now," Mualama said, "back up the Rover until the stone clears."

"All right."

"Slowly!"

Mualama kept his attention focused on keeping the stone steady as Lago backed the Rover up. He was so close, the last thing he needed now was to have it slide on top of him.

After a minute of very slow maneuvering, the stone was clear of the pit.

"Stop!" Mualama yelled. "Lower it," he ordered as Lago got out of the Rover and came to the front. Slowly, the heavy marker went down until it lay on the ground next to the hole they had dug.

"What now?" Lago was staring at the marker.

Mualama picked up the shovels, tossing one to Lago. "We dig some more. The stone was a marker for something that lies underneath." Mualama shoved the tip of the spade into the dirt. Reluctantly, Lago joined him.

Less than ten minutes after they began, Lago's shovel hit something solid. They hurried to uncover the object. When they were done, they both climbed out of the hole and stared down.

"What the hell is that?" Lago murmured as they could now see the entire object.

A black metal pod, seven and a half feet long by three in diameter, lay in the dirt, the surface still shiny after thousands of years in the ground and unmarked where the shovels had struck it.

"A coffin," Mualama said.

"But for who?"

"Let us find out," Mualama said.

Repeating same process, they managed to lift the coffin out of the pit, placing it on the ground next to the marker.

Mualama was running his hands along the side of the black tube, feeling the seam.

"How did you know it was here?" Lago asked. "You told me how you found this site, but how did you know there was a site to begin with?"

Mualama sat down on the tube, resting before finishing the excavation. "I didn't know *it* was here." He tapped the tube. "I learned—as Burton did—that something was here, but I wasn't sure what I would find.

"I—as Burton did—believe that there is a link between many legends in this part of the world. That things that seem unconnected are connected. The presence of the Airlia on this planet gives more credence to that belief."

"A conspiracy?" Lago asked.

Mualama shrugged. "I am not a big believer in coincidence. I believe in cause and effect. I believe that there is a purpose to things. But first, let me test your knowledge."

Lago rolled his eyes but didn't say anything.

"Look at the earth we removed to get to the stone. Compare it to the strata on the side of the hole. Then the dirt we removed to get to the coffin and the depth. Do you think the stone marker was placed on the coffin when it was buried?"

Lago compared the two. "No. They're different."

"Good. You dated the hole as being between two and three thousand years old, based on what we removed from on top, but the strata on the side leading to the depth of the coffin is different, as you've noted. How long do you think this coffin has lain in the ground?"

Lago checked his notes. "This can't be."

"Trust the evidence in front of your eyes, not your flawed knowledge base."

"According to the data, the coffin was buried around ten thousand years."

"Why do you say that cannot be?"

"Because civilization . . ." Lago paused. "It's an Airlia artifact."

"It certainly appears so. You did your research on this part of the world in graduate school, right?"

Lago nodded.

"Africa is too often left out of the annals of history, especially in America. Yet it is most likely the birthplace of the human race." Mualama saw that Lago was about to say something, and he raised a hand. "As you know, it has a legitimate claim to the oldest fossils of *Homo* genus. For example, America can claim humans only thirty thousand years ago! Not long at all when we talk in terms of hundreds of thousand of years.

"Of course," Mualama continued, "we know so little because we've found so little. Pieces of a skeleton here, fragments of an artifact there. We base our entire theory of the development of man on depressingly little factual evidence, yet we call it science and we call it truth. How many times in the past century has the current accepted 'theory' been radically altered by a new discovery?"

"The textbook we used at university was published not long ago," Lago said, "and it had several errors in it."

"Not errors," Mualama corrected, "but outdated 'facts.' " He tapped his foot on the top of the tube. "I wonder what facts this find is going to change."

"But it's an Airlia object," Lago protested. "Not human."

"Consider," Mualama said, "how many things have been discovered that could not be explained. What if someone had found this site *before* the news of what was in Area 51 and the existence of the Airlia came to light?"

Lago bit his lip as he considered the question. "I suppose this would have been the thing that proved we had been visited by aliens."

Mualama emphatically shook his head. "No! You are young and naive. View our society as a deep river, running between stone banks. Do you know what it takes to change the course of that river? To change people's perceptions?

"Even now, with a mile-long alien spacecraft circling our planet, there are many who would close their eyes and say it isn't there. If a mile-long mothership that anyone with a toy store telescope can see clearly doesn't change those people, you think something like this"—he tapped the tube—"would?

"Burton saw something that changed his perception on everything around him. And he was told something— I believe he was told about the aliens having been here on Earth. He dedicated his life to tracking down the truth."

"Did he find it?"

"I think he found out part of it, but not the entire story. And it is the entire story we need." Mualama leaned forward, a thin sheen of sweat on his brow. "Let me tell you some things. I have kept my eyes and my ears and, most important, my mind open for many years. And my mouth shut.

"There *have* been things found that do not fit. There is a dig in Australia where archaeologists found evidence of *Homo erectus,* Neanderthal, and *Homo sapiens* all in the same era. Stages in the development of man that are supposed to be hundreds of thousands of years apart, yet lying in the same time strata.

"There are two places where *Homo* skeletal remains were found at a layer *below* that of Neanderthals. How can that be? There have been numerous strange finds like this. Have you read of any of them?"

Lago shook his head no.

"Of course not," Mualama said. "Because anyone who published such so-called idiocy would be labeled a crackpot. But because of what he had experienced, Burton questioned the status quo. And there have been others. Professor Nabinger was a man who questioned what he saw, who looked where others were too afraid to look. His investigation in the Great Pyramid was based on his discovery of an after-action report hidden in the Royal Museum Archives of Hammond's 1976 expedition that discovered residual radiation in the Great Pyramid. Of course, Hammond didn't publish that report for fear of ridicule and because he couldn't explain his findings. But now we know the reason he found that radiation—the Airlia had left an atomic weapon in the lowest chamber. And I think that Nabinger was not able to do all he wanted at Giza. There is more to the Plateau than meets the eye, and—" Mualama stopped himself, as if suddenly realizing where he was and who was with him.

"But . . ." Lago hesitated.

"Go ahead," Mualama prompted.

"But, like you just said, that radiation was due to the Airlia. That thing you're sitting on is also Airlia, based on the high rune writing on the marker. But the fossil remains—what do they have to do with the Airlia?"

"Good question," Mualama said. "It is one I have been asking myself often. And I don't have an answer. Yet. But I believe they are connected. Perhaps our past is not what we think in more ways than we could begin to conceive." Mualama abruptly changed the subject. "Do you know of the kingdom of Axum?"

"One of the earliest empires in the world," Lago recited. "It was founded around the first or second century before the birth of Christ. The empire covered most of what was now Ethiopia and Kenya. It traded with Greece and Rome during its heyday, while at the same time making contact to the east to India and even China."

"Very good," Mualama said. "You get a B. It is an empire few people know of. Mostly because it was here in Africa and because it was an empire of dark-skinned people, not the most popular or delved-into subject around the world's history courses. But at its height, Axum rivaled any of the kingdoms it traded with— Rome, China, India.

"One subject I have been very interested in is the various legends of Axum." He pointed a long black finger at Lago. "We archaeologists are like detectives. We must investigate the past, and in order to do so, we must gather as much information as possible. I have found the best way to do that is to research the myths and legends of an area. Because there is often much more truth to legend than people realize.

"Many years ago, when I was a student like you, my professor at the University of Dar es Salaam sent me north to Ethiopia. My dissertation was on Axum, and he told me that to do a proper job I must go there, to the land that was the center of Axum's power.

"So I went. I traveled around the country, to many places where scholars have never been.

"At Lake Tana, in northwest Ethiopia, there are many old monasteries. These places have changed little in hundreds, thousands of years. Christianity came early to Ethiopia—to Axum. It was one of the earliest Christian countries in the world.

"Lake Tana, like this crater, is over a mile above sea level in the northwest part of Ethiopia. From the lake's southern end, the Blue Nile cascades down a magnificent waterfall to start its seventeen-hundred-kilometer journey to Khartoum in Sudan, where it merges with the White Nile.

"The lake itself is seventy-five kilometers long and sixty kilometers wide. It is dotted with some thirty-seven islands, many with ancient monasteries and churches that contain valuable religious icons and manuscripts. I visited every single one of those enclaves and learned much. They have not only documents and items that relate to their own faith, but some that are much, much older.

"Christianity first spread to the area around the lake in the fifth century A.D. and is now the dominant religion, but there are also communities of Muslims, Jews, and Animists. Many of the people around the lake and on the islands make a living from fishing, still using papyrus reed boats very similar to those depicted in the pharaohs' tombs of ancient Egypt.

"But even before Christianity, Islam, and Judaism came to this part of the world, there were other faiths. Like many early peoples, the ancient people of Axum worshiped a sun god. Even long after Christianity came to Axum, the Queen of Sheba was reported to be a sun god worshiper. Although she is known now only as the Queen of Sheba and her visit with King Solomon is well recorded, her original title was Queen of Sheba and Axum."

Lago sat on the bumper of the Land Rover, mesmerized by this information as Mualama continued.

"The people of Axum also worshiped other, older gods. In places, there is a strange mixture of these ancient worships and the Christian church. I also learned that someone else had visited all these places before me over a hundred years ago. It took me a while, but I finally learned the identity of this strange white man—Sir Richard Francis Burton. Yet there was no record of these travels in his official biographies. I realized that Burton had led a secret life, and I wanted to know why. I wanted to know what he was searching for in the same places I was traveling to."

"Which was?" Lago asked.

"I think he was looking for a key."

"A key to what?"

"You know, of course, about the Ark of the Covenant?" Mualama suddenly asked in turn.

Lago nodded. "There are rumors, unsubstantiated, that the Ark—if it exists—is in Ethiopia."

Mualama laughed. "See how even now you still guard what you say? 'If it exists'?"

"Does it?" Lago challenged him.

Mualama shrugged. "I don't know. But I suspect something that people have called the Ark does exist.

"The Kebre Negest—The Glory of Kings—is the document that was written during the realm of King Menelik I, the offspring of Sheba and Solomon. It states that when Menelik was a young adult he traveled to Jerusalem and visited his father, Solomon. He returned home to Axum accompanied by Azarias, the son of the high priest Zadok, and brought with them the Ark of the Covenant and placed it in St. Mary of Zion Church in Axum."

"I've heard that, but no one has ever taken a picture of the Ark," Lago said. "It seems like if it was there, it would be one of the greatest archaeological and theological discoveries of all time and people would want to publicize it."

Mualama chuckled. "You are thinking like a westerner. Have you ever been to St. Mary of Zion Church?"

"No."

"Do you know anyone who has ever actually been there?"

"No."

"So these rumors were not enough to make you travel to check them out and you want to be an archaeologist?" Mualama did not wait for an answer. "Thus it is so with many things. There are rumors. Someone says: 'Someone should do something! Someone should check this out!' And they think someone else has, but the truth be known, no one does.

"I have been to St. Mary of Zion Church," Mualama said. "As Burton went in 1877. His biographies said he went to Africa to search for gold, as his finances were desperate, but that is not what he was looking for. Money was not important to him. The search for the truth was.

"At the church there is one monk, each generation, who is given the responsibility to care for the inner sacristy of the church. No one but that monk ever goes into the sacristy."

"That's a nice technique to keep the mystery alive," Lago said, stung by the old man's comments.

Mualama tapped the object he was sitting on. "This mystery—the Airlia— lasted for a very long time while people laughed at things like UFOs. Meanwhile, the Americans were test-flying those craft, the bouncers, at their Area 51 for decades." He wagged a finger. "Do not be so quick to deride things you know little about. I have been to the church, and I spoke with the monk. You have not."

"Do you think the Ark is in it?" Lago asked.

"I spent two weeks there." Mualama seemed not to have heard the question. "The monk told me there were very few visitors. Maybe half a dozen each year. Amazing, isn't that? There are rumors of what even you call a great discovery and only a half-dozen people travel there each year. And no one who had stayed as long as I.

"I'm afraid I was a little obnoxious. I pestered the poor old man every day with my questions. I wanted to know every legend, every story, everything he could tell me. And he did talk to me, finally."

Mualama's eyes were unfocused as he remembered. "One night we sat in the church's courtyard, under a very old tree, and he spoke until the sun rose in the east. He told me strange things and hinted at others, some that he was afraid to speak openly about. Then he had to go to his meditations."

Mualama snapped to, smiling at Lago. "No, I don't think the Ark is in the church, because the monk told me it wasn't. Not directly, but in so many words, he let me know that the Ark had once been in the church. But only for a short while. I think the Ark has traveled to many places."

Lago leaned forward. "Where is it now?"

"Ah, he would not tell me that. But I knew from what he said that it had been moved and that the church was now a blind, designed to confuse the trail. He also gave me clues, places to look for more information. Not directly, but I listened carefully, sorting through all he said, connecting his words with other rumors, legends, I have learned about. I went to England and searched through the source material on Sir Burton. And I found more clues, leading me places.

"And that is what I have been doing for the past twenty years. Looking here and there. Taking a small piece of information from one place and adding it to another. Like bread crumbs from the past, I have followed Sir Richard Francis Burton around the world. I think the manuscript we have, written in a long-dead tongue, tells of Burtons journeys and what he learned. I think I can combine it with what I learned following his trail to have a most interesting tale. We will have to get it translated.

"I, too, went to Lake Tana and visited all of the monasteries. On the island of Dega Estefanos, I went to a very small monastery, cut in the side of a cliff, over three hundred meters above the surface of the lake. You can get up there only if the monks inside lower you a rope. I had to wait four days before they allowed me up."

Mualama paused.

"And?" Lago pressed.

"That is where I found the parchment that told me this site existed. The legends I have studied say the Ark is hidden inside a place called the Hall of Records and that a key is needed to get inside the Hall." Mualama stood. "And now that we have rested, let us see what we have found." He ran his hands along the seam while Lago watched over his shoulder. Mualama staggered back as the lid suddenly swung open, two hydraulic arms smoothly laying the top back.

"Oh my God," Lago whispered.

The skeleton was at least seven feet tall, with disproportionally long arms and legs. The facial bones were different than a human's, elongated, with deep eye sockets. The figure was dressed in a black robe that had withstood the years better than the body. A golden crown— just a band of gold with a large black gem set in the very center—had fallen off the skull. In the right hand was a slender rod, a foot long, two inches thick. On the end of the rod was the head of a lion with ruby-red eyes.

"What is that?" Lago was pointing at the rod.

Mualama reached down and carefully removed the rod from the dead hand. It was surprisingly heavy. He turned it in the light, the setting sun glinting off the rubies and precious metal.

"I believe this is the key."

CHAPTER 10

"Why are we stopping here?" Turcotte asked.

The landing strip outside the bouncer was a desolate piece of concrete cut out of the surrounding tundra. The flight had been a long one—even for a bouncer—north and west over the pole. They'd crossed a large part of Siberia also. Turcotte had followed the route Yakov directed on a map and knew they were now outside the northern Russian town of Tiksa about three hundred miles from the island where Section Four had been headquartered.

Yakov stood and headed for the top hatch. "Information. I think it best if we proceed somewhat cautiously. Would you not agree?"

"The clock is ticking," Turcotte said. He could see a truck heading out from the small control tower building.

"I know that," Yakov said, "but I have learned it is better to go into a strange situation a little slowly with more knowledge than quickly in complete ignorance."

Turcotte agreed with that reasoning, but he also knew it was *his* country and not Yakov's that was being threatened.

Yakov threw open the hatch. "I have someone waiting for us who might have some useful information about who destroyed Section Four, and possibly about the key itself."

Turcotte grabbed Yakov's arm. "What do you mean?"

"I did not want to say anything at Area 51," Yakov said, "but Section Four did not have all of the Airlia artifacts that the Soviet Union gathered. There is no doubt that the KGB also hoarded whatever they found. I have heard rumors that the KGB has an archive of such things hidden somewhere. Perhaps the key is there."

Turcotte gave orders to the pilots to stand down, then followed Yakov. As soon as he cleared the hatch, a bitter-cold wind cut into his exposed skin. A tall figure covered in heavy furs got out of the truck. Yakov wrapped the driver in both arms.

When Turcotte got close, Yakov let go and turned to introduce the driver. "My American friend, Captain Turcotte, this is Katyenka."

Turcotte extended his gloved hand and shook the woman's. He estimated she had to be at least six feet four.

"A friend?" Katyenka repeated as she pulled back the hood on her long fur coat. Her face was startlingly beautiful, with high cheekbones, flawless skin, and deep gray eyes. "That is high praise," she said. "Very few people have been Yakov's friend. I often worried I was the only one still alive he has so branded."

"Let us get out of the cold." Yakov jumped into the driver's seat as Turcotte and Katyenka crowded in next to him.

Yakov floored the pedal, throwing Turcotte back against the cracked vinyl. He gripped the edge of the seat as Yakov tore across the runway onto a snow-covered road at a rate of speed certainly too fast for the slippery surface.

As they fishtailed around a turn, Katyenka looked over at Turcotte. "Yakov tells me you saw Colonel Kostanov die."

"Yes."

"He was one of Yakov's friends," Katyenka said.

"And yours," Yakov said.

Katyenka nodded sadly. "And mine. He was a good man."

Yakov leaned over to Turcotte and tapped him on the chest. "He was once—for a little while—to her what your Dr. Duncan is to you."

Katyenka gave Yakov a glance that Turcotte couldn't interpret. Before Turcotte could say anything, Yakov skidded the truck to a halt outside the small building next to the airfield tower. Yakov jumped out of the truck. He threw open a door and stomped in, leading the way to a small office. Throwing his black coat onto a chair, he gestured for Turcotte to take a chair. Katyenka took off her coat and sat on the edge of the desk.

"A drink?" Yakov held a clear bottle in his hand.

"Something warm?" Turcotte suggested.

Yakov laughed. "What can be warmer than vodka?" He poured three tall glasses.

"How long will it take us to get to the base from here?" Turcotte asked.

"In the bouncer? An hour, no more." Yakov pointed north. "It is on the northern edge of Novaya Zemlya, an island off our north coast. Above the Arctic Circle. We put Section Four there because it is remote. Much more remote than your Area 51. Much of Novaya Zemlya is uninhabitable due to nuclear testing."

Turcotte hadn't yet taken a drink from the large glass of vodka. "When do we leave?"

Yakov sighed. "I know you are worried about the danger from above, and I agree it is a dire and immediate threat, but we must also keep our vision on the big picture, and that is knowing the truth about the past. We have been attacked by *both* groups—the Guides/Mission and The Ones Who Wait/STAAR. There may come a time when we have to choose between them. Indeed, if we find this key Lexina wants, it is not automatic that we should hand it over to her. We must have more information first." He nodded at Katyenka. "Tell us what more you have learned about Tunguska."

Katyenka got up and walked to the small bar. Turcotte thought it quite bizarre, but typical of Russia, that there would be a bar in the office at such a small airfield. He knew Yakov was right once more about gathering information, but he itched to be moving, to be searching for the key.

Katyenka poured herself another glass of vodka. "Not much more than is common knowledge. The commonly accepted theory is that a meteorite exploded in 1908 over Tunguska."

Turcotte found her accent intriguing. He imagined if she had lived in the West, she might have become a model—in Russia she became a spy.

"Exactly who are you?" Turcotte asked.

"She is Katyenka," Yakov said simply.

"That's a name," Turcotte said, "which means nothing to me. Who do you work for?"

"I am not Section Four," Katyenka said.

Turcotte had already checked her hand and not seen the large ring that indicated a Watcher, but the ring could be hidden. "Who do you work for?"

Katyenka spread her hands. "I am GRU."

Turcotte turned to Yakov. "And you brought her into this?"

Yakov laughed. "How do you think I am still alive? How do you think *she* is still alive? She is the spy the GRU picked to infiltrate Section Four. I knew they—and the KGB—would send someone. So we sent spies to infiltrate the GRU and the KGB. It is the way things work in Russia. Except my dear Katyenka decided that she was working for the wrong people after getting a glimpse of what we were doing in Section Four."

"I realized the alien threat was larger than the Section Four threat," Katyenka explained simply.

"So she came to me and offered to be a double agent for us," Yakov said. "That was over six years ago. It is all part of not knowing who to trust. You had a group called STAAR working in the United States, did you not?"

"Yeah." Turcotte nodded. "It was the way The Ones Who Wait could infiltrate our government."

"We have had our Ones Who Wait also," Yakov said. "We don't think they had an official organization here like your STAAR, but they had operatives infiltrated in the KGB and GRU."

"And we believe that The Ones Who Wait destroyed Section Four," Katyenka added.

"Why?" Turcotte asked.

"I don't know," Katyenka said.

"Maybe they were looking for something," Yakov suggested.

"What?" Katyenka asked.

Turcotte wasn't sure how much he should say in front of Katyenka. He noted that even Yakov didn't answer that question, so he thought it best to keep quiet about the key also.

"Have you discovered anything about the KGB—FSB—archives?" Yakov asked Katyenka. "We need to be moving now."

"There is a man at FSB headquarters. A very powerful man. His name is Lyoncheka. I think he is the one at FSB who knows of the Airlia. Who knows what secrets the KGB has kept hidden all these years. As my GRU has hidden records, I have heard rumors of an archives of artifacts and information maintained by the KGB about the Airlia. If anyone would know where it is, it would be Lyoncheka."

Yakov stood. "I will look for him shortly. First, though, let us go to Stantsiya Chyort and discover what happened there and look for what we came here for."

NGORONGORO CRATER
D – 38 Hours, 30 Minutes

"Now that I have some leverage"—Mualama hefted the scepter in his hand—"we can call UNAOC."

"Do you know where the Hall of Records is?" Lago asked.

Mualama smiled broadly. "This was where I thought it was. I think the Hall will be where I believe it is. Far from here."

"Where?" Lago pressed.

"That was the promise Burton made—that he would not reveal what he had seen and where he had seen it. But I think I have figured it out." Mualama tapped the side of his head. "That remains here. With this key and the knowledge, UNAOC will have to allow me to continue. And we will need their help to get to the next place."

Mualama pointed toward the south rim of the crater. "Take the Rover and go to the lodge we passed on the way here. Call UNAOC in New York. Do not tell them what we have, only that we have discovered high rune writing. You can fax them a picture of the stone marker. Do not mention the scepter.

"Try to talk to someone who knew Professor Nabinger. Someone who can appreciate what we have found. Tell them we will meet whoever they send right here."

Less than two miles from where Professor Mualama and Lago were scratching the dirt of the crater, deep under the mirrorlike surface of Soda Lake, Lexina was watching two of her kind die.

She stood over them, a tall, slender figure wearing a gray robe that was worn and dirty from her travel to this location. If Mualama had followed a difficult path to arrive at Ngorongoro Crater, then Lexina's trial had been almost impossible. She'd walked south along the Great Rift Valley, one of the most inhospitable tracts of land on the face of the planet, dwarfing the Grand Canyon in length, running from southern Turkey, through Syria, between Israel and Jordan where the Dead Sea lay—the lowest point on the face of the planet. From there it formed the basin of the Red Sea. At the Gulf of Aden the Rift Valley broke into two, one part going to the Indian Ocean, the other inland into Africa. South of Ngorongoro Crater, the Rift Valley continued for hundreds of miles before ending in Mozambique.

She had swum out into Soda Lake the previous week and found the entrance to the remains of an ancient Airlia base, her new home after spending the past twenty-two years under the ice in Antarctica at Scorpion Base. She was the head of The Ones Who Wait. Since they had been forced to flee Scorpion Base, her small group had scattered across the globe to continue their tasks, but as always, it seemed like all they were doing was reacting to the forces of The Mission.

Her skin was pale and smooth, but the strangest feature visible were her red eyes with elongated pupils. She stood on a black metal floor in a circular room, approximately fifty feet in diameter. Light came from a series of blue, glowing tubes spaced along the vaulted ceiling.

She knew little of this base from the records her kind had kept other than that the Airlia had established it during the height of their domain on Earth. To find it, she had followed ancient markers from the kingdom of Axum.

One of her operatives, Elek, was in Qian-Ling but needed a key to access the lowest level. Two of her other operatives, Coridan and Gergor, had been the ones who destroyed Section Four's base on Novaya Zemlya in their search for the key. In the process of leaving there, they had crossed the contaminated part of the island and now they were paying the price for their rush. However, they had brought her an artifact from the archives of Section Four—a black sphere that could make communications with the computer on the surviving talon. She had found instructions how to use it in the base's data files and taken control of the ship from its autopilot.

The talon was badly damaged and low on power, but the main weapon system could still function out to a limited range, as it had done automatically in destroying the space shuttle *Columbia* approaching the ship; the weapon could also be used on a lower setting as a tractor beam, as Lexina had used it to draw in the Warfighter satellite. She had then established contact with the Warfighter's main computer through the talon, using information STAAR had gathered over the years they had infiltrated the American space program.

Lexina knelt next to Coridan and Gergor and administered more pain medicine so that their distress would not interfere with her work. She knew they had only hours left. She was not overly concerned with their loss, because the previous day she had found a lab deep in the complex where there was equipment similar to what she had used at Scorpion Base to "grow" more operatives.

Reaching into each man's shirt, she removed a gold medallion, shaped like two arms extended upward in worship, strung on a thin metal chain from around their necks and placed the object into her pocket.

She left the two and reentered the main control center for the complex. She had no idea what this place had been, nor did she know how the upper portion had been destroyed.

Her job for all her "life" had been to maintain the status quo. It had been easy as long as the truce held, but once the balance had been upset, things had been happening faster than her group could keep up.

She needed help. Taking tissue samples from both

dying men, she went to a room filled with large vats. She loaded the cells into the base of two of the vats. The controls and setup were similar to what she had had at Scorpion Base. She inserted the samples and turned the machines on.

SOUTH PACIFIC
D – 36 Hours

The *Southern Star* rolled and pitched in the rough fifteen-foot swells. The entire ship vibrated from the engines churning at full speed.

On the bridge, Captain Halls watched the deck as several of the passengers slowly moved along a rope from the forward cargo hatch to the galley below. He felt nothing for them and the misery they were currently experiencing. Idiots, in his opinion.

"Progressives" is what the newspaper called them, and Australia had been hopping full of the lot when he'd left Sydney Harbor to pick up this group in Tasmania. He had the most extreme on board, but there had been thousands of others who would have gladly joined this expedition. Of course, Halls had to be honest with himself: He had those who had been willing to pay the top dollar he had asked.

Despite their money, these people worried him because they believed the aliens held the key to everything good. Halls clutched his side as a spike of pain cut through him.

"Blinking ulcers," he muttered.

"The guardian can cure your problem," a voice behind him startled him.

Halls turned. The Guide Parker had come onto the bridge.

"From the news I'm picking up, the guardian isn't doing much of anything."

"That is because UNAOC forced it to protect itself." Parker walked up next to the captain and stared out the glass. "Wouldn't you retreat and protect yourself if you were attacked?"

Halls had no desire to get into an argument.

"Whatever pain you feel, whatever trouble you have in your life, the guardian will take care of it," Parker continued. "It holds all knowledge."

"How do you propose to get ahold of it?" Halls asked. "It don't seem to be talking to anybody."

"It is talking to Kelly Reynolds, and she will give us safe passage."

"They're not sure that message was really from her," Halls noted.

"Are you an isolationist?" Parker asked. "Afraid to step out of your cave?"

"I'm just a ship's captain," Halls replied.

"That's not going to work." Parker's gray eyes focused on the captain, and he squirmed under the scrutiny.

"I mind my own business," Halls said.

"You can't." Parker said it without raising his voice, but the words carried weight. "No human can. This will reach into every corner of the planet. No one is unaffected by what is happening. It is time for the human race to move forward," Parker said, his voice almost breaking with emotion. "To gain a place in the stars."

"But to take your line of thinking a step further," Halls said, "what if we go out of the cave and there are lions and tigers and bears?"

"If we go with the aid of the guardian and the Airlia, we will not have to worry about those things you fear."

"But," Captain Halls said, "what if the very things you look to for aid are the very things we should be afraid of?"

"Disbeliever!" Parker hissed.

Captain Halls looked out the forward glass of his

bridge to the storm-tossed ocean. He wondered what lay ahead on Easter Island.

But Parker wasn't done. "Every human will have to choose soon. You will either be for or against. There will be no hiding." Parker raised his hand toward the heavens. "You will be either a believer or a heretic. And if you are a heretic, you will burn as they burned in the past!"

AIRSPACE WEST COAST, UNITED STATES
D – 35 Hours, 45 Minutes

"There's a message for you." The copilot of the bouncer held out a headset. They were thirty minutes out from Task Force 78 and Easter Island, and Duncan could see the west coast of the United States rapidly approaching. They really had no idea what the fastest speed a bouncer could achieve. Right now they were moving at over five thousand miles an hour, fast enough for Duncan and the pilots, as it almost outstripped the ability of their radar to see ahead of them and give them time to react.

Duncan put the headset on. "Yes?"

"This is Major Quinn. I've got a strange report that was forwarded to us via the Pentagon."

"Go ahead."

"There's a Professor Mualama who claims to have discovered an Airlia artifact in Tanzania."

Duncan leaned forward, hands over the headset so she could hear clearly. "What kind of artifact?"

"It wasn't specified. The person who sent it mentioned Professor Nabinger."

Nabinger. Duncan remembered the archaeologist who had been with Turcotte and Kelly Reynolds and von Seeckt in the attempt to stop Majestic-12.

Duncan pulled up the mouthpiece, leaned forward,

and tapped the pilot on the shoulder. "Change in course. Tanzania."

The pilot nodded, already used to the strange requests and destinations he had shuttled Duncan and the other members of her team.

Duncan pulled the mouthpiece back down. "Who knows about this?"

"It was relayed through the Pentagon intelligence channels," Quinn said. "So everybody and their grandmother."

Duncan remembered both her friend at USAMRIID being killed and the betrayal within the SEAL team on one of the shuttles. There was no doubt the military was thoroughly infiltrated by all three groups—The Ones Who Wait, The Mission/Guides, and the Watchers. She wondered which of those she was racing to Tanzania right now. The only advantage she had was the speed of the bouncer.

"Anything from Turcotte?"

"Nothing."

"Keep me apprised of any changes. Out." She took off the headset. "A little faster if you please, Major Lewis," she ordered the pilot. The southwestern United States flashed beneath them in a blur and they were over the Gulf of Mexico.

CHAPTER 11

The High Plains that ever so gradually sloped up to the Rocky Mountains contained more than just hundreds of miles of rolling grasslands. Buried into the rocky soil, hundreds of missile silos held the remnants of one of the three legs of America's nuclear triad that had maintained the status quo of mutually assured destruction for decades.

Recent treaties with the other major nuclear powers had downgraded the alert status of the ICBMs nestled in the silos and caused their onboard targeting systems to be directed away from their war targets in Russia and China and left toward what were called Broad Ocean Areas—open spaces of ocean where a launch by mistake would cause the least possible destruction.

In the remote eastern Montana countryside, one of those missiles had been specially modified not to target a location on the surface of the planet but to break the bounds of gravity and go into space with its nuclear payload. This had been done as part of an experimental program designed to come up with ways to try to stop or deflect an incoming asteroid. Whether such a missile would work or not was a matter of debate among the scientists working on the Near Earth Asteroid Tracking (NEAT) program.

Today, however, as the clock ticked down on Lexina's threat, the crew manning the Launch Control Center (LCC) for this missile, code-named Interdictor, were programming it with space coordinates for a different mission.

The surface entrance to the LCC was set in the middle of an open grassy space, about the size of a football field, surrounded on all sides by a twelve-foot-high fence topped with razor wire. No Trespassing signs were hung every ten feet on the fence. The signs also informed the curious that the use of deadly force was authorized against intruders. Video cameras, remote-controlled machine guns, a satellite dish, and a small radar dish were on the roof of the small entrance building, the latter two pointing at the cloudless sky.

A hundred and fifty feet underground, the two members of the LCC crew were dressed in black one-piece flight suits. On their right shoulders they wore a patch showing Earth in the center with a lightning bolt coming off the surface into space. A Velcro tag on their chest gave their name, rank, and unit. Captain Linton was a skinny, dark-haired man. He sported Air Force–issue, black-framed, thick-lensed glasses. The LCC commander was Major Louise Greene, a tall blonde with a no-nonsense attitude befitting her position.

Rows of machinery lined the forty-by-forty room. There was a gray tile floor, and the walls were painted dull gray up to three feet, then Air Force blue to the ceiling. Twelve years before, when Greene started in missiles, the LCCs had been painted colors that psychologists had determined would be conducive to the crew's mental health during their extended tours of duty. That policy had been rescinded because of budget cutbacks and a change in command that had brought in a no-frills policy.

The entire facility was a capsule suspended from four huge shock absorbers, theoretically allowing it to survive the concussion of a direct nuclear strike overhead. The theory had yet to be put to the test, and there was much speculation among missile crews as to whether that bit of 1960s engineering was outmoded.

The main feature of the control room were the two consoles at the front of the room. Above those consoles, various screens showed scenes from the surface directly above, and the adjacent silo this center controlled.

Greene's and Linton's attention was focused on a flashing red light that had just come on.

"Verify Emergency Action Message," Major Greene tersely ordered as she reached over her shoulders and pulled the straps for her seat down and buckled them in, pulling the slack out. The red light was flashing and a nerve-jarring tone was sounding throughout the LCC. She locked down the rollers on the bottom of the seat. Then she hit the keys on her computer.

"I have verification of an incoming Emergency Action Message," she announced.

Linton was reading his terminal. "I have verification of an Emergency Action Message."

The screen cleared and new words formed. "Emergency Action Message received," Greene said. She pulled a sealed red envelope out of the safe underneath her console and ripped it open. She checked it against what was on the screen. "EAM code is current and valid."

"Code current and valid," Linton repeated, checking his own envelope.

Greene's fingers flew over the keys. The blinking message on her screen cleared and new words flashed:

EAM: LAUNCH INTERDICTOR AS TARGETED

"EAM execution is to launch Interdictor," Greene announced. "Give me the launch status."

"Interdictor silo on line. Missile systems show green."

New words formed on the computer screen. "I have

confirmation from National Command Authority that this is not a drill," Greene announced. "Open silo."

"Opening silo."

Four hundred meters from the surface entrance to the Interdictor LCC was another fenced compound. Inside the razor wire topping the fence, two massive concrete doors slowly rose until they reached the vertical position. Inside a specially modified LGM-118A Peacekeeper ICBM missile rested, gas venting.

"I've got green on silo doors," Captain Linton announced, verifying what one of the video screens showed.

"Green on silo," Greene confirmed.

Deep underneath Ngorongoro Crater, Lexina put down the communicator that linked her to Etor. She turned the seat toward the large display panel in front of her. She had the view from Warfighter's imagers relayed to the board and they were zeroing in on eastern Montana—to the coordinates she'd just received.

The excellent equipment put into space by the Department of Defense clearly showed the silo doors opening. Lexina sent her commands to the talon to be relayed to Warfighter.

Inside the LCC there was controlled tension as the pair of officers ran down their checklists.

"Confirm targeting on talon." Greene was never one to leave anything to chance. Even though they'd spent four hours working with Space Command under Cheyenne Mountain to ensure that the Interdictor was targeted on the alien spacecraft, she wanted to check one more time. The talon and Warfighter was passing over the western coast of the United States, and this would be the only time the target would be in range until the deadline, when it would have *Stratzyda* under control. There was a narrow window to launch, and they were going to get only one chance.

"Targeting coordinates confirmed," Linton announced.

"To launch control," Greene ordered. Unlocking their seats, they both rolled along their respective tracks to the middle of the launch control room. The launch consoles faced each other but were separated by ten feet and a Plexiglas, bulletproof wall bisecting the room. A speaker in the wall allowed Greene and Linton to communicate. They locked their seats down in front of their respective consoles.

Greene put her eyes against the retinal scanner and the computer's voice echoed out of a speaker on the console.

"Launch officer verified. You may insert key."

Greene pulled her red key from under her shirt and inserted it into the appropriate slot.

The computer verified Linton's retina and instructed him to insert his key.

"All set," Linton said.

"Let's do it," Greene said, staring through the glass at Linton. "On my three to arm warhead timer. One. Two. Three."

They both turned their keys at the same time.

The LGM-118A was primed to launch. Inside the nosecone was a ten-kiloton warhead, the warhead now live and scheduled to go off on a preset timer when its projected trajectory took it less than four hundred meters from the talon in six minutes.

Major Greene looked up at the status board. Red digits were clicking down from six minutes, ten seconds.

"Ten seconds to launch," she announced. "On my three, turn to launch initiation."

"On your command," Linton echoed.

She watched the number pass through six minutes, five seconds, and her fingers tightened on the key.

Traveling at the speed of light, the laser from Warfighter hit the rocket. The laser cut through the missile, destroying vital components.

Inside the LCC, Greene and Linton caught a glimpse of the laser beam on one of their video screens. Their control board screamed red lights and Klaxons wailed.

"Turn!" Greene yelled.

They both twisted the key to initiate launch. Silence greeted their efforts. For a few seconds Greene and Linton sat absolutely still, looking at each other through the thick glass that separated them. Greene was the first to react. She quickly unbuckled her seat belt, snatching a small radio headset off the side of the console. She glanced at the timer, which was passing through five minutes, fifty seconds.

Greene ran to a hatch on the side of the LCC, punching in her access code. Slowly the heavy steel door swung open. Before going into the tunnel that beckoned, she turned to Linton. "Shut the silo doors." She put the headset on. "I'll be on channel one."

Linton nodded, and Greene was gone, sprinting down the tunnel that linked the LCC with the Interdictor silo. The sound of her boots echoed off the reinforced concrete walls of the tunnel and another steel door a hundred meters in front of her and rapidly coming closer as she picked up the pace, her mind counting off the seconds, estimating she now had less than five minutes.

She reached the door and punched in her code. The door slowly opened, and Greene slithered through as soon as there was enough room. She was at the midpoint of the silo, the bulk of the rocket directly in front of her, five feet away. She turned and closed the hatch behind her, then began climbing up toward the bright daylight above her head.

Inside the LCC, Linton typed in the command for the massive doors to close.

Greene climbed as fast as she could, but it took a precious minute for her to reach the top gantry, which led to the nosecone. She paused for a second as a shadow cut across the silo. The doors were coming down, blocking off the daylight.

She edged out onto the narrow gantry to the access panel for the nosecone. Using an Allen wrench from her harness, she furiously began unbolting the panel, seconds ticking away.

With a solid thud the doors shut, leaving her trapped inside with the missile.

The earpiece came alive with Linton's voice. "Two minutes, thirty seconds."

There were six hex nuts to remove, and she had two out. She scraped her hand, drawing blood, but didn't notice any pain. Everything seemed to be moving in slow motion.

"Two minutes," Linton announced.

She had two more nuts out. As she worked, she mentally ran through the procedure for disabling the timer. In training she had done it in twenty-two seconds. The fifth nut was out.

"One minute, thirty seconds."

She put the Allen wrench into the sixth hex nut. She twisted, but it didn't budge. Greene cursed, putting more pressure on the wrench, feeling the pain as the metal dug into her fingers. Nothing. She paused and took a deep breath.

"One minute."

"Come on, come on," Greene whispered as she torqued the wrench. With a slight pop, the wrench broke in two, a piece of it still stuck in the hex nut. Greene stared at the piece in her hand in disbelief. A simple, dollar-ninety-nine piece of metal.

"Thirty seconds!" Linton's voice had an edge of hysteria.

Greene clawed at the broken piece, trying to get it out of the nut.

"Twenty seconds!"

A fingernail ripped off and she didn't even notice. A part of her mind knew it was too late.

"Ten seconds! Are you in?" Linton's voice was loud in her ear. She took off the headset, wanting one last moment of silence.

Greene slumped back, sitting on the metal gantry. She looked down at her bloody hands and the broken piece of metal. She closed her eyes and unconsciously hunched forward, as if preparing for a strong wind.

The missile, silo, and Greene were vaporized. The LCC, two hundred meters away, was destroyed by the shock wave radiating out. The thick twenty-ton surface doors to the silo were blown into the air and were found half a mile away, but they did help contain some of the blast. A hundred-meter-wide crater, over sixty meters deep, was all that remained where the silo had been.

CHAPTER 12

DAR ES SALAAM, TANZANIA
D – 34 Hours, 30 Minutes

Six hundred pounds of Semtex, a Czech-made plastic explosive, welded to the body of a water tanker truck, had formed the bomb that destroyed the United States Embassy in Dar es Salaam in 1998. Colonel Nakibsu Balele, an officer in the Tanzanian army, had overseen the import of the explosive from a source in the Middle East and personally wired the fuses into the plastique once it was in place on the truck.

That the blast killed only eleven he saw as something of a failure, but whether the goal of the person who had hired him was achieved was not important. The key thing was that he had been paid quite well.

While still a junior major he had been given a cellular phone by a strange man along with a bundle of money. How the man had selected him, Balele never knew. The money was to carry the phone with him at all times, the man had explained. There would be more money, much more, if he followed the instructions relayed by whoever was on the other end when it rang. Balele had not asked what would happen if he didn't answer the phone or follow the orders—he was not that naive. The man had scared him more than anyone else he had ever met. Balele had heard whispers of the man, a figure revered in the terrorist world of the Middle East who went by the name Al-Iblis.

The phone had rung only once in the four years since he was given it, with instructions to pick up the Semtex, wire it, and arrange for the driver to take the bomb to the embassy.

The Americans had blamed Bin Laden, an Afghani, for the embassy attack in Dar es Salaam and Kenya, which was fine with Balele as it kept him in the clear.

Now, as he sat in his office, reviewing training records, the cell phone rang for the second time.

NGORONGORO CRATER, TANZANIA
D – 33 Hours

Professor Mualama and Lago stared in fascination as the disk silently flew into the crater. It was thirty feet wide at the base, sloping up to a small rounded top. The skin of the bouncer was silver and perfectly smooth, without a single seam to be seen. The only thing that marred the perfection of the alien craft were the bright red cargo straps that were wrapped over the rim of the disk.

The craft came to a halt near their position, then came straight down, lightly touching the ground. A hatch opened in the top side and a woman climbed out.

"Good day!" Mualama greeted her.

"Good day, Professor Mualama. I'm Dr. Lisa Duncan from UNAOC." She looked toward the pit and the objects on the ground next to the hole. "Is that what you called us about?"

"Yes."

Mualama and Lago led her over to the coffin and tomb marker. The top was closed, and the long black tube appeared unmarked by time.

"What is it?" Duncan asked.

Mualama answered that by opening the top, revealing the skeleton inside.

"An Airlia!" Duncan knelt down next to the coffin and examined the corpse before turning to the red stone. "What about the marker? Can you read it?"

"Some of it," Mualama said. "I was hoping that with your access to Professor Nabinger's notes, we could decipher the entire message."

"We have accumulated a limited high rune symbolic vocabulary at UNAOC," Duncan said. "But critical parts of Professor Nabinger's notes were lost when he was killed in China. Nabinger was onto something, some way of understanding it beyond the symbols, but whatever that was died with him and he never had the time to tell anyone. He also had the largest high rune database on the face of the planet, and that went down in that helicopter in China with him."

"He made no copies?" Mualama was surprised.

"None that we've found." Duncan stood up. "We're backtracking, looking where he looked, and we've gathered a large amount of information." She pointed down. "This will help."

"With what you do have," Mualama said, "can you make anything of this?"

"That will take some time," Duncan said. "We'll have to take all this back with us."

"This is an archaeological site, protected by the laws of Tanzania," Mualama said.

Duncan arched an eyebrow. "Have you heard what happened in South America with the Black Death?"

"Yes, but I don't see what that has to do with this," Mualama said.

"It's war," Duncan said. "And any piece of information is important. We don't know much about these Airlia, and this"—she pointed at the skeleton in the coffin—"is the first true Airlia body we've gotten our hands on. Examining it could help us greatly in our struggle."

Mualama nodded. "I am willing to give you what I have found if you give me access to whatever notes of Nabinger's you have."

"What we really need," Duncan said, "is a key."

"A key?" Mualama repeated.

"The key to the lowest level of the tomb of Qian-Ling."

"Qian-Ling is in China," Mualama noted. "Why would there be a key for that here?"

"Because it's Airlia!" Duncan was frustrated, her hope crushed. "Who knows where all their artifacts are now."

"I think that . . ." Mualama paused and cocked his head.

"What is it?" Duncan asked.

Mualama held up a hand, hushing her as he slowly turned in a circle. He stopped, facing southeast. "Someone is coming."

Colonel Balele saw the bouncer on the floor of Ngorongoro Crater first. He had seen pictures of the alien craft on TV, but to see one here, now, gave him a moment's pause as the Hind-D helicopter he was on swooped over the rim of the crater toward the craft. The voice on the other end of the phone had told him to interdict removal of an artifact from the crater and to kill all involved.

The voice had also promised one million dollars U.S. if he achieved this goal—more than enough for him to leave Tanzania and retire in style. Also in the message he had read the implicit threat: fail and be killed.

"Sir?" The pilot of the Hind was looking over his shoulder at the colonel.

Balele was standing in the small opening that led to the rear of the chopper, where six armed infantrymen from Balele's command sat.

"Destroy the craft and the people."

The pilot nodded.

———

Mualama shaded his eyes. "It's a helicopter with army markings."

"I think we'd better get out of here," Duncan suggested.

"If we leave this"—Mualama pointed at the stone and coffin—"they will impound it or, worse, destroy it."

"We have no weapons," Duncan said. "The bouncer is unarmed."

The decision was made for them as the 12.7mm machine gun in the nose of the helicopter cut loose. The burst hit Lago, the large-caliber bullets knocking his body to the ground and then, in a grotesque dance, pushing it along the dirt, shredding flesh and bone.

"Nephew!" Mualama headed toward the body, when Duncan grabbed his arm.

"He's dead! With me!" She pulled him toward the coffin.

Mualama rolled into the coffin, Duncan on top of him. She pulled shut the lid—just in time, as the metal reverberated with the impact of the bullets.

The copilot of the Hind armed both outer Spiral antitank missiles. He received a lock-on confirmation from his sight on the grounded bouncer.

"Firing one," he announced. Immediately he hit the missile fire lever again. "Firing two."

As both missiles streaked toward their target, the pilot fired another burst from the nose-mounted machine gun at the long black pod.

Hanging on to the door frame between the pilots, Balele watched both missiles impact on the alien craft. A cloud of dirt and debris obscured the target area.

"Land us next to that black thing," Balele ordered. "We will . . ." He paused as something blinded him. He blinked, and in that time period the unscathed bouncer had halved the distance between the two craft.

"Evade!" was all Balele had time to scream before the forward edge of the saucer-shaped craft sliced into the front windshield of the Hind. The chopper's blades splintered off as they hit the alien metal, and in less than a second the helicopter was cut in half, both parts falling like so much deadweight the three hundred feet to the ground.

Duncan heard the explosions, then seconds later the sound of something heavy hitting the ground nearby and secondary explosions. She felt Mualama below her, the top of the coffin pressing against her back, her eyes seeing nothing but absolute darkness.

"Is there a way to open this from the inside?" she asked.

"I've never been inside before," Mualama replied in a subdued voice, "so I regret to inform you that I do not know."

Duncan reached around Mualama, feeling the bottom of the coffin. She arched her back, pressing against the top, but the metal was unyielding. "This is not good."

"It is better than what happened to my nephew," Mualama said sharply.

The sudden release of pressure on her back was not as surprising as the sunlight that momentarily blinded Duncan. She rolled on her side and blinked.

"Ma'am, I think we'd better get the heck out of here." Major Lewis held the lid up and offered her a hand.

Duncan climbed out of the coffin, noting the burning wreckage of the helicopter and the unmarked bouncer.

She stepped aside as Mualama pulled himself out. The tall African straightened and then gave a slight hiss of pain and doubled over.

"What's wrong?" Duncan asked.

Mualama pointed toward his back.

"Oh, God," Duncan muttered as she saw the piece of white bone sticking out of his back.

"It's not mine," Mualama said. He nodded his head toward the now-crushed skeleton in the coffin. "I felt it go in when we jumped in."

"And you didn't say anything?" Duncan felt around the edges of the six-inch sliver that protruded. She couldn't tell how deep the bone went in.

"Pull it out," Mualama said.

"We can get you—"

"Ma'am." Major Lewis was scanning the crater walls. "Those guys in the choppers might have friends who are coming this way."

Duncan wrapped her hands around the bone and gave one quick, firm pull. The bone slid out, and the only indication of pain Mualama gave was a sharp inhale of breath. She tossed the bone into the coffin and pushed the lid down. When she turned back, Mualama was kneeling over Lago's body.

"Get this and the stone rigged with the cargo netting," Duncan ordered Lewis. "Use the straps he already has around both."

Lewis nodded and turned to the bouncer. Using hand and arm signals, he got his copilot to lift and come to a hover over the objects.

While Lewis was doing that, Duncan walked over to Mualama. She could see the blood still oozing from his wound, but she knelt next to him. She could hear him speaking in a low voice, the words rhythmic and in a language she had to listen to for a few seconds before recognizing it as Arabic.

Mualama pulled a cloth over the dead man's face and slowly stood. "Why is it always the young who die?"

Duncan felt the pressure of time. If someone knew she had come here and tried to ambush them, there was no time to be wasted here. Mualama didn't appear ready to talk, and the coffin wasn't what she had hoped for when coming here.

"We're ready to go," Lewis informed them.

"Come on." Duncan took Mualama's arm.

Mualama pulled his arm out of her grip. "How did they know we were here? No one knew Lago and I were, of that I am certain."

"There are spies everywhere," Duncan said. "We'll sort this out elsewhere."

"Why should I trust you?" Mualama argued.

Duncan spread her hands helplessly. "I can't tell you to trust me. But to be blunt, I don't think you have much choice." She nodded her head toward the burning wreckage of the helicopter. "There will be more like that coming. I don't think you can outrun them in your Rover. And we do have some of Nabinger's notes." She turned for the bouncer and looked over her shoulder. "Your choice."

Mualama reluctantly followed.

CHAPTER 13

"Admiral!" The remote pilot's voice echoed through the communication shack on board the USS *George Washington*. A storm was raging outside, with little sign of abating.

Admiral Poldan hurried over. "What is it?"

"I've got contact with Global Hawk. It's just cleared the shield."

"Global Hawk? I thought it was down. Are you sure?"

"Yes, sir."

The admiral frowned. "What the hell's it been doing? It's nine hours overdue!"

"I don't know, sir."

"Wouldn't it be out of fuel if it had been in the air all this time?" Poldan asked.

"It would be close, sir, but it might be able to stay up this long. It was built for long endurance flights." The pilot was throwing switches. "My contact is weak with the computer. She seems damaged. It's barely moving fast enough to stay airborne." He looked over his shoulder at the admiral. "I recommend we bring her on board. I don't think it can make it back to the mainland. Plus we can download whatever data her imagers picked up."

"You can land it on the flight deck?"

"Yes, sir."

"Do it."

The pilot returned his attention to his controls. "I've got it." His hands delicately played with the joystick. "I'm bringing her in."

"I'll be in flight observation," Poldan said.

The admiral went out the hatch, then climbed up to the observation deck, where the flight operations officer was in command. The rain had lessened slightly, and Poldan could see the entire flight deck but little beyond it.

"Ops, I want you to suspend all launches and recoveries until we get Global Hawk down."

"No problem, sir. I've got only our CAP air cover up, and they cycled over twenty minutes ago, so they won't need to come down for two hours."

"Do any of the CAP planes have visual on Global Hawk?"

"Yes, sir. Eagle Three did a pass."

Poldan picked up a pair of binoculars. He focused on the trailing edge of the flight deck. His crew was running out the safety net to catch the Global Hawk, as it did not have a hook to snag the landing cable, the way carrier planes did. Poldan was impressed as the men strung the net in less than two minutes in the rain on the heaving deck.

"Good job on the net, Ops."

"Thank you, sir. Radar has incoming half a mile out."

"How's the path?" Poldan asked. The last thing he wanted was that Air Force jet jockey in the commo shack crashing the UAV into his flight deck.

"Looking smooth, sir."

"Anything off, even the slightest bit, you get that remote pilot to do a go-around."

"Yes, sir."

Poldan put the binoculars to his eyes. The Global Hawk suddenly appeared out of the mist, gliding down.

"She's smooth and in the path, sir."

Poldan didn't say anything. He watched as the wheels of the plane touched down perfectly, just fifteen feet from the trailing edge. The plane rolled forward and was caught in the emergency net, bringing it to an abrupt halt.

"Maybe we ought to give that Air Force jockey a set of sea wings," Ops said.

"I want my deck clear ASAP."

"Yes, sir."

Poldan lowered the binoculars. He was leaving ops when a startled yell spun him about.

"What the hell!"

The operations officer was staring down at the flight deck. Poldan ran up next to him.

The Global Hawk was—the only word Poldan could use to describe what he was seeing—dissolving. The long wings were drooping down to the flight deck, then disappearing.

Poldan brought the binoculars up and focused. The wings weren't disappearing. They were breaking down into very small parts, those smaller parts flowing across the deck. They reached the legs of a crewman who had been hooking the plane up to be pulled out of the net.

The man's screams reached all the way to the flight operations deck as he was swarmed under.

Lisa Duncan had just finished putting a bandage on Mualama's back when Lewis turned in his seat. "We've got a relayed radio contact that you should hear. It's from Task Force 78 through one of the planes flying cover over the task force relaying from Admiral Poldan to Captain Robinette on the USS *Stennis,* and I thought you might want to listen in."

"Put it through." Duncan picked up a headset and slipped it on. A burst of static came through the earpieces.

"This is Eagle Three. I say . . . Three. Jesus Chr— . . . flight . . . Some kind of . . . what . . . crazy. Over." The pilot's voice was high pitched and excited.

Captain Robinette's voice came through clearly. "Eagle Three, this is Task Force 78. What is your situation? Over."

The static built up to a high pitch and then suddenly it was clear. "Seventy-eight, this is Eagle Three. I don't know what the hell is happening! They're jumping overboard! The *Washington*'s still under way—it's turned for the island at flank speed! But the flight deck. In the rear. It's gone! Gone!"

Duncan leaned forward in her seat, pressing the headphones tight as she listened to Robinette. "Who is jumping overboard? Can you patch me through to the task force commander? Over?"

The pilot's voice had gone up another notch. "The crew! They're going over the side! Something's happening to the back of the ship. About forty meters of the flight deck, it's changing, dissolving. Something. Jesus, I don't know! It was that freaking plane."

"Eagle Three. This is Captain Robinette. Son, you need to calm down. What plane?"

"The Global Hawk! It came back. They landed it on the deck, and now all hell's broken loose."

Captain Robinette spoke again. "Can you patch me through to your flight ops? Eagle Three, do you understand? Over."

"This is Eagle Three." There was a pause. The voice firmed up a little. "Flight ops ordered me not to attempt landing. They said something was happening, something was attacking the ship."

"Can you patch me through?" Robinette repeated.

"Hold on." There was crackling noise. Then a new voice, one that Duncan recognized, came on.

"This is Admiral Poldan. Over."

"Admiral, this is Captain Robinette. What is your situation? Over."

"They're getting control of my ship." Duncan could

hear the shock in the subdued tone of the admiral's voice. "They're taking it over."

"Who has?" Robinette asked.

"Those things. They're *eating* the ship. They've taken over steerage and the engine room. We are on a heading directly for Easter Island. Range eighteen thousand meters and closing at flank speed. They've taken my ship."

"What things?" Robinette asked.

"They came on the Global Hawk. It landed and just began dissolving, breaking down into these things. They're so small, you can't even see them! They tear right through metal. And when they get hold of a person . . ." The admiral's voice broke. "My crew. They're jumping overboard. They're running. You can't fight these things!"

"Admiral!" Robinette's voice was sharp. "What is attacking you?"

"I don't know. You can't even see them. Just this black swarm, but it has no form. I don't know what it is. I haven't been close to it yet."

There was a loud explosion in the background. Duncan could hear voices yelling.

"Admiral?"

"Someone blew up a five-hundred-pound bomb on the flight deck trying to stop them! Jesus." There was a short pause. "Range to shore, seventeen thousand meters and closing."

There was a sharp crack. Some voices yelled in the background.

"God! They've hit the bottom of the bridge island. We're cut off."

Duncan pressed the transmit button. "Admiral, this is Dr. Duncan. What is happening?"

"I've ordered the rest of the task force away at flank speed," Admiral Poldan said. "The pilots are going to have to eject, as they don't have enough fuel to reach land."

Lewis handed her a photo that had just come out of the SATFax. "Imagery from the KH-14 overhead, ma'am."

Duncan looked at it. The upper right was filled with the curving black line marking the edge of the guardian shield. Heading directly for it was the long rectangle representing the *Washington*. The rear half of the flight deck was a swirl of black.

"What the hell is happening to your ship, Admiral?" Duncan demanded. "You've got to tell us before you go into the shield."

"I can see the shield." Poldan seemed not to have heard the question. "It's about six thousand meters dead ahead." There were voices yelling, the sound of shots going off.

"You can't even shoot them," Poldan said. "They're too small and too many of them. They're like a virus, spreading all over the ship. Jesus, they swarm a man under! Oh, God. They're outside the hatch. They're eating through the metal. I'm giving the order to abandon ship."

More shots resounded out of the speaker. A Klaxon reverberated in the background.

"They're here!"

A scream echoed. It lasted for five seconds, then the radio went dead.

Duncan keyed the radio. "Admiral Poldan?"

"The admiral's gone." The voice of Eagle Three was shocked.

"Eagle Three, this is Captain Robinette. You are to clear away from Easter Island."

"Sir, we don't have enough fuel to make landfall anywhere."

"Do as Admiral Poldan ordered. Get close to one of your escort ships and punch out."

"Yes, sir."

"All escort ships, this is Captain Robinette. Close on the last location of the *Washington* and recover whoever managed to get off, then get the hell out of there."

Lewis handed Duncan several more sheets of imagery. She laid them out in front of her. The KH-14 had tracked the *George Washington* as it headed toward the black cover of the guardian shield. Duncan stared at the pictures, focusing on the warped flight deck. Laying the images out in time sequence, she could see the progression of something moving outward from the rear flight deck. In one of the photos an F-14 had sat next to the warp. In the next one, the rear half of the plane was gone. In the next, it was gone entirely.

"Ms. Duncan, this is Captain Robinette."

"Yes, Captain?"

"Do you have the imagery?"

"Yes."

"What do you think?"

"Let me check on something," she said. She pulled out the papers she had been faxed from the NSA regarding what the guardian had accessed through the Interlink.

While she was doing that, Captain Robinette filled her in. "CINCPAC has ordered the rest of Task Force 78 to back off to a minimum of two hundred miles from Easter Island after picking up the survivors."

"What about the *Washington*?"

"We still don't know what happened to it, but at the speed and direction it's moving it'll go under the shield in about ten minutes, and then we estimate it will hit the shore of Easter Island."

"How many people got off?" she asked.

"We don't know yet. It's pretty confused out there right now."

Duncan stopped at a certain page as it suddenly occurred to her what she was looking at. "Jesus, we gave it to the damn thing."

"Gave who what?"

"The guardian. Nanotechnology."

"What?" Robinette repeated.

Duncan was remembering scientific briefings she'd received. "I think the *Washington* was attacked by a virus."

"A virus?" Robinette sounded skeptical. "How can a virus do that to metal?"

"Because the virus is made of metal. Microscopic robots."

"What the hell do they want the *Washington* for?" Robinette demanded.

"To make more of themselves."

CHAPTER 14

EASTER ISLAND
D – 31 Hours, 45 Minutes

A seemingly irresistible force hitting an immovable object. Never in the history of man-made objects had something so large headed for something so solid at such a high rate of speed.

Foam spewed from beneath the bow of the USS *Washington* as it steamed at flank speed, almost forty miles an hour, toward the rocky shore of Easter Island. The alien shield had briefly turned off, allowing it to pass through, and now the land was less than half a mile away. Displacing over a hundred thousand tons, its momentum was so great that even if the order had been given for full reverse to the ship's engine room, there was no way it could avoid hitting the island at this point. But there was no one on the bridge who was capable of giving an order and no one in the engine room who would have been able to respond.

The massive *moai* statues of the Ahu Nau Nau Grouping, just above one of only two beaches on the island, Anakena on the north side, stood tall on their *ahus* stone platform, gazing with stone eyes at the ship rapidly approaching them.

The bow hit the bottom less than a hundred meters from shore. It made the *Titanic* hitting the iceberg seem like a fender bender. Steel sheared the coral off, splintering into the rock beneath even as the ship continued to close on shore, slowing only slightly.

As steel and rock fought, the island gradually won the battle. The *Washington* came to a halt, over two hundred meters of ship out of water and on the beach. Below the waterline, over 150 meters of the ship had been crushed, gouging out a twenty-meter-deep trench in the rock below leading up to the shore. The forward edge of the flight deck had crumpled from the destruction of the ship below.

With the last screech of tearing metal bouncing off the rim of Rano Kau, silence once again came to the island.

"Jesus!" The *Springfield*'s sonarman ripped off his headset and threw it down on the console. "The carrier's hitting the island!"

Standing behind him, Captain Forster could hear the terrible sound of the *Washington* hitting Easter Island, relayed by the one thousand hydrophones arrayed in the sonar sphere in the front end of his submarine, echoing out the phones.

The sound grew louder to the point where every member of the crew could plainly hear it reverberating through the hull. Then silence.

The *Springfield* rested on the bottom, four hundred meters below the surface and just outside the shield. Two foo fighters hung in the water nearby, little golden orbs, three feet across, with the power to destroy the heavily armed submarine.

Even as he tried to imagine what could have happened to the *Washington,* Forster was looking at the displays on the screens in front of him. Able to use only their passive systems, he was working half blind. They had followed the sound of the carrier heading toward the island and now could pick up the other ships in the task force moving about.

"What's that?" Forster pointed at one screen. It "painted" a map of the seafloor around them, leading up to the slightly curved line that indicated the shield surrounding Easter Island less than a mile away. There was now a small anomaly along a curved line, showing how the sound had partially reflected off the alien shield.

"I don't know, sir," the sonarman answered. "It wasn't there before, but the shield went off for about thirty seconds as the carrier went through, then back on."

"Overlay the bottom chart," Forster added.

The computer screen cleared for a second, then the image was superimposed on a hydrographic chart of the sea bottom. A line between Forster's eyes narrowed as he located the anomaly. It was where a very narrow and steep cut bisected the ocean bottom, where the *Washington* had dug a channel out of the rock. The shield had not snapped back into place there because the gap had not existed before. "I do believe we might have found a hole in the shield around the island."

AREA 51
D – 31 Hours, 40 Minutes

Major Quinn had the orbit of the talon plotted on the main board in the Cube with a thick blue line. It was moving slowly eastward over the United States, leaving behind the destruction it had caused in Montana. A thick red line represented the *Stratzyda*'s track, now over the North Pole and heading south across the Atlantic.

Quinn typed in a command and dotted lines, the same colors, shot out from each track. They intersected over the middle of the Atlantic.

"Hoping something changed?" Larry Kincaid stood behind Quinn's command console.

"Someone could have made a mistake in projecting the paths," Quinn said.

"No mistake," Kincaid said. "It's physics, pure and simple. They intersect in twenty-two hours. Let's be glad that Lexina doesn't have any maneuvering control and has to wait for the spin of the Earth and the drifting path of the talon to intersect with *Stratzyda*'s. Then wait again for both to drift over the center of the United States. They both have to drift east, across Asia, the Pacific, and then over target in thirty-one hours."

" 'Over target,' " Quinn repeated. He tried to imagine what it would be like to have the warheads rain down over the United States. "We'd better find that damn key."

QIAN-LING, CHINA
D – 31 Hours, 30 Minutes

Che Lu stared at the notations in Nabinger's notebook until they became blurry and she had to close her eyes and rest. She'd been poring over them, lacking anything else to do.

Leaning back against the rock wall, she felt a moment's despair. All the exits were destroyed, the food and water the mercenaries had carried in wouldn't last forever, and there seemed no resolution in sight to the current situation.

Elek was systematically going through the containers in the large cavern and had made it clear he did not want the humans looking over his shoulders as he did so. Lo Fa had made the wry observation that he hoped the alien/human hybrid found some food soon in one of the containers.

Other than passing such remarks, Lo Fa spent most of his time sleeping. Storing up energy, he called it. It was a sign of the depression she felt that Che Lu didn't even poke fun at her old friend for that. When he wasn't sleeping, the old man wandered the tunnels of the complex they had access to, avoiding going down the central tunnel that led to the lowest level and was guarded by the holographic image of an Airlia and the deadly beam. As long as she had known him, the one trait of Lo Fa's she'd admired was his desire to see new places, to travel to the edges of the maps he had, to—

Che Lu's eyes flashed open. She thumbed through the leather-bound notebook until she found a certain page. Nabinger had written a series of runes down one side of the page along with some numbers next to them. The top rune-number set had the word "Earth" written next to it.

She'd assumed he was deciphering some mathematical formula and considered the page not particularly important. It was apparent he'd been working on it just before coming to China and entering the tomb. She stared at the numbers, comparing what he had translated to the runes. And saw where he had been wrong. Not because he didn't understand the runes, but because he didn't understand the Airlia. She remembered the image that appeared in the central corridor—the hands with *six* fingers instead of five.

The human number system was based on multiples of ten. It made sense that the Airlia system might be based on multiples of twelve. Which meant the numbers Nabinger had been trying to decipher would make no sense to him without that essential piece of information.

Che Lu began recalculating.

STANTSIYA CHYORT (RUSSIAN AREA 51), NOVAYA ZEMLYA ISLAND
D – 31 Hours, 20 Minutes

The bouncer slowly circled. "That is Stantsiya Chyort," Yakov said pointing. "Or was Stantsiya Chyort," Yakov corrected as they could see more clearly.

They were at the northernmost end of Novaya Zemlya, which was an island seven hundred miles long that separated the Barents from the Kara Sea. The base was located in a narrow strip of level land between a glacier on one side and mountains on the other two. The ocean completed the encirclement and isolation.

"Now we know why you lost radio contact," Turcotte said. There was no mistaking the demolished walls and roofs of the surface buildings next to the runway.

"We know why," Yakov agreed, "but we still don't know for sure who is the cause of this."

"We can make a damn good guess," Turcotte said as the plane went into the glide path to land.

"You suspect The Ones Who Wait?"

"Or The Mission," Turcotte said. "We can't forget them."

"No, we cannot," Yakov agreed. "They might well have done this in retaliation for our shooting down the satellite that was brewing their Black Death. Or The Ones Who Wait to prevent us from getting to the sphere that controls the talon." Yakov nodded at the compound. "Fortunately, most of the facility is underground, like your Cube. It might have escaped the wrath of whoever attacked. There was a failsafe device in case of attack. The only way into the underground base would be destroyed."

"Burying the men there alive?" Turcotte asked as the bouncer touched down on the concrete runway.

"Supposedly."

Turcotte remembered the dead scientists at the Terra-Lei compound in Africa—killed when the compound was breached by the UNAOC forces. Everything related to the Airlia seemed to bring death.

"So we can't get to it?"

"Not without major earthmoving equipment," Yakov said.

"Then this trip is a waste," Turcotte said.

"Do not count your chickens before the eggs break,"

Yakov said. "I know of a secondary entrance to the lower level that only a few of us were briefed on. It was the emergency way out if the main elevator destruct was fired."

Turcotte nodded. "Have you been here before?"

"Once, but it was a quick visit. My boss did not want me to be seen often at Stantsiya Chyort, because he felt it would compromise my effectiveness in the field. He was worried like you were at Area 51—eyes and ears everywhere."

Turcotte opened a locker and pulled out two MP-5 submachine guns. He tossed one to Yakov, along with a couple of spare magazines.

"Excuse me, Major?" Katyenka held up her empty hands.

"My apologies," Turcotte said. He drew another MP-5 out and gave it to her. Then he climbed up and opened the top hatch. Once on the ground, Yakov led the way. Turcotte caught glimpses of frozen bodies among the ruins.

"Here." Yakov walked up to concrete bunker. The steel doors had been blown asunder, their twisted remains on either side of a dark opening, like a mouth waiting for its next feast.

Yakov pulled a powerful flashlight out of his pack and shined it in. "Come on."

Turcotte followed, Katyenka right behind him. They went down a corridor until they came to another set of steel doors. Yakov pulled open a panel next to them. He threw a switch, and the doors opened with a hum. A large freight elevator was inside.

"Emergency power is still functioning," Yakov said.

"What kind of emergency power?" Turcotte asked.

Yakov's teeth showed. "Nuclear, of course. It is not like Novaya Zemlaya could get any 'dirtier' from one more bit of radioactivity."

"Who is taking care of the reactor if everyone is dead?"

Yakov was in the elevator, looking around. "It is automated. Can run for months without a human looking at it."

"Right." Turcotte's tone indicated what he thought of that.

Yakov pulled a floor plate up and shined his light down. "The failsafe seems to have failed. Or was made to fail. The shaft is clear."

"One piece of luck," Turcotte said.

"We will not need to use the secondary entrance—it would require many stairs." He gestured for them to enter the elevator. After Turcotte and Katyenka got on board, Yakov closed the doors and the elevator descended.

"How deep?" Turcotte asked after a minute.

"A half mile."

After descending for five minutes the elevator halted with a slight bump. Yakov gently pushed Katyenka to the rear as he put his weapon at the ready.

"This is no time for male chauvinism," Katyenka said.

"It is not chauvinism," Yakov said. "Even with you in front of me, I would still be a target. At least with you behind there is only one target."

Katyenka pushed her way next to Turcotte and Yakov, her MP-5 tight against her shoulder, finger on the trigger.

Yakov shrugged and pushed the button.

The doors slid open.

The bodies were strewn about, fallen where they had been caught by whatever had killed them.

"Is it safe?" Turcotte asked.

"Too late for that." Yakov strode into a large central chamber. He knelt down next to the closest body and turned it faceup. "I would say some sort of nerve gas. If it was still active, we'd be dead. It's dissipated."

The room they were in was circular, with several tunnels going off in various directions.

Yakov had stood up and was slowly turning in a circle, taking in all the bodies. "Everyone," he whispered. "Everyone."

"I am sorry," Turcotte said. He thought of Area 51 wiped out, all the people who worked there killed. He realized it was as vulnerable to attack as Section Four had been—even more vulnerable, as it was more accessible.

"This is most of Section Four," Yakov said. He walked over to a man wearing a uniform, collapsed in front of a red switch. "General Trofimoff, my commander." Yakov checked the switch. "He threw the destruct, but it must have malfunctioned."

"Or been sabotaged," Turcotte said. "Do you think The Ones Who Wait or The Mission did this?"

Yakov pulled his long coat in tighter around himself, even though it was warm in the base. "The Ones Who Wait, most likely," he said. "We captured one of their operatives several years ago and brought him—it—here. They have finally paid us back."

"I think there is more to this than simple revenge," Turcotte said. "Where would this device be?"

Yakov ticked off tunnels, reading the sign over each. "Scientific staff lodging. Mess hall. Communications. Research. Engineering. Power. Storage." He headed for the last one, Turcotte and Katyenka following.

They walked fifty meters down a stone corridor. It ended in a vault door that was standing wide open, the body of a guard draped across the threshold.

They went through the entrance. The chamber beyond was over eight hundred meters long, with alcoves cut into either side every ten meters or so, depending on

what was inside. The alcoves ranged in size from a few
meters wide and high to several that were over a hundred meters deep by fifty high.

Yakov was reading the placards above each. He began
heading down the central corridor, looking left and right.
Turcotte followed. Yakov stopped at one of the smaller
alcoves farther on the left. "It was here."

He was pointing at a table that held an empty frame.

"So that's how Lexina got control of the talon and
that's why they attacked here," Turcotte said. "Her people took the artifact you had. We've failed. I hope
Duncan is having better luck than we are. We need that
key now." Turcotte had continued past and paused at
one of the small alcoves. It was blocked off by a dark
glass wall.

"What's in there?"

Yakov looked at the plaque. "All it says is: 'Recovered
from subcellar, Reich Research, Aviation Ministry, Berlin, 30 April 1945.' " He touched the glass. "It's warm."
He looked around and saw a switch. "Here, let's see."

The tank was backlit, rays of light streaming through
the greenish liquid that filled the tank. And floating inside were a half-dozen objects.

Turcotte stepped back involuntarily. "What is that?"

Five of the objects were six feet long by about twelve
inches thick at one end, tapering to what looked like
three six-inch-long-by-inch-thick projections that formed
a strange tripod at the other end. These were grayish
blue in color. The sixth object was a ball, yellowish,
about three feet in diameter. On the side that Turcotte
could see there were, evenly spaced about six inches
apart, slits about four inches long. There was also a
bump, about four inches high here and there on the ball,
with a fold of the yellow material on the bump. The
ball—and the other objects—was floating in the green

liquid, which seemed to be circulating very slowly, moving them ever so slightly.

"Oh my God!" Turcotte exclaimed as the ball rolled and one of the slits appeared—this one open. A dark black eye peered at the glass.

CHAPTER 15

Larry Kincaid had worked around scientists all his life and was a scientist himself, but he had little patience for the intellectual type whose specialty was so narrow they couldn't program their VCR. The scientist in front of him was one of those, and Kincaid had to force himself to try to figure out what the man was trying to say as he babbled at the mouth.

Joe Forrester was a NASA specialist and the head of the Hubble Telescope division. Forrester fit the NASA geek stereotype to a T, even to the extent of the pocket protector holding his pens and the sophisticated calculator behind the protector. His wire-rimmed glasses held thick lenses, and Kincaid found himself disoriented every time he tried to look the man in the eyes.

Kincaid was one of the few left at JPL and NASA from the early, exciting days of the space program. He wasn't a specialist, but a jack-of-all-trades. He had been mission head for all Mars launches, a job that had thrust him into the spotlight when the Airlia base on Mars had been uncovered in the Cydonia region. He'd brought Forrester to Area 51 to coordinate surveillance on the Airlia base on Mars.

"Hubble is capable of tracking moving targets with the same precision as for fixed targets." Forrester spoke as he typed into his laptop, which was hooked into the secure Department of Defense Interlink. "The images you had of Mars before were just snapshots taken by the Hubble's FOC—faint object camera."

Kincaid had dealt with men like this for decades, so he knew enough to just let Forrester talk as he worked.

"To track a moving object in our solar system we maintain a FGS—fine guidance sensor—fine lock on guide stars, and drive the FGS star sensors in the appropriate path, thus moving Hubble to track the target. Tracking under FGS control is technically possible for apparent target motions up to five arcsec." Forrester looked up. "That is how we were initially able to follow the talon fleet as it came toward Earth.

"However, as happened in that case, this technique becomes unfeasible for targets moving more than a few tenths of an arcsec. What we do then is begin observations under FGS control and then switch over to gyros when the guide stars have moved out of the FGS field of view. If sufficient guide stars are available, it is possible to 'hand off' from one pair to another, but this will typically incur an additional pointing error."

With great difficulty, Kincaid still said nothing.

"Targets moving too fast for FGS control, but slower than seven point eight arcsec, can be observed under gyro control, with a loss in precision that depends on the length of the observation."

"Can you see Mars?" Kincaid finally asked.

"We've always been able to see Mars," Forrester said. "What you want is to see it with the full capabilities of Hubble, and I'm trying to explain to you what is needed to accomplish that." Forrester continued without missing a beat. "The track for a moving target such as Mars is derived from its orbital elements. Orbital elements for all of the planets and most of their satellites are available at STScl. Moreover, STScl has access to the ASTCOM database, maintained by the Jet Propulsion Laboratory—which you have so kindly provided me with through the Interlink—which includes orbital elements for Mars."

Forrester hit a key. "And thus we can get a tight shot, with the best that Hubble has to offer, of the target area in the Cydonia region you gave me. Much better resolution than we had before."

Kincaid stared over the man's shoulder as pixels changed color on the screen and a picture began to appear.

The most noticeable thing that became coherent in the image was the bright reflection from the large solar array from the open "pyramid." It was still intact, no damage from the nuclear explosion apparent. The "Fort" where the talons had taken off from also became visible, the roof still open, the interior empty.

"At least they have no backup ships," Kincaid muttered.

The "Face" on Mars, a massive structure two and a half kilometers long by two kilometers wide, and over four hundred meters high, appeared next.

"I wonder what that thing is," Kincaid said.

"We've taken quite a few shots of the so-called Face," Forrester said. "To those pictures we've applied bit-error correction, reseau removal, and brightness alteration. Then we've projected the images to a standard Mercator view. Two things we didn't do that had been done with the previous photos of the Cydonia region—and which caused much of the controversy whether there was an actual 'face'—were contrast/brightness enhancement and image sharpening. The reason we didn't do those is that using those techniques would create different images, depending on the monitor on which they were viewed, and NASA didn't want to get embroiled in the controversy.

"Another problem with much of the earlier imaging was the problem of accounting for shading. For example, light on one side of a slope can greatly distort the image of a hill. To account for this, we use a technique called shape-from-shading. We have even been able to project images of the Cydonia region so that it appears as if you are viewing it from a ground-level view."

Kincaid waited, still not having received an answer. He often wondered about these men who called themselves scientists—to Kincaid they were technicians, experts at their field of study but with little interest in fields outside their own, and worse, little imagination.

The image of a "face" on Mars had been noted as far back as the 1970s, when the first Viking orbiter had taken pictures. The fact that NASA had never investigated the strange anomaly further until now and called it a natural phenomenon Kincaid knew lay with the influence of STAAR.

"So what is it?"

"Here." Forrester turned his laptop so Kincaid could see the screen.

"Looks like a bunch of rubble," Kincaid said.

"It is," Forrester said.

"Rubble of what?"

"We have no idea."

"Can you print me a copy?" Kincaid asked.

"Certainly." Forrester hit the enter key on his laptop. The printer hummed and a piece of paper rolled out. Kincaid looked at it. Something wasn't quite right. He grabbed a magnifying glass and studied the image. He pulled open a file folder and retrieved an image of the same area made by *Surveyor* before it was destroyed. He put the two side by side and began comparing them.

"What the hell is that?"

There was something in the new image, to the side of the solar panels and Fort, in the direction of the Face. It wasn't there in the earlier *Surveyor* picture. It could be an equipment problem, but Kincaid had a feeling it wasn't.

"Can you get a better image of this spot?" Kincaid

asked, pointing to the small, darker-colored area that disturbed him.

"I can try different spectrums," the scientist said. "Also, we'll get some slightly different angles due to Hubble's and Mars' relative positions changing. Not much, but some." He typed in some commands. "By the way, you were quite correct about the Face."

"What do you mean?"

"Well, it's not a face carved into the surface, as many UFOlogists wanted to believe. But it's not natural either. It does indeed appear to be rubble. As best we can determine, there was a larger structure or mountain there and it was severely damaged."

"By what?"

"We don't know. There doesn't appear to be any volcanic activity in the region, so perhaps an earthquake?"

"Or maybe the Airlia?" Kincaid didn't wait for an answer. "Any idea at all what was there originally?"

"No."

Another piece of paper came out of the printer. The black smear was still present.

"How large is this black area?" Kincaid asked.

The scientist looked at it, then pulled out a clear plastic rectangle with various measurements on it. He measured, then punched into a calculator.

"About five hundred meters long by sixty wide."

"Any idea what it is?"

"No, but it appears to be moving." Forrester pulled a picture out of his briefcase. "This is imagery from last week. Notice the change in location. Appears to be moving from the Fort area toward the Face."

Kincaid tapped the photo. "Keep Hubble on that site."

Forester looked as if Kincaid had just asked him to commit a felony. "Hubble's time has been locked in for over two years. Taking it off-line like that—well, there's going to be a lot of very upset—" The scientist paused when he saw the look on Kincaid's face.

Kincaid returned his attention to the imagery for several seconds, deep in thought. What the hell were the Airlia doing? What had been where the Face was now? And what had destroyed that object, whatever it was? And why were the Airlia sending something across the surface toward it? And what were they sending?

Kincaid reached into a drawer and pulled out a handful of ibuprofen and popped them into his mouth, washing the painkillers down with coffee, hoping it would help with the raging headache these pictures had incited.

He looked up as another of his specialists entered the Cube. This one did not look like the scientist geek; he sported a Fu Manchu mustache, his long hair was tied in a ponytail, and he wore torn jeans and a black T-shirt.

"Give me some good news, Gordon." Kincaid had taken over all scientific aspects of the Airlia investigation for Major Quinn. The newcomer was the computer expert into whose care the STAAR hard drives from Scorpion Base that Turcotte had recovered had been entrusted. The drives had been hastily wiped clean as STAAR abandoned the base, but Gordon was trying to recover the "shadow" of the information that was on them. The major problem he'd run into was that it seemed STAAR had also been trying to recover lost information, so they were two steps removed from what they wanted.

"We're still tracking keywords according to Dr. Duncan's instructions—Key, The Mission, and Ark." Mike Gordon sat down across from Kincaid and rubbed his hands across his eyes.

"Anything?"

"Nothing on those words."

"What do you have?"

"That name of the Guide from the Inquisition—Domeka—we've found it again in a couple of places."

Kincaid held out his hand. "Give me what you have."

Gordon handed over a file.

Kincaid pointed a finger. "Get back to work."

STANTSIYA CHYORT (RUSSIAN AREA 51), NOVAYA ZEMLYA ISLAND
D – 27 Hours, 30 Minutes

"It's dead." Yakov tapped the glass, as one would the side of an aquarium to get the fishes' attention.

"What is it?"

Katyenka had turned on the small computer terminal at the base of the tank. The screen glowed with Cyrillic writing. "It says here it is called Otdel Rukopashnyi."

"What does that mean?" Turcotte asked.

Katyenka translated. "Literally that means 'sections of hands.' They shortened that here to Okpashnyi. According to what I'm reading, they had no idea what it is."

"I heard nothing of this being found," Yakov said.

Katyenka had scrolled down. "As you noted, it was recovered at the end of the Great Patriotic War from the rubble of Berlin."

"Ah," Yakov said. "That makes sense. As I told you earlier, Section Four began during the war, when our aircraft encountered what you call foo fighters. But we had no idea of the scope of what we were dealing with, until we found what the Germans had."

Turcotte was very familiar with the German interest in the alien and occult. "The Nazis were very hot after any sort of strange information or material," Turcotte said. "They were the ones who were the first to realize the significance of the high runes."

"They were also big believers in UFOs," Yakov said. "They had enough information in the records we recovered to make your Project Blue Book look like a thin file.

"They knew the foo fighters were something very different the first time their aircraft encountered them. The Luftwaffe lost many planes trying to shoot a foo fighter down. They also sent many expeditions around the world, searching down clues for anything that seemed abnormal or paranormal. Hitler was obsessed with the subject."

"What does that have to do with Ivan there?" Turcotte forced himself to look at the strange creature.

Katyenka answered that. "They must have found it in the same vault as the German foo fighter and other alien information files. That led the Section Four scientists to assume, besides the fact no one's ever seen anything like that in the natural world, that it is extraterrestrial in origin. It is possible that it is some bizarre creation that came from the Nazi butchers in the camps, but they did not think so."

"It's an organism?" Turcotte confirmed.

Katyenka nodded. "Yes."

"An Airlia pet?"

"They had no idea."

"Was it found with Airlia artifacts?"

"It doesn't say." Katyenka had finished reading the material available. "It does say there were two found. The German scientists did an autopsy on the other one."

"That's one thing?" Turcotte stared at the parts floating in the solution.

Katyenka tapped the glass. "The center part—the ball with the eyes—is the head, as near as they could determine. The Germans found a four-hemisphere brain housed inside a very hard protective covering, much stronger than our human skull. The brain was complex, similar to ours but different in some key ways, besides having twice as many hemispheres.

"The other things . . . well, those are arms, legs, whatever. Each one is the same. The strange thing—well, there are many strange things—is that each arm has a small, complex stem of its own at the thick end, the end that connects with the ball. Perhaps just a nervous system end point, but it appeared to be more than that."

"Why did they take all the arms off?" Turcotte asked, trying to assimilate this information.

"They didn't. That's the way it was found in the Nazi archives. From the autopsy it was determined that the arms . . . well, the best they could figure was that they were detachable and interchangeable. Not only on the main body." She looked up from the computer screen and pointed. "See those humps? That's where the arms attach, but possibly even between different main bodies."

Turcotte blinked. "You're joking. Like I could give you my arm."

Katyenka shrugged. "That is a theory postulated by the scientists who left this record."

"But *what is it*?" Turcotte said. "Where did it come from?"

"We recovered much from the Nazis, but not everything. After all, you got the Airlia atom bomb. And there is much the Nazis didn't find."

Turcotte tried to imagine the thing in the tank alive, the arms attached, the three fingers at the end of each arm moving.

He shuddered.

AREA 51
D – 27 Hours

Lisa Duncan paused in the door of the conference room and surveyed the two men already inside. Major Quinn had an unlit cigarette in his hands, turning it over and over. Larry Kincaid's hands were wrapped around a large coffee mug, dark bags under his eyes, his gaze unfocused. In the corner of the room a clock indicated that Lexina's deadline was only twenty-seven hours away.

She stepped inside, ushering Professor Mualama to a seat near the end of the table. She quickly made introductions.

"What happened in Montana?" she asked Quinn.

Quinn's report was brief. "The NSA authorized use of an ICBM called Interdictor to try to take out the talon and Warfighter with a nuclear warhead. Somehow Lexina must have gotten intelligence about that and fired first. The warhead went off in the silo. Local damage was minimal, as the silo site was remote, but fallout could be a problem. Luckily, there are no winds in the area right now."

"How did Lexina learn of the planned launch?" Duncan sat down at the end of the conference table, Mualama flanking her to the right.

Quinn shrugged. "A leak somewhere. We have to assume STAAR still has operatives infiltrated throughout the military and government."

"Is the NSA planning any further action against the talon?" Duncan asked.

"Not that they will admit to me," Quinn said.

"Anything on the key?"

"No."

"Anything on the runes?" she asked. She'd sent an image of the stone marker ahead via SATCOM to Quinn so the UNAOC high rune experts could take a look at them.

"Nothing so far," Quinn said. "They're still working on it."

"That's helpful." Duncan's tone indicated how she felt about that. "And the skeleton we brought back?"

"Sent to the lab," Quinn said. "It will be examined."

"Any word from Turcotte?"

"Nothing. Last report was he was landing at Stantsiya Chyort."

Duncan turned to her right. "Dr. Mualama, anything you care to say?"

Mualama steepled his fingers together. "It is obvious that the Airlia have been on this planet for a very long time. The discovery of this particular corpse is the first Airlia body that we know of that has been found. The dating of the grave site puts it about ten thousand years ago, or after the destruction of Atlantis."

"We know the Airlia have been here a long time," Quinn said wearily.

"But the thing you don't know," Mualama said, "is how much influence the Airlia have had on our development. Initially, Professor Nabinger believed they had little to do with us after they destroyed Atlantis over thirteen thousand years ago. However, the skeleton site was newer than that, and the marker on top of the coffin was only about two to three thousand years old. Someone put that marker there a long time after the coffin was in place.

"The question that has to be answered is how much interference have the Airlia had in our history? Think of the discoveries by Professor Nabinger in China about the Great Wall and the tomb of Qian-Ling. The possible true purpose of the Great Pyramid that he uncovered. The guardian on Easter Island, the statues there that we now know mimic the Airlia themselves." Mualama leaned forward. "We have to reevaluate everything we think we know about our history."

"We know that," Duncan said. "We've discovered other interference. We know the Guides from The Mission have been active at times throughout our history. We believe the Black Death in the Dark Ages was caused by The Mission. The thing we don't know is why the various Airlia factions have been doing what they've been doing other than it appears to be a continuation of the millennia-old civil war and we happen to be caught in the middle."

A phone buzzed, and Quinn picked it up. He listened for a second, then put his hand over the receiver. "We finally have Captain Turcotte on the SATPhone."

"Put it on the speaker," Duncan ordered. She leaned forward. "Mike, you there?"

Turcotte's voice sounded clear, relayed through Department of Defense satellites from his location in Russia. "Yes."

"The control for the talon?"

"Stolen." Turcotte quickly updated her. "At least we know why Section Four was attacked," he concluded.

Duncan told him of the explosion in Montana. Then she moved on to the actions off Easter Island.

"I think I know what happened to the *Washington*." Duncan had been checking databases about that during the flight back. She'd had imagery of the aircraft carrier relayed to Turcotte's bouncer. "I think the guardian sucked up a lot of information on nanotechnology from the Interlink and used it."

"I've never heard of nanotechnology," Turcotte said. "What is it?"

"It's only a theory to us," Duncan said. "We're several decades from actually applying the theory."

"It looks like it took the guardian only a couple of days to go from theory to application," Turcotte noted.

"It makes sense," Duncan said. "If I was the guardian, nanotechnology would be the way I would go."

"And what way is that exactly?" Turcotte asked.

"The best analogy I can give you," Duncan said, "is to think about the way computers deal with information. They can process it, change it, and reproduce it by themselves at practically no cost. They do that by breaking the information down to bits, the most basic level, and then manipulating or reproducing it.

"Imagine if a machine could do the same thing structurally at the atomic level. The real kicker to it is that it is almost like inventing a new virus, a machine virus, because the nanomachines are capable of taking new material, manipulating it molecule by molecule, and reproducing. A nanorobot can break down a molecule, change it, and eventually make another nanorobot."

"So that was the virus that invaded the *Washington*?" Turcotte asked.

"Yes. The nanorobots were able to take apart the material of the *Washington* at the molecular level."

"Jesus," Turcotte exclaimed. "What about the people these things touched?"

"I don't know," Duncan said.

"There were over six thousand people on board the *Washington*," Turcotte said.

"I know that. The Navy picked up almost four thousand crew members out of the ocean. They jumped overboard when Admiral Poldan gave the order."

"And the other two thousand crew? We don't know what happened to them?"

"From Poldan's last transmissions, we know some of them were killed. The rest, well, I would have to assume they have been . . . the only word I could use is captured."

"Can nanotechnology affect humans?" Turcotte asked.

"In various ways, yes."

"Goddamn!" Turcotte exploded. "We stopped the Black Death and now we have this?"

"Nanotechnology," Duncan said, "is the wave of the future in almost every area. It will revolutionize practically everything we know. Think of machines built at the molecular level able to go inside our bodies and help maintain them. Machines that can attack cholesterol at the molecular level in our bloodstream. Or be designed specifically to attack cancer cells.

"And nanotechnology removes waste in construction. Since the building is done at the molecular level, there is no excess or lost material. It is also extremely efficient of energy. It's like"—Duncan paused, searching for an analogy—"like having a machine that is a paper copier, except dealing with machines rather than paper images—it would be able to make copies of anything.

"A nanometer is one-billionth of a meter," Duncan continued. "You get about ten atoms per nanometer. What I think the guardian has mastered that we can't do yet is be able to work the atoms individually and place them where it wants. We've barely begun to work at microtechnology, which are small robots you can see. You can't even see a nanorobot.

"I call it a virus, because it's the mechanical sibling of the organic virus. Capable of replicating on its own, operating at a level even smaller than that of organic viruses."

"What is the guardian going to do now that it has mastered this?"

"I don't know," Duncan said.

"We'd better come up with something," Turcotte said, "because it just sucked up the most powerful weapon system on the face of this planet. How many nuclear warheads were on board the *Washington*?"

"Eight."

"Great."

"Don't forget that the *Washington* also had two nuclear reactors," Duncan added. She leaned forward, and her voice lowered. "I think this is going to force UNAOC's hand. They're going to have to attack Easter Island."

"Then you'd better hope those two thousand sailors are really dead," Turcotte said.

"Even if they aren't," Duncan said, "when you have a virus, sometimes you have to cut off the infected part."

"Jesus!" Turcotte exclaimed. "That's a bit cold."

"I didn't mean it like that," Duncan quickly said. Her hands were pressed against the side of her head. The others in the room were watching her, not able to offer any support.

"I know you didn't, but is that the way UNAOC is going to look at it?" Turcotte asked. "When I was getting ready to go on an operation, we always had to ask ourselves some hard questions. One of those questions was what we would do if we had someone wounded and he couldn't keep up with us.

"It's real easy in the movies for that guy to volunteer to stay behind, or for someone to make the decision to leave that guy behind with a pack of cigarettes in one hand and a gun in the other, but in real life it's a whole different ball game. Because the question we would ask was what if it was me, not some other guy." His voice was tight. "Me that was the one who was wounded. The one we were talking about leaving behind. The one on Easter Island we're talking about nuking."

"I understand, Mike, but this is out of our hands now."

"I know, but goddamn, two thousand men! And Kelly Reynolds, let's not forget she's still there."

Duncan sighed. "Mike, let's let UNAOC take care of this. The good thing is that Easter Island is very isolated. Whatever the guardian has planned, I hope we can contain it. Let's keep our focus on finding this key. That's the most immediate problem."

"What about Che Lu?" Turcotte changed the subject.

"There's not much we can do about that either. We

haven't heard from her since the nuke went off. The Chinese have sealed their borders."

"Goddamn," Turcotte swore. "This is ridiculous. We're not only fighting the aliens, we're fighting ourselves again."

"Mike, I know that. We have to do the best we can."

"And if it's not good enough?" There was a short pause. "Does anyone there have anything useful?" Turcotte finally asked.

"I will try to interpret the high runes on the stone," Mualama said. "I believe it will lead us to an even more significant find."

"I have something." Kincaid opened a folder. "My computer whiz guys have extracted more from the Scorpion hard drives."

He handed a copy to each person and read it out loud so Turcotte could get it.

Appendix 1 Cross-References The Mission &
Domeka
  (research reconstruction and field report)
  10/21/92—Cordian
Overview:
  While investigating the role of The Mission in the Inquisition, specifically the trail of Galileo for heresy in 1624, I discovered that the Fiscal Proctor, one of the key men responsible for prosecuting the case, apparently was a Guide.
  We know that through the Dark Ages to the Industrial Revolution, The Mission was based in Europe, most of the time in Italy. It exerted strong influence on the Roman Catholic Church, reaching its zenith during the Papal Inquisition.
  Domeka was the name of a Fiscal Proctor, an extremely powerful man who was instrumental in

many key prosecutions designed to stem the growth of human knowledge.

The Ones Who Wait counterattacked the power of The Mission in Europe, infiltrating the forces of both the Reformation and Counter-Reformation, which seriously weakened The Mission's influence via Rome. Even more interestingly, The Ones Who Wait subverted The Mission in an area Domeka and his comrades never suspected—the arts. It is no coincidence that most great scientists who escaped the net of The Mission at this time were also artists first—such men as Da Vinci.

However, Domeka—using various names—keeps reappearing throughout the history of The Mission. In Appendix 2 to the Crusades, Domeka is a key figure in forming several of the early crusades. The cross-reference in this instance is the emergence of Domeka as one of the early Spanish explorers in the New World. I found documentation that he accompanied Cortes during the conquest of Mexico. It must be remembered that King Montezuma greeted Cortes with the legend of Kon Tiki Viracocha (see ref. 6:32–4) weighing heavily on his mind. This led to the almost miraculous victory by Cortes and the conquering of Mexico City.

{data degrades—retrieval failed}

"This is most interesting," Mualama said.

The others in the room looked up from their copy of the downloaded document.

"If The Mission influenced the Crusades, they might have had an ulterior motive," Mualama continued.

"Of course they did," Duncan said. "They wanted to keep the human race in check."

"No." Mualama shook his head. "I am speaking of

something much more specific. Europeans going to the Holy Land—perhaps The Mission was searching for something?"

A new voice came out of the speakerphone—Yakov's deeply accented rumble. "And Kon Tiki Viracocha—the god that the Aymara in Tiahuanaco worshiped. Who was this Domeka? Was he Kon Tiki?"

Duncan put down the printout. "This is more information that leads nowhere. We need information that tells us about the key and where it might be. Right now—"

The door to the conference room opened and Mike Gordon stepped in. "Sorry to interrupt," he said, sounding not sorry in the least. He waved a piece of paper at Duncan. "I thought you better see this right away.

She took it and read it out loud. " 'Appendix Two, cross references The Mission and Domeka. Research reconstruction and field report. Dated ten, twenty-one, ninety-two by Coridan.

" 'Overview: While recovering information about the Inquisition I pulled up a partial file about a figure named Domeka. No doubt a Guide who participated in the Crusades, the Inquisition, and the Spanish exploration/exploitation of the New World.

" 'It is interesting to speculate that Domeka might not be one person but a rcincarnation using a guardian imprint of the same mind on different subjects. Because the alternative—that the Domeka involved in these events is the same person—means that this individual has lived for over a thousand years, the latter figure devolved from the most recent revelation, that Domeka was a member of the Nazi party in the 1930s and a close confidant of the Führer.

" 'There is no doubt that The Mission was intimately involved in the Nazi death camps. Also, the numerous operations mounted by the Nazis that have a direct bearing on Airlia artifacts:

" 'Bimini/Atlantis search by submarines, 1930s.

" 'The Great Pyramid SS expedition, 1941.

" 'Tunguska expedition, 1934.

" 'The Spear of Destiny, also known among us as the key of destiny!' " Duncan's voice rose on the last sentence.

"Does it say where this Spear is?" Turcotte's voice was as excited as hers.

Duncan looked up from the paper at Gordon.

He shook his head. "Data retrieval failed from that point on. We're still looking through the rest of the hard drives."

"There might be another person—" Turcotte began, but Duncan's mind had already raced to that conclusion.

"Von Seeckt," Duncan hissed as she threw the printout down on the conference table. "He knows more than he has told us."

Yakov's bitter laughter came through the speaker. "I told you that you could not trust the Nazis."

Duncan stood. "Mike, get back here as soon as possible."

"Roger that," Turcotte answered.

"Major Quinn and Mr. Kincaid. I want to know more from the hard drives—anything at all about the Spear of Destiny or keys—and I want the medical evaluation of those bones, ASAP."

"Yes, ma'am," the two answered in unison.

"Professor Mualama. If you could help our linguists decipher what is on the stone you brought, it would help tremendously." She turned for the door. "Let's move, people. The clock is ticking. I'm going to see von Seeckt."

EASTER ISLAND
D – 26 Hours, 40 Minutes

Kelly Reynolds was more "alive" than she had been since she'd made contact with the guardian. It was as if the alien computer no longer needed her but didn't want to discard her yet, just in case. The part of her mind that was still her self, her identity, found that darkly amusing, reminding Kelly of her mother, who could never throw anything out and as a result ended up with a garage full of items she might need someday but never did.

Kelly didn't think someday would come in this case either. The guardian was reaching into the world now, bringing what it needed to it. Kelly "knew" of the fate of the *Washington,* and the message the guardian had sent with her name on it.

The guardian was doing thousands of things at once, absorbing information, giving commands, testing theories, planning actions, in communication with Mars. And Kelly knew that although it made human computers look likes abacuses in comparison, the guardian was still only a machine.

So as it learned about humans through her, she learned about it.

CHAPTER 16

STANTSIYA CHYORT (RUSSIAN AREA 51),
NOVAYA ZEMLYA ISLAND
D – 26 Hours, 40 Minutes

Yakov, Katyenka, and Turcotte braved the cold wind blowing off the Arctic Ocean and up the valley that held Stantsiya Chyort. The desolation of the site was reinforced by the shattered buildings. The bouncer waited nearby, ready to take them home.

"Your Dr. Duncan is very aggressive." Katyenka broke the silence. She had listened in on the SATPhone conference call to Area 51.

"At least somebody is," Turcotte said.

Yakov had been quiet ever since they'd come up to the surface, but he finally spoke. "There is a possibility this Spear key might be here in Russia."

"Where?" Turcotte demanded.

"If the Germans did find this key, then they probably would have had it in Berlin, and we overran Berlin at the end of the Great Patriotic War."

"Wouldn't Section Four have gotten any Airlia artifacts?" Turcotte asked.

"Not necessarily," Yakov replied. "The KGB and GRU always accepted the tenet that knowledge is power. Knowledge about the Airlia and their artifacts is turning out to be the ultimate power, is it not? Even fifty years ago there were some in the KGB and GRU who were afraid of the power Section Four potentially wielded. What if Section Four discovered an alien weapon was a major concern. How would the balance of power be maintained?"

"So the key might be in the hands of the KGB?" Turcotte impatiently asked.

"Yes." Yakov reached into his greatcoat and pulled out a flask. He offered it to Turcotte, who shook his head, then Katyenka, who took it.

"Westerners do not understand the new Russia." Yakov screwed the cap on the flask after she handed it back. "In many ways it is worse now than under the Communists. We had a system then, one that the people understood. Now there is chaos. We Russians have become capitalists." He gave a bitter laugh. "So much so that the most powerful force in this country is the Mafia. Everyone is playing for a position, trying to get as much power as they can in the vacuum the overthrow of the communist regime left. So, given that, even if the FSB did have something, I have no idea where that material is now."

"Lyoncheka knows where the archive is," Katyenka said. "He works out of FSB headquarters in Lubyanka."

"Then we must go to Moscow and talk to this fellow," Yakov said. "It is as simple as that."

"We cannot fly into Moscow in that thing"—Katyenka nodded at the bouncer—"and expect to be able to accomplish our mission quietly."

"We will fly to an airfield outside the city, where I have a contact," Yakov said. "He will get us into the city." He turned to Katyenka. "Then I go into Lubyanka to visit this Lyoncheka."

Turcotte knew the name Lubyanka. During the Cold War, just the mention of the famed headquarters for the KGB on Red Square was enough to make prisoners break down.

"Let me have a second," Turcotte said. He walked away and pulled out his SATPhone. He dialed the number for the phone that had been assigned to Captain Billam and ODA 055.

It was answered on the second ring. "Billam here."

"It's Turcotte. I'm heading to Moscow, and Yakov is going into Lubyanka to talk to an FSB official. If he doesn't come out, I'm going in after him. If I don't come out, you come in after both of us."

Billam's response was immediate. "You're joking, right?"

"I don't joke, Captain."

"Lubyanka. FSB headquarters. In the middle of Moscow. Rescue you. Right. Got it."

"I'll update you once we're in Moscow."

"Roger that."

"Out here."

Turcotte flipped the phone shut and headed for the bouncer, remembering Duncan's last words—she wanted him back at Area 51 as soon as possible and that time was running out. He didn't think he should update her on this side trip. If the key was in Russia, then he would find it. She had enough on her mind right now. "Let's get going."

QIAN-LING, CHINA
D – 26 Hours

Che Lu had not worked on mathematics this hard since she had attended college over fifty years before. But there it was on the paper finally, the two sides of the equation she had worked out: transforming a twelve-digit system to ten, and given the known on one side as the earth's diameter—12,753 kilometers.

The result was a number she hoped was the Airlia standard of measurement.

Given that, she went to work on the next line on the notebook, which detailed a location using two variables. Nabinger's notes indicated one variable was a measurement in Airlia units from the South Pole. The other was a longitude distance from a vertical line along the Earth's surface, much like the 0-degree line that went through Greenwich, England; unfortunately, Nabinger didn't write down what the Airlia 0-degree line was, if he had known it. Also, it went in increments of twelve, not ten.

Still, though, as Che Lu thought about it, she realized she could come up with the set of numbers. Then she would have a definite latitude for each set of coordinates. Then it would be a question of maneuvering the longitude to knowns—and she had little doubt that Qian-Ling, Easter Island, and most likely the Giza Plateau were three of the sites listed.

She went to work.

MARS
D – 24 Hours

The steel point scraped against the reddish-brown rock, sliding a few millimeters before finding purchase. If this had been Earth, there would have been sparks and sound. But in the thin Martian atmosphere there was neither. The point was at the end of an articulated leg two meters long, one of eight that came out of a center pod.

On both the top and bottom of the center pod were small globes at the end of a forty-millimeter stem, the sensors for the device allowing it 360 degrees of observation above and below.

The legs continued their way along the surface until it reached the site. Following its orders, the mech/worker reached with its large grasping arm and picked up a boulder. Carefully balancing the rock, it slowly stalked across the Martian surface until it was over two kilometers away, then it dropped the burden. It was not alone, just one of thousands of similar devices, like an army of giant ants moving across the surface.

It turned and went back the way it had come. And every ten minutes, another worker scurried out of a tunnel and joined the line of workers digging.

EASTER ISLAND
D – 22 Hours

What had taken the workers at Newport News Shipyard three years to put together was being torn apart in a matter of hours. The guardian had had the microrobots power down the two nuclear power plants for the moment, to prevent meltdown.

The large island where the bridge had been was just a frame. Most of the flight deck and the planes that had been on it were gone, already taken apart and examined. As the side plating was being removed by swarms of microrobots, steel girders poked into the air, like the ribs of some massive dead dinosaur.

As quickly as it was being taken apart, it was also being reassembled, in some cases the new construction being much superior to the old.

Of the 6,286 men and women who had been on board, most had escaped. Many of the rest had been killed when the ship was taken over. They were the lucky ones.

Along the edge of the main runway, the remaining hundreds of bodies were laid out, their arms and legs pinned to the ground by U-shaped brackets slammed into the ground by a large mech/robot, kin to the ones digging on Mars. The sailors were spread in clumps of ten, covering a large portion of the runway's edge, each group set in a circle, heads toward the center. All of the captives were unconscious, the result of a large electromagnetic burst by the guardian once the ship was inside the shield.

But as time went by, the men and women began to come awake, and as they did, a different type of robot went down the line. It would roll up to a group, stopping just outside the circle. A tube extended out the front of this mech and would be positioned directly over the center of each cluster.

The tube would spray a small cloud, then move on.

Behind it, as the various forms of the nanovirus settled onto the prone bodies, other mechs pulled up to record the results and forward it to the guardian.

Some went as the guardian had predicted, others not so well, as the screams of the men and women indicated.

AIRBORNE, NEVADA
D – 21 Hours

Lisa Duncan watched the Nevada desert flow by below the UH-60 Blackhawk helicopter as she headed from Area 51 to Nellis Air Force Base. She was thinking about the time she'd flown in the other direction, toward Area 51, prepared to shut down Majestic-12. So much had happened since then, and she felt every new truth she uncovered led to more mysteries.

Her musings were cut short by her SATPhone buzzing. She opened the phone and pressed on. "Duncan."

"Dr. Duncan, this is Lexina."

Duncan closed her eyes and shifted gears. "Still need your key?"

"Your time runs short."

"You knew the space shuttles were going to be attacked, didn't you?"

"I knew the automatic defenses on the surviving talon were still operating."

"You allowed those people to get killed. I thought you were here to protect humans. You destroyed Section Four to get the control for the talon."

"You are learning," Lexina said, "but much too slowly."

"You killed many in Florida when you destroyed *Atlantis,*" Duncan continued.

"I must be given the tools I need to do that job," Lexina said. "I need the key."

"You destroyed our missile in Montana and killed our people there."

"You were going to attack the talon, and I could not allow that. The longer you play your games, the more dangerous it becomes."

"*'More* dangerous'?" Duncan repeated. "We just barely stopped the world from being wiped out by the Black Death manufactured by The Mission—with no help from you, I might add—and you're talking about things getting worse? The only worse I see is you're attacking us now along with The Mission."

"Give me the key."

"Give me answers."

The phone went dead.

AREA 51
D – 20 Hours

Mualama was not a professor of languages, but he didn't feel that handicapped him. In fact, as he watched the UNAOC linguistic experts with their computers pore over the high rune text on the grave marker, he realized that not being an expert could be an asset. He was not bound by preconceived notions.

He did know much about hieroglyphics. He'd been in most of the major archaeological finds in Egypt during his lifelong quest. He'd even met Nabinger on two occasions, although the other had not shared his passion for the Ark and other artifacts just as Mualama had not shared the other's passion for the high runes and Atlantis. And Nabinger had been the foremost interpreter of the runes and he, Mualama, had been just an archaeologist, not a linguist.

On a large computer screen at the end of the room, the UNAOC scientists had put up the symbols they knew the translation for, but it was less than a sixth of the writing on the marker.

Mualama had another advantage. He had a very good idea what the message on the marker might be about. On top of that, he also knew the mythological names the runes stood for.

So while the scientists chattered among themselves and consulted their computers, Mualama sat in a corner on a high stool from which he could look down on the marker. He had a pad of paper and a pencil in hand, along with the Nabinger interpretations of high runes that UNAOC did have. And slowly he began to write down what he saw.

In his backpack rested both Burton's manuscript and the scepter. He was not prepared to show either to the UNAOC people until he was sure of his suspicions. He was beginning to feel he could trust Dr. Duncan, but someone had leaked word of his discovery in Ngorongoro and that someone had to be affiliated with the Americans. He had spent decades searching, and a little caution was most appropriate now, especially since this had cost Lago his life.

NELLIS AIR FORCE BASE, NEVADA
D – 20 Hours

Lisa Duncan stared down at the old man lying in the hospital bed and tried to control her emotions. He should have been dead, but he still clung to life, although why he did, Duncan had no idea.

"Can you wake him?" she asked the doctor who had accompanied her to the room.

"He's resting and—" the doctor began, but Duncan cut him off.

"I don't care about his rest. I don't care if talking kills him. Wake him up. I have the authority to order you to do it, and that's exactly what I'm doing."

The doctor stared at her for a few seconds, then went over to a tray and removed a needle. "I can't take responsibility for—"

"I don't want to hear it," Duncan said. "You work for the government, start taking responsibility for that decision." She pointed. "That man worked at Peenemünde, helping to develop V-1 rockets. He was a member of the SS, and he's been lying to us all along. Don't try to make me feel anything for him other than contempt."

The doctor held the needle out to Duncan. "You do it. You take responsibility."

Duncan took the needle, held it vertical, tapped the side to clear the air, squeezed a little of the fluid out, then inserted it into the IV line and pushed the plunger. She removed the needle and waited.

After a couple of minutes, the old man's eyelids fluttered. While she waited, Duncan considered how to approach the former Nazi and scientist. Von Seeckt had been the key to her initially discovering information about Area 51 and Majestic-12. It was while investigating the history of Operation Paperclip that she first came across the name Werner von Seeckt.

Officially, Paperclip began in 1944 as the war in Europe was winding down, but Duncan felt that the real beginning of Paperclip was when von Seeckt was shipped over from England to the United States several years before that.

Von Seeckt had been captured by British Commandos in Egypt while he was on his way back from a most unique mission. The Nazis had interpreted high rune symbols and a map on a stone in the water off of Bimini to indicate that there was something in a secret lower chamber of the Great Pyramid of Giza. Von Seeckt, a young scientist of the Third Reich—and a member of the SS—had been chosen to accompany the military team that traveled to Egypt to investigate this, even as war raged across the desert and the Desert Fox, Rommel, closed on the British forces.

Von Seeckt and his companions broke through a wall in the Pyramid, discovering the chamber and finding a black box inside that they couldn't open. In their attempt to return to their own lines they were ambushed by the British and von Seeckt and his box captured. Eventually the radioactive box—along with von Seeckt—ended up in America, because when the Majestic scientists finally opened it, they found a nuclear weapon that gave the Americans great insight into what they were trying to do in the Manhattan Project.

Since 1942 von Seeckt had lived in the desert at Area 51, subsequently joined by other Nazi scientists formally brought to the States under the auspices of Operation Paperclip. As the war in Europe was ending, the United States government—and the Russians, of course—were already looking ahead. There was a treasure trove of German scientists waiting to be plundered in the ashes of the Third Reich. That most of those scientists were Nazis mattered little to those who invented Paperclip.

While other Nazis were being tried as war criminals, German scientists were being interviewed by American intelligence officers from the JIOA, Joint Intelligence Objectives Agency. Despite the fact that President Truman signed an executive order banning the immigration of Nazis into the United States, the practice went on at a feverish pitch in 1945 and 1946, all in the name of national security.

Majestic-12 had picked up Werner von Seeckt—an undisputed Nazi—and several other scientists used in the early work on the bouncers and mothership. While some of the former Germans working on the NASA space project were highly publicized, the vast majority of the work covered by Paperclip went on unobserved. When news of the project became public, the government claimed that Paperclip had been discontinued in 1947. Yet Duncan had affidavits from an interested senator's office that the project had continued for decades beyond that date.

Now that they had the information from Devil's Island about The Mission, Duncan was willing to cut her government a little bit more slack. It appeared as if The Mission had been behind Operation Paperclip as a means to siphon some of their best minions out of the crumbled Third Reich into new countries where they could continue their work.

While the German physicists had gone to MJ-12 and the German rocket scientists had gone to NASA, the largest group of Nazi scientists involved in Paperclip had disappeared—the biological and chemical warfare specialists, the foremost of whom had been General Hemstadt, who had died at Devil's Island and helped invent the new Black Death The Mission had deployed in an attempt to wipe out humanity.

Von Seeckt's eyes opened wide for a second, he saw Duncan, and they shut just as quickly.

"Schutzstafeel," Duncan snapped in German. "Look at me, you SS pig."

Von Seeckt's eyes flashed open, and she could see the anger. "Do not talk to me like that," the old man rasped. "I saved you. I warned you of the danger in Area 51."

"Why?" Duncan leaned over his bed. "That's what I want to know. Why did you do that?"

"I am old. I knew it would not be good to fly the mothership, and I wanted to make amends."

"You lie."

Von Seeckt's shoulders slumped. "Believe what you will."

"I want the truth."

" 'Truth.' " Von Seeckt repeated the word as if it were a curse.

"I want the key."

"Key?"

"The key to the lowest level of Qian-Ling. The Spear of Destiny."

Von Seeckt closed his eyes and said nothing.

Duncan decided on another approach. "Who was Domeka?"

The eyelids flashed up. For the first time since she'd met the old man, Duncan saw fear in those pale blue eyes. Even faced with death from the cancer eating his insides, von Sceckt had never shown fear.

"Domeka." Duncan repeated the name.

"Ahhhh—" Von Seeckt let out a moan.

Duncan walked over to the cart and picked up another needle. She inserted it into the IV line as von Seeckt dully watched her.

"I will kill you right now if you don't tell me the truth."

The old man's face was slack, his eyes unfocused. "Kill me, then."

The threat went out of Duncan's voice for the moment. "You told Turcotte that you wanted absolution for your work on the Manhattan Project. You told him you had lived in fear all your life and you wanted to do something good. Something right. You told him what Oppenheimer said when the Trinity bomb—the first man-made atomic bomb—detonated in 1945. Did you mean any of that, or was that just lies like everything else you have said?"

"I told truth." Von Seeckt seemed to be coming back to the room, to his reality.

"Some truth, but not all of it. Tell me all of it. The war—the war against the aliens and their minions— we're going to lose it if we don't know the truth. You're human, you have that at least. Tell me!"

"Human?" The left side of von Seeckt's face twitched. "You know nothing about what human is."

"Then tell me!"

"Domeka." Von Seeckt now spoke the name with awe. "Where did you hear the name?"

"Tell me where and what *you've* heard of him." Duncan relaxed her thumb over the plunger.

"Heard of him?" Von Seeckt winced as he sat up a little. "Heard of him? I think Domeka was a name he had very early. Very early. It is Latin, you know. It means 'leader.' So maybe he was a Roman? But he predates Rome. Oh yes. He is old. I don't know what his real name is. His names are legion. Even during my life he went by many names, so which name I first heard, I could not tell you."

Duncan pulled the needle out of the IV feed.

"Ah, where to begin?" Von Seeckt was lost in thought for a few moments. When he began speaking again, the change in subject matter startled and scared Duncan.

"Hitler was a failure," von Seeckt finally said. "Historians have traced his life. It is known. So how did such a failure end up almost ruling the world? He was gassed in the First World War—the War to End All Wars, it was called. He had an undistinguished military record. Certainly there were many, many thousands of veterans who had shown more courage, more leadership than Hitler during that war.

"After the war he lived off his deceased mother's savings. He went to Vienna to become an artist but was refused entry into the Academy of Fine Arts. He tried next to get into the School of Architecture and was again refused.

"What did he do then? He was an angry young man. Bitter at his treatment. So he went to the library." Von Seeckt started to laugh, which immediately turned into a spasm of coughing.

Duncan waited the old man out. At the first mention of Hitler her skin had gone cold. She feared what von Seeckt was going to say, but she knew she had to hear it—no one had ever claimed the truth would be good.

"Do you know what was in the Hofberg Library in Vienna?" Von Seeckt didn't wait for an answer. "Oh, there were books. Yes. Many books. Many books on the occult. On strange histories. Things we know now are true about our past but were looked at then as being like a cuckoo clock. Crazy." Von Seeckt whirled a bony finger around his head.

"But there was something else in the library. An ancient spear. Said to be the Spear of Longinus." Von Seeckt paused. "Do you know what that is?"

Duncan sat down on a stool to collect herself. "Longinus was supposed to be the legionnaire who stabbed Christ on the cross."

"'Supposed to be'?" Von Seeckt laughed, and this time there was no cough. He seemed to be gaining strength with each passing minute. "I agree, I agree. I do not know if Longinus was real. But there was a spear in the library there, and it was claimed to be Longinus's. The Spear of Destiny. And a tool of destiny it turned out to be, as it shaped Hitler's destiny regardless of its origins or its real purpose.

"Hitler was obsessed with the Spear and the legends that surrounded it. He would stand in front of the case holding it for hours on end, staring at it. He himself later claimed that seeing the spear was the one event that changed the course of his life. Of course, he was lying."

"What do you mean?"

Von Seeckt snorted. "You think simply seeing an old spear could change a person like that? No, there was more to it than that. The Nazis didn't appear out of nothing. The stage had to be set. There was a man in Vienna during those days. A man named List." Von Seeckt suddenly stopped speaking.

Duncan waited, then the pieces came together. "List was Domeka?"

Von Seeckt graced her with the ghost of a smile. "I believe so. The name he used for this phase of his life was Guido von List. He first came to notice as a member of Austrian Alp Society, which used the 'heil' greeting, which had roots in early German paganism. List claimed to be a channel, a man with a connection to an ancient group of German shamans called the Armanen. The emblem of List's group was the swastika. And their written language was one of runes."

"Jesus," Duncan muttered.

"You can find these facts in many history books," von Seeckt said. "They are not secret anymore. But until the Airlia came to light, it was thought an odd historical footnote, and it has been too soon for stodgy historians in their ivory towers to catch up to recent events. To reevaluate all this information, which is now much more important than anyone gave it credence.

"List even wrote a book about runes in 1908. He extensively quoted a Roman historian, Tacitus, who lived in the first century A.D., yet didn't attribute the material to a source document in his bibliography. How could he do that?"

Duncan felt overwhelmed. "Was Tacitus also Domeka?"

"Perhaps. List was interested in many objects of the

occult. The Spear, certainly. But also the Holy Grail. The Ark of the Covenant. Someone who was close to Hitler in those early days in Vienna said that Hitler told him that List conducted strange rituals and that Hitler himself was the subject of one of them. A rite of purification. Purification of the race, of the blood. That was when Hitler really changed."

"What did List do to him?"

Von Seeckt ignored her. "Do you know how Nabinger found me here? Found us? He got my SS dagger from an Egyptian—a Watcher—at the Great Pyramid. On one side was my name. On the other the word 'Thule.'

"Thule was the cover name in the 1930s for the secret societies of the occult in Germany. For List's followers. For Hitler's. The Society of Thule brought Hitler to power. There was even an exposé book written about it in 1933, called *Bevor Hitler Kam*—Before Hitler Came. Of course, the author was assassinated, and all copies of the book seized and destroyed by the SS.

"The Society of Thule believed in Atlantis—ah, they were not so foolish now that we know what we know about the Airlia base there, eh? They believed that the original inhabitants of Atlantis looked very much like the statues on the island of Rapa Nui—Easter Island. Ever more remarkable, is this not?"

"How did they have this knowledge?"

"After the war such ramblings were considered the ravings of crackpots. But these crackpots brought Hitler into power. Thule's inner circle was dedicated to communicating with a nonhuman, more powerful intelligence."

"The Airlia?" Duncan felt as if her head were spinning. "A guardian computer? Was there one in Germany? How many guardians are there?"

Von Seeckt's frail shoulders moved under the hospital

gown in what might have been a shrug. "I do not know. Have you ever heard of the Ahnerbe?"

Duncan shook her head. She didn't have time for this. "Where is the Spear now?"

Von Seeckt ignored her question. "Not many people have heard of the Ahnerbe. It was the Nazi Ancestral Research branch. It was the core of forming the SS, the Schutzstafeel—what you called me when you walked in. The secret to that group was they were very, very interested in genetics.

"I was sent to the Great Pyramid, the Pyramid of Khufu on the Plateau of Giza, to search for the black box, which we found. There were other SS groups sent to search for things that the Führer wanted. For the Grail. The Ark. Other relics of legend." Von Seeckt was silent for a few moments before speaking again. "It would all have been folly. The muttering of madmen, except for the forty-seven million people who died in the war Hitler began."

Von Seeckt slumped back in the bed, his face drawn.

Duncan stood. "Tell me more. Tell me about the Spear!"

"I am tired," von Seeckt muttered. "I must sleep now."

Duncan didn't care how the old man felt. "The spear from the library—was it really the Spear of Destiny?"

"Do you think such a powerful thing would be left on display in a library?" von Seeckt asked in turn. He looked out the window. "The Night of the Long Knives," von Seeckt said. "June thirtieth, 1934. Hitler purged his own party, the SA, and shifted allegiance to the SS. Two months later, he proclaims himself Führer and all the military are to swear personal allegiance to him—not to the country, but to a man. Remarkable, isn't it?"

Duncan was growing frustrated by von Seeckt's refusal to answer the all-important question of where the

Spear was now. "I need to know—" she began, but the old man cut her off with a wave of his frail hand.

"Yes, yes, the Spear. In 1938, when Hitler annexed Austria, the very first day, he went to the Hofmuseum and took the so-called Spear of Destiny. He had it shipped to Nuremberg, which the Thule group believed was the spiritual capital of Nazi Germany."

"But that wasn't the real Spear of Destiny." Duncan had focused on von Seeckt's use of "so-called."

"No, but by having a public one, he could hide the real one," von Seeckt said. "The farce continues to this day. According to legend, it is the spear of the Roman centurion Gaius Cassius Longinus which was thrust into the side of Jesus when he was on the cross. There are four different objects that are claimed to be the Spear. One is supposed to have been sent from the Ottoman Sultan Bajazet the Second to Pope Innocent the Eighth in 1492 and was placed in one of the columns supporting the dome of Saint Peter's Basilica. Another is supposed to be in Paris, brought there by Saint Louis following his return from the Crusades in the thirteenth century. The third—which I have seen—is in Cracow in Poland, but it is a copy of the last one which most believe to be the real Spear located in Vienna—the one Hitler saw in the library. This one has a long and strange history."

"And it's in Russia now?" Duncan asked.

"No. That one is back in the library. The real Spear of Destiny is none of those four, but rather an Airlia artifact. It looks like a spear, though, so perhaps that is how it was mixed up with the Longinus spear story. Who knows?"

Duncan felt her heart race. "You've seen it?"

Von Seeckt nodded. "We had it with us when we went to the Great Pyramid in 1942."

Duncan waited for him to continue.

"I don't know where Hitler got it," von Seeckt said. "I

saw it only once. The patrol leader, an SS major, carried it. He never let it out of his hands. I think they knew it was a key, they just didn't know what it was a key to. They thought maybe a door in the Great Pyramid. So we had it. Of course, it was not for there. We had to break through the wall to find the bomb."

"What did it look like?"

"In a black case. Metal—some kind of Airlia metal, but not the black like the skin of the mothership. It was silver. Very sharp. Perhaps sixty or seventy centimeters long by ten wide. Like a spearhead. It had a point on one end and a hole for a staff on the other."

"What happened to it?"

"When we were ambushed by the British commandos, the patrol leader escaped into the darkness. I never heard of the Spear again. Either he made it back to Germany with it, or the Arabs caught him in the desert and took it. It is most likely the former."

Duncan grabbed the edge of the bed. "If he made it back to Germany, where would it be now?"

"The Russians." Von Seeckt's voice was a whisper now, his energy drained. "They took everything after the Great War. Everything."

Mike, Duncan thought. He was in the right place, just looking for the wrong thing. "And if the Arabs got it?"

"The Watcher of Giza. Kaji. It would probably end up in his hands." Von Seeckt's eyes closed. "I must sleep now."

Duncan stood and strode out of the room. As soon as she was in the hallway, she pulled out her SATPhone and punched in the code for Turcotte's phone.

CHAPTER 17

"Many of my countrymen have entered that building and never come out," Yakov said. "The sky over our heads is the last bit of freedom they ever saw."

Turcotte was impressed with Lubyanka. In the center of downtown Moscow, it dominated the square that had the same name. Seven stories high, the building was covered with yellow brick, giving it a dour facade. It had taken Yakov several frustrating hours to track down exactly where Lyoncheka's office was and to set up a meeting. Turcotte had felt every minute of those hours pass by with a sense of impending doom, as if he were in the midst of a high-altitude jump but he had no parachute and the ground was approaching with inevitable disaster.

"There is Dyetsky Mir." Katyenka nodded toward the large building on the opposite side of Lubyanka Square. "Children's World. It is the largest toy store in the world. I always thought the contrast of the two buildings facing each other was quite interesting. What is the word—ah, yes, ironic—that is it?"

The three were seated at a small bistro on the south side of the square. The shop was a pathetic attempt to imitate European coffeehouses. Whatever was in his cup, Turcotte doubted a coffee bean had had anything to do with it.

"They even give tours now in the building behind the main one you see," Katyenka said. "They have a KGB museum there. There is a disco in Lubyanka itself, on the first floor, part of a club for retired KGB. There used to be a statue of Felix Dzerzhinsky—the founder of the Cheka, the first communist secret police—in the middle of the square, but that was taken down in August 1991, when we became enlightened."

Yakov laughed at that last statement. " 'Enlightened'?" He turned to Turcotte. "I have tried to explain something to you that I do not think can be explained." He tapped the side of his head. "The Russian mind. It is a very strange place. We lived for so long under the Czars, then the Communists. That was bad enough. But add on top of that the threat from the outside world. The invasions over the centuries. From Napoleon to Hitler.

"You Americans have no idea what we have suffered. You did not even suffer a million casualties in your two-front battles in the Second World War. We don't know how many of our people died. Some say twenty-seven million. One out of every four men, women, and children. With such threats the desire for power here is different than in your country. You have a Donald Trump—we come up with a Stalin. Money is not an end here, but a means to an end. The end that powerful men in Russia desire is to be able to defeat one's enemies. To crush them."

Yakov pointed a long finger at Lubyanka. "When I go in there, remember that." A waiter passed by, and Yakov barked at him in Russian. Seconds later, there were three vodkas on the table. "Drink," Yakov said. He lifted his glass and downed it. He nodded at Katyenka. "I will see you later."

"And you also," Katyenka said. She stood and walked off, disappearing into the crowd in the square.

Yakov placed a hand on Turcotte's shoulder. "If I am not back in . . . let us say an hour, I recommend you go home."

"What is Katyenka doing?"

"She is checking in with her boss. Remember, she

doesn't work for me and she has to keep up the illusion that she works for the GRU."

"Make sure you get back here in an hour," Turcotte said. "I don't want to have to go in there after you."

"You go in there after me, that makes two of us not coming out," Yakov said.

"I'm not leaving without you."

"Easy to say now," Yakov said. "You might feel differently in an hour."

Turcotte checked his watch. "We have eighteen hours. Exactly." His SATPhone buzzed. He flipped it open. "Yes?"

"Mike, the key is known as the Spear of Destiny. Either the Russians got it from the Germans at the end of the Second World War or it's in Egypt. You need to turn around and go back to Russia."

Turcotte digested that information, before responding. "I'm still in Russia, Lisa. Downtown Moscow to be exact. And if the Russians have it, Yakov and I are on the right trail."

"Good. I'm going to Egypt to check that possibility out." She relayed the information she'd gotten from von Seeckt about the Spear and what it looked like.

Yakov was staring at Turcotte across the table, his bushy eyebrows arched in question.

"Be careful," Turcotte warned.

"You too."

Turcotte turned slightly away from Yakov. "I mean it. Be careful."

There was a slight pause. "I know you do. And you know I meant it also. I've got to get going. Out here."

The phone went dead. Turcotte turned to Yakov and relayed Duncan's information.

Yakov stood. "The KGB must have the Spear. I will find out."

"Remember what I said," Turcotte reminded him.

"I will." Yakov walked off.

Turcotte flipped open the SATPhone and punched in a new number.

"Billam here."

"It's Turcotte. I'm sitting across the square from Lubyanka. Yakov is going in."

"This guy Quinn is pretty good," Billam said. "He got us floor plans for Lubyanka. We could land the bouncer right on the roof and work our way down. Any idea what floor you'll be on?"

"By the time you get there, if I need you, I'll know."

"We're locked and loaded," Billam said. "We can be airborne in thirty seconds and the pilot of the bouncer says he can get us there in thirty-six minutes."

"Let's hope you don't need to come," Turcotte said. "I want you to keep on top of Dr. Duncan also. Out here." He closed the phone and put it in his pocket, then checked his watch.

AREA 51
D – 17 Hours, 40 Minutes

Major Quinn walked up to Professor Mualama. "How's the translation going?"

"Most interesting," Mualama said. He reached into his backpack and pulled out the scepter. "I now know where this goes."

Quinn stared at the artifact. "That's Airlia."

"Yes. I found it in the coffin."

"Goddamn!" Quinn exploded. "When the hell were you going to tell us you had that?"

"When I knew what it was," Mualama said.

"We've been searching for the key to Qian-Ling and—"

"It is not the key to Qian-Ling," Mualama interrupted him. "I knew that from the very beginning. But what I didn't have to know is where it was the key to and if I could trust you."

Quinn had seen this before, in the dark days under Majestic. Information was compartmentalized—in this case the threat from Lexina—so much that those who had pertinent information weren't aware it was pertinent. Secrecy was sometimes a necessity, but always with a cost.

"And you know where it goes?" Quinn asked.

"Yes."

"Don't move." Quinn pulled out his SATPhone and called Duncan.

LUBYANKA, MOSCOW
D – 17 Hours, 30 Minutes

"We have cooperated with United Nations Alien Oversight Committee as directed by our president and parliament," the man seated across from Yakov said. His name was Lyoncheka and he wore a very expensive suit, something that was not unusual here in the halls of the FSB headquarters these days. Yakov knew that the reason Lyoncheka could afford such clothes was that he had strong ties with the Mafia here in Moscow. It was the new way.

"It is your organization," Lyoncheka continued, "that was penetrated. It was your facility that was destroyed. Why do you come to me?"

"Because I believe the KGB withheld alien material and records from Section Four. Material recovered at the end of the Great Patriotic War."

Lyoncheka leaned back in his deep leather chair. His desk was huge, made of expensive wood. The windows behind him opened onto Lubyanka Square. It was on the third floor, which Yakov knew meant much prestige, because the office of the head of the KGB, now the FSB, was on the same floor, just three doors away.

The KGB had changed its name to FSB, but Lyoncheka had the same look Yakov had always associated with the KGB. A thick, solid body that did not fit well inside the tailored suit, heavy-lidded eyes that rarely made direct contact, and a total lack of anything remotely resembling happiness in his features. The sort of man that would choke his own mother to death if it would advance his position and increase his power.

"The KGB no longer exists," Lyoncheka said.

"You have all the records from—"

"No, we don't," Lyoncheka interrupted. "Much was destroyed in the change of power from communism. We are a free country now. As such we cannot maintain the type of records the KGB used to have. And"—Lyoncheka smiled without any humor—"there were many incriminating records that could not stand the light of day so the individuals who were mentioned in them spent many a late night shredding and burning."

Yakov was impressed that Lyoncheka could say that without the slightest hint of sarcasm in his voice. Yakov realized it was time to switch his approach. Appealing to Lyoncheka as a member of the government was obviously futile. He would have to approach the man's more basic side, the part that worked hand in hand with the Mafia.

As with any other country, there had always been crime in the Soviet Union, and there was crime now in the new Russia. Yakov knew that under the Communists, the top criminals had been in bed with the government, their actions controlled. If anything, since the change, it was now the government that was in bed with the criminals.

In the decade following the fall of communism, the Mafia had grown to the point where it rivaled the government for control of the country. Those who were smart—and ruthless—like Lyoncheka had seen the handwriting on the wall very early on. The previous year Russia had taken in a total of $60 billion in Western goods; over half of that had been imported illegally by the Mafia. Yakov knew that in the streets of Moscow, the murder rate was standing at approximately a hundred Mafia-related killings a *day*. And no one was being arrested for those crimes.

"I believe UNAOC would pay for any Airlia-related information," Yakov said.

Thick bushy eyebrows lifted in mock amazement. "Are you trying to bribe me? That is a crime."

"I cannot bribe you," Yakov said, "because you say you do not have the information I am seeking. I just mentioned that UNAOC would probably pay for that information. It is you who are making the connection between that statement and yourself."

"Very cute." Lyoncheka leaned back and steepled his thick, sausagelike fingers. "I do not enjoy playing word games. Tell me, do you know who destroyed Stantsiya Chyort?"

"I do now. The Ones Who Wait."

Lyoncheka nodded. "It is a terrible shame. The Americans are having trouble also. Their Area 51 was attacked from the sky, was it not? And there have been reports of a nuclear explosion in the—what do they call it—their heartland? And one of their shuttles destroyed on the ground. Their government vehemently denies such stories, of course. I also understand their fleet off Easter Island has had some trouble?"

"I know nothing of any of that."

"But you want information from me?" Lyoncheka pulled a bottle out of a drawer and two glasses. He poured a generous amount into both. He shoved one across his desk, and Yakov picked it up.

"To Mother Russia," Lyoncheka proposed.

"To Mother Russia," Yakov agreed, but his hand paused at Lyoncheka's next words.

"I do not think you put your country first."

Yakov put the glass down on the desk and waited for the other man to continue.

"You will toast our country, yet you work for the Americans."

"I do not work for the Americans," Yakov said.

"You let your Section Four comrades get killed, yet you immediately go to the American Area 51 instead of coming home. You seem in no desire to avenge the deaths of your comrades."

"There are larger issues," Yakov said.

"Larger than Russia?"

"Larger than Russia."

"There is nothing larger than Russia," Lyoncheka said flatly.

"The world is larger than Russia," Yakov argued.

"Not to me." Lyoncheka took a drink. "Not to me, comrade. I served the Soviet and I serve the new state, but it is all the same to me. The old women cleaning snow off their steps with whisk brooms, the children playing in the parks, the men working in the factories. I serve them." He abruptly changed directions. "The Americans' Majestic-12 was infiltrated by these aliens, was it not?"

"Yes. Their minds were affected by an alien computer they uncovered at Tiahuanaco in Bolivia. They brought it back to their lab at Dulce in the state of New Mexico. It directed them to fly the mothership, working most likely because of a program that was activated when they uncovered the guardian."

"I know all that," Lyoncheka said. "Don't you think it highly likely that maybe some of our own people have also been so affected?"

Yakov nodded. "I have always considered that a possibility."

Lyoncheka lifted his glass, unwrapped his index finger from around it, and pointed it at Yakov. "You think me, perhaps?"

"Perhaps."

"Would I know if I was?"

Yakov blinked. "I don't know."

"And if you were, would you know? Would I?"

Yakov didn't say anything. He wondered where this was heading.

"Section Four caught one of these human-alien creatures . . . didn't you?"

"Years ago," Yakov acknowledged. "It chose to die rather than be questioned. We autopsied it and found evidence of cloning. And some nonhuman genetic material."

"Yes, but the others, the humans affected mentally by this guardian computer, they are not so easy to discover. They are just like you and me. The Americans had one on their shuttle crew who killed his shipmates," Lyoncheka said. "And then there are these Watchers—who blew up that other shuttle. So many groups, so many enemies. And now they are tightening the noose. The American President is threatening our president with retaliation if Stratzyda is used against his country, even though we no longer control the satellite and can do nothing to stop it.

"I am neither progressive, saying let us work with these aliens, nor am I isolationist, saying let us ignore them. You cannot ignore a threat. I am Russian. I say we fight them." Lyoncheka leaned forward and his voice dropped. "But they are all around us. They have tried to get to me before. You can trust no one." A large meaty fist slammed down on the top of the desk.

"To stop them we need something," Yakov said. "Something from the Archives."

Lyoncheka cocked his head. "What exactly do you need?"

"A key. With it we can stop Stratzyda."

Lyoncheka remained still for a minute before he spoke. "The Archives you look for exist. I can give you some help. But you must remember, Russia comes first." Lyoncheka slid a piece of paper across the desk. "Meet me there, this evening."

AREA 51
D – 17 Hours, 30 Minutes

Quinn turned the scepter so that the ruby eyes glittered in the overhead lights of the conference room. It was not what von Seeckt had described. "It's heavy. There's something inside."

Mualama nodded. "I suspect it is some sort of machine that functions as a key."

They both looked up as the door to the conference room slammed open and Lisa Duncan walked in. She had raced back to Area 51 from the Nellis hospital after getting Major Quinn's report that Professor Mualama had withheld an artifact—a key.

Quinn placed it down on the table, and Duncan picked it up. She wasted no time on recriminations. They had seventeen hours before Lexina's deadline.

"What do you think it opens?" she asked Mualama.

"I've made a barely legible translation of the marker. Knowing that this"—he tapped the scepter—"is a key pulled it all together."

Duncan had no more patience. "It goes to the lowest level of Qian-Ling?"

Mualama frowned. "Qian-Ling?"

"The tomb in China."

"Dear lady, I know what Qian-Ling is. And there is a reference to China on the tablet." He pulled out a notepad and flipped through it. "Here. It says: 'Admiral Cing Ho—In the Year 2038—brought the power and the key. The power stayed. The key was passed on to the ones from the inner sea.'"

"Is *this* the key to Qian-Ling?"

"I do not think so."

Duncan closed her eyes to collect her thoughts. "What is 2038 from the Chinese calendar in the Western calendar?" she asked.

Mualama thought for a few moments. "Six fifty-six B.C."

"Who was this Admiral Cing Ho?" Duncan asked.

"I do not know."

Duncan looked at the translation for a few seconds. "The power—could that be the ruby sphere we found in the Great Rift Valley?"

"Very likely," Mualama agreed.

"But if the Qian-Ling key was passed on"—Duncan tapped the scepter—"what is this?"

"A different key," Mualama said.

"'A different key.'" Duncan sat down and put her head in her hands. After von Seeckt's disclosures, she had to force herself to focus. "One thing at a time. You say this isn't the Qian-Ling key?"

Mualama was patient. "No, I don't believe so. According to the marker, it is—"

Duncan held up her hand. "Okay. Do you know where the Qian-Ling key is?"

"If it is the key discussed on the stone," Mualama said, "it was passed on to those from the inner sea, which means the Mediterranean. In 656 B.C., that could be one of several groups of people. Rome was not yet founded, but the Greeks controlled a good portion of the Mediterranean. The Assyrian Empire, which ruled from Turkey along the crescent of the eastern Mediterranean to Egypt, was still in power, although its capital, Nineveh, was sacked not long afterward, in 612 B.C."

"In other words, you have no clue where the key mentioned on the stone went," Duncan summarized.

"That key, yes. Although I suspect there may be other ways to try to track it down."

"How?"

"*This* key might lead us to information that will lead us to *that* key," Mualama said. "In fact, this key may lead us to the truth. The entire truth."

"What do you mean?" Duncan asked. "If not Qian-Ling, What is the scepter a key to?"

"I suspect a room. A hiding place."

"A room where?" Duncan demanded.

"I believe it is the key to the Hall of Records."

"What Hall of Records?" Duncan asked.

"According to legend," Mualama said, "there is a hidden chamber that contains the entire lost history of mankind. Going back much further than our current recorded history. To the island of Atlantis and a fantastic kingdom on the island."

"We know Atlantis did exist," Duncan said, "so maybe this Hall of Records exists. But wasn't the Hall destroyed when Atlantis was blasted?"

"Not according to legend."

"In what form are the Records kept?"

"I don't know, but whatever form it was, I believe it was kept in the Ark of the Covenant," Mualama said. "Ms. Duncan, you must bear with me. I have spent many years tracking down legends and rumors. My translation of the runes was tainted by my own knowledge, so some of what I think I know will disagree with some of what your UNAOC scientists think. I don't—"

"Professor," Duncan interrupted him. "I have seen many strange things in the past month. Things I never dreamed existed. So please, speak freely. My belief is that by the time our scientists figure all this out, it will be much too late. As you say, perhaps this Hall of Records will tell us where the Qian-Ling key is, and we desperately need that. I trust your intuition—you did find the grave site, after all. And I do want the full story of how you did that when we have some time."

"All right," Mualama said. "I believe this record of history is contained in the Ark of the Covenant. I believe for most of its existence the Ark was stored inside the Hall of Records. I also believe, though, that this record may have had other names throughout our history."

"Where is this hidden Hall that holds the Ark?" Duncan asked.

"According to the marker, it is located under the Highland of Aker, in one of the six divisions of the Duat, along the Roads of Rostau."

Duncan simply stared at Mualama, waiting for him to say it in English.

"I believe what we are looking for is hidden underneath the Great Sphinx on the Giza Plateau."

Giza again, Duncan thought. All the more reason to go there now.

Mualama continued. "The Sphinx has always been something of an enigma. Archaeologists can't agree on when it was built, but they do agree that it was constructed at an earlier time than the three large pyramids behind it."

"How much earlier?" Duncan asked.

"Anywhere from five to six thousand years before the pyramids," Mualama said.

"So it could have been built at the same time that Atlantis was flourishing under the Airlia," Duncan said. She signaled with her hand to Major Quinn, who began quietly accessing one of the portable computers built into the conference tabletop as they spoke.

Mualama responded to Duncan's statement. "Yes. There are those who claim the Sphinx is twelve to thirteen thousand years old, dating to around 10,000 B.C."

"Do you think it is that old?" Duncan asked.

"I have been there," Mualama said. "I believe it very well could have been built that long ago. Have you ever thought about Egypt's history?"

"What do you mean?" Duncan asked.

"Egyptologists." Mualama's voice showed his contempt. "There is so much they ignore or don't think about. The alignment with the stars of the entire Giza complex. Even though the pyramids were indeed built around the time they say, they never quite explain the alignment with the various star systems that the shafts in the three pyramids have. The alignments suggest that while the pyramid complex was built in the Fourth Dynasty, between 2613 and 2494 B.C., it was *planned* around 10,450 B.C. With modern computers that can scroll back through the star charts—using a method called precession—this is obvious, but no one speaks of it.

"But the most fascinating thing, the most amazing ignored fact, is the lack of development in ancient Egypt. It's as if we are supposed to believe that for almost four thousand years of rule, nothing changed, nothing developed. The civilization just sprang fully formed into being with the reign of the Pharaoh Menes and pretty much stayed at the same technological level all that time. Think of it. If you were an archaeologist a thousand years from now and you excavated Cairo, would you not be able to see a vast difference between buildings from the nineteenth to twentieth centuries? Just a hundred years. But we look over the course of thousands of years in ancient Egypt and all is the same. You know how they date the Sphinx? Someone scribbles a name in hieroglyphics somewhere and the 'experts' say, aha, it must have been built then!

"They ignore the state of the rock, the construction, the weathering, and they focus everything on the stela between the paws. The dating of the Sphinx, according to the experts, is all based upon a single syllable on a stela found between the paws. Even though the experts agree that the stela is not of the same age as the Sphinx, that it was placed there later. It is dated to the Pharaoh Thutmosis IV, who ruled from 1401 to 1391 B.C., who tried to clear the Sphinx of the sand that constantly surrounded its body.

"He put a stela, a stone tablet, between the paws, and on the thirteenth line it has the word *Khaf,* which Egyptologists say refers to the Pharaoh Khafre, who ruled between 2520 and 2494 B.C. and thus must have built the Sphinx, according to their inductive logic.

"I have seen this stela. You cannot even read the writing anymore, as the stone has deteriorated so badly over the years. The only way they even have an idea what was written there is that someone made a copy of what was written. So it is a case of a copy of writing on a stone not contemporary with the Sphinx, all relying on one word, being the leading case for dating the Sphinx to the realm of Khafre.

"Something that is interesting about the stela is a line that says the Sphinx is the embodiment of great magical power from the beginning of time. Even most Egyptologists agree that there were three eras to ancient Egypt if one studies the texts of the early Egyptians. The first was the time of the Neteru, or gods. Most people consider this not a real time but rather a mythological time, which saw the gods go through various struggles, ending with the accession of Horus, the son of Isis and Osiris. The second phase was that of Shemsu Hor, which means the followers of Horus. This ended when Menes unified the Upper and Lower Kingdoms and started the first dynasty of pharaohs. All our focus has been on the time from

Menes forward, because it was believed that the two earlier ages were mythical, but what if they were real?

"What if the Neteru were the Airlia? In myth, the Neteru were said to have fair skin and red hair, most unusual for that part of the world, but very fitting for the Airlia, don't you think? And what if the Shemsu Hor were the humans who survived Atlantis and began civilization in Egypt?"

"What you're saying," Duncan interrupted, "is that if the Great Sphinx was built around 10,000 B.C., then it might have been made by the Airlia."

"Or humans who followed the Airlia's orders. There is much about the Sphinx that is strange. Because it lies in the shadow of the Great Pyramid, the Sphinx has not had as much attention paid to it as it should. It is quite remarkable in its own right.

"First you must consider what a sphinx is. No one quite knows whose face is that on the Sphinx. In fact, it is very likely that the original face was altered at a later date during one of the many restorations of the Sphinx.

"The Great Sphinx is called the 'father of terrors' by the Arabs, which is a strange title. One has to wonder where that name came from. It sits on the west bank of the Nile and looks to the east, into the rising sun.

"The main body of the statue was carved out of a huge, solid, limestone rock. I don't know the exact dimensions," Mualama said, "but it is quite large."

"The face is nineteen feet from the top of the forehead to the bottom of the chin." Major Quinn was looking at his laptop screen. "It's slightly wider than high. The body length is a hundred and seventy-two feet and the total height from base to top of the head is sixty-six feet.

"According to official and accepted records," Quinn continued, "it was built around 2,500 B.C. and the likeness is that of King Khafre. But we all know that we have to read official records with a jaundiced eye," he added.

"That is indeed so," Mualama said. "One interesting aspect about dating the Sphinx is that a study of the surface concluded that the base and the stones on the temple wall around it were eroded by water. As we all know, the Giza Plateau lies on the edge of the Sahara Desert, a region which has been dry for nine thousand years. However, there is speculation that before that time, about ten thousand years ago, the area was heavily vegetated and the Nile much larger than it is now, forming lakes. Which might account for the water erosion.

"Another interesting aspect is that although the main body of the Sphinx was carved out of a solid block of limestone, the base, the paws, and the wall around it were made of blocks of limestone, much like the Great Pyramid. The difference is that the blocks around the Sphinx are much larger than those used in the pyramids. The largest weigh two hundred tons. If one wonders how the ancient Egyptians moved the blocks that made the pyramids, you truly have to marvel how these huge blocks were transported so long ago. Modern engineers are stumped as to how this could have been done, as there are only two cranes in existence today that could move such heavy stones.

"It is believed that there is an entrance to a network of underground tunnels between the paws of the Sphinx. If the Ark is hidden anywhere, I would say it is underneath. According to legend, there are two gateways to the Roads of Rastau, one on land and one in the water."

Duncan put the scepter down. "We can sit here all day and chat about the Sphinx, but I think the best thing is we take a look. Professor Mualama and I will go to Egypt."

"What about permission?" Mualama asked. "The Egyptian government has had most curious policies regarding investigating the Sphinx, particularly the network of tunnels that are supposed to be underneath it."

"I'll contact UNAOC and have them get in touch with the Egyptian government," Duncan said.

"Egypt is slightly to the right of center," Mualama said, "as far as the isolationist movement goes. The Muslim fundamentalists are very much against having anything to do with the Airlia."

"I'll emphasize to UNAOC that this has the highest priority," Duncan said. "It's all we can do."

"There is something else," Mualama said.

"What?"

Mualama pulled out an oilskin-wrapped package. "This manuscript. It is written in Akkadian, an ancient tongue." He briefly gave Duncan the background of the papers and Sir Richard Francis Burton. "If we can translate this, it might be of use. I believe it will be important with regard to whatever is inside the Hall of Records. It might also talk of the key you seek."

"Why did you hold the key and this manuscript back from us?" Duncan asked, although she already had a good idea what the answer would be.

Mualama confirmed her suspicions with one word. "Trust."

"Major Quinn?" Duncan pointed at the manuscript. "Think you can find someone who reads Akkadian?"

"I can try."

The door to the conference room opened and an enlisted man handed a file folder to Major Quinn. He opened it and checked the sheet of paper inside.

"What is it?" Duncan asked.

"The results of the tests you requested the UNAOC doctors perform on von Seeckt and the results from the examination of the Airlia skeleton." He pulled the paper out and handed it to Duncan.

She scanned the two pieces of paper. "Goddamn!"

she exclaimed. She tapped Mualama on the arm. "Let's go."

MANHATTAN, NEW YORK
D – 15 Hours

The sniper had been in position for forty-eight hours. He sat in the room the way he had been trained, the muzzle of his weapon two feet from the window. Only amateurs would rest the barrel on the window and allow the end of the weapon to poke out. The room was dark, and he was invisible to anyone peering at the window from the outside.

He had a perfect angle of fire along First Avenue. The previous day he had counted the flags that lined the edge of the United Nations from Forty-second Street to Forty-eighth. One hundred and eighty-five, in alphabetical order, from Afghanistan to Zimbabwe, north to south. Even at the place that was supposed to help unite the world, each country had to fly its own flag.

The sniper had pulled the dresser over to just in front of the window, and the bipod for his weapon rested on it, the metal legs scratching the finish, but that was the least of his concerns. He had the butt plate swung up and resting on top of his shoulder, taking the rest of the weight of the M93.

The weapon, with ammunition, topped out at twenty-six pounds. He had broken it down into three parts—detachable stock, receiver with barrel, and magazine—to carry it to the room. Then he had carefully reassembled it. The scope was bolted to the top of the barrel, and he had zeroed it in the previous week at a farm in upstate New York. The barrel was made of match-grade chrome alloy with a matte black polymer finish. There was a large flute at the end to reduce some of the muzzle blast signature.

The gun was so big and heavy because it fired a .50-caliber round. A half inch in diameter and almost six inches long, it was the bullet that fighter planes in World War II had fired from their wing guns. Using that large a round gave the gun a range of over a mile, although the kill zone the sniper had delineated for his target was only six hundred meters away. The large caliber ensured that when the bullet hit, it would do devastating damage. In fact, the primary use of the M93 was not called sniping but strategic operations target interdiction—using the weapon to hit critical components in such systems as microwave relay towers or on jet fighters sitting on a runway.

But a bullet was a bullet, the sniper's instructors had harped at him during his training.

He removed his eye from the scope and checked the watch lying flat on the desktop. The target window was open. He had been given a folder that said this was the earliest the subject left. The sniper used his right hand to pull up on the bolt and slide it back. The top bullet on the magazine of ten slid up, and as he pushed the bolt forward, it slid the round into the magazine well, seating it tightly in place.

He put his right hand on the pistol grip, curling three fingers and his thumb around it as his forefinger slid through the trigger guard and lightly touched the thin metal sliver.

He leaned forward and peered through the scope. He began to control his breathing, taking long, shallow breaths. He could maintain this position for hours if needed. He could feel the rhythm of his heart and let it become like a metronome inside his head.

For a moment that rhythm sped up. He pulled his head back and shook it, feeling a spike of pain bisect his brain. He looked about, as if surprised at his current situation, the gun, the muzzle pointing down First Avenue, the United Nations to the left, then the eyes glazed over, his face twitched in pain, and he leaned back into position. Slowly the twitching stopped, the tension went out of the face.

Below, Peter Sterling, the head of UNAOC—the United Nations Alien Oversight Committee—exited the main UN building and headed for his car waiting at the curb on First Avenue. His patrician face was lined with the stress of the past weeks, but he walked with a bounce, his mood lightened by recent inroads he'd made on the Security Council. He almost had them convinced that the UN should take a tougher stand on all interactions with the guardians, the Airlia on Mars, and all other factions involved with the aliens. While the isolationist movement was gaining ground in the General Assembly, Sterling hoped to sway the Security Council to pass a resolution to allow UN-sanctioned forces to try to track down The Mission, to completely isolate Easter Island, and to resume digging at the destroyed American research facility at Dulce, New Mexico to discover what had been down there.

The Remington trigger was set at 2.5 pounds pull. The sniper drew in a long, shallow breath and held it. The reticles were centered on target, leading very slightly to account for the target's pace. His mind was in rhythm with his heartbeat, and in the space before the next beat, he smoothly pulled back on the trigger.

Sterling's mind was focused on how to get the Russian on his committee, Boris Ivanoc, the number-two man, to be more enthusiastic in getting his Security Council member to vote for the resolution, when the .50-caliber bullet made that the last thought he would ever have.

The half-inch-wide bullet splintered through skull on

the right side of Sterling's head, plowed through the brain, and took the entire left side of the head with it as it exited, splattering the sidewalk beyond for twenty feet with blood, brain, and fragmented pieces of bone.

The sniper had no doubt the target was dead. But he wasn't working on the rules he had been trained on. The fact that something overrode years of repetitive training echoed somewhere in the back of his brain, like a leaf blowing in the wind, but he couldn't grab on to it.

He pulled the bolt back, placing another round in the chamber, and aimed. Two cops were moving tentatively toward the body, everyone else having scattered. The sniper centered the reticles on what remained of the target's head. He didn't bother to wait between heartbeats—the target was stationary and at a range where he would hit one hundred times out of one hundred. He pulled the trigger.

The bullet smashed into the remains of the head and effectively finished decapitating Sterling. The two cops dove for cover, screaming into their handheld radios for backup.

The sniper removed the butt plate from over his shoulder and put the rifle down on the desk almost reverently. He walked over to the window. People were pointing up, having a general idea of where the shots had originated from due to the loud report of the .50-caliber weapon. He climbed up onto the windowsill in clear view of those below and teetered there for a second.

He paused as a memory fought through the alien conditioning. He remembered visiting the United Nations as a child, on a school trip to New York City. He tried to pull up more of the memory, but a black curtain slid down over that part of his mind.

He stepped out into space. He felt no fear as he fell the fifteen stories. The impact of the pavement brought an instant of release from the conditioning, the horror of what he had done, of what had been done to him. Then he died.

CHAPTER 18

OUTSIDE THE KREMLIN, MOSCOW
D – 14 Hours

Turcotte had the MP-5 tucked inside of the long coat that Yakov had given him. He was pressed back in the shadows under the Moskvorestkiy Bridge, which spanned the Moskva River near the walls of the Kremlin. Katyenka was farther down Kremlevskaya Naberezhnaya, hiding in the vegetation on the slope that came down from the walls of the Kremlin to the river, while Yakov was in the open, waiting for Lyoncheka.

Turcotte had almost called in Billam's team for support, but he knew doing that would take them away from being able to support Duncan, and he had just received word from her of the assassination of Sterling prior to leaving the hotel they were staying at. Until he absolutely needed the team, he wanted to leave it untasked.

At the appointed time, a figure appeared, down the walkway from the north, from the direction of St. Basil's Cathedral in Red Square. Turcotte slipped the submachine gun's safety off. He could hear intermittent traffic going across the bridge, but otherwise all was quiet.

Yakov turned to face the newcomer, arms out from his side.

"Good evening, comrade," Yakov greeted Lyoncheka.

"Whoever you have covering you," Lyoncheka said, "bring them into the open. Now."

Yakov signaled for Turcotte to come out.

Lyoncheka turned, hand snaking inside his coat, only

to have Yakov's massive paw grab his arm. "Easy, comrade. He's a friend."

Lyoncheka shook his head. "There are no friends." He peered as Turcotte came up to them. "And an American—you are the one who destroyed the alien fleet."

It was a statement, not a question, so Turcotte remained silent.

"I will have to trust that since you did that," Lyoncheka said, "you are not working for either of the alien groups or the Watchers."

"That is good," Yakov agreed. "What do you have for us?"

"Come with me." Lyoncheka pointed to the west, where the walls of the Kremlin loomed. "I will show you what you want to see."

They began walking along the river, the sounds of their boots echoing off the Kremlin walls.

Yakov paused. "There is someone else here. Another friend."

"You have too many friends for the business you are in." Lyoncheka's voice revealed his anger and fear. "Where and who?"

Yakov signaled, and Katyenka appeared out of the darkness.

Lyoncheka shook his head as he recognized her. "She's GRU! This is too much. I promised to help you"—he tapped Yakov on the chest—"not a committee."

"We're in this together."

"No, *I'm* not," Lyoncheka argued.

Turcotte curled his finger around the trigger of the MP-5, but he didn't pull the gun out. He waited for Yakov to defuse the situation.

"Comrade, you have come this far," Yakov said. "Sooner or later, you are going to have to take a stand against these aliens and their minions. Take one now.

Stratzyda will be over the United States in less than twelve hours."

Lyoncheka spit. "On your head be it. There is no time for games. Come." He clambered up the slope toward the Kremlin. They reached the large wall that surrounded the compound and Lyoncheka turned west, the other three following.

When he reached a portal through the wall blocked by a steel gate, Lyoncheka pulled out a plastic card. "We have modernized from the locks and chains that used to secure the compound." He slid the card into a small opening, then punched in a sequence of numbers on a numeric keypad.

The gate slid open and he led them in. A second steel gate blocked the way into the Kremlin proper, but Lyoncheka turned to the left where another keypad was located. He slid another card through that, entered a new code, and the stones rumbled back, revealing a descending stairway.

"Come, quickly," Lyoncheka urged them.

They crowded down the stairs to a landing. The stones shut behind them. The only illumination came from a couple of flickering fluorescent lights on the ceiling. Turcotte tightened his grip on the gun, fearing an ambush in the confined space. The only other apparent exit was a solid steel door at the end of the landing.

Lyoncheka leaned over a new security device next to the door. Turcotte recognized it as a retinal scanner, the top of the line in identity checking. Lyoncheka waited as the laser scanned across his eyes, then the door opened, revealing a descending corridor. "Come."

Lyoncheka led them into the corridor. The walls were painted a dull green, the floor gray. It went straight as far as they could see in the dim lighting. The steel door shut with a thud.

"During the Great Patriotic War," Lyoncheka said as

they walked, "Stalin had a very large bomb shelter built under the Kremlin. Then, during the Cold War, the various premiers continued building deeper and deeper shelters. The desire was to have a command-and-control center and living quarters that could survive a nuclear attack on the Kremlin itself. This was eventually expanded to have underground connections to various other government agencies.

"Billions and billions of rubles were spent. This network we're in connects to many places under Moscow. There is even a secret underground rail line that goes over eighty kilometers outside of the city to the alternate national command post."

Lyoncheka opened a heavy door. "This way. We are under the Great Kremlin Palace right now. About eighty feet below the surface."

The tunnel was smaller and older. Cut right out of the rock, the walls were not finished and a thin sheen of moisture glistened in the faint glow of naked lightbulbs strung every twenty feet. Several of the lights were burned out.

They went about a hundred meters, then another door blocked their way. This one was wooden and very old, with iron bands across it. Turcotte noted a small electronic eye to the left and above the door, a strange thing given the apparent age of the tunnel and door.

Lyoncheka waved at the eye. With a hiss of hydraulics, the door swung open and they entered.

A sheet of thick, bullet- and blast-proof glass bisected the room and the top of a desk. A door made of the same thick glass was to the right.

A middle-aged woman, her hair gray, her body stout, looked up from a video screen on the desk. "Look what the wind has blown in," she said. Her words carried to their side via a small speaker. Her hands were not visible.

"Pasha!" Lyoncheka greeted her.

The woman was all business. "Step forward, through the metal detectors." Behind her, two large steel doors were closed.

Turcotte noticed the detectors on either side of the door. He stepped through, the alarm beeping and a red light going off. Each of the others did the same, with the same results.

"Your friends carry weapons. Tell them to slowly remove them and place them in the bin or they will be dead in five seconds."

A panel on the front of the desk slid up, revealing two antipersonnel mines, pointed at them, and a metal bin.

"Nine." Pasha's voice was cold.

"Do as she says," Lyoncheka advised.

Turcotte glanced at Yakov.

"Eight."

The large Russian pulled his submachine gun from under his coat and placed it on the desk. Turcotte and Katyenka did the same. All weapons had been deposited by the time she got down to four.

"Back through the detector," Pasha ordered.

Each stepped onto the elevator and back off. This time there was no alarm.

"You vouch for these people?" Pasha asked Lyoncheka.

"I would not be here if I did not." Lyoncheka pulled a Western cigarette out of a pack and placed it in the bin. The door slid shut. Pasha reached down, and her hands appeared for the first time, the cigarette in one, an AKSU folding-stock submachine gun in the other. She slipped the sling for the AKSU over her shoulder and picked up a lighter from the desktop, firing up the cigarette.

Turcotte recognized the weapon—top-of-the-line commando issue in Russia. A shortened version of the

AK-74, an updated model of the venerable AK-47, but firing a smaller 5.45mm round, more in line with modern thinking that a smaller, faster bullet was more devastating in causing wounds than a slower, larger bullet. She picked up a large satchel, which she looped over her shoulder.

"You have not been here for months," Pasha said. She took a deep drag, then eyed him through the smoke and thick glass.

Lyoncheka spread his arms. "Ah, Pasha, you know the life of the spy. We are always being ordered to go here and there and—"

Turcotte was surprised at the change in the FSB man. He almost seemed human.

"I checked on you," Pasha said. "You have been in Moscow for the past three months."

The glass door clicked open.

"Ah." Lyoncheka walked through the door and around the desk, almost bumping his head on a low beam that cut across the ceiling. He placed his large hands on her equally large shoulders. "Pasha, Pasha, Pasha. I've thought of you. On those cold nights when—"

"Oh, stop it." She nodded at Yakov. "I know of him. He is Section Four. There are whispers of trouble at Stantsiya Chyort."

"It was destroyed," Lyoncheka confirmed. "Everyone killed."

Pasha's eyes immediately flickered toward the tunnel door and back. "They are getting closer."

" 'They'?" Yakov asked.

Pasha ignored him. "Things are still very strict here, Lyoncheka. There are still screams coming through the pipes." She nodded toward a small heating vent on the wall.

"There are larger dangers now," Lyoncheka said. "We need to access the Archives."

Lyoncheka reached inside of his shirt and pulled out a key. Pasha did the same. They walked to opposite ends of the room where two control boxes were bolted to the wall. Each inserted their key, then Lyoncheka counted to three. They turned at the same time.

"If we do not do this correctly," Lyoncheka said, "the Archives will be buried."

The steel doors slid open, revealing a large elevator. The five of them entered, Pasha pushing the button to close the doors.

Turcotte felt a slight lessening of his weight as they descended. "How deep are we going?"

"A half mile," Pasha replied.

"Who runs this place?" Yakov asked.

"I do," Lyoncheka said. "The Alien Archives were established by the KGB right after the Great Patriotic War. Section Four was the official response, but of course the KGB trusted no one. As did the GRU, the military's intelligence service," he added with a sideways glance at Katyenka. "So we had three organizations trying to keep things secret from each other as much as anyone else.

"As we became aware of the alien organizations and their infiltrations into human society, we in the KGB realized we had to reduce the number of people aware of the Archives to a minimum." A smile without humor crossed Lyoncheka's dour face. "After many years and purges, Pasha and I have become the minimum. Even the current director does not know of the existence of these Archives."

Turcotte thought about that. What good had it done the Russians to bury their knowledge like this? In a way, he knew that Lyoncheka had played into the aliens' hands while trying to protect what he had access to from them. The cult of paranoia had a very high price.

The elevator halted with a slight jar. The doors rumbled open. A dank corridor, lit with an occasional light, beckoned.

"We do not have much money for maintenance," Lyoncheka said. "And what little we have, we spend on security devices." He stepped off the elevator. "This way."

He led the way down the corridor fifty meters from the door.

"How much farther?" Katyenka asked.

"The Archives are much deeper," Lyoncheka said. "The elevator was the easiest descent. It gets harder from here."

"Any more gates or security devices?" Katyenka asked.

"No," Lyoncheka said. "We are—" He didn't finish the sentence, as Katyenka slashed the sharpened point of a plastic ice-scraper across Pasha's neck, severing the carotid artery in a spray of blood. Even as Pasha's body fell, Katyenka's other hand grabbed the AKSU and brought it to bear on the three men.

"I told you!" Lyoncheka turned toward Yakov. "I told you not to—" He never finished the sentence, as Katyenka fired a single round. It hit the side of Lyoncheka's head, a small black hole on entry, and ripped out the other side, taking a large portion of brain, blood, and skull with it.

Turcotte had not moved throughout, and he remained still as Lyoncheka's body slumped to the floor.

"Katyenka." The resignation and disgust in Yakov's voice expressed how he felt. "Why?"

Katyenka had the gun trained on the Russian, but Turcotte knew she would stitch him full of holes before he made half the distance to her.

Katyenka shook her head. "I do not need you, comrade, so do not irritate me."

Turcotte noticed movement. He forced himself not to

look directly. Out of the corner of his eye he saw Pasha, lying in a pool of expanding blood, slowly moving a hand down her side.

"I thought you trusted her," Turcotte said loudly. "You Russian pig!"

"Shut up, both of you." Katyenka shifted the muzzle between the two. "You are children groping in the dark."

Yakov turned and grabbed Turcotte's coat by the lapels. "Don't talk to me like that, you American slime."

Turcotte could see that Pasha had pulled something small and black out. A thumb flipped open a red cover, revealing a switch. At that moment, Turcotte knew what she was going to do and he almost alerted Katyenka, but his discipline prevailed.

With her dying effort, Pasha pushed down on the remote switch. The charges that lined the elevator shaft they had just departed went off in rapid succession. Farther down the corridor, a secondary explosion fired less than a second after the first, destroying the tunnel and trapping them.

Katyenka howled in rage and spun about, firing at Pasha on automatic. The bullets slammed into the already dead body, pushing it down the corridor. Yakov took advantage of that lapse to attack her by the expedient method of tossing Turcotte at her.

Turcotte was prepared for that, twisting in the air and grabbing at the gun as he hit her. He bit back a curse as his right hand closed on the hot, stubby barrel of the AKSU, flesh searing, just as it had in Germany months before.

He ripped the gun out of her hands as Yakov grabbed her arms, pinning her against the wall of the tunnel. The last of the charges went off and the elevator doors buckled as rock and stone filled the shaft. Dust billowed out from both ends of the tunnel, further decreasing visibility.

"Who are you?" Yakov yelled at the woman struggling in his arms.

Turcotte trained the weapon on her, even as she kicked at the large Russian holding her captive. Yakov solved that by snapping one of her arms like a twig. Katyenka hissed in pain.

"Do it again and I break the other," Yakov warned. "Who are you? Who do you work for?"

Katyenka spit at him. Her body spasmed, then her eyes rolled back. She went limp.

Yakov held her with one hand while he checked the pulse in her neck with the other. "Ahh!" He laid her on the floor. "She's dead."

"How did she do that?" Turcotte asked.

Yakov was staring down at her sadly. "I trusted her. Almost."

Turcotte knelt next to the body. He pulled up her eyelid and felt . . . a contact. He pulled it off. Below was a red iris in a red pupil. "The Ones Who Wait."

Yakov nodded. "They wanted whatever is in the Archives. Lyoncheka must have fooled them all these years, and we led her straight to him." Yakov went over to Pasha's body. He grabbed the satchel off her shoulder. He pulled out a pistol, which he stuck in his belt, and several grenades, both fragmentation and flash-bang, dividing them between himself and Turcotte. Then he covered her face with her jacket.

Turcotte stood and checked his watch. The clock was still running. In a perverse way he was bolstered by the attempt by Katyenka to betray them. It meant there was a very good chance they were on the right path. After all the delays once they had reached Russia, this one was the most positive.

"Let's go." Turcotte strode off down the corridor. Yakov followed, leaving the bodies lying on the floor.

Colonel Tolya waited as his men pried open the elevator doors. As soon as they were far enough apart, he leaned in, shining a powerful light down. Through the cloud of dust he could see the shaft blocked by rubble. He pulled back and signaled for his men to let the door shut.

Tolya was a colonel in the GRU, the intelligence arm of the Russian army. He took his orders—and the money for him to follow them—from Katyenka, and she had been most specific about how far behind he was to follow and what he was to do. This destruction of the elevator had not been in the instructions, but he did have a backup plan.

He had a metal case slung over his shoulder that he swung around to his chest. He thumbed the combination to the right setting and opened the lid. He pressed the on button and an active matrix display came alive. The screen was split, and a dot glowed on both sides. The left showed horizontal displacement, while the right vertical. The object that the tracker was ranging in on was a highly radioactive isotope.

"Who has the plans?" Tolya yelled.

"I do, sir." A young engineer lieutenant hesitatingly came forward, looking out of place among the heavily armed GRU commandos clustered around Tolya.

The engineer unrolled a set of yellowing paper on Pasha's desk. "These are very old, sir. I do not know if they have been updated. The underground tunnels and chambers below the city have been the province of numerous organizations, some of which did not want others to know what they were doing."

Tolya simply stared at the lieutenant, then used a pencil to point at the plans. "North of us about three hundred meters. Down about eight hundred meters."

The engineer bit his lip as he made the mental adjustments while looking at the charts. "This shaft is listed. It intersects a deeper cross-tunnel, here. That leads to this intersection, which runs to the point you want."

"Can we get down there?" Tolya asked.

"It will take a while. We have to go to this downshaft below the Armory in the Kremlin," the lieutenant said. "And then . . ." The lieutenant paused when he realized no one was listening. Tolya was already moving.

AREA 51 TO NELLIS AIR FORCE BASE
D – 10 Hours

Duncan was once more watching the desert flit by below, this time through the skin of the bouncer. "Before we go to Egypt, there is one last thing I must do," she informed Mualama. "There is a man I must talk to. His name is Werner von Seeckt."

Mualama nodded. "Von Seeckt was with the German party in 1942 that recovered the Airlia atomic weapon from inside the Great Pyramid."

Duncan was startled. That information had been close-held. "How did you know that?"

"I have been many places over the years in my travels," Mualama said. "The Giza Plateau I have visited many times. I believe Sir Burton knew something of the black box von Seeckt recovered."

Duncan could see the Nellis Air Force Base hospital coming up quickly as the pilot directed them to the helipad. "Why didn't he let people know?"

"He made a promise. Everything I have discovered, I have done so by tracking his movements and unraveling the riddles he left to get around his promise. The manuscript should yield more information."

Duncan shook her head. "The English and their sense of honor."

"Honor is a good thing," Mualama said. "It might be the most important thing in the path leading to truth."

Duncan was going to say something, but the bouncer touched down on the Nellis hospital helipad. "Let's go."

EASTER ISLAND
D − 9 Hours, 50 Minutes

The sun shone down on Easter Island, revealing a ghastly scene. Several of the clusters of subjects the guardian had gotten from the *Washington* were dead. On orders from the guardian, the mech/biomanipulator checked that by sticking a needle into the bodies. There was no response. But other clusters of subjects were more promising, the bodies obviously still alive, given the cries for help and the struggling against their bonds.

But it was the living clusters that simply lay there that interested the guardian most. The mech/biomanipulator stalked up on steel legs to one group. The imager noted the steady rise and fall of the chests. Eyes were open, but staring up, slightly averted from the sun's rays.

The guardian took the slightly averted eyes as a good sign—it meant the autonomic nervous system was still working properly, taking care of the body. It instructed the mech/biomanipulator to remove the U restraints pinning one group of this type to the ground. The ten men remained motionless, despite the restraints being removed.

Then the guardian accessed a new program, sending out commands.

One by one, the men began to stagger to their feet. One couldn't do it. He collapsed, tried to get up, then the body was still. Two made it to their feet but then crumpled to the ground and rose no more.

The other seven remained standing. With jerky motions they began moving. Over half fell on the first step. Two didn't get up. Within three minutes, all ten were down and dead.

But the guardian had learned much. It issued new instructions to its nanovirus-producing robots.

Caught in the thrall of the alien computer, Kelly Reynolds's mind was still alive, although her body was thoroughly invaded by various nanoviruses. The mind was connected to the guardian via the golden electromagnetic field, and she received information from the computer even as it extracted it from her.

Like a withering vine, she was kept against the side of the pyramid. As her mind received the same images the guardian did of the men of the *Washington* being tested and tossed, a tear rolled down one cheek, the only sign she was alive.

She studied the data as the guardian did. As the guardian spewed out a series of orders to the various nanoviruses that had been implanted, recovering the effective ones, directing the ineffective to be broken down and reconfigured, Kelly focused her mind, mimicking the process by which the guardian had drawn information from her.

The tears on her cheeks mingled with sweat as the extreme effort to get a coherent thought into the proper format strained her to the utmost.

It was a small command, insignificant in the flow of hundreds of thousands of decisions and orders being calculated and sent by the guardian every second. It fell into the stream, a small blip, and raced along the pathways.

NELLIS AIR FORCE BASE, NEVADA
D – 9 Hours, 40 Minutes

Duncan stared down at the old man in the bed for several moments as the drugs did their work and brought him into consciousness.

"You've lied to us all along." Duncan wasted no time on greetings. "Have you ever told the truth?"

"I have told you more truth than you know," von Seeckt said.

"Did you tell me the truth about the Spear of Destiny?"

"Yes."

Duncan wasn't sure whether to believe him or not, but she wanted to get to what she had just learned. "There was more to the SS, wasn't there?" Duncan asked. "A secret rite of passage, wasn't there?"

When von Seeckt didn't respond, Duncan pulled out a piece of paper. "I had your blood analyzed against the blood we drew from the hybrid STAAR personnel. You have traces of the alien blood in you. Tell me how."

"After all these years it is still there?" von Seeckt marveled.

"How did you get it?"

"When I joined the SS, I was given an injection. To purify me, to bring me back to my roots, I was told. You tell me how much I lie—think of that lie that the Nazis perpetrated. Purity of the race, we were told, when in fact the opposite was being attempted.

"In a way, though, most people have never realized what the purity concept was about. Historians have focused on the efforts by the Nazis the eradicate the unpure in the camps, but never much on the efforts to develop the pure.

"Again, List was in on it. He had a partner named Lanz, who was a defrocked Cistercian monk. Lanz's group was called the Order of the New Templars."

"Templars?" Mualama interrupted. "I have heard much of the Templar Knights interwoven with the history of the Ark. The original Templars—"

Duncan kicked Mualama, out of sight of von Seeckt. Getting the archaeologist's attention, she shook her head very slightly. "Tell me about Lanz," she said to von Seeckt.

Von Seeckt's eyes shifted between Duncan and Mualama.

"Answer," Duncan snapped.

"Lanz was from Vienna, the bitch city that eventually gave birth to the Hitler of the Third Reich. Lanz desired to become a Knight Templar, even though that group had officially been disbanded for many centuries. He chose the next best thing—at age nineteen he entered the Cistercian Monastery of the Holy Cross. A year after being in the order he wrote a bizarre paper about a vision he had from the time of the Crusades, of a godly man treading upon an animal-like human being. He believed that vision delineated the pure line of man treading on the unpure.

"After he was kicked out of the monastery for carnal desires, he founded his order. The symbol was the swastika. The slogans: Race fight until the castration knife, and Love thy neighbor as thyself—if he's a member of your own race!

"He bought a castle in lower Austria and flew the swastika flag above it. He believed that his pure beings had electromagnetic-radiological organs and transmitters which gave them special powers."

"Like foo fighters or a guardian computer?" Duncan asked.

Von Seeckt spread his hands. "This is all secondhand knowledge to me. I am repeating what I have read and heard from others. I don't know exactly what Lanz meant by that. Hitler and Lanz first ran into each other in 1909. They met several times after that. Most interestingly, Hitler had Lanz barred from publishing anything after the Nazis took over Austria in 1938. List and Lanz together had a very strong influence on Hitler, something he turned his back on after his rise to power."

"What exact influence did Lanz have on Hitler?" Duncan asked.

"Lanz did what you're trying to do," von Seeckt said. "He looked backward in time. To the origin of mankind, or at least his version of it. He divided early man into two groups. The ace-men and the ape-men. The former, of course, were white, blond, and blue-eyed, and responsible for everything noble and good. The latter was every other racial trait. In German the ace-men were called the *Asings* and the others the *Afflinge*. The *Afflinge* always threatened to contaminate the purity of the *Asings* through interbreeding." Von Seeckt coughed. "The image of the Aryan woman being raped by the impure was one Hitler and his minions used in many posters to rally support to his cause."

"Lanz developed a scorecard by which he could grade candidates for his organization. So many points for eye color, skin, hair, even the size and shape of the skull. It was called the Rassenwertigkeitindex."

Von Seeckt's mouth twisted in an evil smile. "They urged members to breed with women of the same traits, but even then they knew women could not be trusted, Ms. Duncan. Women were the source of all evil."

"Spare me the lecture and give me the facts," Duncan said.

"That is a fact," von Seeckt replied. "That is the way the groups that eventually formed the Nazis felt. It was brought out in the purification rights of the SS."

"How did the SS get the Airlia blood?" Duncan asked.

Von Seeckt shrugged. "I assume from one of those hybrid creatures. What I was injected with was a negligible amount."

"But enough to still be present over fifty years later," Duncan noted. "Does it have anything to do with the fact you are still alive? The doctors can't understand why you haven't succumbed yet to your illnesses."

"Perhaps," von Seeckt admitted. "I don't know. I was very young at the time and—"

"Don't start with the lies again," Duncan warned. "Was The Mission running Hitler?"

"No one ran Hitler," von Seeckt said. "I believe The Mission—through List or Domeka, if you wish to call him that—got Hitler started. But he went too far. Hess was Hitler's partner, the man who shared his prison cell, who helped write *Mein Kampf*. Everything went well for a while, but then Hitler began spinning out of control. When Hess saw what was happening, he flew to England in 1941. No one has ever adequately explained why he did that. I will tell you why. He was looking for The Ones Who Wait. Seeking help in stopping Hitler."

"Why England?" Mualama spoke for the first time. "Why would he seek those alien-human creatures there?"

"I don't know," von Seeckt said. "Hess was a true believer; Hitler an opportunist. They did find a small syringe on Hess when he landed in England," von Seeckt noted. "But nothing more was ever said of it. Perhaps he brought a sample of the blood the SS was using."

"It was reported the syringe held poison, so Hess could kill himself if his mission failed."

Von Seeckt laughed. "No one knows exactly what his mission was, so how could anyone know that? Besides, he obviously didn't kill himself." Von Seeckt shook his head. "It was crazy. Hitler sent an expedition to Tibet to search for the remains of giants who he believed had walked the Earth in ancient times. Herr Hitler, our mighty Führer, listened to his occult advisers who told him the winter of 1941 would be a mild one and he need not equip the troops on the eastern front. History tells us what a fantastic mistake that was. Thousands upon thousands of Germany's finest troops froze to death because of that 'vision.'

"But we fought and we believed. We were trained to. We had *Kadavergehorsam*—cadaver obedience. That is steps beyond what you Americans call blind obedience. I was an SS scientist, but my training was just as difficult. We had to do brutal things to teach us not to feel. To obey without question.

"There was an inner circle to the SS. Twelve officers who met at a monastery in Wevelsburg where Himmler would preside."

"Twelve?" Duncan repeated, thinking of Majestic having the same number. "Were they Guides?"

"I do not know," von Seeckt said. "Probably."

"Was there a guardian in Wevelsburg?"

"I don't think so," von Seeckt said. "People whispered the inner circle met at Wevelsburg, but who knows where they really went. Hitler and the SS spent the war searching, always searching."

"For what?" Duncan asked.

"To find where the true Spear of Destiny went," von Seeckt said. "Hitler knew it was a key. A key to something very powerful. Hitler thought it must be to a weapon. With that weapon, he would rule supreme on the face of the Earth. Ah . . ." Von Seeckt sighed. "But he never found where the Spear went."

"I will ask you one more time," Duncan said. "Have you told me all you know about the Spear?"

"Yes."

"You believe it is in Russia?"

"Yes."

"Let's go," Duncan said to Mualama.

"Where are you off to?" von Seeckt asked.

"That need not concern you." Duncan paused at the door. "One last question. You stopped the mothership flight because you worked for The Mission. Even they couldn't allow the ship's drive to be detected. Isn't that so?"

Von Seeckt nodded. "I worked for The Mission as a young man. The mothership not flying was the one, absolute rule."

"So there is a danger out there in space," Duncan said.

"So it is written, and so it has been passed down even among The Mission."

CHAPTER 19

As the clock ticked through nine hours, the blue line representing the talon intersected with *Stratzyda*'s red line on the master board at the front of the Cube. Major Quinn and Kincaid watched from the rear of the room, hoping that each would continue on its same trajectory.

"How long?" Quinn asked Kincaid.

"We'll know in about a minute," the JPL man answered.

There was silence in the room as every eye watched the screen that relayed data from Space Command buried deep under Cheyenne Mountain on the other side of the Rocky Mountains from Area 51.

The screen blacked out for a quarter of a second as a new update was posted.

Both lines moved a fraction of an inch adjacent to each other to the east.

The dotted line indicating *Stratzyda*'s normal orbit disappeared.

"Ah, hell," Kincaid muttered.

CHAPTER 20

VICINITY OF EASTER ISLAND
D – 8 Hours, 30 Minutes

Captain Halls had skirted the American fleet, running to the west of where he guessed it was. He'd maintained radio listening silence the whole way in, but nothing seemed to have changed regarding UNAOC's stance toward the island or its status.

He knew the Americans might pick him up on radar, but his hope was that he could get close enough to let these lunatics overboard in their rubber zodiacs and then run for home before they sent someone to investigate.

But so far there hadn't been any sign of the Americans and Easter Island was directly ahead. At least he assumed it was. All he could see out the front of his bridge in the early-morning light was a dark hemisphere on the ocean's surface.

"Doesn't look like they want visitors," Halls said.

"We will be accepted," Parker said.

A roar overheard startled both of them. An F-14 banked and came around for another run.

"They will not stop us," Parker said.

Halls watched the plane race by, the pilot wiggling his wings.

"I think he wants to talk to us," Halls said. He started for the radio room, when Parker put an arm out, blocking him.

"No. We will not be interfered with." He pointed at the circling jet. "These are the people who attacked the Airlia. Who killed Aspasia. We will not talk to them!"

"Then I suggest you get your people in gear and get

overboard," Halls said. "That plane has got a radio, and I'm sure they're calling someone."

Parker left the bridge without a backward glance. Halls watched the progressives climb into their zodiacs, sixteen to a boat. The small convoy circled the *Southern Star* until all were launched. Then the ten boats headed directly for the black shield. The F-14 came low between them and the island, the pilot almost touching the wave tops, but they went on.

"Turn on the radio," Captain Halls ordered his first mate. "Put it on the speaker."

There was a crackle of static. Then a voice came on, speaking urgently.

"Unidentified ship, this is the USS *Thorn,* representing the United Nations blockade of Easter Island. You are to turn on a heading of nine zero degrees immediately."

Halls reached down and picked up the microphone on the wall in front of him. "This is the *Island Breeze*. We will assume a heading of nine zero degrees."

The voice lost its officialness. "Who am I talking to?"

"This is Captain Halls of the *Island Breeze*. I am complying with your orders."

"Captain, this is Captain Norris. We've been trying to raise you for the past thirty minutes. Who the hell are in the small boats our pilot sees heading toward the island?"

"I am not responsible for them," Halls said. "They're a bunch of progressives going to greet their almighty computer."

"Good God, man, you have no idea what's going on and neither do they. You have to stop them right away!"

"They're not my responsibility."

"By the law of the high seas, they were passengers on your ship, and you're abandoning them in harm's way," Captain Norris retorted.

"What's the big deal?" Halls wanted to know. He looked ahead. The first zodiacs were within half a kilometer of the shield. "They're just going to hit that shield, bounce off, and come on back. They . . ." Halls paused, his hand still on the send as something came out of the shield. "What the devil is that?"

It looked like a black cloud, but it kept shifting in shape very quickly, as if it were alive.

"Full speed, hard port," Halls ordered. The nose of his ship very slowly swung in the direction of the zodiacs. Halls could see Parker standing up in the lead boat, hands in the air, as if supplicating the dark cloud.

The F-14 banked hard away from the shield. That made Halls think. "Full astern," he yelled into the tube leading to the engine room. "Hard starboard," to the helmsman.

"I'd get out of there!" Captain Norris confirmed his decision over the radio.

"What's going on?" Halls demanded.

"I don't know," Norris said, "but whatever is on that island took down the *George Washington*."

Halls swallowed. He'd seen the *Washington* one time in Sydney Harbor. He knew there was no comparing his ship to the carrier.

The black cloud descended onto the boats, swarming over the people inside. As his ship ponderously turned away, Captain Halls watched the people in the zodiacs collapse and flail about.

"Get us out of here, Helm," Halls said, even though he knew the ship was moving as quickly as possible.

But then the people in the first boat began resuming their positions. Halls pulled up his binoculars. He trained them on that zodiac. Parker was standing once again. The man was looking directly back at the *Island Breeze*. His body was twitching, but the eyes were steady, glowing with the same insane light Halls had been witness to the entire voyage. But something was different. Halls twisted the focus on the glasses, then his fingers froze on the knobs. The skin of Parker's face was rippling, as if there were something alive just under the surface. Halls shifted to the other people in the boat—all had the same thing happening to them. One of the women stood up, her hands ripping at her own face, blood flowing through her fingers, her mouth contorted in a scream Halls could not hear. She staggered to her feet, then fell overboard.

In another boat, a man was pounding his chest, screaming. He flopped back, his legs drumming against the floorboards of the zodiac. Then he was still.

The black cloud was gone, but Halls could see that the rubber pontoons of the zodiacs were covered with a black film that was moving on its own in surges.

Halls went back to the lead boat. Parker's mouth moved; he was yelling something to the people in his boat and the other zodiacs nearby. Halls lowered the glasses. Two of the zodiacs turned and headed for the *Island Breeze,* throttles wide open, the boats planing out. The others continued toward the shield wall.

"More speed!" Halls yelled into the tube to engineering.

Halls knew the zodiacs could catch his slow-moving freighter. He focused on the lead boat chasing him. A man was standing in the prow. As Halls watched, the movement under the man's skin stopped. The man's face twitched in a wide smile that was not pleasant at all.

The two zodiacs had already halved the distance to the *Island Breeze*. Halls knew there was no way he was going to escape.

The F-14 Tomcat came in so low that Halls thought it clipped his mast. There was a line of smoke on the left side, and Halls could hear the whine of a high-speed gun firing.

The 20mm bullets hit the surface in a column of water spouts until they struck the lead zodiac. The milk-bottle-size bullets made short work of both the rubber boat and the people in it. The F-14 climbed and turned.

Halls pulled his binoculars up. The second zodiac had not wavered in the slightest, completely ignoring the fate of its partner. It was less than three hundred meters from the *Island Breeze* and still closing. Each of the people on board was totally focused directly ahead at the ship, their faces blank of expression.

The Tomcat came in from the left this time and ripped the boat to shreds. Halls saw one of the people take a direct hit from the 20mm round, the upper chest completely disintegrating and the body flying forty feet before landing in the water.

The Navy jet made two more runs, bullets churning up the sea where both boats had gone down.

"Goddamn," Halls exclaimed, watching the merciless strafing.

The radio crackled to life. "This is Captain Norris. You are to maintain a heading of nine zero degrees until in sight of my ship. At that time you will be prepared to be boarded. Is that clear?"

"Perfectly clear," Halls replied.

MOSCOW
D – 8 Hours, 30 Minutes

"This is not good," Yakov said.

Mike Turcotte stared at the pile of fresh rubble that blocked the tunnel in front of them and didn't have the energy to respond to that most brilliant observation. They had gone about a quarter mile from the scene of their fight with Katyenka, the tunnel slowly bending to the left and still descending. They had not passed a single door or side passageway in the time it had taken them to traverse that distance to the other blockage Pasha had initiated. They had already dug through one pile of rubble, eating up precious time. Now here was a second.

Instead of answering, he grabbed a block of concrete, picked it up and carried it about twenty feet back the way they had come, and dropped it. He returned to the blockage and picked up a second piece. By the time he dropped it, Yakov had picked up a hunk of rubble and joined him.

They worked in silence and in a small dust cloud for an hour, slowly making their way farther down the corridor. Finally, Turcotte sat down and took a break, Yakov joining him. The Russian pulled his always-ready flask out of a pocket and offered it to Turcotte, who shook his head.

"Did you suspect Katyenka was one of The Ones Who Wait?" Turcotte asked.

Yakov sighed, then answered. "If I had suspected, I would never have allowed her that close, and certainly never allowed her to, how do you say, get the drop on us back there."

"Then my next question is, why didn't you suspect her?" Turcotte rubbed some dirt off his forehead. "You're the one that's been lecturing me all along to trust no one."

Yakov was silent for a long time before answering. "She seduced me." He forestalled Turcotte by speaking with a wave of his hand. "Not so much with the body— although she did do that, but here." Yakov thumped his hand on his chest. "I have spent so many years doing this, traveling all over the world. I thought I was a man with no heart, but every man has a heart. I realize now I was hard on you about Dr. Duncan, because in my own mind I knew I was being foolish with Katyenka, allowing her too close. But I could not admit it to myself. It is an old Russian saying that when something another person is doing bothers you, look to yourself. Because I did not, here we are, trapped."

Turcotte stood. "Let's get untrapped."

Colonel Tolya's patience was running out. His patrol of twenty commandos was gathered behind him as he kneeled next to the engineer lieutenant, trying to make sense of the various plans unrolled before them on the tunnel floor. The earth underneath Moscow was a warren of tunnels, shafts, and man-made caverns burrowed out over decades of Cold War survivalism.

"Which way?" Tolya asked for the third time since they'd halted. The dot had not moved except in relation to their moves. But it seemed as if every time they got close, they had to take another tunnel that took them farther away.

Sweat dripped off the lieutenant's chin—even though it was cool in the tunnel—and splashed onto the top map. "Sir, I think we need to backtrack to the last intersection. I believe we should have taken a right there, not a left."

"You 'believe'?" Tolya checked his watch. Katyenka had instructed him to be no more than five minutes behind, and he had been close behind the walls outside the Kremlin to her group entering the tunnel. He had a feeling things had not worked out the way Katyenka had planned.

Tolya reined in his anger. He pointed back the way they had come. "Let's go."

AIRBORNE
D – 8 Hours

"What were you going to say about the Knights Templar?" Duncan asked. The bouncer was at 40,000 feet altitude, moving swiftly west to east, already over the Atlantic, approaching Africa.

Professor Mualama had been unusually silent as they left the hospital at Nellis Air Force Base and boarded the bouncer for the trip to Egypt. Duncan had not interfered with that silence, as she was also trying to sort out the information von Seeckt had given them. Quinn had informed her that Turcotte was not answering his SATPhone, which was further unsettling news.

Mualama stretched his long legs out in front of him. "I think the answer to that lies in Burton's manuscript. We are searching for pieces just as he did over a century ago. He dedicated a lifetime to it."

"What pieces?" Duncan asked.

"Pieces of legend and myth that are something else entirely. I think Burton discovered how many of the pieces ended up where they currently are. Learning that will tell us something of where they came from, which will tell us, perhaps, how they should be put together, which, in the end, I believe will be the most important thing."

Duncan followed that line of reasoning to an extent. "Why did Burton make such a secret of what he was doing?"

"He made a promise not to reveal something he had learned. Also, you have to remember there was no urgency to his revealing the truth. The world seemed unaffected by the aliens or their followers during his day."

"Lucky him," Duncan said. "Let's hope we do a better job than our predecessors, because we don't have much more time."

AREA 51
D – 7 Hours

Captain Billam had a map of the world spread out in front of him on top of the conference table located just off the Cube.

"Big operational area," his team sergeant, Greg Boltz, noted.

"We can make it smaller," Billam said.

"How?" Major Quinn had just walked in the door along with the bouncer pilot, Major Remmick.

"Duncan is going to Cairo and Turcotte is in Moscow." Billam placed a finger on each location. He turned to Major Remmick. "How long can you hover?"

"If I let go of the controls," Remmick said, "we remain stationary until I touch the controls again. So we can 'hover,' as you put it, forever."

Billam slid his two fingers together. "If we stay here, over the Black Sea, we'll be halfway between Duncan and Turcotte and a hell of a lot closer than we are now." He looked up at Quinn for approval.

"Get moving," Quinn ordered. He held up his hand as they headed for the elevator to Hangar One. "Two things. I've got your SADM waiting up there for you. And I put it in a rather interesting package."

NGORONGORO CRATER
D – 6 Hours, 30 Minutes

The two bodies were fully formed inside the clear tubes filled with an amber liquid. Lexina recognized the figures, even though both heads were covered with a black helmet from which numerous leads extended through the top of the tube to the console in front.

She had watched Coridan and Gergor, comrades for many years, die just hours before. And now she was watching the completion of the rebirth of their bodies. There was only one more step and it would be done.

Lexina took out the two Ka necklaces she had removed from around her comrades' necks. Going in front of Coridan's tube, she slid the two upraised hands into a receptacle on the console. They fit perfectly. A golden glow suffused the panel as the memories and personality encoded on the Ka were sent to the blank mind that waited under the black helmet.

Lacking, of course, were the memories the two men had accumulated since the last time the Ka were updated. And even the original programming had degraded over generations of use as bodies wore out and new operatives were needed. Lexina herself knew there were gaps in her own mind, things she should know and didn't. Skills she should have—that generations of Lexinas back to the beginning of The Ones Who Wait had had—that were no longer present.

After several minutes, the glow went away. The amber fluid drained out of the tube. Lexina opened it and removed the helmet from the body, cradling the new Coridan in her arms as she took him out and laid him on the floor.

Coridan gasped for air, the eyes flickering open.

"Welcome back, old friend," Lexina greeted him.

VICINITY OF EASTER ISLAND
D – 6 Hours, 30 Minutes

The USS *Anzio* was a *Ticonderoga*-class guided missile cruiser. It cost over one billion dollars to build, and its primary purpose was to be a carrier battle group's primary defense against air attack. Its job was to defend the battle group's aircraft carrier at all costs—a job that, it could be argued, it had failed in, given that the *Washington* was lost.

That fact did little to improve the morale or temper of the crew. That no one could have guessed the returning Global Hawk was the threat it had turned out to be did little to assuage that feeling. The presence on board of more than eight hundred survivors of the *Washington* not only crowded the ship, it added to the burning desire for revenge.

The *Anzio* had already earned a battle star in the war against the Airlia by dropping the nuclear weapon that had—they thought—destroyed the foo fighter base north of Easter Island.

When the message came in, via high-frequency radio from Pearl Harbor, for it to prepare a nuclear weapon to be fired against Easter Island, the initial feeling among the crew was one of anticipation. But when the fact that almost two thousand members of the crew of the *Washington* were missing behind the black shield they were now ordered to penetrate and destroy, sunk in, the mood became more somber.

As they had against the foo fighters' base, the weapons specialists on board the ship opened up one of their BGM-109 Tomahawk cruise missiles and began disabling the electronic guidance equipment.

The captain of the *Anzio* also sent a message to the long-suffering crew of the *Springfield* to prepare for action.

In response to the command she had slipped into the system, the microscopic machines that had thoroughly infiltrated Kelly Reynolds's body began to leave, traveling through her bloodstream and out the needle that had been inserted in her neck by the guardian.

When the last one departed, the part that was still Kelly Reynolds was now larger and stronger than it had been since she'd come down into the chamber deep under Rano Kau. She still had the mental link via the golden tendril coming out of the guardian itself, but that was weaker than before, because the alien computer had relied on the nanovirus to a great extent after infecting her with it.

With her small degree of freedom, Kelly now tried something new.

CHAPTER 21

Not once had Turcotte or Yakov discussed the possibility that the blockage might extend farther than they could dig. In a strange way, that felt good to Turcotte, reminding him of his classmates at Ranger and Special Forces schools, where he'd worked with the other students on difficult tasks without having to chat about it or discuss the impossibility of the obstacles before them. In such situations talk was wasted energy and time.

Turcotte knew that they were getting closer to the deadline with each passing minute, but he had long before learned to focus his mind on the most immediate task at hand. He was doing everything he could right now. His training and his experience had taught him to avoid panic by taking things one step at a time.

His hands were bleeding from the concrete and stone he'd been lifting and carrying, the pain past the point of sharpness, into a numb, pounding ache. As he headed into the narrow opening they had excavated, Yakov slid out, tumbling large chunks of concrete with him. Turcotte slithered past, along the fifteen-foot-long dig. Several times concrete beneath him moved, which highlighted the possibility that blocks above might collapse. It was dark when he reached the end and he worked by feel, carefully discerning the size of a piece of rubble with his hands, then slowly pulling it out.

Turcotte knew his limits, and he had a very good idea how far past those limits he could push his body. He estimated being able to work about three more hours before having to rest. Then the next work segment would be more difficult to begin because of aching muscles and scabbed-over wounds. And shorter because of less energy. The largest concern he had was lack of water. Taking it one step past how long he estimated he could work, Turcotte figured he and Yakov had about two days of life if they didn't break through.

Checking his watch, he realized that was about five or so hours more than everyone in the United States had if he did not find the key.

CAIRO, EGYPT
D – 5 Hours, 30 Minutes

Duncan and Mualama's arrival in Cairo was not as inconspicuous as they would have liked. Thousands mobbed the edge of the airfield where the bouncer came in for its landing, eager to see the alien craft on its first visit to Cairo despite the early hour. Duncan would have preferred landing directly at the Sphinx site, but the Egyptians had refused them permission to do that and directed they arrive at the airfield.

Duncan had no idea how word of the visit had been leaked, but she had to assume that it had occurred somewhere in UNAOC. The two quickly disembarked, eager to move to the Giza Plateau. The head of Egypt's Supreme Council of Antiquities (SCA) was waiting for them with a car, looking none too happy. Mualama had told her that he had met Dr. Hassar before, at archaeological seminars, but he had never really talked to the man. Hassar's first words to them were not positive.

"Get in the car, quickly," Hassar snapped, holding the door open and looking at the crowd anxiously.

Duncan and Mualama scooted in, followed by Hassar, who barked at the driver in Arabic to go. As the car headed for the airfield gates, Mualama stuck out his hand. "I am pleased to be here, Dr. Hassar."

Hassar ignored the hand; his attention was focused outside the thick window. He rapped a knuckle against the glass. "Bulletproof. I had to call in a favor from a friend of mine in the Foreign Ministry to get this car." Hassar pointed at the crowds. "They are not all here because of the bouncer. Word has slipped out that you want to attempt to go under the Sphinx. There are many who oppose doing that."

Based on what Mualama had told her, Duncan had known they would be flying into a hornet's nest. The SCA had long resisted all attempts by archaeologists to do any work around the Sphinx. Egypt also had a very bad reputation with regard to foreigners, women in particular. The Muslim fundamentalists believed so strongly in fighting the inroads of what they considered decadent Western culture that attacks on tourists were not uncommon.

Duncan decided to cut to the heart of the matter. "Do you oppose it?" she asked.

Hassar seemed surprised at the directness of the question and the source. "Yes, I do. But not because I believe it is sacrilegious or I despise foreigners, as the fundamentalists do."

"Why, then?" Duncan asked.

"Because it is a waste of time."

Mualama leaned forward in the seat. "There are open spaces under the Sphinx. That has been proven through various seismic readings."

"Yes, I know," Hassar conceded. "A Japanese team using ground-penetrating radar found a hollow to the south of the Sphinx. Not a large one, mind you. Readings indicated a space just a few meters across."

"And they found a similar hollow on the north side of the Sphinx," Mualama added. "Which indicated there might be a tunnel going completely under the entire structure."

"Doubtful," Hassar said.

"I am more interested in what lies near the paws," Mualama said.

"The altar found between the paws was added later. By the Romans. You know that."

"I believe the Hall of Records lies *under* the paws," Mualama said.

Hassar sighed. "The Hall of Records? Cayce's 'visions'? The ramblings of a madman."

"There may be more to his theories than scientists like us would like to admit," Mualama said.

"Ahh!" Hassar slapped his forehead in disgust.

Mualama knew where the other man's reactions came from, but his own wanderings and studies over the years had forced him to reevaluate many preconceived notions. The name Cayce had come up numerous times during Mualama's studies, always quickly discredited by scholars and scientists. Edgar Cayce was an American, born in Kentucky in the late nineteenth century, who died in the last year of World War II. He was considered one of the world's greatest psychics—that thought brought a smile to Mualama's lips—if one believed in psychics.

"Cayce was a great believer in the myth of Atlantis," Mualama said. "And now we know that Atlantis did exist."

"There is not yet any empirical proof that Atlantis existed," Hassar argued.

"We have the word of Professor Nabinger," Mualama said. "And the stones off Bimini. And the history of the Airlia."

"Nabinger was corrupted by the guardian," Hassar said firmly. "Why are you willing to believe Nabinger, yet UNAOC is putting the surviving members of Majestic on trial? Both were in contact with the guardian, were they not? Do you simply prefer what you heard from Nabinger?"

They had passed the outskirts of Cairo and the three great pyramids were in sight across the Nile, the Sphinx crouched in front between the pyramids and the river.

Mualama was incredulous. "How do you explain the mothership, then? The bouncers? The Airlia on Mars?"

"I don't have to explain them, and I don't have to believe that there was an island of Atlantis." Hassar stabbed his finger into Mualama's chest. "I have had those people pestering me for years to dig under the Sphinx."

"What people?"

"An organization that honors Cayce and thinks he was a true—a true—" Hassar sputtered, searching for a word, then gave up. "I have responsibilities. This entire Plateau"—he waved his hand out the window as they passed the first pyramid on the right—"is in my care.

"Do you know how much damage pollution from Cairo causes on the stones? Do you know how many people come here with their crackpot ideas about the pyramids and the Sphinx? And want to run tests? I have people who want to hold religious—or what they call religious—services inside the Great Pyramid. I've had actual requests from people who want to commit suicide at the very top—they believe that they will pass on from there directly to a better life!"

He turned to Duncan. "Like your Heaven's Gate people, there are many who believe they can transport themselves to a better life, and many think the pyramids or the Sphinx are their gateway. It has gotten much worse in the past month."

Mualama spread his hands to calm the other man down. "But Cayce was right about some things that you now know are true. He was right about another room under the Great Pyramid. The one the Germans found in World War II with the bomb in it. And was redis-covered later by Edmunds. You've been in there! And Cayce told of that room long before the Germans found it."

Hassar wasn't willing to give away anything. "A good guess. There were others who speculated that there was more under the Great Pyramid than had been found. It was an easy prophecy to make. What about all the other prophecies of Cayce that have not come true?"

Mualama didn't answer that question. "I believe there is more under the Sphinx than has been found."

The car came to a halt. The Great Sphinx looked down on them, the aged and beaten face lit by spotlights.

The stepped out of the car. It was relatively quiet, the tourists long gone, the sound of the city a murmur. Duncan felt her inner soul stir under the gaze of the Sphinx as she thought of the generations of humans who had passed in front of it and as she tried to imagine who had built it and why, so many thousands of years ago.

"Let me make one thing perfectly clear," Hassar in-terrupted Duncan's reverie. "I did not agree with my government's initial decision to cooperate with UNAOC. I did not agree that you two should be allowed to come here."

Duncan looked at this man who had been in charge of perhaps the world's greatest archaeological sites for de-cades. Who had done nothing in all those years to fur-ther man's understanding of his own past. She wondered what would have happened if Hassar had found evidence of the Airlia on the Plateau before the debacle at Area 51. She realized he would have most likely been ridi-culed, branded a fool.

"Why do you not agree?" Mualama asked.

"Because it is dangerous," Hassar said. "You know what happened at the Valley of the Kings several years ago to that tourist group. The fundamentalists here do much more than talk. They shoot."

"Fear is never a good reason to not act," Mualama said.

"You are a scientist first," Hassar said. "You do not understand."

"What do you mean?"

Hassar stared at the other man as if he were crazy. "This alien thing. The Airlia. It affects people. Each in their own way. You are excited because it brings the past to life and proves things you long believed. But very few people are archaeologists or anthropologists, and very few people care about the future or the past. They care about their lives in the here and now. The things that are important to them in their little world.

"And it is through that prism that they see the Airlia." Hassar pointed up. "It is with that perception that they look at the mothership overhead. But there are many who won't look. Who refuse to believe."

Mualama and Duncan remained silent, listening to the Egyptian official.

"Religion." Hassar drew the word out. "Do you know how the world's various organized faiths have reacted to the events of the past month? To the proof that there is life —at least was life—on other planets? That our planet had an alien outpost on it over ten thousand years ago? That aliens were here on Earth before Christ, before Mohammed, before Buddha?"

Duncan had a good idea of what Hassar was talking about, but Mualama had not followed the news much on his travels around the world, nor had there been much opportunity once he was there to keep up on current events. "No, I don't," he said.

"It is not just the recognized organized religions," Hassar said. "I mentioned Heaven's Gate—those people killed themselves to get on a spaceship they believed was

in the tail of a comet. Now we have real spaceships! Do
you know how many people have committed suicide
around the world in the last several weeks? There are so
many new cults. Yesterday I was reading about one
formed around the alien base on Mars that worships the
'Face' at the Cydonia site.

"And then there are those who are afraid. They fear
the unknown. They fear retribution for the destruction
of the Airlia fleet. Rome is in turmoil. The Pope issued a
statement that said nothing with many words, as that
office is prone to do. Do you know what this does to
their center-out view of the universe? What of the Airlia? If God exists, then he had to have made them too.
Did they have a Son of God visit them to spread the
good word? Did they have a prophet like Mohammed to
show them the true path? How does all that fit in?
Where do we humans fit in, then? What happens to our
relationship with God?

"There are some who believe the appearance of the
Airlia to be the second coming of the Christian God-
child." Hassar forced himself to calm down. "Rest assured, Dr. Duncan and Professor Mualama, that *those*
people are not thrilled that UNAOC killed Aspasia.
They are the driving force behind progressive groups in
numerous countries.

"But Catholics are not a great concern here. Islam is
the religion that rules in this part of the world." Hassar
reached out and put his hand on Mualama's shoulder.
He pulled him over to a stone just in front of one of the
large paws and they sat down, Duncan following. "I will
tell you how the Airlia fits in according to Islam.

"As the Catholics have their angels and demons, Islam, according to the Koran, has its own version of
other-than-human creatures: Al-Malak and Al-Jinn. Al-
Malak are the beings of light. Al-Jinn are those who
were created before man. It is written in the Koran that

Mohammed, Allah be praised, was sent to be a messenger to both man and the Al-Jinn."

Mualama stirred impatiently, the closeness of the Sphinx and the weight of the scepter in his pack pressing on him. "Every Holy Book has writings of other beings," Mualama said. "Angels and demons and devils."

"True," Hassar acknowledged, "but Muslims are the true believers. Their religion comes first in all things. The word of the Koran is law. And either way, this does not bode well."

"Either way?" Mualama knew that Hassar's perception was slanted a certain way because he was a Muslim.

"If a Muslim chooses to interpret that Airlia are the Al-Malak, then they are angels and UNAOC has struck against the beings of God. If the Airlia are Al-Jinn, that means they are the devil—but the Koran says even the Al-Jinn can be saved. The leader of the Al-Jinn is named Al-Iblis, but he is also described in places as being an angel or a demon."

"Dr. Hassar," Duncan began, "perhaps if—"

"I have heard Professor Mualama speak," Hassar cut her off. "At the Pan-African Conference last year. Your topic was the power of myths and legends. Don't you understand? What is happening here in Egypt is happening everywhere in the world. Angels or demons. Progressive or isolationist." Hassar slapped the ancient stone they were sitting on. "This is not some intellectual pursuit you are talking about. Ah!" Hassar threw his hands into the air. "What you see so clearly with your own perspective, others see very differently."

"UNAOC has gotten approval from your government for us to look," Duncan said.

"UNAOC *had* permission," Hassar corrected her. "Do you know that Sterling was killed in New York? Shot?"

Duncan nodded. She wondered on the flight here

which alien group had been behind the killing or if it had been the work of human fanatics.

"There have been other killings around the world," Hassar said. "This has made my government reconsider. Your request has been put in abeyance."

"What does that mean?" Duncan asked.

Hassar shrugged. "That means I stick it on the stack of hundreds of other similar requests that will never be granted."

"We came here in good faith—" Duncan began, but the Egyptian cut her off.

"And I met you in good faith. I am trying to be reasonable. You are poking a stick into a nest of angry scorpions for no reason."

"There is a reason," Duncan said. "Why do you say there isn't?"

"Because you are risking much for nothing. There is *nothing* under the Sphinx." Hassar pulled a photo out of the inside of his jacket and handed it to Mualama. Duncan leaned over to see.

It was a faded black-and-white image. Two men, pith hats guarding them against the harsh sun, stood just to the left of the spot Mualama and Hassar were currently occupying.

"This was taken in 1922," Hassar said.

"And?"

Hassar pointed to the right paw. "They opened the door you want to open between the paws. And found an empty room."

"I will hire a local crew to help move the stone." Mualama handed the picture back.

"Please." Hassar gripped Mualama's forearm. "Please do not do this."

"I have to." He placed his large black hand over the other man's. "I will respect the Sphinx. But I must look."

Mualama reached into his pack and pulled out the scepter. He tilted it in front of Hassar, the ruby eyes glinting.

Despite himself, Hassar was interested. "What is that?"

"A key," Mualama answered.

Hassar took it out of Mualama's hands. He turned it, feeling the weight. "Where did you find it?"

"Ngorongoro Crater."

"Ngorongoro," Hassar mused. "The Garden of Eden, so some say. Just lying there on the ground?"

"No."

Hassar waited.

"It was in a coffin. There was a marker above the coffin. The marker directed me here."

"Who was in the coffin?" Hassar asked.

"An Airlia body." Mualama took the scepter back.

Hassar sighed and looked out toward the Nile. Duncan could well imagine the conflicting feelings the Egyptologist was experiencing. His entire life had been dedicated to promoting Egypt's past, and in the past month all the supposedly known "facts" had been tossed on their ear.

"Was a spear found here?" Duncan asked.

Hassar frowned. "Excuse me?"

"During World War Two. Was a spear found in the Great Pyramid?"

"No."

"Where is Kaji?" Duncan asked.

"I know no one named Kaji." Hassar stood. "As I told you. You do not have permission to do anything in this area."

"We will not leave," Mualama countered.

"You touch any stone, dig anywhere on this Plateau," Hassar said, "and I will not be held accountable for the results. You have been warned."

MARS
D – 5 Hours

The steel claw flashed down, spearing through the Martian soil, and struck something solid that wasn't rock. All the mechrobots came to a halt as the information was relayed back to the control center underground.

New commands were sent and the mechrobots began to dig more carefully, scraping away the soil. Soon black metal was exposed to the light of the distant sun for the first time in many millennia. The edges of the metal that met the light were twisted and scarred from some terrible force.

Inch by inch, foot by foot, more of the wreckage was uncovered.

MOSCOW
D – 5 Hours

Turcotte's fingers scrambled, trying to get a grip on a small piece of concrete, when the block fell *away* from him, out of his reach. He had to think for a second through his exhaustion to realize what that meant. He pushed himself forward, ignoring the sharp edges that dug into his stomach, and peered. There was only darkness. He reached out, hands probing.

His left hand went as far it could reach and touched nothing. He held his breath and cocked his head. Very faintly he could feel air flowing over the skin on his face.

"We're through!" he yelled back to Yakov. "Come on!" Turcotte pushed himself forward and tumbled free, into the undamaged tunnel beyond the blockage.

Behind him, Yakov heard the yell. He squirmed into the tunnel to follow the American. As he got near the end, the going got much tighter. The only other time Yakov had wished he were smaller was when he had been caught in an ambush in Afghanistan. He pushed his wide shoulders through the narrow opening, hearing cloth rip. He exhaled, making his rib cage as small as possible, and held his breath. He pushed with his legs and fell free.

As Turcotte grabbed him, the top of the tunnel they had created imploded, leaving them in pitch black.

"The power line to the lights must have been cut," Yakov said.

"You think?" Turcotte's voice held an edge of sarcasm. "And, of course, we didn't bring a flashlight. The Boy Scouts would not have given us a merit badge for this exercise."

"Speak for yourself," Yakov said. A glow of light came out of the penlight in the Russian's hand, as bright to the two men as if it were a searchlight. "Let's go." Yakov strode off down the tunnel, Turcotte close behind.

After ten minutes, they had to make their first decision. The corridor split at a Y intersection. Yakov shone his light down each. The left fork was narrower and went down; the right stayed the same size and level.

"Well?" Turcotte asked.

"Flip a coin?" Yakov suggested.

"I say we go left. Seems like lower would be where the Archives are."

"Makes sense," Yakov agreed, and he bent over so he could fit in the five-and-a-half-foot-high tunnel.

As they went down, Yakov suddenly paused. There was a noise to his left. He shined the light in that direction. Several sets of eyes gleamed back at him. He cursed.

"Rats," he warned Turcotte.

Turcotte noted something else. "Check out the walls."

Yakov pointed the penlight. The walls were no longer concrete, but iron. Swinging the light around, Yakov showed that they were now in an iron pipe, five and a half feet in circumference. Streaks of rust circled about them, and the air was growing fetid.

"We might be in the drainage system," Yakov suggested.

"Let's keep going."

"Maybe we should take the other—" Yakov paused as a groaning noise came from beneath their feet. Both men looked down as Yakov pointed the light that way.

"Oh, crap," Turcotte muttered as cracks in the iron radiated out from under Yakov's feet and down the pipe faster than his eye could track. He looked for something to grab on to, found nothing, then the pipe gave way beneath him.

He slammed onto metal curved underneath him—another pipe, but this one was angled—and before he could slow his momentum, Turcotte was sliding after Yakov, going faster and faster as the pipe angled closer to the vertical.

Colonel Tolya cursed. He had been less than two hundred meters from the bug when it had begun moving. As he watched, the glowing dot moved horizontally and at an incredible pace vertically, dropping down on the screen so fast that Tolya had to quickly adjust the scale to keep the dot from disappearing.

"We need to go down, very far down," Tolya told the engineer as he watched the screen, wondering how the others could be moving so quickly.

He wished he could call in more help, but he was uncertain how much more loyalty he could buy. Everything was for sale in Russia, and using the money Katyenka had given him, he had hired these men from among the contingent that guarded GRU headquarters in Moscow.

The other problem he had was lack of communications. FM radio didn't work in these tunnels, so for all he knew the ones he sought might have even escaped, but he doubted that. Either Katyenka had dealt with things and no longer needed him, or she'd failed and no longer needed him. Regardless, Tolya's task was to find the Archives and kill anyone else who found them.

CHAPTER 22

At the Grumman plant in Calverton, California, an F-14 Tomcat took six months to make it from the beginning of the assembly line to the end. The micro- and nanorobots on Easter Island reversed that process in two hours. They carried the pieces of the airplane off the wreck of the *George Washington* and laid them out on the tarmac of the Easter Island airfield.

The guardian integrated information it had gathered over the Department of Defense Interlink and the objects lying on the concrete runway. Two parts of the plane especially interested it right now: the AN/APG-71 radar and the AIM-54 Phoenix missiles that had been attached under the wings.

The guardian examined both objects, then gave orders. A cluster of microrobots swarmed over both, breaking them down into portable pieces, then trekked up the side of Rano Kau to the highest point. Then, just as quickly, they put it all back together with some minor modifications.

The AN/APG-71 radar was placed on a tripod. A line to power the radar was run from the thermal coupling underneath the volcano. An antenna for the radar was constructed in fifteen minutes nearby, mounted on a rotating base.

With five kilowatts of juice surging through it, the radar system came alive, reaching out over seven hundred kilometers. It picked up the lurking fleet, located well over the visual horizon three hundred kilometers off-shore.

The AIM-54 Phoenixes were mounted on racks, pointed out to sea. The Phoenix was the navy's top-of-the-line weapon, costing over a million dollars apiece. Its range was over a hundred kilometers, with an onboard computer that allowed it to obtain and lock on to fast-moving targets. A link was established between the system and the guardian computer and all was set.

Below the shadow of Rano Kau, more people were moving about, the survival rate growing higher as the guardian continually adjusted its microvirus to control their nervous system.

MOSCOW
D − 4 Hours, 58 Minutes

Turcotte pulled himself to a sitting position. "Yakov?" His voice echoed, indicating he was in a large open space. "Yakov?" The ride in the tube had gone on for an extremely long time, then he had suddenly fallen into space, dropped at least ten feet, and landed on a solid floor that had knocked the wind out of him.

"Yes, yes." The Russian's rumbling voice came from somewhere to the left.

"Do you have the light?"

"I dropped it when I fell out of that tube," Yakov said. "It should be somewhere close by."

Turcotte reached down and felt the ground beneath— pitted concrete that was slightly damp. He stretched his arms out, testing to see if everything worked properly. He felt bruised but not broken. The muzzle of the AKSU had caused the most damage, digging into his left side and leaving a bloody gouge and sore rib in its wake. He edged toward Yakov's voice, carefully checking the surface in front of him. He had no idea how deep they were, but they had slid for a long time.

"I've got it," Yakov suddenly announced. "Damn bulb is broken. There is another in the handle. Wait."

When the penlight came on, it speared through the dark. Turcotte followed the light as Yakov slowly swept it in a circle around them. They were on a rough concrete floor—check that, Turcotte realized as the light halted on a massive spring to his right running up into the darkness above, he was on the concrete roof of a bunker. Turcotte knew that such shelters were hung on huge springs and placed on shock absorbers, in the hope that whatever was inside could sustain a nuclear blast this far underground. Looking up, he could just see the opening of the pipe they had fallen from. Probably an air conduit, Turcotte guessed. The walls beyond the edge of the concrete roof were of raw rock. There was about ten feet of separation between the edge of the bunker and the cavern wall.

"There." Yakov switched the direction of the light.

There was something ten feet in front of them, sticking up a few inches. Turcotte and Yakov crawled over to it—it was a metal hatch with a round latch on top.

Yakov glanced over. "What do you think?"

"I think we're lucky to be alive," Turcotte answered.

"Should we see what is inside?"

"Definitely."

Yakov stuck the end of the penlight in his mouth, clamping down on it with his teeth. With great effort, muscles straining in the dark, they turned the rusted latch. It gave way slowly, emitting great shrieks of protest.

"If there's anyone in there, they know we're coming," Turcotte said.

"I don't think anyone has been down here in a long time."

The latch finished turning. With all their might, Yakov and Turcotte pulled up on it. With a clang, the hatch fell open. A faint light shown up out of the hole. Turcotte leaned over and looked down. The floor was over fifteen feet below, a steel ladder leading down to a flat concrete floor. The light came from the right, but even sticking his head down into the opening, he couldn't see, as the concrete top was more than three feet thick.

Turcotte lowered his legs into the hole, holding himself in place with his hands on either side of the opening. "I'll let you know if it's safe."

"I'll be right behind you," Yakov said. "We have nowhere else to go."

"What is this?" Tolya asked the lieutenant. A narrow tunnel, obviously very old judging from the tool marks on the wall, was at the end of the more modern shaft they had been following. Shining a light down the tunnel, Tolya could see that it descended and was curving slightly to the left. Tolya checked the tracker. His object was very far below and slightly to the left front.

"Uh—sir, that's not on any chart I have. According to what I have, this is the end."

"Then I no longer need you?" Tolya turned, the muzzle of his submachine gun pointed at the other officer, his finger resting on the trigger.

The engineer's face had gone pale. "We have to get out, sir, don't we? I have the charts. The—"

Whatever else the man was going to say was stifled in a three-round burst that knocked him against the side of the tunnel. Tolya grabbed the map case and slipped the sling over his shoulder. "Now I have the charts."

He signaled for the men to continue.

VICINITY OF EASTER ISLAND
D – 4 Hours, 45 Minutes

On board the *Anzio* the ship's sophisticated radar array picked up the probing finger of the AN/APG-71 radar. Alarms rang and the ship turned hard away from Easter Island. Missile and gun crews went on maximum alert until it was realized that the radar was not approaching and there were no inbound missiles.

"What the hell does it mean?" Captain Breuber, the commander of the *Anzio,* demanded of his chief weapons officer, Lieutenant Granger.

"From the signal," Granger said, "it appears to me that the radar is ground based, not moving. It's definitely located us. But at that range, there's nothing that was on board the *Washington* that can reach us."

Breuber considered that. "But there was plenty that could intercept an incoming missile, wasn't there?"

Granger nodded. "Sidewinders, Sparrows, and Phoenixes. Besides the ship's own SAMs and air defense guns."

Breuber rubbed his chin. "Which means we have a problem for our launch."

"Yes, sir."

"Can we beat the AN/APG-71?"

"That's top of the line, sir. The best our Navy has."

"Lieutenant, I know that. I want to know if we can beat it. Because if we can't, our Tomahawk is not going to be able to do the job it's supposed to."

"Well, we built it, sir. We have the specs on it." Seeing the look in his commander's eyes, Granger quickly answered. "Yes, sir. We can beat the radar."

"All right. Anything from the *Springfield*?"

"No, sir, but they had to have heard the message."

"Good." Breuber looked to the horizon, beyond

which lay the shield covering Easter Island. "Not much longer now."

QIAN-LING, CHINA
D − 4 Hours, 25 Minutes

Che Lu came up behind Elek. The hybrid creature was standing at the top of the tunnel that descended to the lowest level of Qian-Ling. Twenty meters in front of Elek, the holographic image of the Airlia was playing. The legs and arms were longer than a human's, the body shorter in comparison. The head was large, covered with bright red hair. The skin was pure white, without a mark. The ears had long lobes that almost touched the shoulders. The eyes were bright red under fierce red eyebrows, and the pupils were elongated like a cat's.

The figure wavered in the air, the descending corridor behind dimly visible. The right arm was raised up, a six-fingered hand on the end, palm open toward them. A deep, guttural sound echoed up the tunnel, coming from the figure, but the language was singsong. The figure spoke for almost a minute, then faded out of sight.

"Do you know any more than when we came in here?" Che Lu asked as Elek turned from where the image had been and spotted her.

"I know the key isn't here. I know that the guardian doesn't know where the key was sent."

"That was important enough for all those men you brought here to die for?"

"If the key is not here, it allows others to search elsewhere," Elek said simply. He regarded her with his red eyes. "What have you discovered? Anything worth the deaths?"

Che Lu shook her head and lied. "No."

"There is something else I have learned, though," Elek added. "A way we can open up a door to the outside world." He turned and walked away, heading down toward the cavern. Che Lu followed, curious to see what could get them out of their current trap.

Elek strode among the black boxes that filled the floor and halted before a large one, about twenty meters wide by thirty long. He went to a hexagonal panel in the center of the short side. Che Lu could see that the hexagon was divided into numerous smaller, six-sided sections.

Elek pressed on several of them in a pattern too quickly for Che Lu to keep track. The panels were lit with an inner light, revealing high rune markings on each small section. Elek stared at it for a little while, then again ran his hands across the panels, almost as if playing a musical instrument, so quickly did his fingers move.

With a rumble, the black cover slid back. Che Lu moved to the side along with Elek to see what was revealed. Lo Fa came walking up, alerted by the strange noise.

"What is it?" the old man asked as the cover came to a halt. He blinked as he took in the form. "It is a metal dragon!"

A large, silvery device, ten meters long by four wide, rested on a cradle of black metal. It was indeed shaped like a dragon, with a high arced neck above a sleek body. The two eyes were dark red and glittered in the light coming down from the bright orb overhead. The mouth was open, revealing a row of black teeth. Two short, stubby wings poked out from the body, extending less than two meters on each side. It appeared to have been damaged at one time: A long black smear about a meter wide on the left side extended from just forward of the wing to the base of the tapered tail. At one point along the smear the silver skin had been breached, revealing wires and tubes inside.

"It is Chi Yu," Che Lu said. "The Dragon Lord of the South who fought with Shi Huangdi!"

GIZA PLATEAU, EGYPT
D – 4 Hours

The moon highlighted the face of the Sphinx. Professor Mualama had watched the shadow of the night horizon creep down the face inch by inch over the last several hours, his attention caught between the marvel in front of him and searching the road leading to Cairo for Duncan to arrive.

He had located the block he thought needed to be removed. It was on the right paw, at the base. He'd knelt in the sand and cleared away the bottom of the stone with his bare hands. If he had had his own vehicle and equipment he would have tried to open it himself, but Hassar had left him standing between the paws after Mualama turned down his offer to return to Cairo. Duncan had gone with Hassar to try to contact UNAOC and get Sterling's successor to put pressure on the Egyptians.

For the hundredth time, Mualama looked to the road, searching for his crew. He checked his watch. He walked between the paws once more, feeling the weight of the scepter in his backpack. He placed his hands on the stone and pressed his palms flat. He could feel the time, the millennia that had passed since the stone had been shaped.

He looked once more to the road.

What he didn't notice was the figure standing on the temple wall that surrounded the body of the Sphinx. Wrapped in dull-gray robes, the figure had not moved once the entire evening, waiting as Mualama waited.

VICINITY OF EASTER ISLAND
D – 4 Hours

Captain Forster had walked through the entire ship, poking his head into every compartment where a member of his crew was, personally making sure they were all ready for the upcoming mission.

He could see it in his men's eyes that they didn't have much optimism that they would be able to escape. Hearing the *Washington* hit the island had been a rather devastating experience. If whatever was on the island could take down an aircraft carrier, what chance did they have? Plus, they had all been nearby when the *Pasadena* was destroyed by the foo fighters, hearing their sister ship go down into the depths, the sound like that of popcorn popping as bulkheads gave way.

After going on all decks, from the rear of the sonar sphere in the bow to the engine room adjacent to the reactor halfway back in the sub, he returned to the control room. Not long now.

AREA 51
D – 3 Hours, 25 Minutes

Larry Kincaid studied the new imagery from the Hubble under a magnifying glass. The "Face" had definitely changed in the last forty-eight hours. He looked up at Forrester, who had just brought the photographs to the Cube conference room. "Well?"

"The black smear is an army of robots, average size about six feet long."

"What are they doing?"

"Excavation," Forrester said. He pointed. "These four piles are the rubble they've taken off the top of the 'Face.' A rather large amount. Estimates by imagery specialists put it on the order of—"

"What are they excavating?" Kincaid interrupted the scientist.

Forrester slid another photograph across. "This is the latest. They've reached whatever it is, but they haven't fully cleared the surface area. You can see this small area in the top right quadrant. Appears they've reached some structure made of the same black metal as the mothership."

Kincaid's pulse doubled its pace. "Another ship?"

Forrester shook his head. "I don't believe so. It's something else."

"What something else?"

"We don't know yet."

The possibilities that he could imagine raced through Kincaid's mind, and then he realized it was the possibilities he couldn't imagine that scared him the most.

MOSCOW
D – 3 Hours, 25 Minutes

The interior of the chamber was one large concrete vault, stretching over a hundred meters in each direction. Steel beams ran from floor to ceiling every ten meters. It was filled with crates, dimly lit by the glow of a half-dozen lightbulbs dangling from the ceiling. The ladder they'd climbed down was in the exact center.

"Someone must come down here to change the lightbulbs," Turcotte said. "So there has to be a way out."

Yakov pointed toward the left. "There is a door over there. I would think maintenance of this room was Pasha's job."

"This is the Archives?"

"We best hope it is. I would prefer not to fall through any more pipes." Yakov rubbed dust off the side of the nearest crate, exposing Cyrillic writing. " 'Recovered from German Aviation Ministry, 1945.' "

Turcotte looked around and spotted a rusty crowbar resting against one of the crates. "Let's see what we've got." He jammed the edge under one of the borders and pried it up. After several minutes' work, he had the side

off, revealing a thick glass surface, heavily covered in
dust. The case was six feet high by four wide and deep. It
looked as if it had not been touched in decades, as did
most of the piles of boxes and files in the room.

Turcotte rubbed the sleeve of his shirt against the
glass, leaving streaks, gradually clearing a few inches. He
leaned forward.

"Oh, jeez!" he hissed, stepping back as he saw the
dark black eye staring back at him out of the yellow-
colored orb, the sphere floating in some liquid.

"Ah, Okpashnyi's twin," Yakov noted. "We are in the
right place."

Turcotte looked more closely. He could see the crude
sutures where the sphere had been put back together
after autopsy.

Turcotte checked the other crates nearby. There were
several wood boxes with the Nazi eagle stenciled on
them. He flipped open the lid on the closest one. It was
full of files. He pulled the front file out. A drawing of
Okpashnyi was the first piece of paper in there.

"You read German?" he asked Yakov.

"A little."

"Can you tell which of these are important and which
aren't? Which one holds the Spear if it is here?"
Turcotte asked.

"I will check."

As Yakov moved about rubbing dust off crates,
Turcotte pulled out his SATPhone. He knew it wouldn't
work this far underground, but it was a sign of the straits
they were in that he flipped open the cover anyway and
pressed the on button. As he had expected, nothing but
static came out of the earpiece.

"This is strange." Yakov's voice floated through the
room.

Turcotte walked over to where the Russian was prying
open the top on a crate. "What do you have?"

"Files reference the Ark." Yakov pulled a folder out of the crate and opened it. He quickly read the opening page. "An after-action report from an SS reconnaissance."

"Where?"

"Turkey." Yakov's lips were moving as he read. "In 1942." He turned a page and held out a photo. "Aerial recon."

Turcotte took the black-and-white picture. It showed a snow-covered mountainside. "What am I looking at?"

"Mount Ararat."

"Ararat." Turcotte made the connection. "Noah's Ark?" He shook his head. "Wrong ark."

"When you are not certain what you are looking for," Yakov said, "you cannot afford to ignore anything." He was looking at the photo. He tapped the corner with a thick finger. "What is that?"

A long object was embedded in the ice. Turcotte had some experience with overhead imagery, but the quality of this photography was poor. "Probably a spur of rock."

"Or Noah's Ark?" Yakov asked.

"What the hell does that have to do with anything?" Turcotte asked, even as he threw the folder into Pasha's satchel. "Let's keep looking. We've got to find the Spear."

CHAPTER 23

The hours just before dawn were von Seeckt's favorite. He would lie in his bed, looking out the window at the desert, the darker mass of the mountains in the distance. Above the mountains were the stars, and he often thought about seeing those same stars as a child in the mountains of southern Germany. Sometimes he even thought he could see the mothership pass by overhead; the newscasts said one could occasionally see it with the naked eye when the tumbling ship reflected light.

He remembered the first time he saw the mothership, nestled in its crater inside the cavern now known as Hangar One at Area 51. World War II raged around the planet, but all he could do was stare at the long black, cigar-shaped alien craft and feel the impact of how puny man was, how insignificant in the true scale of the universe.

He was not surprised when the door to his room silently swung open, letting in light from the hallway. The door closed just as quickly, returning the room to its original dimness.

A dark figure moved across the tile floor and stood at the side of the bed, looking down on the old man.

"Do it quickly," von Seeckt said.

The figure didn't move. "What have you told them?"

"I have done as instructed. I told them nothing they didn't already know or wouldn't have found out soon. Just enough to get them going in the right directions. They have people looking in Moscow and at the Giza

Plateau. They look for things we have searched for. Maybe they will have better luck."

"Luck has nothing to do with it," the figure said. "It is all about power and knowledge, and ours is growing."

"If we were so brilliant, why did it come to this?" Von Seeckt looked out at the desert. "Spare me the speech."

"Have they found the Spear of Destiny?"

"I don't know."

"What about the key *we* seek?"

"I don't know." A hint of a smile played across the old man's lips. "You ask me many questions after boasting how your knowledge was growing."

"I don't have time for games. The Ark of the Covenant?"

"They seek that at Giza as many have sought it there in the past. There is no reason to believe they will have any more success."

"I think you are wrong there." The figure pulled out a small device, which it hurriedly whispered into, then returned to its resting place. "What else have they found?"

Von Seeckt was still looking out the window, but he waved a hand to take in his room. "Does it look like I'm in the information loop from the Cube?"

"Then you are no longer needed."

"You had already decided that before you came in," von Seeckt said.

"True—" The word reached von Seeckt's ear at the same time as the black blade made of alien metal punched through the skull into the brain, killing him instantly.

MOSCOW
D – 2 Hours, 50 Minutes

They had been slowly descending in what Tolya suspected was a large spiral for quite a while now. He had no idea how deep they were, but he suspected that if a nuke did hit Moscow, they would not be immediately killed. They were circling the object, so he felt reasonably certain this would lead them to the target.

"Sir!" The commando backed up from the steel door he had just opened, his finger on the trigger.

Tolya edged around the man to see what had caused his reaction. It was the first door they had encountered in quite a while. It had taken two men to unscrew the latch that held it shut. Tolya doubted that Katyenka or those who had been with her were on the other side, but he saw no need to pass it by.

Tolya shone his light into the opening. A large chamber was revealed, the end of which was blocked by the numerous objects poking up from the floor. Tolya's brain had to process what he was seeing for a few seconds before it accepted the reality—hundreds of mummified bodies impaled on stakes set into the floor.

Like a moth drawn to light, Tolya slowly walked into the chamber. Not only directly ahead, but left and right, the bodies stood like a forest of the dead. Tolya had served in the GRU and had been in Siberia, seen the secret gulags and the horrors perpetrated there, but even that didn't compare to this.

His gaze came closer, able to make out details, and he saw a heavy wooden chair bolted to the floor. Leather straps were looped over the arms and legs. Tolya realized that someone had bolted people into that chair, left them there to stare at the dead. His gaze went up. Rails lined the ceiling, with chains dangling here and there. He realized that was the way each body had been conveyed to position over a stake and then lowered.

Tolya could sense the men behind him, peering in from the doorway. He knew he should give some orders, get moving back down the corridor, but he was unable to stir. He tried to see a far wall in any direction, but all that was visible were bodies. There could be thousands here. He looked at the closest one. The face was brown, stretched, mummified, tight against the bone underneath. The naked body was just as shriveled. Tolya could detect no sign of violence other than the wood stake the body was impaled on—more than enough to cause a slow, agonizing death that Tolya was loath to imagine too closely.

Then he noticed something else in the room: a large wooden cart with a metal device on it. He finally stirred, taking a few steps closer to the apparatus. There were large glass bottles on the lower level of the cart. Thin rubber hoses led from the bottles to the metal device on the top. Other hoses came out of the top of the device, with large-gauge needles on the end. There was writing in German on both the bottles and the metal device. A swastika was emblazoned on the side of the cart.

Tolya stared at it for almost a minute before he connected the setup with the state of the bodies and realized what the device was designed to do. Draw blood.

The bodies had been drained to just before the point of death, before being lowered and impaled.

Why was so much blood needed? The question reverberated in Tolya's mind, and he took an involuntary step backward. He shook his head, turned on his heel, and marched to the door, shoving the commandos out of the way. He pulled it shut behind him. "We continue."

Eyes looked back at him blankly. Tolya raised his voice. He jabbed the muzzle of his sub down the tunnel. "We continue!"

AIRBORNE
D – 2 Hours, 25 Minutes

"Wild." Sergeant Boltz was looking down between his feet at the surface of the Black Sea twenty-five feet below.

The bouncer was motionless after a rapid flight across the Atlantic, through the Mediterranean, then across the middle of Turkey to their current position. The interior was packed with not only the twelve men of the A-team but their weapons, equipment, and ammunition.

Strapped tight against the side of the bouncer was the black coffin that had been recovered from Ngorongoro Crater. And carefully packaged inside the coffin was the atomic bomb that Quinn had procured for them at Turcotte's request.

"All right." Captain Billam was leaning over a large plastic case that contained demolitions. He spread out two map sheets. "Let's pay attention." The men gathered around, the inner circle kneeling, the outer peering over their shoulders.

"Let's work some contingencies for going into Moscow and Cairo."

QIAN-LING, CHINA
D – 2 Hours, 25 Minutes

Elek had disappeared inside of Chi Yu, the beast of Chinese legend, crawling through a panel just under the tail. Che Lu and Lo Fa were left standing outside, marveling at the detailed dragon the metal had been formed into.

Both were startled as the dragon lifted off the floor of the cavern several feet, hovering silently in the air. Che Lu could well imagine the fear such a beast would inspire among the peasants of ancient times.

The neck twisted, the dragon head going to and fro. Then the body slowly turned clockwise in a complete circle before the robot settled down on the floor once more.

The panel opened, and Elek exited.

"What good does that do if we are stuck in here?" Lo Fa demanded.

Elek looked down at the old Chinese man. "When the time comes, we will not be stuck in here."

MOSCOW
D – 2 Hours, 25 Minutes

The tunnel finally ended. A steel door blocked the way ahead, and Tolya held up his fist, stopping the small group of commandos with him. They had slowly spiraled down for so long that he estimated they were over a mile below the city of Moscow. Whatever was behind that door had to be very important, of that he had no doubt.

And the one he tracked was behind that door, the direction finder assured him.

CAIRO, EGYPT
D – 2 Hours, 15 Minutes

Hassar was startled out of a fitful sleep as the door to his bedroom was kicked open. He sat up, then froze as two small red dots centered on his chest. He could see the two men holding the submachine guns flanking a third shadow, a tall figure dressed in a black robe. That figure scared him much more than the men with the guns.

"I have done as instructed, Al-Iblis!" Hassar held his hands up in supplication, giving the figure a name that was whispered about throughout the Arab world. "I have not allowed them a permit."

"It is far past permits now," Al-Iblis said. His voice was low and barely above a whisper, yet it hissed as if a snake were speaking. "Why did you not tell me they had the key?"

Sweat was pouring off Hassar's forehead. "I did not know what it was."

"You lie," Al-Iblis said. "You have been here too long. You wonder what secrets the Highland of Aker holds. You are a fool. You do not even know who Aker is, do you?"

Hassar was thrown off by the question—all Egyptologists knew who Aker was. "Aker was the lion-god who guarded the gates of the horizon and allowed the sun to enter the sky each morning and leave each evening."

Al-Iblis laughed, but there was no humor to it, and the harsh sound sent a chill down Hassar's spine. "A god! Aker was a bureaucrat given a job which he did only too well."

Hassar was totally still, afraid to intrude on the thoughts of the creature in front of him. He could not see the face hidden by the dark hood, and he had no desire to. As far as he knew, no one had ever seen Al-Iblis's face. The name was a legend in the Middle East, a figure that Western intelligence agencies had a skimpy file on, who skirted around all the terrorist groups; a name mothers used to scare their children into going to bed.

Al-Iblis took a step closer to Hassar's cowering form. "If it is to be about gods, then so be it. The time for pretense is fast fading. You must seal off the Plateau with your soldiers and allow no one in, no matter what happens. I will deal with the infidels. Is that clear?"

Hassar's head bobbed in agreement. "Yes, Master."

MOSCOW
D – 2 Hours, 10 Minutes

"Captain!" Yakov's voice echoed through the cavern.

Turcotte had the duffel bag full of files, grabbed those he deemed important with only a cursory examination of the diagrams or photos enclosed. "What?"

"I think this is it."

Turcotte rushed to the center of the chamber, where Yakov was standing over a crate he had smashed open.

The Russian lifted out a metal box as Turcotte arrived. It was steel, inlaid with gold and black bands, about two feet long by ten inches wide and high. The top was hinged. Looking closer, Turcotte recognized the black bands as being made of the same metal as the mothership and other Airlia artifacts.

Yakov had the box in his hands, turning it around, looking at it from all angles. "According to the invoice, this was recovered from beneath 77 Wilhemstrasse in Berlin on the first of May, 1945."

"And that means?" Turcotte asked.

"77 Wilhemstrasse was the address of the Reichskanzlei. Underneath it was the Fuehrerbunker."

"Hitler's bunker?" Turcotte already knew the answer. "Where he died?"

Yakov held the case next to his head and shook it lightly. "It's heavy, but nothing's moving that I can hear. Look . . ." Yakov rubbed off some of the dust and dirt that covered the top of the box.

There were markings on it. It took Turcotte a second to recognize them. Not high rune characters, but Chinese. He tapped the top. "That's the same character that was on the obelisk marker in the Ethiopian cavern where we found the ruby sphere." He remembered Nabinger's translation. "Same name. Cing Ho. The Chinese explorer who went to Africa and the Middle East in 656 B.C." Turcotte turned the clasps and opened the lid.

A long sliver of highly polished metal, two feet long by less than four inches across at its widest, the edges razor sharp, tapering to a needle point at one end and a round hole at the other for the acceptance of a shaft. "The Spear of Destiny," Turcotte whispered as he grabbed the shaft end and lifted it out of the case. "We need—" He was interrupted as the door to the chamber imploded and the sharp crack of plastic explosive going off ripped across the room.

Turcotte shoved the Spear back in the box and dove to his left, swinging up the AKSU as he moved. He blindly fired a burst in the direction of the door and heard the crack of bullets coming back in his direction. Lying on his belly, he peeked around the crate he was using for cover. He saw several men in camouflage smocks slip through the now-open door. Turcotte fired a three-round burst and one of the figures slammed against the wall and slid to the floor, leaving a trail of blood.

The reaction was swift as a hail of bullets ripped into the wood around him, scattering splinters and causing Turcotte to press so hard against the floor that he could distinctly feel the buttons on his shirt push into his chest.

He heard a pistol firing and knew Yakov was giving him covering fire. He slid backward, putting more distance between himself and the invaders. Having relocated, Turcotte rolled onto his back and pulled two grenades off his vest. If there was one lesson he had been taught in Ranger and Special Forces school and had had reinforced in combat, it was to move swiftly and decisively when ambushed. Turcotte knew there was no time to "let the situation develop," as Pentagon briefers liked to say.

"Yakov!" he yelled.

"Here!" Somewhere to Turcotte's left as he lay on his back.

"The ladder in six seconds on my go. Flash-bang in five."

"I'm ready!"

"Go!" Turcotte yelled as he pulled the pins. He tossed both grenades, arching them just below the ceiling toward the door. He squeezed his eyes shut while he pressed the palms of both hands over his ears.

Even with that, his ears rang as both grenades exploded. Turcotte jumped to his feet and dashed for the ladder, firing the AKSU one-handed over his shoulder.

Out of the corner of his eye he saw Yakov's large form moving in the same direction, also firing.

The bolt on the AKSU closed on an empty chamber as Turcotte reached the ladder. He took it two rungs at a time, climbing up. He could hear bullets cracking by, but he hoped the camouflaged men were firing blindly, the grenades having done their work. He reached the top and was almost shoved through by Yakov climbing up between his feet.

They sprawled onto the top of the bunker. Turcotte reached for the hatch to slam it shut, but Yakov's large hand grabbed his arm. "Wait a second," Yakov growled, his head cocked, listening. His other hand pulled two HE grenades off his vest. They looked like OD green Ping-Pong balls in his large hand. He let go of Turcotte's arm and pulled the two pins, still waiting.

Voices were yelling below in Russian. There were a couple of bursts of automatic fire. The sound of movement. Yakov tossed both grenades through the opening and then slammed the hatch shut. Turcotte heard the explosion through the metal and the immediate screams of the wounded. Yakov turned on his penlight and stuck it between his teeth. The Russian whipped his belt off and looped it around the handle, ensuring that the hatch could not be opened from below.

"Do you have the key?" Turcotte asked.

Yakov tapped his chest. "Inside my shirt in its case."

"Now what?" Turcotte asked Yakov as they slowly stood.

"The power, the air, must come down here somehow," Yakov said.

"I think we came down the air shaft," Turcotte noted.

"Let us take a closer look." Yakov was already walking toward the edge of the bunker. Turcotte followed.

"One thing you must understand about Russians," Yakov said as he shined his light along the cavern wall, slowly walking along the edge clockwise, "is that anyone building a shelter like this would plan a second way out. There is no other reason to have the hatch in the top, is there?"

Turcotte could think of several reasons, but he saw no point in disagreeing. Yakov stopped so suddenly that Turcotte bumped into him.

"There." Yakov was shining his light at a six-inch-wide metal beam that spanned the ten-foot gap. At the far end, a dark opening waited. "Let us leave this place," Yakov said as he stepped onto the beam and gingerly made his way across.

Turcotte waited until the Russian was on the other side, then followed.

CHAPTER 24

GIZA PLATEAU, EGYPT
D – 2 Hours

"They're stalling at UNAOC. The Russian Ivanoc now chairs the committee, and he's afraid. It's as if everyone is holding their breath hoping this deadline passes and nothing happens." Lisa Duncan had just arrived back from Cairo, to find Mualama still sitting between the paws of the Sphinx, impatiently waiting.

"Why do you not call for some help of your own?"

Duncan had considered calling in the Special Forces team from Area 51, but she had a feeling the Egyptians would react violently to such a blatant transgression of their national boundaries. And she wasn't exactly confident that Mualama knew where he wanted to go or what he expected to find. An exact definition of what the Hall of Records would look like had been one fact absent from all the information the archaeologist had given her. Overriding that reasoning, though, was the fact that she wanted the team free to be able to help Turcotte, since it looked like he was more likely the one on the trail of the needed key.

"Everyone's afraid to rock the boat— And who the hell are you?" Duncan was looking over Mualama's shoulder at the robed figure that had just appeared out of the darkness.

"My name is Kaji." The old man's face was like part of the desert, his skin dark brown, full of deep lines. A worn turban was wrapped around his head, a gray robe over his frail shoulders.

Mualama turned in surprise. "The same Kaji who was with Professor Nabinger under the Great Pyramid?"

"There has always been a Kaji here. My father, and his father before him, and thus it has been for as long as there is a memory."

"You were with von Seeckt when he opened the lower chamber of the Great Pyramid," Duncan said.

"What does that matter?" Kaji asked. "That is the past."

"It matters," Duncan said. "You took von Seeckt's dagger. Did you take anything else from the Germans?"

Kaji considered her. "You have something in mind?"

"I don't have time to play," Duncan said. "Did you take the Spear of Destiny from them?"

"No." Kaji looked at Mualama. "You have been searching for many years. I have heard stories of the tall black man who travels far and asks many questions."

"And your people have been trying to hide the truth from me every step I took," Mualama said.

"My great-grandfather went with Burton into the Roads of Rostau and never returned," Kaji said.

Duncan forced her way between the two men. "What do you want with us?" she asked Kaji.

Kaji shifted his gaze from the African to her. "I understand you have found something else. A key."

"Christ!" Duncan exclaimed. "Is there any such thing as a secret anymore?"

"I know all that happens on the Highland of Aker," Kaji said. "Do you have the key?" he pressed.

"Yes," Duncan said.

"Then nothing is safe, and as it has been told through the generations of my family, it is time," Kaji said. "I will take you to see what it is you seek."

"I seek the Spear of Destiny," Duncan said. "Is it here?"

Kaji's answer was blunt. "I do not think so."

"Then we're wasting our time here," Duncan said.

Mualama placed a large hand on her shoulder. "There is nowhere else to go. Your friend Turcotte is on the best possible trail for the Spear. What lies hidden here could be just as important."

Duncan considered that. "Why is it time now?" she asked Kaji.

"No one has ever had the key before," Kaji said simply.

"What is it the key to?" Duncan pressed. "The Hall of Records?"

"The truth," Kaji said.

Duncan checked her watch. She knew there was nothing else she could do right now about the Spear—it was in Mike's hands. If she could find something here, it might give her some leverage with Lexina. "All right. Let's find the truth."

Kaji extended a hand toward the causeway that led from the Sphinx to the Great Pyramid. "This way."

MOSCOW
D – 2 Hours

Sweat had soaked through Turcotte's shirt, drenching his combat vest. The access tunnel Yakov had discovered had immediately turned into a vertical shaft about fifteen feet wide that went up as far as the light from the small penlight could illuminate. Thin metal stairs ringed the shaft, and they had begun the long trip up.

Turcotte had no idea how long they had climbed, and the light showed no end yet. Even Yakov had to stop now every twenty or thirty sets of stairs and lean against the wall to catch his breath. Turcotte's calves burned as he forced himself upward, one step at a time.

"Wait," Yakov gasped, halting once more.

Turcotte didn't have the energy to answer. Yakov turned off the penlight and the shaft was plunged into darkness. At least for the first minute. Then Turcotte noticed that he could make out, very faintly, the stairs above.

"There's a light on above us," he noted.

Yakov nodded. "The top of the shaft."

"Where do you think we're coming out?" Turcotte asked.

"With the luck we have had," Yakov said, "I would say the middle of Red Square during a military parade."

"Our luck's bound to change," Turcotte said.

"But not necessarily for the better," Yakov commented, then began climbing toward the light.

THE GIZA PLATEAU
D – 1 Hour, 50 Minutes

Kaji swung the gate open, the dark tunnel leading into the Great Pyramid beckoning.

"Why do you have access to the Pyramid?" Duncan asked as Kaji locked the gate behind them.

"I am the *wedjat* of the Highland of Aker," Kaji said, as if that explained everything.

"What about Hassar?" Mualama asked as they headed down the entrance tunnel.

"Hassar is a lackey of a government which fears secrets of their own past," Kaji said.

Duncan was overwhelmed simply by the aura of the surroundings. The light from their flashlights disappeared into darkness far down the tunnel. She thought of the age of the Pyramid, the first men who had walked down this corridor when it was completed. The weight of stone above her, the sheer massiveness of it all. Even being on the deck of a *Nimitz*-class carrier was nothing compared to this. The sound of their shoes on the stone echoed off the rock walls and then into silence.

Kaji pointed. "That is the way up to the Queen's Chamber, the Grand Gallery, and the King's Chamber beyond." He nodded his head toward a narrow tunnel that descended. "That is the way we must go."

They went down. Duncan knew this was the way that von Seeckt must have gone over fifty years earlier. She imagined the SS soldiers scurrying down the same tunnel on their secret mission, and that brought to mind all that von Seeckt had told her.

Kaji suddenly stopped and put his hand on one of the stone blocks on the right side of the tunnel. The stone rotated, and a secret tunnel was opened to them.

"It has been many years since anyone has gone this way." Kaji ushered them through.

They hustled down the tunnel, passing between the smoothly cut stone walls.

Kaji paused once more, opening another stone block. Duncan could see that two tunnels, one on either side, were now open.

"To the right links back up with the lower chamber of the Great Pyramid," Kaji said. "Where your von Seeckt and the Nazis found the black box."

"If you are a Watcher, why did you guide the Nazis there?"

Kaji coughed and bent over to catch his breath before answering. "I didn't. They knew where they wanted to go without needing assistance from me. I went along to see where they went and what they would do. And they were too many to stop. And by allowing them to find one of the six divisions of the Duat, the other five remained secret. Sometimes trade-offs must be made." He pointed. "We go to the left."

Duncan glanced at Mualama. She had a feeling both

of the men were holding something back. She saw little reason for Kaji to guide them to the Hall of Records, and she didn't think that Mualama had told all he knew.

She noted when they were no longer in the Pyramid, as the walls changed from stone blocks to a tunnel bored through solid rock.

"We are heading toward the Sphinx?" Mualama asked.

"Yes," Kaji answered shortly.

"What is that noise?" Duncan asked, hearing a distant roar.

"The River of Aker." Kaji was walking steadily down the tunnel, his leather sandals shuffling along the dusty floor. "The Nile makes a loop under the Highland and then back again."

"How far do these tunnels go?" Duncan asked.

Kaji suddenly stopped and was looking at the wall on the right side. "I have not traveled all the tunnels, so I do not know." He pressed his hand against the wall and the outline of a stone appeared, then slid up into a recess above. Duncan had never seen the likes of that technology, and she knew it had to be Airlia.

Kaji motioned for them to go through. They squeezed past and he followed, the door shutting behind them, the outline melding into the rock and disappearing.

Kaji began hacking, and Duncan knew from the sound that he was seriously ill. When he was able to get his breath, he pointed down the tunnel where darkness waited. "The Hall is that way."

Duncan shined her flashlight where he pointed, but it was as if the very light was being sucked into the darkness. "What is that?" she asked.

"The Old Ones had strange ways," Kaji answered. "You must go through the darkness to come into the light."

"I think you should go first," Mualama said.

Kaji shuffled forward and disappeared into the darkness.

"Do you trust him?" Duncan asked.

Mualama shook his head. "No. I believe his great-grandfather tried to kill Sir Burton down here."

"Thanks for letting me know that now."

Mualama stepped forward. "But we will never know what is on the other side unless we go." He disappeared, leaving Duncan alone.

She stepped forward toward the darkness. It was unlike anything she had ever seen, as if the light were being absorbed by the air. Her ears popped from a decrease in pressure as she continued forward, moving by feel, totally blinded. Her stomach spasmed as she almost fell to her knees, but she forced herself to continue moving. The experiences reminded her of the feeling she'd had when Majestic had operated the gravity drive of the mothership in Hangar Two.

She blinked as she was abruptly blinded by light.

"That is the Hall of Records," Kaji said, but Duncan barely heard him as she stared down at the Black Sphinx on the floor of the cavern.

MOSCOW
D – 1 Hour, 45 Minutes

Yakov shoved the grate at the top of the stairs away and climbed up, Turcotte following. They were in a room illuminated by a few bulbs. Turcotte blinked, adjusting to what was to him a brightly lit area. There were several large objects in the room, and he had to look at them for several minutes before he recognized what they were: elegant horse-drawn coaches.

"Where the hell are we?" Turcotte asked.

"Remember when I said luck could always get worse?" Yakov asked in turn. "If I am correct, we are in the basement of the Kremlin Armory."

"And that's bad?" Turcotte walked around one of the carriages to the lone door in the room, a thick heavy wooden one with metal bands across it.

"The Armory is where the greatest treasures of Russia are housed," Yakov said. "These carriages were probably used by the czars—there is always an exhibition of one or two on the main floor. The Fabergé eggs are housed above us; the crowns of the later czars; the Icon of the Virgin of Smolensk."

"And?" Turcotte tried the handle on the door. It turned freely. As far as he was concerned, it seemed things were getting better.

"Do not open that door. I would wager you a large amount of money," Yakov said, "that you will trip an alarm if you open it. And there is always a heavily armed platoon of guards on standby in the Armory itself and over a battalion of men stationed on the grounds of the Kremlin."

Turcotte stopped turning the handle. Yakov came over and examined it, then pointed. "A laser along the inside. Open it more than a quarter inch, and you will trigger the alarm. There are many more such alarms once we get through the door. It is, as you Americans say, out of the frying pan, into the fire," Yakov summed up his take on the situation.

Turcotte checked the AKSU. He had four rounds in the magazine and no spares. "How are you doing?" he asked Yakov.

The Russian held up the pistol. "Two bullets left. And I would prefer to kill as few of my countrymen who are just doing their job as possible."

Turcotte reached into his shirt and pulled out the

SATPhone. "Let me see if I can get us a fire extinguisher."

SPACE
D – 1 Hour, 30 Minutes

The talon passed over the west coast of the United States, Warfighter and *Stratzyda* in its nearby wake. Four hundred miles below, millions of unsuspecting people went about their business in San Francisco.

NGORONGORO CRATER, TANZANIA
D – 1 Hour, 30 Minutes

Underneath Soda Lake in the center of Ngorongoro Crater, Lexina had tried calling Duncan once more but received no response. She went to the second number she had—direct access to the Cube at Area 51.

The SATPhone was answered on the first ring. "Major Quinn."

"There is not much more time." Lexina didn't waste time on an introduction. "I want the key."

"We'll get you your key," Quinn said. "It's taking us a little while."

"How can it take you so much time when you already have it? I will do as I promised. To show you I mean what I say, watch *Stratzyda*." Lexina cut the connection. She turned to the black sphere and forwarded commands to the talon's computer, which in turn controlled *Stratzyda*.

SPACE
D – 1 Hour, 28 Minutes

Directly over Oakland, two long doors that even the makers of *Stratzyda* had hoped would never be opened, slowly slid apart, revealing the blunt nosecones of the cobalt bomb reentry vehicles.

AREA 51
D – 1 Hour, 27 Minutes

"Goddamn Russians" was Kincaid's comment as the front screen relayed the view from a ground telescope of *Stratzyda*. "All the crap that went wrong with Mir, you'd think this wouldn't work after all these years."

"They've always been better at making weapons than anything else," Major Quinn said.

"The President has this, doesn't he?" Kincaid asked.

"It's being relayed to the War Room," Quinn confirmed. "But with Interdictor destroyed, there's not much anyone can do."

"Where the hell is Turcotte?" Kincaid muttered.

"Oh God!" Quinn exclaimed, looking up at the screen. "She isn't waiting!"

With a puff of a small rocket firing, one of the reentry vehicles separated from *Stratzyda*. It moved away, gravity pulling it down, the small engine orienting its path on an angled trajectory.

"Where's it heading for?" Quinn demanded of the people monitoring the equipment in front of him. The *Stratzyda* was over Stockton, California.

"We don't have a solid lock yet," one of the technicians responded. "It's in a glide path rather than a direct downward shot. Warhead passing through three hundred and fifty miles altitude, descending rapidly."

The view on the screen switched to the tracking imagery from Space Command.

Quinn breathed a momentary sigh of relief as the black line indicating the warhead edged eastward, away from Oakland and San Francisco. "Give me a targeting and impact point and time!" he yelled.

Kincaid had shoved one of the technicians out of the way and was rapidly typing into a computer. He stiffened as numbers appeared on the screen. He swiveled around on the seat. "Time to impact is four minutes. Target and impact point is right on top of us."

CHAPTER 25

The reentry capsule angled into the atmosphere over the Sierra Nevadas, the heat shield leading the way. Thirty seconds later it crossed the California/Nevada border at two hundred miles of altitude. Drogue plates, less than ten inches long and six inches wide, popped out perpendicular on the side of the capsule, slowing it enough so that it would not burn up.

AREA 51
D – 1 Hour, 25 Minutes

"Seal the Cube!" Major Quinn ordered.

"Two minutes to impact," Kincaid announced.

A heavy steel door, over two feet thick, slowly swung shut over the only exit out of the underground complex, sealing off the elevator to the surface.

"Do you think that will make a difference?" Kincaid asked Quinn.

"We're going to find out, aren't we?" Quinn snapped in reply. He nodded at the door. "That's not the important thing. What's critical is that our air-filtration system works. The bomb should go off in the air to maximize the spread of the cobalt."

"What about all the people still on the surface?" Kincaid asked.

Quinn's silence was answer enough to that question.

AIRBORNE
D – 1 Hour, 24 Minutes

Over target, the reentry capsule split in two, the pieces ripping away into the air at 5,000 feet altitude. A drogue chute popped open on top of the bomb itself as it drifted down. A built-in sensor on the bottom of the casing ranged a radar beam to the ground below and received immediate bounce-back, giving the arming system relative altitude. The detonator had been preset many years before the launch to go off at 3,000 feet relative altitude above target.

AREA 51
D – 1 Hour, 23 Minutes, 30 Seconds

"There it is!" Quinn pointed at the corner of the front screen, where the feed from one of the surface video surveillance cameras had picked up the small dark dot of the deployed parachute directly overhead. "Any second now." Quinn's voice had dropped to a whisper and all activity in the Cube had ceased.

Breaths were held as the parachute grew larger, and now a small black object could be detected hanging below.

"How high?" Quinn asked.

"Passing through four thousand feet," Kincaid replied.

The ring of Quinn's SATPhone caused everyone to jump. For the first time, Quinn didn't jump to answer. His gaze was fixed on the screen.

"Three thousand, five hundred," Kincaid announced.

The phone continued to ring.

"Three thousand."

"Damn it!" Quinn snatched the phone. The bomb

could clearly be seen now. "Quinn!" he yelled into the phone.

"Do you believe me now?" Lexina's genderless voice was barely audible.

"Can you stop it?" Quinn felt a bead of sweat trickle down his neck.

Kincaid's voice echoed through the Cube. "Two thousand, five hundred."

"Give me the key," Lexina said. "In a little over three hours, *Stratzyda* will be over the center of your country, the warheads able to blanket it completely."

"Two thousand!" The strain was getting to Kincaid, his voice rising.

"When you are ready to be serious," Lexina said, "you can contact me—SAT Code two-four-bravo-six-nine-eight."

"Wait!" Quinn yelled into the phone. "Can you stop the warhead?"

"One thousand."

Quinn looked up at the screen. The camera was panning from the vertical as the bomb rapidly descended. It followed as the black orb slammed into the desert floor less than a hundred meters from the control tower on the edge of the runway.

"The warhead is one of six that are nonfunctional," Lexina said. "Rest assured, though, that the other twenty-six will work quite well." The SATPhone went dead.

CHAPTER 26

Duncan had to grab Mualama twice to keep him from falling off the stairs that led to the floor of the cavern. The African archaeologist's legs moved numbly, his eyes focused on the Black Sphinx. They followed Kaji and finally ended up standing just in front of the large, dark face with glinting red eyes. The statue between the paws loomed above them, mounted on a six-foot-high black pedestal.

Duncan stared up, even more impressed with this than she had been the first time into Hangar Two and seeing the mothership. The stone copy on the surface was majestic, but this held an overwhelming sense of power.

"The key." Kaji had his hand out.

Mualama pulled the scepter out of his pack.

"Hold on a second—" Duncan protested, but Mualama didn't appear to hear her as he handed the artifact to Kaji.

The Egyptian held it in his hands reverently. "Generations of my family beyond the horizon of known history have watched the Highland of Aker and guarded the way to the Hall of Records."

"When was the key taken away?" Duncan asked.

Kaji seemed surprised that she spoke. "I do not know."

Duncan was tired of mumbo-jumbo talk and bowing before Airlia artifacts. The Watchers had known of this hidden Sphinx and the Hall of Records since before recorded history—at least according to Kaji—yet they had kept it hidden, which she had a feeling was the way the Airlia and their lackeys—both sides— would have preferred it.

"You don't even know what's inside, do you?" Duncan pressed.

"It is the Hall of Records," Kaji said.

Duncan shook her head in disgust. "That's a name for something when you don't have a clue what it exactly is."

"The Ark of the Covenant." Mualama intruded on the conversation, stirring out of his Sphinx fog. "That is what is inside the Hall of Records."

"And what is the Ark?" Duncan's voice was sharp.

Mualama's eyes came off the Sphinx, and Kaji looked up from the scepter. Duncan finally had their attention. She pointed at the Sphinx. "Forget your preconceptions. Forget your legends. Neither of you knows a damn thing about what is really going on. I don't either." She jabbed a finger into Kaji's chest. "You're setting us up. I know that. He knows that." She nodded at Mualama. "He's just too caught up in his search to let that stop him. You'll leave us down here to die once you have the key and open the Hall.

"You don't think The Mission isn't on our trail?" Duncan asked. She didn't wait for an answer. "You Watchers are out-of-date. Humans can't sit back and simply observe anymore, because the truce between Aspasia and Artad is over. Your man knew that deep in the Amazon when he alerted us to the Black Death." With her free hand Duncan pulled a ring out of her pocket and showed it to Kaji. "This is his ring. He was a Watcher, and he died taking a stand. It's time for you to take a stand. To make the sacrifices the generations of your family who have guarded this place have made worth something."

She pulled the 9mm pistol that Turcotte had given her

out and held it at her side. "I'm tired of people playing games with hidden agendas. My agenda is I want what is in there, whatever it is." She gestured with the gun. "So let's open it up."

Kaji reached out and took the ring from her. He turned it in the light of the false sun, noting the eye design on the face. "It is the sign of the *wedjat*," he agreed.

"Open the Hall," Duncan pressed.

"We will see. . . ." Kaji paused and cocked his head. "Someone has entered the Roads of Rastau."

"How do you know?" Mualama asked.

"I can sense it." The first display of emotion that Duncan had seen played across Kaji's face for the briefest of moments. "They have my son."

"The Mission is coming," Duncan said. "You can let us in the Hall or let them in. Your choice. You know you will not be able to save your son, and that the line of Kaji the *wedjat* on the Highland of Aker will end today."

Kaji quickly turned and walked forward between the paws of the Black Sphinx.

"What does the stela say?" Mualama asked, referring to the six-foot-high, polished black stone that rested against the chest of the Sphinx at the end of the open space between the paws and upon which rested the statue. High runes were carved all along the face of the stone.

"I do not know," Kaji said.

Duncan had a feeling he was lying, but the stone could be examined later. She had no idea how far away The Mission's people were. Mualama pulled out a small camera and took a picture of it. In the very center of the stela was a proportional drawing of the scepter.

Kaji held up the scepter and placed it on the image. He pressed it against the stone for several seconds. Duncan was startled as the glowing orb overhead blinked out for a second, then came back on. The surface of the stone shimmered and the scepter began sinking into it, absorbed into its own image. Kaji let go of it and stepped back next to Duncan and Mualama.

"What now?" Duncan asked as the scepter completely disappeared into the stone.

"I do not know," Kaji said.

"I would think that—" Mualama began, but he shut up as the stone smoothly slid down, revealing a six-foot-high opening into the body of the Black Sphinx. The passageway beyond had several steps down into it, was eight feet high with curved and straight walls of the same black metal. A thin line of blue lights along the center of the ceiling illuminated the way.

Duncan put the gun away and walked into the corridor, the men following her.

AREA 51
D – 1 Hour, 10 minutes

Quinn's SATPhone buzzed once more. "Quinn here."

"This is Captain Billam. We need the floor plans for the armory inside the Kremlin."

Quinn had to stop for a second to run that request through his brain one more time, the image of the bomb lying on the sand still burned into his mind. There was an explosive-ordnance disposal team there now, preparing to make sure the bomb had actually malfunctioned. Quinn did not envy them their job. "How am I supposed to have access to that?"

"I don't know, sir, but Captain Turcotte said you had access to a lot of information."

Quinn looked down at the people working in the Cube. His mind was already processing through the various intelligence agencies he could contact. He knew

Turcotte was right—the information would be somewhere in the system. "I'll get it to you."

"In ten minutes?" Billam pressed.

"I'll try."

"Do better than try, sir," Billam said. "We'll be over Moscow in eleven minutes."

"Tell Turcotte when you see him that time is getting short," Quinn added before Billam could cut the connection.

"I think he knows that," Billam commented dryly.

MOSCOW
D – 1 Hour

"Time to target?" Turcotte had the SATPhone pressed against his ear.

"One minute out." Captain Billam's voice was loud and clear.

"Ready?" Turcotte asked.

Yakov nodded.

"You sure you can do this?" Billam was looking over his two demolitions men's shoulders.

The senior demo man, Metayer, was unrolling a length of detonating cord. "We got the floor plans for the building from Area 51, but it doesn't give composition, so we're worst-casing it." He inserted a fuse into the top of the shaped charge. "We're ready."

Billam looked through the floor of the craft at the outskirts of Moscow rapidly rushing beneath them, streetlights casting their glow, a few cars puttering about. He hoped the building wasn't occupied and that Metayer hadn't overdone the charge to the point of killing those they were trying to rescue.

"Thirty seconds!" the pilot called out as he adjusted

course, dipping down to fly less than ten feet above the surface of the Moscow River.

The two engineers climbed up the ladder to the top hatch, balancing the shaped charge between them. Below, two more men of the team waited with the second charge the demo men had prepped.

The Moskvorestkiy Bridge appeared directly ahead. The pilot edged forward on the controls, and they flew under the bridge. Just as quickly, the pilot increased altitude and they buzzed the wall of the Kremlin, banked left, missing the spires of the palace by less than two feet, and dropped down onto the roof of the armory.

"Go!" Billam's order was unnecessary, as Jones and Metayer already had the hatch open. They slid down the side of the bouncer and onto the roof. As Jones prepared the charge on its tripod, Metayer ran a tape measure from the southeast corner of the building. He dropped the end of the tape on the spot, ran back to Jones, and helped him carry the forty-pound charge there. They scampered back up the side of the bouncer, unreeling the det cord.

Jones pulled the fuse igniter, and the charge shattered the early-morning calm. A focused cone of blast and heat cut through the roof of the armory, but Jones and Metayer were already running up with the next shaped charge, which was attached to a rope. They lowered it into the hole the first had created and repeated the process, even as the rest of the team was unloading two more charges and other gear. Billam was in the hatch, the SATPhone pressed against his ear.

Turcotte and Yakov heard the first charge go off and ducked behind one of the carriages, eyes on the ceiling. The fourth charge blew a ten-foot-wide hole in the center of the room.

"You're through!" Turcotte yelled into the SATPhone, struggling to be heard over the clanging of alarms.

The two men ran forward, jumping over debris, and stood underneath the hole, looking up.

The team sergeant, Boltz, was now the only one near the blast site. The others were getting back on the bouncer. Boltz had two duffel bags at his feet, ropes going from them to clamps on the side of the bouncer. At an arm signal from Billam, he kicked both bags into the hole that ran through the center of the armory.

Weights in each bag made sure they fell, coiled rope playing out. A burst of automatic fire from the adjacent palace caused Boltz to duck. He spotted several guards on the roof of the other building. Several more bursts of fire caused him to crawl toward the bouncer, putting it between him and the firing.

Turcotte grabbed one of the duffel bags, pulling out the harness on the end of the rope, while Yakov took the other.

"I hope the pilot is good," Yakov said as he buckled the harness around his legs and waist.

Turcotte looked up. The sides of the blasted shaft were mostly irregular, with several I-beams sticking dangerously out. "I hope so—" His next words were lost as the ropes tightened and both men were jerked off their feet.

Sergeant Boltz had a harness around his waist, a rope keeping him from sliding off the side of the bouncer. He wore a headset that allowed him to speak to the pilot, and he ignored the occasional bullet that pinged off the side of the alien craft as he looked down the shaft, watching the two men get pulled up as the bouncer rose straight into the sky.

A round fired from the roof of the palace skipped off the side of the bouncer and hit Boltz in the left side, ripping through flesh and coming out his upper right back. He collapsed, dangling from his harness as Turcotte and Yakov cleared the top of the shaft that had been blown.

The bouncer began to accelerate, moving south while also gaining altitude.

Hanging a hundred feet below the bouncer, Turcotte and Yakov had linked arms to give them some stability as they were buffeted by the fierce wind. They hung on that way until they were forty miles south of the city, where the pilot brought them in for a gentle landing in an empty field. As soon as his feet touched down, Turcotte unhooked from the harness.

The bouncer landed forty feet away, and the team's medics were out of the hatch and seeing to Boltz's condition. Captain Billam, after making sure Boltz was alive, headed toward the two rescued men.

Yakov knelt in the recently plowed field, running his fingers through the earth. "I never though I would be so glad to feel dirt."

Turcotte pulled the bag with the files and Airlia box off his shoulder and opened it, making sure the items were still inside.

"You have the Spear?" he asked Yakov.

The Russian tapped the box inside his shirt.

Turcotte looked up as Captain Billam loomed over them.

"Have you heard from Dr. Duncan?" Turcotte asked.

"We have no contact with her."

"Damn it." Turcotte pulled out his cell phone and punched in the code for the Cube as they climbed on board the bouncer. Quinn answered promptly.

"No word?" Turcotte had the SATPhone against his

ear, watching as Yakov searched through the duffel bag. The bouncer was heading south, the Black Sea not far away.

Quinn's voice was clear despite the distance. "Last report Dr. Duncan sent was that she was going with Professor Mualama under the Sphinx. The NSA is relaying me imagery that shows the Egyptian army sealing off the Giza Plateau."

The knuckles on Turcotte's battered hands turned white around the phone. "She's been betrayed."

"We don't know," Quinn said. He quickly filled Turcotte in on Lexina's call, the status of *Stratzyda,* and the nuke lying on the surface above the Cube. "What are your orders?"

"My orders?" Turcotte asked.

"Dr. Duncan left instructions that we were to take orders from you if she was out of contact. You're in charge."

"How do I contact Lexina?" Turcotte asked.

Quinn forwarded him the SATPhone access code Lexina had given him.

CHAPTER 27

Duncan could see that the corridor opened up about fifty feet ahead. She walked quickly, hearing the sound of Mualama and Kaji behind her. The room she entered must have been in the exact middle of the Sphinx. The ceiling was twenty feet overhead, the walls spreading out with twenty feet of space between, and the far wall was thirty feet away.

Exactly in the center of the room, four poles held up four horizontal rods ten feet from the floor. At the top of each pole was a replica of the end of the scepter, a head looking down on them, all oriented toward the entrance, ruby eyes glittering. A thick white cloth hung from the rods, concealing whatever was inside.

Duncan looked about. To the left, against the wall, were several racks of what appeared to be various garments.

Duncan started to walk forward when she noted that the four heads on the top of the poles were slowly turning, tracking her. She stopped. "Someone tell me what's going on?"

"Ahh—" Mualama was watching the heads. "There is a legend that the Ark must always be hidden behind a veil—much like those cloths. It must be hidden because anyone who lays eyes on the Ark of the Covenant and is not one of the chosen priests will be consumed with fire. While the Ark was in Israel, it is said that Nadab and Abihu, two of the four sons of Aaron the High Priest, entered the area behind the veil and were killed by the burning fire.

"Even when the proper procedures were followed, it is said that the Ark would sometimes send off sparks and kill those who carried it or were around it."

"And you were going to tell me this when?" Duncan asked as she backed up a step.

"There are so many legends." Mualama shrugged. "It is hard to know what is important and what isn't."

"The one about getting consumed by fire is kind of important." Duncan was watching the four heads. They were in their original positions, oriented on the entrance, which was where she was standing with Kaji and Mualama. "You knew about this, didn't you?" she asked the old Egyptian. "You would have let me walk into—" She stopped, at a loss for words and knowing exactly what it was she had almost stepped into. "Any suggestions?" she asked.

Mualama pointed to the left. "They must be the accoutrements for those who tended to the Ark."

Duncan went to the racks, Mualama following. Kaji remained in the entrance, still just staring at the veil, his head cocked as if he were listening to something behind him.

"How long do we have?" Duncan called out to him.

"Ten minutes, maybe more, maybe less," Kaji said.

"Can we close the Sphinx from the inside?" she asked.

"The door will close only when the scepter is removed," Kaji said.

Duncan turned to Mualama. "Do you know anything about these clothes? Will wearing them allow someone to get inside?"

Mualama nodded. "When the Ark was in the temple in Jerusalem, the high priest wore a white linen robe, much like this." He lifted it off the rack and tried to put it on. It was much too small for his large frame. He held it out to Duncan. "You must wear it to get to the Ark."

Duncan reluctantly took the garment and slipped it over her head.

"On top he wore the *meeir,* which is this." Mualama handed her a sleeveless shirt, blue in color with gold fringe. "On top of that went the *ephod.*" He held out a coat of many colors.

When Duncan took it from him, she almost dropped it. "Why is it so heavy?"

"Metal threads connect the various colors," Mualama explained. He picked up two stones from a shelf on top of the rack. "These fasten it on the shoulders." He helped her with it, still speaking. "The names written on these stones are those of the twelve sons of Jacob. As you can see, six names on each. According to legend, they give the wearer the power of prophecy."

"I just want to see what's behind curtain number one," Duncan said. Her words were flippant, but she felt a change wash over her body as the stones were fastened at her shoulders. A tingling on her skin, as if a slight electric current were passing through. She realized she was going back through time, donning the garments of ancient priests.

"And the last piece." Mualama held up a breastplate. A dozen jewels were attached to the wool with golden thread. Duncan had no idea what each stone was, but she had no doubt they were very precious. Mualama looped the neckpiece of the breastplate over her shoulders and it came to rest on her chest, fitting into a depression on the *ephod* perfectly. It was heavy, and she felt it pull her forward slightly before she adjusted her balance.

Duncan was startled when Kaji suddenly spoke. She had not seen or heard him walk over. "This is the *essen,*" Kaji said, pointing at the breastplate. "It is a symbol of righteousness and prophecy. The bearer must be true of heart and mind, or it will not protect you."

Kaji reached out and Duncan almost pulled back, but she remained still as he adjusted the *essen*. He tapped two deep pockets, one on each side. "These are empty now. They held the *urim* and the *thummin*."

" 'Held,' " Duncan repeated. "Where are they now? And what were they?"

"The way by which the prophesier spoke to God," Kaji said. "I don't know where they are now."

"Great," Duncan said. "Any other important parts missing?"

"This." Kaji lifted a crown consisting of three bands, stacked one on top of another. "Each band represents two things. The three worlds of existence—heaven, hell, and the earth. And the three divisions of man—spiritual, intellectual, and physical."

"What does that have to do with the Airlia?" Duncan bowed her head and allowed Kaji to place the crown on her. She would have felt ridiculous except for the fact that she was inside the Black Sphinx and she knew The Mission was coming.

"It was the way ancient man tried to deal with things they could not understand," Kaji said. "You are ready to view the Ark. If you are pure, you will survive. If not . . ." He didn't seem too concerned either way.

"What about the *urim* and *thummin*?" Duncan shuffled a few steps toward the veil. "Will I be safe without them?"

"I do not know," Kaji said.

"Great," Duncan muttered.

AIRBORNE
  D – 35 Minutes

The blue water of the Mediterranean was below the
bouncer as Turcotte punched in the SATPhone code. As
soon as it was answered, Turcotte began talking.

"I have the key."

There was a short pause, then Lexina spoke. "Where
are you?"

"Where do you want the key delivered?" Turcotte
asked instead of answering.

"You do not have much time. I will follow through on
my threat."

"Then tell me where you want it delivered."

"Forty-two degrees north latitude, one hundred and
five degrees east longitude."

"I want Che Lu and whoever is with her in exchange
for the key," Turcotte said as Captain Billam thumbed
through an atlas, searching for the coordinates.

"You are in no position to make demands."

"You are in no position to turn me down," Turcotte
snapped back.

"It is of no import. You can have the old lady. The
clock is still ticking."

The phone went dead, and Turcotte looked at where
Billam's forefinger was pointed. A spot in Mongolia, in
the middle of the Gobi Desert, with no roads or towns
within hundreds of miles. "Let's go."

EASTER ISLAND
  D – 30 Minutes

Kelly Reynolds existed in a netherworld of physical stasis
and extreme mental activity. She was barely aware of her
body, pressed up against the guardian computer, surrounded by the golden field. The metal probe along with

the nanomachines had been removed from her body through her insinuation of the commands in the steady stream she could monitor coming out of the guardian computer.

To penetrate into the guardian itself, to examine its database, was a different story. She'd had "visions" of the building of the *moai* on Easter Island, of the Giza Plateau at the height of its glory, and even the current situation with the nanovirus swarming over the crew of the *Washington* and the ship itself.

Her delicate probing, like trying to consciously manipulate a dream in a half-awake stage, had come across something quite intriguing: a large pathway for data in and out of the guardian, like an electronic superhighway among secondary roads, but empty of traffic. It originated in the core of the guardian, and Kelly found her psyche there, alone in the empty conduit. She "followed" it out of the guardian, her mind ranging along the pathway until she reached an abrupt end, where the data link had been severed.

How she knew these things she couldn't consciously elaborate, but her subconscious was picking up enough for her to have realizations. It suddenly came to her where this data superhighway had gone and why it was no longer functional. The Easter Island guardian was a complicated machine, far more powerful and aware than any computer made by humans, but Kelly now knew it had once been only one piece of a whole system. She "saw" it as the guardian had once seen it—a network of guardian computers on Earth, the one at Cydonia at Mars, on board the mothership, others in places she couldn't quite grasp all linked together. And on Earth there had been one guardian that every other guardian on the planet had been linked to. The place where the data highway had been linked to.

That guardian had been on Atlantis, and for a moment Kelly thought the reason the pathway had been severed was that the master guardian had been destroyed when that island had been blasted by the mothership.

But the data recorded indicated otherwise. The severing had come *after* Atlantis was destroyed and the Airlia split into their two factions.

That meant the master guardian had been removed from Atlantis prior to destruction. But the machine was no longer active; the core of it had been removed. She saw the removal of the core by two Airlia, the vision startlingly real to her, then the vision went black, as if a TV had been turned off, and she knew that was when the highway from the Easter Island guardian—indeed all the other guardians on Earth—had been severed from the master.

Kelly knew that Duncan and Turcotte had to know the master guardian existed, and they had to know the core also existed. She turned her attention once more to the string of data the guardian was moving outward into the world and slowly worked her own small, very discrete bits of data into it.

QIAN-LING
D – 28 Minutes

Without ceremony Elek had escorted Che Lu and Lo Fa into the metal dragon immediately after getting a call from Lexina. The interior was as elegant as the exterior. A series of half a dozen red chairs faced forward in the belly. One center seat was in front with a black globe centered in front of it, a wide screen beyond showing the view outside.

"What is this thing?" Che Lu asked as Elek took the forward seat.

"A weapon. Built from scrap during an ancient war."

Elek placed his hands on the black sphere. Che Lu could see that they were lifting off the ground even though it felt as if they had not moved.

"Between Shi Huangdi and the Empress of the South?"

Elek shrugged. "That is your legend. There have been many battles over the millennia between the Guides and The Ones Who Wait, and the humans who have chosen sides. This is another one." The dragon was now facing the rubble in the wide tube that led to the surface. Elek pressed on the top of the sphere, and a lance of red came out of the mouth, blasting rock aside, opening a path to blue sky beyond.

"But this one is different," Che Lu said, which earned her a sharp glance from Elek as he edged the machine into the tunnel.

"This is the final one," he said. "There will be no more truce, and only one side will prevail."

GIZA PLATEAU
D – 25 Minutes

Duncan forced himself to move toward the veils. The heads tracked her once more, the four sets of ruby eyes fixed on her movement.

Duncan almost jumped as a flash of light came out of the frontmost, right-side head. A red beam struck the ground in front of her, quickly ran up her body, stopped on the *essen* for two seconds, continued on to the crown, then disappeared. She froze, waiting for more, but there was nothing.

She reached the veil. Kneeling, she lifted the bottom of the veil and then stepped inside.

CHAPTER 28

GOBI DESERT, MONGOLIA
D – 18 Minutes

Sand dunes stretched as far as the eye could see in all directions. Turcotte's boots sunk into the sand a couple of inches as he walked around the bouncer, checking out the terrain with a set of binoculars. Nothing.

"Sir!" Master Sergeant Boltz was digging in the sand with his hands.

Turcotte hurried over. "What is it?"

Boltz pointed. "Something is buried here."

Turcotte could see part of a piece of granite exposed by Boltz's digging. Stomping his boot down, Turcotte could feel something hard underneath, indicating that the stone extended quite some distance. Turcotte checked his watch. Time was indeed getting short, and there was no time to investigate this strange find.

He turned to Captain Billam, who had the rest of his team deployed in a defensive perimeter around the bouncer. "Here's what I want you to do."

VICINITY OF EASTER ISLAND
D – 15 Minutes

All was ready on board the *Anzio*. The flight path for the Tomahawk had been calculated so that the missile would fire up, reach apogee, then glide down toward Easter Island, letting gravity make sure it hit the center of the top of the alien shield. The warhead in the nose was fitted with a time delay, calculated to go off ten seconds after the missile passed through the shield.

A flight of four F-14s was already between the launching ship and Easter Island, making sure the airspace was clear. Captain Breuber had all the authorizations he needed to launch, but he hesitated. He knew the *Washington* and what was left of her crew were under that shield.

He also knew that the *Springfield* was ready. They had picked up banging noises from the submarine in Morse code indicating the crew was ready to execute their part of the plan. Sent through the same rudimentary communication system was the interesting information that there might possibly be a slight opening in the shield on the ocean bottom. There was no way to factor that into the plan other than to direct the *Springfield* to change the target of some of its wire-guided torpedoes to try to take advantage of the chink in the armor.

The loss of the space shuttles, the explosion in Montana, the assassination of the Secretary of Defense and UNAOC chief, topped off by the inert nuke landing at Area 51, had added impetus to the decision to take out Easter Island just prior to the deadline from Lexina. The information about the Chinese attack on Qian-Ling had been downloaded from the National Security Agency, and while it confirmed the fact that the shield was not totally impervious to a nuclear blast, it made it all the more imperative that they get the warhead through the shield before detonation, given that the guardian was buried deep under Rano Kau.

"Lieutenant Granger, is everything ready?" Captain Breuber asked.

"Yes, sir."

"Launch in ten minutes," Breuber ordered.

"Yes, sir."

SPACE
D – 10 Minutes

The doors on *Stratzyda* slid open once more. It was passing over Wichita, Kansas, and soon would be in optimal position to blanket the United States with its cobalt bombs. Even with one gone and five others inert, the remaining twenty-six were more than enough to finish the job envisioned by its Soviet creators during the height of the Cold War.

Adjacent to *Stratzyda,* the imaging equipment on board Warfighter scoured the face of the planet, searching for any last-minute assaults from below, the reactor powered up, the laser ready to lash out at the speed of light.

GOBI DESERT
D – 10 Minutes

"What the hell is that?" Captain Billam had his binoculars pointed toward the south.

Turcotte directed his in the same direction and spotted what appeared to be a metal dragon rapidly approaching through the air. "Have your men stand by," Turcotte ordered. He'd seen much in the last couple of months, but a flying dragon ranked up there with the strangest.

The dragon came to a hover about twenty meters away, then slowly settled onto the sand. Out of the rear came Elek, Che Lu, and the old man Lo Fa. Turcotte was glad to see the professor and her bandit comrade.

Elek gestured for the two to stay put as he strode forward toward Turcotte. "Give me the key."

Turcotte pulled the black case out of his pack and opened it, revealing the Spear of Destiny to Elek. The alien/human hybrid held out his hand, but Turcotte

shook his head. "It goes in there. You take it all."
Turcotte nodded his head toward the long black coffin
that had been recovered from Ngorongoro Crater by
Mualama. Captain Billam ran over to the coffin, opening
the lid just enough to slip the case holding the Spear in.

"Release my friends," Turcotte said.

Elek gave a dismissive gesture, and Che Lu and Lo Fa
came over to stand next to Turcotte.

"It is good to see you once more." Che Lu's wrinkled
face split in a wide smile.

Turcotte smiled in turn but kept his attention on Elek.
"Tell Lexina to stop *Stratzyda*. I want it released by the
talon. Along with Warfighter."

"Have your men load the coffin into the back of the
dragon," Elek ordered. "Then I will call Lexina."

As Billam directed four of his team to do that,
Turcotte checked his watch. Less than eight minutes.
"What is this place?" he asked.

Elek's attention was on the men carrying the coffin to
the dragon. "This is where the *ordon* of the Great Khan
was first raised and last taken down. Chi Yu knows the
location, so it was easiest to meet here."

Turcotte had no idea what Elek was talking about.
The coffin was inside, and the men returned. "I want
confirmation that *Stratzyda* has been aborted."

"Talk to Lexina." Elek turned and walked away.

"Damn." Turcotte pulled out his cell phone and
punched in the code he had been given by Quinn.

There was no answer on the other end. The dragon
lifted and headed to the south.

AREA 51
D – 8 Minutes

Major Quinn looked up as Larry Kincaid slid a piece of paper in front of him. "Another message from the guardian pretending to be Kelly Reynolds."

On the screen at the front of the room a live view of the deck of the *Anzio* was being relayed via secure Interlink. A red digital clock counted down to the launch time and had passed through three minutes.

Quinn quickly read the message:

> *The Airlia have meant no harm. They have only been protecting themselves. They have coexisted in peace with us for thousands of years. They have protected us from outside forces that would destroy our world. It has only been the interference of Majestic-12 and people from Area 51 who have caused the recent troubles.*
>
> *I have talked with the Airlia still surviving on Mars, and I know all this to be true. They are trapped now, but even so, they hold no ill feelings toward us.*
>
> *The recent events in South America were the results of a NATO secret experiment in biological warfare. The death of Johnny Simmons was caused by your own people when they tried to rescue him from your Majestic-12. There is a guardian that supersedes all others.*
>
> *They can help us, but they must be left alone. In turn, the promise not to take any action that can affect us negatively.*

"This doesn't make any sense," Quinn said.

"It's the same damn message as last time." Kincaid sat down and pulled out a pack of cigarettes, offering them to Quinn, who took one. Ignoring the large signs on the wall prohibiting smoking, they both fired up.

"No, it's different," Quinn noted. "Was it sent the same way?"

Kincaid shook his head. "No. Just over FLT-SATCOM, not to the Internet or any of the other modes from last time. So the Navy people have bottled it up. They're worried it's an attempt by the guardian to forestall their Tomahawk launch."

Quinn read the message one more time. "It's as if the guardian's replaying the message but it added the part about that reporter Johnny Simmons and a master guardian for some reason." He sat up straight. "It's Reynolds."

"What?"

Quinn tapped the piece of paper. "It's Reynolds. She *is* sending us a message. She's the only one who would mention Simmons—he was her friend. She saw him jump to his death after they rescued him from Dulce. It has to be her."

Kincaid frowned. "What's she trying to tell us?"

"That she's alive and free of the guardian," Quinn said. "And that she knows something—there is a master guardian that can affect *both* the Easter Island one and the one in Qian-Ling." He looked up. The digital countdown clicked through 3:00 to 2:59. "We've got to get them to stop."

VICINITY OF EASTER ISLAND
D – 7 Minutes

The Tomahawk leapt out of its hatch, flame roaring out of the bottom. It headed almost straight up, angled slightly toward Easter Island. Only then did Captain Breuber pick up the phone that linked him by satellite to Area 51.

"It's too late," he told Major Quinn. "And even if it wasn't, I wouldn't stop the missile. It's war here, Major. And we're going to win it."

Breuber looked out the thick glass at the front of his bridge, watching the Tomahawk going higher and higher.

AREA 51
D – 6 Minutes, 30 seconds

"Damn it!" Quinn slapped away the mike from in front of his face. He looked up at the front screen. *Stratzyda* was just minutes out from launching position.

"Turcotte turned over the key to Elek, but he can't get ahold of Lexina to confirm *Stratzyda* has been aborted." Larry Kincaid had a SATPhone to his ear.

"And Duncan?"

"No word."

"Is *Stratzyda* shut down?" Quinn asked.

Kincaid shook his head. "Doors are still open, and the talon still controls it."

VICINITY OF EASTER ISLAND
D – 6 Minutes

"Power up, lock on targets, all systems fire when ready!" Captain Forster snapped out the orders, and his crew leapt to action. He turned to his helmsman. "Get us up and away from here."

"Aye, aye, sir."

For the first time in many days, the *Springfield* was under way, lifting off the bottom, the single screw turning, giving it thrust.

"Torpedoes away!" the weapons officer announced. "Hatches ready to open on Tomahawks when we surface."

Four MK-48 torpedoes shot out of the tubes and headed—two each—for the foo fighters.

"Bogies bearing in on us," the sonarman warned. "Torpedoes running true on bogies."

"Get us to the surface, helm. Weapons, launch as soon as we are up."

"The shield is down!" Lieutenant Granger's voice cut across the hubbub of tracking the Tomahawk inside the operations center of the *Anzio*.

"It's back up," he yelled almost immediately.

"What's going on?" Captain Breuber demanded.

"AWACS has multiple missiles in the air!" one of the radar operators called out.

"From where?" Captain Breuber spun around.

"From Easter Island," the man replied.

"I thought AWACS blocked the radar." Breuber looked at Granger.

"They've got the frequency it transmits blocked," Granger said.

"Well, it's not working." Breuber leaned over the radar operator. "What are the missiles targeted on?"

"One each on the F-14s on CAP and one for the Tomahawk. A harpoon heading for the *Springfield*'s location."

"Get the Tomcats out of there!" Breuber ordered.

"A Phoenix can't take down a Tomahawk," Granger said, his voice full of forced confidence. "It's too fast."

Breuber was watching the radar. All four F-14s were heading back toward the carrier with afterburners on.

"They're out of range of the Phoenix," the radarman announced.

Breuber didn't move. The four dots representing his aircraft were still being tracked by four dots representing the Phoenixes. The screen showed the Tomahawk was closing on the island, another dot closing on it.

One of the pursuing dots caught a Tomcat. Both blipped out of existence. "Evasive maneuvers!" Breuber yelled into the mike to the pilots of the three remaining craft.

"It's on me!" a pilot yelled.

Another pair blipped out.

"Eject!" Breuber ordered. Both remaining pairs disappeared.

"Did they get out?" he demanded of the radar operator.

"I don't know, sir."

"I thought they were out of range."

"They were, sir."

"They were of a normal Phoenix." Breuber was still watching the screen. The Tomahawk was less than forty kilometers from Easter Island. He wasn't surprised to see the remaining Phoenix close on the cruise missile.

"That's impossible," Granger whispered.

The nuclear-tipped Tomahawk was less than twenty kilometers from the shield when the Phoenix overtook it. Both dots disappeared.

"That's impossible," Granger repeated.

Captain Breuber rubbed his forehead. "That thing took our weapons and made them better." He picked up an intercom to the bridge. "I want another hundred kilometers between us and this island. Now! Flank speed! Get ahold of *Springfield*!"

"We've got hits on both bogies!" the weapons officer yelled.

"Target's destroyed?" Captain Forster demanded.

The sonarman immediately doused the momentary euphoria. "Negative. Both targets are holding, though, not closing."

"What the hell?" Forster muttered, trying to make sense of the foo fighters' tactics.

"We've got incoming from above!" the sonarman suddenly screamed. "Harpoon, impact in five seconds."

Every head in the control room looked up, as if they could see the missile coming down toward them. Shoulders tensed as each man waited for the explosion of the warhead, to be followed by the implosion as water rushed in and killed them.

A thud reverberated throughout the ship as the missile struck the top of the submarine's deck. But there was no explosion. Forster felt blood in his mouth from where he had bit his tongue at the sound. "A dud?"

Relief flooded across the crew's faces.

A Klaxon sounded, returning the looks of anxiety.

"Status?" Forster spun about to his executive officer.

"Breach in the hull, sir." The XO was looking at his status boards, his forehead furrowed. "I don't get it. We're not taking on any water, but something's coming through the hull."

Forster checked the screen himself. The alarm was coming from the hull just above the room in front of the combat center. He strode forward, slipping through the hatch. The men working there were all looking up, but nothing was happening—at first.

Forster's eyes widened as the metal itself seemed to shimmer, changing from gray to black.

"We have no contact with *Springfield,* sir!"

Captain Breuber turned in his command chair. "Status?"

"She's heading for the shield. We've lost her."

VICINITY OF EASTER ISLAND
D – 4 Minutes

Duncan stood perfectly still, her mind trying to accept that what she was seeing in front of her was the object of legend. The Ark rested on a waist-high black platform. It was about three feet high and wide, and a little over four feet long. It was gold-plated, and the two long poles that were used to carry it were poking out on either end through the rings on the bottom of the Ark.

The most intriguing aspect were the two "cherubim" on the lid. They were shaped exactly like miniature versions of the head of the Black Sphinx, with ruby-red eyes, and as soon as she had entered the veil, both had slowly turned and fixed their inhuman gaze on her. Red light had flashed out from both heads, run over her garments and crown, and then stopped. But the heads were still focused on her presence.

Duncan felt the same menace from the two sphinx heads as from the ones on top of the poles. She forced herself forward, taking very careful steps until she was at the Ark itself. The two sphinx heads now faced each over the lid.

SPACE
D − 3 Minutes

The stubby snouts of the reentry vehicles for thirty-one cobalt nuclear warheads pointed down toward Earth.

NGORONGORO CRATER, TANZANIA
D − 3 Minutes

Lexina had listened to her cell phone ring over and over again. She had confirmation from Elek that he had the key. She knew what had happened at Easter Island to the American fleet and that the war was alive once more. She also had a very good idea of what the next escalation of the war was going to consist of. And America was currently more of a threat than an asset.

It was a simple, dispassionate decision, similar to many her predecessors had made.

The phone rang once more, and she stared at it, not answering.

GOBI DESERT, MONGOLIA
D – 2 Minutes, 30 Seconds

"They're going to nuke the States anyway, aren't they?" Captain Billam asked as Turcotte turned off the SATPhone.

"Not if I can help it," Turcotte said. He pulled a black box out of his shirt pocket and flipped open the cover. "Let's get their attention." There were a series of buttons on it, and he pushed the first one.

Elek spun about in his seat as a high-pitched shriek came out of the black coffin. He stopped the dragon, leaving it in a hover, and went back to the black tube. He swung open the lid, and the irritating noise stopped. The black case holding the key lay at the foot of the coffin.

At the head of the coffin was a shiny metal cylinder about three feet long by two in diameter. Turcotte's voice startled Elek, coming out of a small speaker taped to the hood of the coffin.

"You're looking at a twenty-kiloton-yield nuclear weapon. I don't know what that machine you're in is made of, but I know it's enough to take out the key and you. Now that I know you're listening, I suggest you tell Lexina to answer her phone."

Turcotte's SATPhone rang. He checked his watch before he opened it. Just under two minutes before *Stratzyda* released the warheads.

"Now do we have a deal?" Turcotte asked as soon as he pushed the on button.

"I will stop *Stratzyda*," Lexina said. "Take *your* nuclear weapon off-line."

"That's not good enough." Turcotte had his watch in front of his face, watching the numbers tick off. "I want you to have the talon release *Stratzyda* and Warfighter into orbits that will never coincide again. Agree or I will destroy the key."

There was a long silence—forever, in Turcotte's opinion, as he watched twenty seconds tick off, bringing it under one minute before *Stratzyda* activated.

"It will be done."

CHAPTER 29

AREA 51
D – 2 Minutes

"*Stratzyda* is closed." Kincaid was staring at imagery just downloaded from Space Command. "She's floating free, distancing from the talon."

Major Quinn slumped down into his seat, all energy gone after the events of the last three days.

On the other side of the conference table, Kincaid was shuffling through other photos he'd downloaded— copies of the latest imagery from Hubble of the Cydonia region of Mars. The four piles of rubble were larger, and the camera was now able to make out a small cleared area that revealed a spiderwork of black metal.

"What the hell is that?" Kincaid murmured.

GIZA PLATEAU
D + 3 Minutes

In the chamber outside the veil, Mualama turned his attention from the center to the corridor as the sound of boots tramping on the metal floor echoed against the walls.

Kaji stepped into the passageway with his hand held up. "You cannot trespass here."

"You are a fool, old man," replied a low voice that made the hair on the back of Mualama's neck stand on end.

Mualama stepped behind Kaji and saw a tall figure in black robes in front of a group of armed men. A hood hid the man's face. Near the back of the group, two men held a young Egyptian man captive.

"I have heard of you, Al-Iblis," Kaji said. "Even you cannot pass here."

"I have your son," Al-Iblis said. "The next in the line of the *wedjat* of the Highland of Aker. The last in the line." He waved his arm, and one of the commandos slid a knife across the young man's neck, bringing forth a gush of blood.

Kaji screamed something in Arabic and leapt forward, to be met with a swing of Al-Iblis's right arm. Mualama saw something flash in the light, a thin black blade that sprung from under the flowing sleeve. It sliced through Kaji's neck, and the *wedjat*'s head toppled from his body even as the dead man's hands reached for Al-Iblis. Slowly the body collapsed next to the head. Mualama stood still as the blade retracted, disappearing into Al-Iblis's sleeve.

"You are Professor Mualama." Al-Iblis made it a statement, not a question. He saw the medallion around Mualama's neck. "I gave that to Burton in Mecca long ago. But he betrayed me."

"That was over a hundred years ago!" Mualama said.

"I have walked the Earth before the dawn of your time," Al-Iblis said. "My names have been many and woven into legends on every land. You are the one who has been tracking the clues left by Sir Richard Francis Burton. Very smart. My man almost had you in Brazil. I have also tried to learn what Burton knew. I came close once, many years ago."

"You are Domeka?" Mualama remembered what he had been briefed on at Area 51.

"That was one of my names for a time," Al-Iblis allowed.

"What is your real name?" Mualama asked, trying to stall, wondering what Duncan was doing.

Al-Iblis shifted his dark gaze past him, toward the veil. "Duncan is in there. We will wait for her."

GOBI DESERT, MONGOLIA
D + 3 Minutes

Turcotte pushed the autodial for Duncan's SATPhone and listened to the phone ring and ring.

"Orders, Major?" Captain Billam was in front of Turcotte.

Turcotte shut off the phone. He knelt down and picked up a handful of sand, letting it pour through his fingers. He remembered landing in the desert on the other side of the world after destroying the Airlia talon fleet. Another desert, the same war, taken to another level, and now he was out of contact with Duncan.

"Load up," Turcotte ordered.

"Destination?" Billam asked as they headed toward the bouncer.

"Egypt."

EPILOGUE

Deep under the Giza Plateau, Lisa Duncan placed her hands on the lid of the Ark of the Covenant. A surge ran through her body, a feeling of power. A red glow suffused both of the cherubim-sphinxes and extended over the lid, encompassing her.

She could no longer hear those outside of the veil that surrounded the Ark. Her world was the Ark, the gold under her fingers. She grabbed the edge of the lid. She felt suspended in time, beyond the reach of everything she had ever known, not even of the Earth anymore. She lifted the cover. A golden glow blazed out, overpowering the red as the lid went up. It locked in place in the vertical, revealing the chamber inside.

Robert Doherty is the pen name for a bestselling writer of military suspense novels. He is also the author of *The Rock, Area 51, Area 51: The Reply, Area 51: The Mission,* and the forthcoming book in a new series, *Psychic Warrior.* Doherty is a West Point graduate, a former infantry officer, and Special Forces A-Team Commander. He currently lives in Boulder, Colorado.

For more information, you can visit his website at: www.nettrends.com/mayer